For all the adventurers out there.

COPYRIGHT

All rights reserved in all media. No part of this book may be used or reproduced without written permission, except in the case of brief quotations embodied in critical articles and reviews. The moral right of Atif Khan as the author of this work has been asserted by him in accordance with the Copyright, Design and Patents Act 1988.

This is a work of fiction. Names, characters, businesses, places, events and incidents are either the products of the author's imagination or used in a fictitious manner. Any resemblance to similar events is purely coincidental.
Published in the United Kingdom 2016 by Atif Khan
(8F Consultancy)

Cover illustration Copyright Atif Khan 2016.
Cover illustration designed by Leanne Edwards
www.shardelsbookcoverdesigns.com

Copy Proof Editor: Aneela Khan

International Standard Book Number:
ISBN-13: 978-1530359172

WWW.FACEBOOK.COM/TIMESTOPPERBOOK

*In loving memory of
Sahim Raja.
The only unsinkable ship
is our friendship.*

FACTS

Mayan Civilisation –

All references to the names of Mayan gods are accurate. The Kukulkan pyramid and the Temple of Warriors and their location in Chichin Itza are factual places in Mexico that still exist today.

2012 Doomsday predictions –

The Web Bot project is a real computer programme and any references made to its predications are factual.

The Mayan Calendar is a real artefact that ended abruptly on 21st Dec 2012 giving rise to the notion that the Mayans believed the world would end on Dec 21st, 2012.

References to global catastrophes that have occurred prior to 2012 in this book are also factual.

The I-Ching is a real ancient divination text that predicted the end of the world in Dec 2012, any doomsday references to it are factual.

TARGET PRACTICE

The elevator doors slid closed and began to descend as Adam looked at his G-Shock watch. It read 5:48pm. *Almost 6pm. I've got 2 floors left. I can make it out at midnight. I've got plenty of time.* Adam instantly wished that he could un-think that last thought. He didn't want to jinx himself. *Be positive, you can do this.* The elevator stopped at floor 2. *Ding.* The doors slid open. He looked at the wall and there was another A4 sheet of paper.

TIME MASTERY

Adam stepped out of the elevator but then heard a click, *SWOOSH.* He turned his head and something dark bolted towards him. It was so fast he could barely see it. It hit his shoulder, spinning him and knocking him to the ground. His shoulder burned in agony as he felt something wet on his shirt. *Oh my God, that's my blood! I'm hit!* Adam grabbed his right shoulder and winced in pain. *Was that an arrow?* There was blood running down his arm and his jacket and shirt were torn through. The hallway on this floor was set up like a shooting range, and he was the target.

2 MONTHS EARLIER

It happened again. Tonight, it was the worse it had ever been. Adam woke up soaked in a pool of sweat in his bed, and despite it being a hot summer night, he was shivering. Cold, and damp, he groaned, knowing that the usual ritual of finding a change of pyjamas and having to change the sheets was now upon him. A task he rather not undertake half asleep at 3am. Unfortunately, it was a necessary evil if he wanted to enjoy his last few hours in bed.

Adam rubbed his eyes in the bathroom mirror. He was only sixteen, but he looked and felt drained right now. Looking at his reflection he wondered when he'd grow out of this embarrassingly horrid puberty phase. Although his voice had finally broken and somewhat settled, his facial hair was sparse and embarrassing and the mild acne didn't do him any favours either.

'Ah man, not another one.' he grimaced as he poked the blotchy red mound. He quickly scanned the rest of his face for other newcomers, but thankfully there were none.

Back in bed and wrapped in the light summer duvet, he felt cosy in his fresh pyjamas and crisp new bed sheets. He lay there, now wide awake, wondering what had happened. *Man, why can't I just dream of unicorns like normal people?* He could never quite remember his nightmares afterwards. He tried closing his eyes and recalling the last part of it just before he woke up, but there were no images, there were no sounds, just a sickly feeling in the pit of his stomach, like being hungry and full at the same time. But the headaches were the worst part. The dull pounding and spinning would take ages to die down. It reminded him of the feeling he got immediately after getting off a rollercoaster. At least, this time, he didn't break anything. His last nightmare had somehow left him across the room. He only awoke once he heard his mirror smash into a hundred pieces.

He lay there in the dark and tried distracting himself, sometimes thinking of something else helped. He knew exactly what would take his mind off the pain. He closed his eyes and there she was, like an angel of peace, serenity and joy; Nikkita. The most beautiful girl in school. But despite being good friends with her, she had no idea about his true feelings. Adam envisaged her floating towards him. He smiled to himself as he closed his eyes, and before long sleep washed over him.

FRIENDS LIKE THESE

Adam loved London during summer. He felt that the cityscape came alive during the warm summer evenings. There was something mesmerising about gazing at Canary Wharf and the buildings that surrounded it during sunset, watching all the pinks and purples in the sky turn darker and darker as the sun went down. Adam often gazed out of the balcony from his two-bedroom council flat in Poplar watching tiny lights in the buildings flicker as people left the office for the day. He liked living in the east end of London it was always busy and buzzing with life. He wondered how amazing it'd be to finally move out of this flat and get his own place away from his mum and younger sister; his own space. Suddenly, his cell phone beeped as a text arrived from Zee.

We're @ the park blud, come down!

'Going out Mum!' Adam yelled to his mother.

'Where are you going?' She asked unsurprised. She knew that Adam and his friends usually hung out in Mile End park during the holidays. She'd caught him drinking there once and now knew perfectly well what sixteen-year-old boys got up to unsupervised. His mother knew him a lot better than he thought she did. Despite her concerns about his social life, talking him out of meeting with his friends was pointless. They'd argued about it many times before. To her, he was still that little boy who she used to dress and take care of, but he was now turning into a man, and that meant letting go of the reins a little. They had agreed a suitable compromise, a reasonable curfew, that must never be broken, set for 11pm sharp.

'Out!' He yelled as he twisted his foot into his trainers. 'Meeting Zee in the park.' Adam grabbed his keys and wallet. 'Phone, check. Wallet, check. Keys, check.' He muttered to himself.

'Well, be back by 11 okay? You remember our deal right?' The last time Adam was out he wasn't home till 11:45 and he was now out of warnings.

Alright, alright! Man... thought Adam, Man I can't wait to get my own place. 'Yeah, yeah.' He replied, annoyed that she felt he needed reminding.

It was only a short walk from where Adam lived and he took the path he always did, through the in-roads and back alleys. He had walked this route to the park hundreds of times and he was there within seven minutes. He didn't usually have to search hard to find his friends. They were exactly where they always were, sat on top of the small hill in the park by the swings.

'Sup bro!' yelled Zee from on top of the hill as he staggered to his feet. He was clearly already high. Zee was like a weed smoking machine. No time of the day was too early or too late. The only time he wasn't high was when he was on his way to buy more weed. Adam helped him up and laughed at how red Zee's eyes were.

'Bro, you look proper red-eye Jedi', Adam joked.

Zee smiled. 'Dude, I've got this sick haze, just picked it up, you've got to try it, banging bruv, banging!' Zee often got overly excited when he'd talk about cannabis. In fact, he'd get overly excited talking about most things, whether it'd be about a girl he liked, or a car he drove, or the day he'd had. Zee's passion often misled people into believing something was a lot better than it actually was, but not Adam. Adam knew better. Ironically, it was exactly this personal attribute that Adam loved about Zee, there was never a dull moment when he was around, and his stories, although exaggerated, were enjoyable nonetheless. Adam didn't need a weed sales pitch. He needed the pick-me-up and would've smoked anything.

'Zee you said that last time, and that weed last time was dusty man.' He said as he shook his hand and gave him a one armed hug.

Zee took another pull of the joint. 'Junior, just try it!' Adam had become accustomed to being called Junior by Zee. They first met during work experience last year and the boss was also called Adam, to avoid confusion the office began referring to the boss as "Senior" and the younger Adam got the less prestigious nickname of Junior.

'Hey, you.' a voice called out. Nikkita was sat with her long legs crossed and stretched out in front of her on top of the hill smoking a cigarette. She was beautiful, and at that moment, in the evening light, she looked gorgeous. Her tight white vest top accentuated her curves, and the blue denim short-shorts always made men, young and old, stare. Adam tried not to gawk at her toned legs stretched out on the soft grass. She turned on her side to face Adam and smiled. They'd been in the same class since they were eleven-years-old. Adam secretly liked her then, and he secretly liked her now. It was only after he turned fourteen that her group of friends and his group of friends started hanging out together. He was fairly certain that having access to drugs and alcohol was what gave them common ground. But hanging out almost every day built a strong bond between them all.

'Hey.' Adam replied, smiling as he tried to remain smooth. 'Loving the tan.' he joked as he pointed to her pasty white legs. Getting little digs on her usually helped ease his nerves.

Nikkita blushed as she became self-conscious about her bare legs. 'It's a work in progress.' She joked. 'You love them really!' Her Turkish heritage had blessed her with a skin that glowed during summer. However, it had been a particularly cold spring in London this year. It was almost the end of June but her pale legs were a far cry from the tanned shade of brown they usually were by now. Adam caught himself staring and looked away.

'Yo!'The voice took Adam by surprise, it came from behind him but he didn't need to turn around to know who it was. 'Took your sweet time playa!' Adam spun around and saw Adil walking towards him. As if pre-programmed to do so, they both raised their right hands and clapped them together, with hands gripped, they pulled each other in for a brief one armed hug.

'Damn dude, didn't even see you there,' Adam was glad to see Adil, but he suddenly recalled that Adil had a prior appointment today. 'Wait, what the heck are you doing here? I thought you said you had a job interview today?'

'Already done it.' he replied smugly. 'They called me up this morning and asked if I could come in earlier.' Adil extended his hand to Zee who took a quick pull of the joint before handing it over to him. 'Someone backed out, so I thought heck with it, why not, just get it over and done with,' Adil took a deep inhalation. 'I've been cacking myself about this interview all week so the sooner it's over with, the better.' He let out the smoke slowly, watching the smoke billow out.

Adam looked at his friend up and down, it wasn't often he got to see him in a shirt and trousers. 'Coming straight from the interview?'

Adil realised Adam was referring to his attire. 'Yeah, if I went home first mum wouldn't let me out again without making me eat, and sort my room out.' He took another inhalation on the joint. 'Didn't want to be late to the party.' He smiled as he exhaled the thick cloud of smoke and passed the joint over to Adam.

Adam took a drag. 'Well at least you're getting interviews bro.' he exhaled sharply and resisted the urge to cough. 'How'd it go anyway?'

'Ah man, I don't know.' Adil stared down at his feet, brushing the blades of grass with his shoes. 'Most of it went well but I think I messed up one of the questions, but sod it, it's done now. So no point worrying about it, let's just see what happens'.

Adil's ability to remove stress from his life was enviable. It was evident from his childhood that he would be destined for great things. He was a naturally gifted child and excelled in school. A "straight A" student and part of almost every extracurricular kids club imaginable. It was a mystery to Adam how, despite all his geeky habits, he was never really bullied at school. 'You know you're probably gonna get it.' Adam replied in an uplifting tone handing the joint back to Zee.

'Thanks, bro.' Adil looked up and smiled. He loved how Adam always supported him and made him feel sure of himself.

'So ladies,' Zee interjected as he pulled out a large zip lock bag from his pocket filled with fluffy green buds. 'are we gonna talk, or are we gonna smoke!?' Zee wrapped his arms around them both and marched them to where Nikkita was sat still bathing in the final few rays of the sun.

Adam smiled as he dived into his pockets and produced a box of cheap cigarettes and rolling paper. 'Let's smoke!'

∞

It had just past 10:45pm and Adam knew that he would get into trouble if he didn't leave soon. Summer had just begun and he didn't want to be grounded for any of it.

'Guys, I'm gonna head off, I'm proper buzzin' and my mum is gonna kick my arse if I'm not home before eleven.'

'Dude, what are you, a baby?' Zee jibed in an obvious attempt to get Adam to stay. Zee also lived without his father, but unlike other kids his age, his mum seemed pretty relaxed with him being out regardless of the time. Everyone in the group wished that their mum was as chilled as Zee's. He always got to stay out till the party was well and truly over, and then some.

'Bro, you know what my mum's like; "her house, her rules" and all that crap.' Adam hated that saying. It was his mother's trump card whenever the argument wasn't going her way.

Adil was sat gently swinging on the adult swings nearby, he was just staring across the park in the darkness clearly thinking about something. 'You know what we should all do?' he suddenly chimed. 'Get a place of our own and split the rent. It'd be so much fun. I'm sure that if we all got jobs we could afford it.' It was common for moments of inspiration to descend suddenly and without warning whenever they smoked marijuana. Adam often wished that he kept a notepad on him whenever they smoked, some of the conversations were mind blowing new perspectives on life. The only problem was that they were too high to remember them afterwards.

'Sure, I'll just cash in my trust fund shall I?' Nikkita joked.

'No seriously, it'd be totally do-able if we all chipped in together.' Adil had clearly been thinking about this for some time.

Adam threw his arm over Adil's shoulders 'Dude, as much as I'd love to, it's not going to work, we're all broke and we're all jobless. You've also forgotten to factor in our parents, credit checks and the deposit.' Adil began to realise that in reality, it wasn't so simple.

Adam sensed that Adil seemed slightly dejected by his response. 'Maybe one day man, when we're all a little older and a little richer.' Adam comforted. 'Anyway guys, I seriously gotta jet, so I'm out.' Adam went through the usual goodbye routine of high-fives and one armed hugs with the guys. He finally approached Nikkita and gave her a gentle hug and a kiss on the cheek. It was their little tradition. The girls in the gang always got a hug and a peck on the cheek. In a strange way it made Adam feel grown up. Recently however, his friendly goodbye hugs with Nikkita were lingering just a little longer than usual. He noticed that the hugs were a bit tighter, and the previously innocent kisses were beginning to slowly creep closer to the lips. Adam kissed her goodbye and felt the edge of her lip on his. His heart pounded as he pulled away pretending not to notice. He stared at Nikkita to gauge her reaction, but she just smiled and stared back completely un-phased.

'Err, by the way,' he said breaking the awkward tension. 'what happened to Tania and Claire tonight?'

Nikkita smiled as she realised Adam was trying to diffuse the awkwardness of the semi-kiss they'd just shared. 'Tania's out with her boyfriend, I think they've gone to the cinema. I don't know about Claire.'

'Claire's with her mum.' Adil interjected, oblivious to any awkwardness. 'They've gone shopping, Lakeside I think.'

'Cool, well, when you speak to them tell them I said hi.' Adam began walking towards the park gate. 'Zee, call me tomorrow if you wanna do something yeah?'

'Safe, Junior!' He yelled back. 'Laters!'

Adam pressed the button on his white G-SHOCK watch and his dial instantly illuminated into a bright turquoise. *10:51, bang on time.* He walked as quickly as he could through the familiar streets he grew up in. His head was still swimming with the effects of the marijuana. It was a pleasant, hazy feeling, but something in his mind was feeling strange right now.

Adam had been smoking marijuana for over a year now, ever since his uncle Sam first introduced it to him. Sam never felt like an uncle to Adam, not in the traditional sense. Sam was Adam's Dad's younger brother. A small seven-year gap meant that whilst growing up they often hung out at Sam's house where he lived with Adam's Grandma.

Grandma Sheila was awesome and loved Adam to bits. She was notoriously harsh on her own kids, but she was never harsh with Adam, he was her first and eldest Grandchild. Grandma Sheila had a strong work ethic and ran her own jewellery stall at Queen's Market in East Ham near the West Ham football grounds in London. On the weekends she'd leave at 5am in the morning, rain or shine, and sell her fashion accessories until well past 8pm. He was only twelve when he started helping Grandma run the stall on Saturdays. Occasionally he'd make £5 a day, but if it was a particularly bad day, he was content in being paid in sweets from the sweet shop around the corner.

Grandma's busy life meant that the house was pretty much Sam's for most of the day, he was a university student and often had cool older friends over at the house. Sam loved spending time with Adam and they'd often cruise around in Sam's car, play board games, watch movies and smoke the occasional cigarette. Adam didn't always like the taste or the smell, but the habit began to grow on him.

One day Sam took Adam to visit Ross, a new friend Sam met at university. Adam was mesmerised as he watched Ross prepare a marijuana joint with delicate precision and attention to detail. To Adam, when Ross had finished, the joint looked like a piece of art; beautifully shaped and packed full of cannabis.

Having rolled up, Ross grabbed his lighter and looked up at Sam, 'Is it cool?' He asked referring to the fact that Adam was in the room with them.

'Yeah man, Adam's safe.' Sam assured.

Adam smelled the wondrous aroma instantly fill the room as Ross lit the joint. It was a strange sweet sickly smell, but he liked it. To Adam, it definitely smelled better than cigarettes. Before long, the joint found its way over to Adam. He looked over at Sam for approval.

'Just a little tug,' Sam warned. 'take it easy, it's strong.'

Adam sucked on the joint as if it were a cigarette and inhaled the thick unfiltered smoke. He instantly began coughing and spluttering.

Ross burst into laughter. 'He warned you it was strong dude. That blast you just took was Rasta level man.'

Sam took the joint away from Adam. 'You okay?'

The coughing soon passed and Adam was transported to a comfortable dream like state. 'Yeah...' Adam replied suddenly feeling very drowsy. Adam melted into the sofa with a smile on his face, laughing uncontrollably at the slightest provocation for the rest of the afternoon. Adam knew from that day, he loved marijuana. Coincidently, his friends at school also started getting into it, which made getting hold of it a lot easier. By the time he turned fifteen almost everyone he knew smoked it at social get-togethers.

But despite being familiar with its effects, walking home from the park right now the marijuana was having an odd effect on him.

Adam had to stop for a moment. He knew that his mum would ground him for sure if he was late, but he was feeling dizzy and almost tripped over as he missed the kerb. *Damn, Zee was right, what the heck is in this weed?!* He placed his palm on a gritty brick wall to stabilise himself. Everything was swaying. The building, the road, the streetlights, everything was moving. *Wait, this isn't the weed. Weed doesn't do this, what the heck is going on?!* He tried to shake his head and clear his mind, but it only made it worse. The more he focussed on the road, the more things were moving. He suddenly realised that he had felt this feeling before. Something was familiar about all this, but he couldn't think straight. The motion in his head was making him dizzy, he had to sit down.

'Don't sit down, if you sit down now, you won't get back up, keep going!' He urged himself. He knew he had to make it home. *Don't sit here on the street like a homeless crack-head Adam, don't do it.* This was his neighbourhood, he was worried that if anyone saw him like this it'd get straight back to his mum, and she'd kill him if she found out he'd taken drugs. He held his head in his hands and closed his eyes to help stop the swaying. Nothing was working. He rested against the wall and slowly slid down until he was sat on the floor, completely incapable of movement.

Every so often he opened his eyes to see if the swaying had stopped, but it was unrelenting. No one was around to help him. He sat there mentally crippled, all alone and isolated. *Help me God.* It seemed his prayer had been instantly answered as he looked up and out of nowhere, he saw something at the far end of the alleyway. Everything was moving so dramatically that he wasn't sure whether it was the shadow of a wheelie bin, a person, or an angel. But whatever it was, it wasn't there before. As he tried to focus it seemed to look like someone was standing there, just watching him.

'Help.' Adam pleaded.

But the shadow just stood there. Adam had to close his eyes, he was about to vomit. He couldn't take the swaying anymore. With his eyes closed, he mustered a much louder call.

'Help!' he yelled.

He took a deep breath and opened his eyes to look up again, the figure had moved, he could now tell that it was a man, walking towards him. The light was behind him in an otherwise dark alleyway making him appear as black as a silhouette. Adam tried to focus. Only the outline of his frame was distinguishable. But Adam noticed he was tall, and wearing a dark jacket and big boots. *Thank God. Someone's here to help.*

Suddenly he realised why all this was feeling so familiar to him. *My nightmares*. He recalled his most recent episode only ten days ago. They started when he was just thirteen-years-old. They occurred once every few months. But over time they began occurring more and more frequently. Being a teenage boy, he preferred to keep his embarrassing secrets hidden. He didn't tell his friends out of fear of ridicule, and kept it from his mother because he knew she'd make a huge fuss, worry unnecessarily, and insist on spending hours waiting in the A&E department of a hospital, only to be told by an over-worked NHS Doctor that everything was fine, and to go home. But as he sat there paralysed on the cold hard road, he regretted his decision. He wished he had told everyone.

With his nightmares now on his mind, the swaying and dizziness got worse, everything in his vision was now violently shaking. It was like an earthquake rapidly escalating up the Richter scale in his mind. He couldn't take it anymore, his stomach turned as the motion sickness took hold and he threw up on the side of the road. His head dropped as everything began to fade to black. With his last few moments of consciousness, he saw the dark figure of the man in the black coat and boots walking towards him. It was too late, the darkness took over and everything went black.

Trapped in the darkness, Adam called out into the pitch black void of his empty mind. *Help me.*

Although the words didn't reach Adam's physical lips the dark stranger seemed to respond to them. He stood above Adam's limp body directly beneath a streetlight, his face masked in shadow. Adam tried in vain to open his eyes, but his body simply refused to obey. Despite his inability to see, he could feel the stranger was close. He felt a strange aura emanating from within him that he couldn't quite comprehend. He knew he was in the presence of someone strong, and not just in a physical sense. Instead of feeling fearful, an unusual sense of comfort washed over Adam. As if he had just met his guardian angel.

'You're nowhere near ready Adam.' His voice was warped as if it had been slowed down on a record player, but it pierced straight through the darkness and the physical words painted themselves in colourful red paint in Adam's mind. In his mind's eye, he looked at the words and he focussed on the last word of the sentence. *He knew my name.* But Adam was sure he'd never met this person before.

Adam began to hear a sound. He wasn't sure if it was in the physical world, or just in his mind. The paint before him began vibrating. The sound was like the annoying monotone of a television channel when the broadcasting signal had ended for the day. The paint began vibrating harder and harder as the piercing tone grew louder and louder. As the tone peaked into a deafening noise the words suddenly shattered in his mind and Adam lost all consciousness. Everything went dark.

Adam woke up and realised he wasn't in the alleyway anymore. For a moment he didn't know where he was. He looked around as he cautiously got to his feet, he realised that he'd been sitting on the floor half propped up against the wall. He then recognised the recycling bins, he turned around and looked for more familiar landmarks and realised he was actually outside his own council block. *What the hell?* A mixture of relief and confusion overwhelmed him. He checked his watch; 11:21pm. *Damn! How did I just lose thirty-one minutes!* He tried to recollect how he'd got here.

Then, like a tsunami, everything came flooding back. He remembered his seizure, his blackout, the strange man in the boots, everything. Instinctively he scanned himself to check if his phone, wallet and keys were still with him. After a quick self pat-down, everything checked out okay. He opened his wallet to ensure nothing had been stolen. His bank cards, national insurance card and Game store card were all still there, along with his two crumpled £5 notes. He finally breathed a sigh of relief and realised that his gut feeling about the man was right, he was a good guy. His panic faded and was immediately replaced by gratitude. He looked up and thanked God for sending an angel to his aid at his time of need. *Zee and Adil are gonna freak when they hear about this one.* He headed towards the security door that led to the internal lifts. As he used his fob to buzz himself in, his mind began to clear and more unanswered questions began to arise. *Wait, how did he get me back here?* Then Adam's face turned pale. *How did he know where I lived?*

Adam's head was a mess. He didn't know what problem to focus on first. It was now 11:24pm and Adam knew he was in trouble with mum when he got home. *There goes my summer.* Dejected, he pressed the button for the 3rd floor knowing that this time, his mum wouldn't let it slide. The lift doors slowly closed as it jerked and hummed to life slowly hauling him up. *I can't tell her the truth, she'd worry too much and never let me go out again.* He cycled through excuses in his mind to see if he could dream up anything even remotely plausible enough to save him. *The buses were running late. No, the park is too close for a bus. Wait, I got mugged. No, no, that would just make it worse. The police...?* Adam felt a spark of inspiration. *Yes, the police stopped us! That would work! Yeah, it wasn't my fault! I'll tell her the police questioned us for hanging out in the park after dark.* It was plausible enough, the police presence in the area over the past few years was significantly higher than it used to be and everyone had noticed it. Officers were often seen patrolling the parks around east London watching out for kids Adam's age. *Perfect.*

Adam opened the door to the flat as quietly as he could, but the latch on the lock seemed extra loud tonight. CLICK-CLACK. He winced as he closed the door behind him. He illuminated his oversized G-Shock watch. *11:28pm. Crap! Please be asleep, please be asleep.* As he peeped inside he noticed all the lights were off, but a familiar glow was coming from the living room. *Dammit! TV's still on. Mum's definitely awake.* He crept quietly towards his bedroom, trying to avoid her altogether. He figured it'd be easier to deal with her in the morning.

'Adam!?' bellowed his mum. 'Get in here, now!'

Adam let out a heavy sigh. There was no avoiding her tonight. *Time to face the music.* He walked towards the living room, now feeling free to make as much noise as he wanted. *No need for stealth now.*

'Hey mum.' He said, trying to be as nonchalant as he could.

'What time you call this?' Adam could tell by her tone that she was livid. 'It's almost midnight!'

Midnight? Adam checked his watch again. It read 11:29pm. His mother usually over-reacted when trying to prove her point, especially when it came to time. 'Mum, it's not even half-past yet. Look.' He raised his wristwatch to her face.

Sharon slapped his arm away. 'Do you remember what you promised me?' She gave him a look that made him feel like he was six-years-old again.

'Mum, it's not my fault, I swear. We got stopped by police and-'

'Stopped by police?!' she gasped. Raising her children right was everything to Sharon. She'd raised her children alone ever since their dad disappeared. Adam's father went to work one day and just never came back. No goodbye, no note. Just... gone. Raising two children on benefits was hard and they never had much money, but Sharon did the best she could with what she had, and for the most part, they were happy.

As far as Sharon was aware, Adam had never been involved with the police before. He knew that unless he came up with a good story right now, things could go from bad to worse.

'Mum, don't freak out, it was nothing, they thought we were causing trouble, but we weren't. I swear. After that they just let us go.' Adam saw the worried expression wasn't leaving his mother's face and he began to doubt whether this was a good story to use. *Should've bloody said I was mugged!*

Sharon respected the law and actually liked police officers. The only experience she had with them was when they investigated her husband's missing person case. They were extremely thorough and helped her get back on her feet when she had no one else to turn to. 'Adam, tell me the truth, what happened? What did you do? The police wouldn't stop you for no reason.'

Adam was pleased that at least she was buying the story. But he wasn't out of the woods yet. 'Mum, I swear, I did nothing, Zee, Adil and Nikkita were with me, you can call them and ask them if you want.' He knew she would never do that, not in the middle of the night at least. 'We were all just chilling in the park and it was almost eleven. I was actually leaving to come home and the police walked by.' He kept firm eye contact and tried to sound as believable as he could. He read somewhere that visualising the fake scenario in his mind made telling it a lie more realistic. He started imagining his own story. 'They saw me walking away and must have thought I was walking away because I had something to hide. So they called me back and the two officers searched and questioned us. They didn't find anything and told us to go home.' If he were an actor on stage, this is where he would have paused for a standing ovation for his amazing acting skills. He held her gaze and tried to look as genuine as he could, he tried not to think about how this situation had just become an astronomical lie involving the police. He was making it up as he was going along and hadn't thought it through this far. But there was no backing out now. He was all in. He had to tread carefully, one inconsistency, one slip-up, and she'd know something was off and catch him out.

Sharon's worry dissipated somewhat. She now had a more inquisitive look upon her face. 'Questioned you?' She probed as she stood up, her hands now firmly on her hips. 'What did they ask you?'

Adam wasn't expecting to go into details. The question caught him by surprise. 'Err...drugs, they wanted to know if we had drugs on us.' Adam instantly regretted bringing up the subject. *Dammit, why didn't I say knives, or Guns, or Bazookas! Dumbass.* His mind reeled back to the time when his mother found a tiny bag of cannabis in his school uniform. He'd managed to convince her at the time that it was his friend's and that he didn't smoke himself, but that lie just made his mother sceptical of all his friends, which was just as bad, if not worse, for his social life. Sometimes there was no winning with her. In retrospect, he wished he'd just confessed to it back then. But knowing his mother, she'd have him in rehab by now.

'Drugs!' Sharon blurted as she walked to the lights and flicked them on. Adam expected this. He was smart enough to know that red eyes were a dead giveaway. As usual, he'd used eye drops before leaving the park but wasn't sure if the violent seizure he experienced had caused his eyes to redden again.

She looked into his eyes carefully and then up and down to see if there was anything out of place. When she was finally satisfied she walked over to him and slapped his arm. 'And what did they find?' she asked expectantly.

'Nothing. I told you. If they had, I'd have been in jail right now.'

'I don't want you hanging around with that Zee anymore.' She never had anything against Zee per se, but whenever there was trouble, Zee always seemed to be around.

'Mum, Zee is cool. He had nothing to do with any of this you're making such a big deal about this just like I knew you would.' He tried to act annoyed. He then took a deep breath, pretending to calm himself down. 'Please mum, I'm tired and I just wanna go to bed now. Is that okay?' He tried to soften his tone and lay on the charm reminding her that he was still her baby boy.

'Get lost.' She conceded. 'I'll let you off this time. But next time you're not home on time, you can stay out permanently. Don't bother coming back!'

Adam had heard that threat before and he knew she was being dramatic. Adam turned around and let out a quiet sigh of relief. *Frekkin' close one.* He headed down the narrow hallway and towards his bedroom.

Sharon took a deep breath and sighed as she sat back down. She had no idea how to manage him anymore. Sometimes she'd wonder; *would he have been more sensible had his father been around?* To her, he was still her little boy, trying to be a grown up. But handling a child was very different to handling a teenager. 'There's food in the fridge if you're hungry.' she called out.

Grateful to finally be alone in his room Adam now had time to think. *What the hell happened back there?* His mind was spinning with what felt like endless unanswered questions. *Who was that man? Why did he help me? Why did I black out like that? How did he know where I lived?* Just as he felt like he was losing his mind something clicked. It was only a small part of the puzzle, but it was a glimmer of light on an otherwise dark mystery. *My nightmares,* he recalled. There wasn't much to go on since Adam could never quite remember what happened in his nightmares, nor recall what exactly made them so terrifying. But there was a strong connection with what happened on the street today and the feeling he felt immediately after having a nightmare. He rattled his brain to think of any obvious patterns or triggers that caused the nightmares. He considered his dietary habits to see if he was reacting to something, or having an allergic reaction. But he was certain it wasn't that. He pondered if his night terrors were related to his mental state of mind just before going to bed, he recalled events that occurred prior to his seizures but no obvious patterns jumped out at him. He knew that they weren't fear related, they weren't stress related either. Nothing made sense. They seemed completely random. The only pattern he could spot was that over the past few months they had been occurring a lot more frequently. But today was different, today, for the first time the night terrors crossed over from the realm of childish nocturnal nuance into a real waking, crippling disability.

Suddenly, Adam became worried. *What if I'm sick? What if there's something wrong with my brain?* Adam had no idea what the symptoms of a brain tumour were so he decided to investigate. He walked over to his desk, sat on his swivel chair and flipped open his laptop. His desk was cluttered with semi-complete coursework from various classes. *Damn, gotta hand that essay in soon.* He reminded himself as he tidied up the pages waiting for the laptop to boot up. He nostalgically browsed through his vintage pile of classic Hip Hop CDs that he no longer listened to, but couldn't bear to part from. His messy room was merely an extension of his cluttered desk. His clothes were scattered on almost every inch of the floor, his mother always nagged him about the mess, but as far as he was concerned he had a system. His mother only ever made the mistake of clearing his room once. Adam couldn't find his favourite hoodie for a week after that and insisted it was her fault. Since then, his mother stopped clearing his room as long as he promised her to be tidier. His walls were plastered with posters of 2pac, Notorious B.I.G. and other famous rappers, along with posters of his favourite movies, most of which involved gangsters, guns, and drugs. He loved movies by Quentin Tarantino. A large black and white poster of Samuel L. Jackson and John Travolta from the famous gun-pointing scene in Pulp Fiction dominated his main wall. He must have watched that movie a hundred times. It was the first time he truly fell in love with the gangster movie genre. He loved acting out the Pulp Fiction scenes with his friends. He once went through the entire movie in his head and accurately rearranged the scenes in chronological order. He was proud of the accomplishment even though his friends thought he was crazy and had way too much time on his hands. The login screen chimed to life and Adam spun back around and logged in.

Adam Googled the words;

BRAIN TUMOR SYMPTOMS

Google instantly returned the results, all 25,000,000 of them. Adam clicked on the first link on the UK's NHS website. He read through the symptoms and gulped as he felt a sense of dread overcome him. *Headaches, memory problems, pressure on the brain, dizzy spells, seizures and fits. Oh my God, I've got most of these symptoms.*

He took his time and read through everything, from symptoms to surgery. He finally turned away and looked at himself in the mirror in despair. *I've got a brain tumour.* He became depressed and anxious, and the happy buzz from the marijuana completely faded away.

The only thing that didn't make sense to him was why he wasn't having fits. The website said that sufferers usually have seizures. But then it suddenly all made sense. *My nightmares, aren't nightmares... they're seizures!* Adam recalled how his nightmares were occurring more and more often, and today what he suffered in the alleyway was a full blown daytime seizure.

Adam spun back around to his laptop and typed in;

ODDS OF SURVIVING A BRAIN TUMOUR

The results weren't good. 40% of those diagnosed died within the first year, and only 20% survived five or more years. Adam's heart sank as he slumped back into his chair. His shock turned into sadness as he contemplated how he'd tell his mother. The thought of dying so young and leaving behind his family and friends broke his heart. *How long do I even have left? There's so much stuff I'll never get to do.* He closed the laptop screen and slowly made his way back to the living room where his mother was still sat watching Gems TV.

'Mum, I have to tell you something.'

Her maternal instincts could tell from the way he said those words that this was going to be bad news. 'What is it, Adam?' her voice was cautious and she braced herself.

Adam wasn't going to beat around the bush with this. 'Mum, I think I have a brain tumour.'

She closed her eyes and shook her head to help process what she just heard. 'What?!' She replied, hoping she had misheard. She was prepared for almost anything, but she wasn't prepared for that. 'What makes you say that?' She questioned sceptically.

This was it, time for the truth. 'I've been... I've been having these nightmares and headaches for a couple of years now and they come and go, and it's no big deal. But today I had one in the street. Mum, it was so bad that I just collapsed.' Sharon gasped and realised that he wasn't joking about this. 'Someone helped me home while I was unconscious. I didn't tell you 'coz I knew you'd get worried.' Sharon stared at him lost for words. Adam could tell she was trying to process the bombshell he was dropping on her. 'I've just been researching the symptoms on the internet, and I can't hide it from you anymore, I'm scared now. I think I need to go to the Doctors.' Adam broke eye contact from his mother. Her eyes were filling with the type of empathy only a mother was capable of, and seeing it made the whole thing feel real. 'I think I have a brain tumour.'

Sharon's eyes were wide with shock. The voices on the television felt distant and muted as if the hosts of the show themselves had realised how serious the conversation was and considerately turned their own voices down. The light from the TV was projected on to Sharon's face in the otherwise dark room.

'Turn the light on Adam.' Her voice was soft and concerned.

Adam flicked the switch and sat on the sofa across from her. In the light, Adam witnessed a look he had never seen on his mother before. She sat there in stunned silence. But he could tell her mind was racing and she couldn't collect her thoughts to speak. She looked up at Adam and as she did a single tear ran down her cheek, seeing it made Adam emotional too and he looked up at the ceiling to stop his own tears from falling. She quickly wiped it away and tried her best to compose herself.

'We're going to the hospital right now.' She commanded, her voice cracked with emotion.

Adam knew she'd say that. 'Mum, please.' He begged. 'It's the middle of the night, and I'm really tired. It's not an urgent situation and they're going to take forever to see us. I don't want to sit on those hard plastic chairs all night.'

Both Adam and Sharon had a lot of experience of going into the A&E department at odd hours of the night. Sidney suffered from asthma and occasionally had attacks so bad that going to the hospital was the only option. She knew

Adam had a point. The nurses wouldn't prioritise him as they wouldn't consider the situation an emergency. 'Are you sure you don't want to go right now, it'll only take ten-minutes in a taxi? How are you feeling now?'

'I'm fine now. Just... tired.'

She walked over and inspected him closely, and other than looking a little drowsy he looked completely normal to her. 'Okay fine.' She conceded. 'But first thing tomorrow morning, make sure you're dressed by 9am we're going to the Doctor's office. I want Dr Dutta to take a look at you properly.

'Ok mum.' Adam agreed.

'Hey, do you want anything? Are you hungry?'

'I'm okay mum, just want to rest.' Adam got up and began walking to his room.

'Set your alarm for 8am. Let's be there first so we don't have to wait long.'

'Will do mum.' Adam closed his bedroom door. He took a deep breath and breathed out sharply. *Boy, that was tough.* He glanced at the clock. It was approaching 1am and he knew he didn't have long to go before he had to wake up again. He hated waking up early.

Dressed in his pyjamas and now laying in bed, he reflected on the conversation he just had with his mother and realised that he felt so much lighter as if a burden had been removed. It reminded him of a saying he'd heard somewhere; *A problem shared, is a problem halved.*

Sharon sat there staring at the television, but all she could think about was Adam. Tears were streaming down her face and she considered the possibility of losing him. *I'm not going to let that happen. No way.* She got up and turned off the T.V. and prepared for bed, tomorrow was going to be an important day.

RECRUITMENT

As night descended in the West End of London the street lamps and neon signs rejuvenated the concrete streets with a new vitality. Parts of London were transformed once the sun set, becoming unrecognisable from their prior forms. During the day, the busy banks and popular landmarks dominated, only to become deserted icons of history during the night. But then magically, the derelict and intricate alleyways became arteries of life as shops lit up bright signs attracting tourists like moths to a flame. Tourists flocked to affluent Knightsbridge to see the sights and visit the prestigious department stores that Knightsbridge was famous for. Above the streetlights in an 8th-floor penthouse apartment, Belkin gazed down on all the shoppers rushing around, busy in their own lives, oblivious as to how vulnerable their world was to an impending doom. He caught his own reflection in the window pane. He looked deep into his dark eyes. The tall, muscular figure staring back looked all but forsaken, yet at the same time, determination to complete the mission was burning within him.

The door clicked and swung open, Belkin didn't need to turn around to know it was Sash. She walked through the hallway and into the open, square shaped living room of the apartment. The penthouse was beautifully minimalistic with a striking red, white and black theme running throughout. The suite was encapsulated with floor to ceiling glass windows all around that provided amazing panoramic views of London. But the penthouse itself was more than just a home, it was headquarters.

Sash removed her shoes before she stepped down into the recessed lounge area. She knew how much Belkin hated people walking over the plush white carpet in outdoor shoes. She sat down on the white leather sofa with her feet up, waiting for Belkin to acknowledge her.

'Well?' She finally said, impatiently. 'Where is he?'

'Sash, he's not ready.'

'What?!' she exclaimed in disbelief. 'We've been watching him for years! He's showing the signs.' Adam had been on their radar for several years. His heritage made him a strong potential candidate.

Belkin continued to look out the window. 'If we engage him before he's ready, we run the risk of losing him altogether.' It was clear to Sash that Belkin didn't want anything to jeopardise the mission. 'I've been thinking about this for a while,' he continued, 'the next step is critical. Had it not been for the fact that we're on a deadline I'd have left it another year.'

'Belkin, weren't you the one who told me that Timestoppers should be aware once they're sixteen at the latest?' Sash recalled how young she used to think that age was when she first started out in this business. But now, she wished she could condition them at the age of ten. The hardest part was the training, most just weren't mentally prepared.

'As a general rule, yes,' Belkin replied. 'Sixteen is the age the process dictates, but Adam...' Belkin paused to turn and face Sash. 'Adam is different.' Belkin seemed bothered about something as if there was something else on his mind. Sash rarely saw Belkin this concerned.

Sash had never known Belkin to swerve off plan, it was completely out of character. 'The plan was to intercept today, judging by what you're saying, he's obviously not here. So what happened?'

'It's... his trigger.' He paused as if to recall the scene he witnessed earlier. 'They're seizures, and they're nothing like I've ever seen before.' Belkin walked down into the square shaped recessed lounge area and sat across Sash. 'His power is immense. I've never seen a Timestopper collapse and blackout from his trigger before.'

'He blacked out?' Sash sat up. 'What exactly happened?'

Belkin explained how Adam collapsed in the alleyway before he had the chance to talk to him. He described the seizure Adam experienced and explained how someone else suddenly appeared and carried him home unconscious as he hid out of sight. He described how he followed the stranger who carried him to his block of flats and left him there before disappearing into the night. He explained how he continued to watch him to make sure he woke up safe and was in a fit state to go home. Belkin believed that it was a sign that tonight wasn't the night they were destined to meet. He had to be patient and try again.

Sash started considering causes for the seizures, and wondered who the mystery man was. She went through his file in her mind, a file she had helped create and knew inside out. 'Do you think it's the cannabis habit reacting with his abilities?' She wondered.

'It's unlikely. Belkin replied. 'Alexander smoked cannabis and it didn't affect him like this.'

Sash wasn't expecting to hear that name, and for a moment she lost her train of thought. Poor Alexander. What a sweet boy he was. One of the hardest parts of the job was keeping professional boundaries. But over the years she learned to develop a wall. It kept her cold and detached. It helped with the emotional turmoil of losing candidates on missions or during training. Belkin's point was valid, prior Timestoppers used cannabis recreationally with no adverse effects on their abilities. There was no correlation between the times when Adam was intoxicated and the occurrence of his seizures, they seemed completely random.

'We will uncover the mystery behind his trigger and train him accordingly in time.'

'And the man?' Sash inquired.

'A good Samaritan perhaps, or maybe a family friend. I can't be sure. I didn't get a look at his face. But he knew where he lived. Oddly, he didn't wait for Adam to come around. Nor did he take him up to his flat. It's suspicious.'

Belkin stood up and walked towards Sash. 'Our first step, as you know, is an introduction. But we'll take it slow with Adam.' Belkin paused and looked into the distance recalling previous failures. 'I don't want to make the mistakes I've made with the others.'

'The others weren't your fault Belkin. They knew what the risks were. You did your best with them, we all did.'

It was obvious Sash was trying to comfort him, but Belkin didn't need comforting, he needed results. 'I have every faith that Adam is the one we've been looking for. I can't afford to get it wrong with him. There's not enough time. Everything about engaging him must be perfect.' He paused and looked at Sash. 'Therefore I'm changing protocol.'

Sash raised her eyebrows in exaggerated surprise. 'Okay...'

'This time, you're going to make First Contact.'

Sash couldn't hide her excitement. 'I'm honoured.' She smiled. She'd never been trusted with First Contact before. It was usually a make or break situation and Belkin always handled it. Excited by the news, Sash began thinking of creative ways to attract Adam's attention. 'Do you have something in mind,' she queried, 'or am I in complete creative control?'

'No, this one is yours.' Belkin replied. 'I think you can handle it, and I'd like to see the style of your approach.'

'Alright!' Sash beamed. 'Belkin, you won't regret it.'

Belkin smiled back. 'I know.'

HEALTH CHECK

Adam stared at himself in the mirror of his bathroom. He looked at the small clock on the bathroom ledge. *Crap, it's already 8:45!*' He was already dressed but hadn't eaten breakfast and his belly was rumbling. But today he couldn't tell if it was rumbling because he was hungry, or because he was nervous.

'Adam! Hurry or we'll be late.' called Sharon from the kitchen. 'We have to be there early for emergency appointments or we'll be sitting waiting all day.'

'Let's go, mum. I'm ready.' Adam walked into the kitchen and noticed Sidney having her breakfast watching Judge Judy on the small kitchen television. Adam wondered whether his mother had told his sister what was going on.

'Sid, your brother and I are going to the Job Centre, not sure how long it'll take but call me if you need me.'

Sidney sniggered and almost choked on her cereal. 'Aw, is mummy coming to help you talk to all those grown-ups eh Adam?' Sidney and Adam used any chance to get in digs with each other. Back when they were kids, handling Sidney was easy. If she got out of line a few punches from big brother did the trick. But now the game had changed, fighting was no longer an option, and his physical advantage counted for nothing in verbal warfare.

'Shut up Sid, they said I needed her signature, alright!' Adam almost surprised himself at how quickly he was able to create a plausible lie. Sharon stared at him uncomfortably. He read her eyes, she was clearly unhappy about lying any more than necessary. Adam remained quiet after that and ate his breakfast as quickly as he could. He wished he could tell Sidney the truth right now and watch that smug little smile disappear off her face. But despite how he sometimes loathed her, he knew that deep down she cared about him, and he had to admit, he cared about her too. He didn't want her to worry until all the facts were clear.

'Come on Mum.' Adam said as he shoved the last spoonful of cereal in his mouth. 'Let's get this over and done with.'

∞

'Mr. Newton... Mr Adam Newton'
'Yes. Here.' Adam got to his feet and walked over to the receptionist, his mother following closely behind him.

'The Doctor will see you now.' The receptionist smiled as she gestured towards the doctor's office.

Adam looked at his mum for comfort. Up until now, he'd been desperate to see the Doctor about his problem. But right now it felt like he was about to face his executioner. *What if it's bad news? I know it's going to be bad news.* Adam shook his head and tried to think positively, he tried to belittle the situation in his mind, but his mind wasn't going to be fooled so easily. He approached the door to the doctor's office and placed his hand on the handle. He paused as he took a deep breath and exhaled sharply. *No turning back now.* Mustering all his courage he pressed down on the door handle, pushed it open, and walked in.

'Ah, Adam, how are you? It's been a while.' Dr Dutta welcomed as he stared down at a pile of papers on his desk.

Adam held the door open for his mother. 'I'm good thanks.' Adam said as he cringed at the sterile smell of the doctor's office.

'If you're good then why have you come?' The doctor chuckled.

Adam hadn't been in the room for five seconds and he already felt like an idiot. Adam pondered how it was odd that people often answered out of habit rather than actually answering honestly; social conditioning at its finest. 'Well, actually, I'm not so good.' He corrected.

The doctor finally looked up and pushed his spectacles up the bridge of his nose. 'My, you've turned into quite a handsome young man.' He turned and faced Sharon. 'Mrs. Newton, it's nice to see you again. Please, take a seat.'

'Thank you so much for seeing us at such short notice.' Sharon began. 'I know how busy you are.'

'It's what I'm here for Sharon.' Dr Dutta replied as he wrapped his stethoscope around his neck and walked around the desk. He perched himself on the corner beside Adam. 'So young man, what seems to be the problem?'

Adam explained his nightmares and the incident on the street. He tried his best to describe the feeling of sickness and dizziness before the blackout he experienced.

After listening carefully the doctor placed his stethoscope in his ears and placed the diaphragm on Adam's back and listened to his heart for a few seconds. The doctor went back to his seat and checked through Adam's file. 'Adam, have you suffered from a cold or fever recently?'

'No.' Adam shook his head as he replied.

'Have you had any head injuries, any fights at school, any knocks during football?'

Adam took a moment and thought about it. 'I've had a few bumps during football, but nothing serious, and nothing to my head.'

'I see...' The doctor leant forward. 'Adam, I have to ask you an important question and you have to answer me honestly, don't worry about getting into trouble. Okay?'

'Okay...' Adam wasn't sure what this question was going to be about, but by the tone of the doctor's voice, he could tell that it was something he probably didn't want to answer in front of his mother.

Dr Dutta looked Adam straight in the eyes. 'Do you, or have you taken any drugs or alcohol recently?'

Adam physically gulped and instantly felt his face redden with embarrassment. It was the worst thing the Doctor could've asked him. He considered lying but there was too much at stake. He glanced at his mother and saw nothing but genuine concern for his wellbeing in her eyes. He looked back at the doctor and realised that he had to be honest.

'Yes...' he replied sheepishly. 'I've smoked a little weed over the last few days, but not much.' Adam wondered what was worse; the brain tumour, or his mother's wrath now that she knew he was a pothead.

'Anything else? Alcohol? Other Drugs?'

'No, just the weed.' Adam admitted.

'And how often do you smoke?'

'I'd say... two or three spliffs in a week.'

'Okay.' Doctor Dutta started scrawling on a notepad. 'Anything else you think I should know Adam?'

Adam sat there and thought for a while. He wasn't sure what that question meant. But he knew that there was nothing left to admit to. 'No. That's it.' Adam looked at his mother, to his surprise she didn't look angry, nor upset. But Adam knew that it didn't mean he wasn't in trouble later.

Dr Dutta finished scrawling and dropped his pen on the desk. He pushed his spectacles up and looked at Sharon. 'I suggest we send him for an MRI scan, it's designed to detect abnormalities in the brain. If something's wrong it's likely to pick it up.' Doctor Dutta turned back to Adam. 'In the meantime Adam I'd highly recommend you avoid any intoxications of any sort. I don't think that's the cause, but we need to rule it out.'

'Okay.' Adam nodded his face pink with embarrassment.

Doctor Dutta sat back on his chair and began scribbling on his notepad again. 'I'll make a referral for you today. The hospital will be in touch shortly with a date. I'll mark it as urgent.'

'Thank you, Doctor.' Sharon looked at Adam with a smile on her face.

'That's alright, just keep an eye on him, no driving or operating machinery, or anything else that could be a hazard if he suddenly has another seizure. These things can get worse, and can occur at any time.'

'Yes, of course, Doctor.' Sharon replied.

The Doctor tore off a prescription and handed it to her. 'Here's something for the headaches if they occur again. Follow the dosage on the box, no more than three tablets within twenty-four hours'.

Sharon took the prescription and they both stood up to leave. Adam wasn't sure how he felt about all this. He didn't get the answer he was hoping for, just another appointment, and this time in a hospital. *God, I hate hospitals, well at least I don't have to wait in A&E.*

FIRST CONTACT

Adam stood out on his balcony and stared out at the familiar city skyline. It was a hot evening in July, and everything looked beautiful. No matter how often he stood there and gazed at the same cityscape he always saw something new. Sometimes a new building, sometimes a new light, but what he loved most, was the sky; every day it looked completely different. But today Adam wasn't looking at anything in particular. Today he was just staring into the abyss lost in his own thoughts.

It had been a week since his visit to the doctor's office and Adam hadn't seen his friends once. He felt bad for avoiding them, but right now all he wanted was to be left alone. He knew Nikkita, Zee, Adil and the rest of the gang would suspect something was wrong since it wasn't like him to spend his summer holidays indoors. But Adam couldn't tell them, and he didn't want to lie. Right now, avoiding them was the only thing he could do, and he hated it.

Thanks to his researching skills Adam had become very familiar with the process that was likely to be involved if they did spot an irregularity with his brain. But knowing about the process offered him little comfort. *Why me?* Adam contemplated as he stared at the traffic moving slowly below. He looked at his watch but it was too dark to tell the time without illuminating the dial. He pressed down on the large **G** symbol and the watch instantly burst to life, emitting its usual super-bright turquoise glow. He glanced down at his watch to read the time, but something was wrong. The numbers had all disappeared, his entire display was blank. It was just a bright turquoise screen displaying nothing. Adam shook his wrist and looked again and suddenly he noticed letters slowly scrolling across the dial.

y–o–u–r–e– n–o–t s–i–c–k

Adam froze and felt his heart rate rise in shock. He stared at the message, he shook his wrist again, wondering if it was a glitch, but it didn't go away, the words just scrolled over again and again. *What the damn? I must be trippin'!* Adam began to panic, someone or something was communicating with him and he had no idea how to react. For a moment he wondered if his watch was trying to comfort him as if it were a toy from a Disney movie that had come to life to reassure him that all will be well. He chuckled at the thought. But he couldn't deny that there it was; a message, relevant to him on his wristwatch.

Someone's watching me. Adam's eyes darted around. He was outdoors in plain sight. Anyone with binoculars could be watching him from any one of thousands of locations right now. *But how are they controlling my watch?* Adam continued to look around and just then, beneath him on the road, a parked black Mercedes roared to life, it switched its lights on and sped off down the road, turned left and disappeared out of sight around the corner. Adam tried to catch the number plate but it was too small and too dark to make out the characters. He glanced back at his watch, the light had switched off. He pressed the button and it burst into life again, and staring back at him was the time; 11:01pm. *I really am losing my mind!*

Lying in his bed bouncing a ball against the wall, Adam was once again in deep thoughts. His mind desperately trying to solve the mystery of what he'd just witnessed. In a way he was thankful, the strange occurrence offered a welcome break from constantly worrying about his health. All he could focus on now was the surreal experience he just had. *The message... the car...my watch...* The thoughts circled in his mind over and over relentlessly. He retraced his steps and was certain he never took his watch off, and there was no way someone had taken it off him and tampered with it. He flipped open his laptop and tried to describe what happened to see if the search engines would return any answers. He scrolled and scrolled through thousands of results but nothing seemed relevant. He read something interesting about radio controlled text messages, but the device receiving the message had to be configured too, and he was certain his wristwatch didn't have the required hardware within it for such a thing to be possible. But then, it suddenly dawned on him. *Oh my God*. Adam closed the laptop and spun around to look at the mirror. *The alleyway guy!* Suddenly, he realised that his watch could have been tampered with by the stranger who helped him when he was unconscious.

CONFIDANT

Adil looked at his Seiko watch, it was almost 11:15am and despite having lots of errands to run in his new job he felt distracted. It had been over a week since he'd spoken to Adam, and it was unlike Adam to avoid his calls. Adil decided to take a break and he grabbed his cigarettes and lighter. He turned towards his manager who was on a call and made the internationally recognised gesture for "I'm going for a cigarette break" by tapping his index and middle fingers to his mouth. His manager nodded and spun around on his chair to continue his call. Adil grabbed his phone and headed for the designated smoking area in the staff car park to the rear of the building. He lit up the cigarette and took his time with the first couple of drags, watching the smoke as it escaped his mouth. With the cigarette gripped in his lips, he unlocked his phone and opened up his list of contacts and tapped on the call symbol beside Adam's name.

The phone had been ringing for a while, and after the fifth ring Adil was almost certain Adam wasn't going to answer and started wondering what he should say on the voicemail, but suddenly the call connected.

'Hello?' Adam answered in a croaky voice.

'Wow Adam, still asleep? Bloody alright for some eh?' Adil joked.

'Adil, bro, how you doin' man? Damn, what time is it?'

'It's almost midday you ragamuffin. Where the heck you been? I ain't seen you in time. You ain't even congratulated me on my new job yet.'

Adam tried to shift through the hazy memory banks in his mind. 'What job? Where you working?'

'Remember that interview I went to a couple of weeks ago? Well, it came through man, they offered me the job the next day! Can you believe it? I'm working in St. Pauls now.'

'No way man, that's awesome!' Adam beamed, genuinely happy for Adil. He knew that if there was anyone who was going to be successful in life from the group, it was probably going to be him. 'Congrats dude, sorry I've been offline lately, just had crap to deal with man.' Adam felt guilty for being such a recluse. His best friend had got his first job and he didn't even know until now.

'Seriously dude, what's up with you these days?' Adil complained. 'You've been away and we've kinda missed having you around, the rest of us all still hook up every day. The gang's been asking after you. People are starting to talk.' Adil was always straight-up with Adam, neither of them ever felt that they had to sugar coat anything that was on their mind.

'Really? Damn.... what's everyone been saying?' Adam frowned.

'Well for starters, that your mum has got you on lockdown for something major, is that true?' Of all the theories people had to explain Adam's disappearance, this one seemed the most plausible to Adil.

'No man, I've just been on a weird flex lately.'

'Bro, if you can't tell me, who can you tell?' It was hard to ignore Adil's sincerity as it shone through in those simple words.

Adam paused for a moment, he had no intention of telling anyone about this, but suddenly a sense of loneliness overcame him and Adam reasoned that confiding in his best friend might help him deal with it better. *I gotta tell him.*

Adam realised that he couldn't keep himself isolated like this any longer.

'Okay, Okay...' Adam sighed. 'Adil, look something's going on and I wanna tell you in person. But you gotta meet me somewhere so we can talk properly, I can't tell the guys yet, just you, and you gotta swear on your mum's life that you won't tell anyone, cool?' Adam had gone all in. He still wasn't quite sure if telling Adil was the right thing to do, but his heart was begging him to share the burden with someone who'd understand.

'Hell man, this sounds serious.' Adil frowned, he could tell from Adam's tone something was wrong and now wasn't sure whether he should be curious or concerned. 'Dude, you know me. Bro-code for life. I won't tell anyone.'

'Okay, what time do you get off work?'

'I get out of here at 5:30. I can come down to Mile End if...'

'No.' Adam interrupted. 'Not around here, let's meet in St. Pauls, I'll come to you.'

'Okay, no probs, so how about the Cafe Nero by the Merrill Lynch building, they've got a nice quiet basement seating area, best place for a private chat. It's always dead down there.'

'Yeah that's fine,' Adam confirmed. 'I'll find it. I'll be there at 5:30.'

'See you then man.'

'See you then.'

∞

Adil sat there in stunned silence as Adam spilt his guts about everything; the nightmares, the blackout, the stranger he saw on the street, the Doctor's appointment, his watch message, and finally his imminent MRI scan.

Adil stared at Adam in shock. 'Mind....blown, bro.' He finally blurted. Adil didn't know how to feel about what he had just heard. His head was struggling to process everything. *What advice does someone give in a situation like this*? He wondered. But then he looked up at his best friend and realised that coming up with a plan or solution wasn't what Adam needed right now. Right now he needed a friend. A friend who would throw an arm over his shoulder and tell him that everything would be okay. Simultaneously, Adil's sympathy was tainted with a sliver of anger that his best friend had been in such grief alone. 'This is crazy dude, why didn't you tell me sooner?'

'I didn't know how to. Besides, nothing is really confirmed. The MRI scan has to be done first. Then I'll need to wait for the results before I know for sure. I just wanted you to know so you don't think I'm skanking you. I wanna just forget about all this stuff, but I can't. It's always on my mind, and I know that if I see the guys they'll sense something's up and keep pressing me till I tell them. I don't want their pity, man. And they're gonna tell everyone, and it'll only get worse. So I thought I'd just avoid everyone and stay indoors. But now I'm going insane and needed to talk to someone I could trust.'

Adil wondered what he would have done if he were in such a situation. He quickly realised that he would've probably done the same and hidden himself to avoid the questions and negative attention.

'Okay so I get the health stuff,' Adil began, 'but what you said about that bloke has got me worried man. You sure he actually physically picked you up and brought you home?'

'Bro, I was knocked out. But I'm pretty sure he did. I got a weird feeling that this guy is linked to the message I got on my watch too.'

'Man, are you sure you saw a message on your watch? What pills they got you on?' Adil joked. 'I mean, that's some serious James Bond, mission impossible stuff right there.'

'The message was clear as day bro. I know what I saw, and I'm pretty sure he was in that Merc that took off right after.'

Adil sat in deep thought rubbing the stubble on his chin for a moment. 'Well, to be honest, just looking at the plain facts the guy seems pretty decent.'

The remark caught Adam by surprise. 'Decent?' He laughed.

'Think about it, I mean, he saw you collapse, he took you home, he didn't rob you, and now he's communicating through your watch, telling you that you're not sick and you've got nothing to worry about.'

Adam couldn't deny that Adil had a point. He slumped back in his chair for a moment and pondered the notion that maybe, just maybe this person wasn't some serial killer psycho. 'Well... well I guess you're right. But it makes me wonder, if he is behind all this, why is he being so mysterious about it? He clearly knows something that I don't, so why doesn't he just talk to me like a normal human being?'

'I don't know.' Adil admitted. 'That's what makes me nervous. Just keep your wits about you in case you see him again.' Adam nodded in agreement. 'So when's your MRI scan anyway?'

'Thursday.'

'This Thursday?'

'Yup.'

'Man, that's quick. NHS usually takes ages for my appointments!'

'They don't hang about for things like this. They act fast if they think you have something serious.'

Something serious. Those final words hung in the air like a bad smell, and a sombre mood suddenly fell upon both of them. They both sat there for a moment in silence, dwelling on the possibility of it all being real. Adil had no idea what to say or do to make his friend feel better.

'Bro, just know you can rely on me for anything ok. Through thick and thin I'll be there for you, I'll take Thursday off work and come with you.'

'Thanks, bro, but it's ok. Mum's coming with me, and I made her promise not to tell anyone, so I don't want her to know, you know.'

'Okay, okay. But as soon as you get out call me and tell me how it went.'

'Yeah cool.' Adam nodded.

'By the way, the guys are wondering what's going on with you and they're asking me on a daily basis if I've heard from you, what do you want me to tell them?'

'I don't know man.' Adam groaned. 'Just tell them I've been staying with my uncle's family in Birmingham for a couple of weeks.'

'Birmingham? That's a bit random.'

'Got a better suggestion?'

Adil thought for a moment and then shook his head. 'Not really.'

'Guess it'll have to do then.'

'Fine, Birmingham it is, and when exactly are you coming back from your imaginary holiday to Birmingham?'

Adam figured out the dates in his head. 'Hmm... tell them, next Saturday. By then I should have my results and I'll know one way or the other.'

'Cool, next Saturday.' Adil confirmed.

'If it's good news then happy days, and if not, then I'll just face the guys and tell them the truth. I won't be able to hide it forever and I can't keep living like this.'

As the reality of the situation was sinking in Adil felt a sudden wave of sadness overwhelm him and felt his eyes well up. The pang of emotion caught him off-guard and he quickly looked upwards as he took a sip of his cappuccino avoiding eye contact. 'Man, I still can't believe all this is happening.' He croaked before clearing his throat.

Adam noticed the wet shimmer in Adil's eyes and felt blessed that he had a friend who cared about him this much. He knew that telling him was the right thing to do and he felt better for doing so. 'Oi, I ain't dead yet so hold off on the waterworks.' Adam teased trying to make light of the situation.

Adil felt embarrassed and laughed, 'Shut up, I ain't teary over you! I burned my mouth on that last sip.' He lied. 'Anyway, what you gonna do for the next couple of days till your scan?' He asked quickly changing the subject.

'Same thing I've done for the past two weeks. Play on my PlayStation I've been stuck on this one Boss battle for ages, I swear it's gonna be the death of me!' He stopped and looked up at Adil as he realised what he'd just said. Adil looked back and after a few moments of silence they simultaneously burst into laughter.

PROTOCOL 8F

'I think it's time.' Sash concluded. 'Remember what you said, I'm in complete creative control, right?'

Belkin was thinking the same thing. He'd already waited long enough for this moment, and the clock was ticking. He should've intercepted Adam a long time ago. But he was worried, worried about Adam's lineage, he wasn't just some potential candidate. He sat there running through the plan in his mind, again and again, cross-referencing it to the milestones he had by now memorised. He had to achieve the goal before the ultimate deadline, and the deadline was approaching fast. He estimated that he was already running four-weeks behind schedule, and they hadn't even started with Adam yet, he was the key. He swivelled his white leather chair away from his desk and gazed out of the window of his office. Like the rest of the apartment, the office was minimal, with classy modern furniture and the same white, black and red theme running through it. The office felt clean and light. It was a place that Belkin used for solitude, problem-solving, and creating strategies.

'Belkin, you know what's at stake.' Sash continued. 'If you want me to succeed in recruiting him and giving him a fighting chance at success we need to act now. Hell, we needed to act last month!' Sash didn't understand why Belkin was procrastinating like this. It wasn't like him at all. He of all people knew it took years to train some candidates before letting them out on field ops, and most didn't even make it past training.

'Okay.' Belkin said flatly. He felt the gravity of the word on his shoulders. It felt heavy as if he had just agreed to execute somebody.

'Okay?' Sash echoed in pleasant surprise.

'You're right Sash. You are in creative control of his First Contact. Besides Adam is now mature enough to make his own decisions, legally he's no longer a child once he's sixteen.'

Sash looked into Belkin's eyes. 'Legally? Wait, have you been worrying about his legal age all this time?'

Belkin broke eye contact and looked away. 'I made a promise to his father. The Newton family has done more than their fair share for this cause and-'

'And nothing.' Sash Interjected. 'Joseph was a great man. A hero. Given the situation, I'm sure he would've wanted this for-'

'Look Sash,' Belkin cut in. 'We don't know what he would've wanted, but Adam is now old enough to decide for himself. My oath to Joseph expired when he turned sixteen. My morality has kept my hands tied. But I've decided that saving the world by risking the few demonstrates greater morality. I just wished I didn't know his father so personally.' Belkin stood up and walked to the bookshelf scanning the books within it. 'But like I said, the world is more important than my personal sense of guilt.'

'You're doing the right thing Belkin, you've tried finding other candidates and I know you didn't want to involve Adam. But it looks like he might be the one after all.' Sash watched Belkin pause at a book on the shelf before sliding it out. 'Want me to call the team and get this started?'

Belkin nodded in agreement as he looked at the cover of the book in his hand by Sun Tzu; The Art of War.

Over the past few years, Belkin travelled across the world and scouted a small elite team of naturally gifted individuals that he brought back to London. Considered outcasts and freaks of nature in their home countries, with

Belkin, they were a unified force. This was the mission his crew had been waiting for.

'Tell them that we're commencing Protocol 8F. Tell them to rendezvous here at headquarters 7am tomorrow morning.'

Sash beamed, she couldn't hide her excitement any longer. She felt that Belkin had been mentally detached over the past couple of months, but now suddenly he was back. The old Belkin, the Belkin she admired and respected.

'Right away, Captain.' Sash said as she turned and headed for the door.

'One more thing Sash.'

Sash stopped halfway out the door and spun around. 'Yes?'

'Were we able to obtain a copy of Adam's MRI test results?

'Yes, all negative. He's stressing over nothing. I guess one good thing about telling him the truth is that he can stop worrying about his health.'

'Good. Intercept Adam tonight.'

'Tonight?' Sash wasn't expecting that. She paused and raised an eyebrow.

'Is there a problem?'

'Nice to have you back Chief.' Sash smiled.

THE WOMEN

Adam was playing Call of Duty on his PlayStation when he heard the doorbell ring. It was just after 2pm and he wasn't expecting mum or Sid back from the market till at least 5pm. *God, mum and her damn GEMs TV.* It was well known that Sharon had a habit of ordering cosmetic jewellery from late night TV shows. Adam groaned as he rested the controller unable to pause the real-time online game knowing full well it would ruin his kill streak. He ran towards the door, turned the latch and swung it open.

'Surprise!'

'Nikkita?... Hey!' Adam exclaimed in shock as his heart began to race. She looked gorgeous. Her dark blonde hair bounced in the wind and hugged the soft contours of her face. She looked prettier than usual today. At first, Adam couldn't figure out what it was, and then the penny dropped. *She's wearing make-up.* He'd never really noticed make-up on her before, not even for the school disco. The make-up wasn't excessive, but it made her eyes sparkle, and her lips seemed more prominent and voluptuous. She looked as if she was getting ready to go on a date.

'Everything okay?' He asked anxiously. Nikkita had visited Adam before, but didn't usually make unannounced visits like this, and she never visited alone. 'Wha-what's going on?' He stuttered trying to act as cool as possible.

'Wow, that's nice isn't it?' She scoffed. 'A friend comes over to ask after you, and you don't even invite them in!'

Adam smiled to hide his embarrassment. 'Come on in, hun.' He said as he stepped aside. 'You know, you could've at least called love, you're lucky I'm not in my underwear!' He joked as she walked in.

'Hmm... shame.' Nikkita giggled as she made her way to his room and looked around. 'Goodness me Adam, did you get burgled last night? Look at the state of this place!' She jibed as she noticed his clothes all over the bed and floor. She glanced at the television and noticed the action in the video game still in full swing. 'Video games Adam? Shouldn't you be looking for a job or applying to college?'

'I'm learning important skills through these games Nikki.'

'Oh really?' She smiled. 'Like what exactly?'

'Hand-eye coordination, problem-solving, strategy, tactics, teamwork, you name it! It's more practical than school. Trust me, games ain't like Pac-Man anymore, I'm developing real life-skills.'

'Real life skills?' Nikkita laughed. 'When's the last time you led an Alpha Squad out to battle?'

'Well, maybe not the situation,' Adam chuckled. 'but mentally it's useful. I mean some of the puzzles in these games take me hours to figure out, but once you do, there's nothing in the world more satisfying.'

'Oh really?' Nikkita teased. 'Nothing at all?' She said as she raised an eyebrow.

Adam felt his cheeks flush. Nikkita was known for teasing and flirting with the guys from time to time but right now he wasn't sure if she really liked him, or if she was just joking around.

'Well...' he conceded. 'There might be one thing.'

'You are so full of crap Adam.' Nikkita laughed as she playfully slapped his arm. She turned towards his bed and moved his clothes to one side before sitting down and making herself comfortable. 'So what's going on with you lately? Where the hell you been the last couple of weeks?'

Adam hesitated in responding. He had been expecting the question, but he was still stuck for words. 'I'm sorry babe,' Adam finally confessed. 'I've just been going through a lot at the moment and needed to be alone for some thinking time with the family.' Adam didn't want to talk about it. The truth was that he wasn't playing video games because he enjoyed developing life skills. It was because they distracted him from his problems. For the first time in weeks, someone had come over and made him forget all about it.

'I just don't want to talk about it right now, but either way, it'll be over this week and I promise to be myself again.' He smiled.

Nikkita had no idea what that meant, but her instincts were telling her not to pry. 'Ooh, such a man of mystery.' She teased. 'Maybe that's why all the girls are crazy over you at school.'

Adam blushed as he laughed off the comment. 'Whatever.' He smiled. He looked at her and in that very moment he realised why he liked her so much. She had the innate ability to make any situation pleasant, he rarely felt awkward around her, and if he did, she could cast her magic and somehow make everything better.

'I'm sorry. You must have me confused with some other guy.' He joked back.

'Your name is Adam right?'

'Yes.'

'You live with your mum and sister right?'

Adam smiled as he realised she was taking this joke all the way. 'Yes.'

'You're awesome at Call of Duty right?'

'Yes, dammit, yes!'

'Sorry, you were right, I *do* have the wrong Adam.'

They both burst into laughter as Adam sat on the bed beside her. 'Hey, wanna learn how to play Call of Duty?'

'Learn?' Nikkita laughed. 'I'm a pro. Pass me the controller, you better have my guns unlocked.'

Adam handed her the controller both stunned and sceptical. 'You really know how to play?' He quizzed.

'Where's that... oh, here we go.' Nikkita barely heard Adam as she cycled through the options until she found the guns and equipment she was looking for. 'Okay, my class is set.' She said as she made some final tweaks. 'Yup, let's do this.' She turned and looked at Adam who was looking back at her completely dumbstruck. 'Oh and any map except Wasteland. God, I hate that map.'

'Sure,' Adam replied in amazement. 'how about Rust, that's a good map. Rust okay?'

'I love Rust! You're going down buster!' She beamed.

Adam began selecting the options and started the game. *Oh, my god, she's perfect.*

∞

Nikkita received a call from her mother and had to leave suddenly. Adam could tell her mother was angry with her about something, he didn't want to pry and didn't protest when she told him she had to go. He could tell she was having fun, which made saying goodbye even more difficult. He kept recalling the look of longing in her eyes as she left. *I should've kissed her, I'm so stupid.* He kept telling himself.

Sharon and Sidney had been back a while now. Sharon was cooking in the kitchen and Sidney was on the phone in her room. Sheer boredom kept Adam playing until the online game lobby lost its connection and the PlayStation network couldn't re-connect to the online servers. Frustrated, he threw his controller aside and sat there thinking about what other games he had. Suddenly his phone beeped alerting him to a new text message. Adam smiled before he even picked up his phone. *I bet its Nikkita.* Adam unlocked his phone and noticed something he'd never seen before. The sender was 'Unknown'. *What? Unknown?* He frowned as he looked at the screen. *I didn't know you could withhold a text message ID.* Adam opened up his inbox to read the message;

Adam, you are not sick. You are special. We can help each other. I'm outside, we should talk- Sash.

Sash? Who, or what is Sash? Adam read the message five times before he was able to register what he was reading. He was petrified. *Man, what is this crap?* Adam felt his heart rate rise and adrenaline course through his veins, he felt a sense of nervous anxiety, the kind he felt when he was about to get into a fight with someone after school and it was just minutes before the bell rang. He got to his feet and walked over to the window and peered outside. It was getting dark, but there was still a decent amount of daylight. He couldn't see anyone, just a row of cars parked up as always. Suddenly he noticed a very expensive Mercedes. He knew he hadn't seen it before and amongst the usual cars it stuck out like a sore thumb. Adam stared at the car a little longer. *Wait, that's the car I saw that night I got the message on my watch!* It was all making sense now. *They're here to talk to me, to tell me what the hell is going on.* The curiosity was becoming overwhelming. He paced up and down his bedroom trying to think about what he should do. *Hell with it.* Adam grabbed his socks. As he was putting them on he wondered what they'd tell him. The words on the text message kept looping in his mind. *Special.* Adam chuckled to himself. That word could mean anything in this politically correct world these days.

'Mum! I'm going out!' Adam yelled.

'What?!' Sharon bellowed 'Where are you going?' It had been a while since Adam had told her he was going out and she was happy that he'd be getting off the games and into the fresh air. He'd been cooped up at home for weeks. But her maternal instincts were telling her that something wasn't right.

'Just out to see Zee, I'll be back in a bit not going far just getting a game from his house.' He slipped his feet into his trainers he grabbed a game of his own and stuffed it down the front of his jeans. He opened his bedroom door and headed straight for the front door of the flat.

'Ok, but be back before 11pm, ok?' She yelled back.

'Ok mum, I will.' Adam opened the door and checked he had his phone, wallet and keys. The three things he always checked for before leaving. He patted his pockets. *Check. Check. Check.*

He took a deep breath. *This is nuts.*

He pressed the elevator call button and waited for it to arrive. Suddenly his phone bleeped again. It was another text message from the same unknown number:

'Come to the car, you'll know which one.'

Adam knew exactly which one. He finally reached outside and looked around for the car. It was a lot darker now, but someone had noticed him and he suddenly saw car headlamps flick on. He walked up to the car cautiously and noticed that it was a brand new S- Class Mercedes. *Nice.* The windows were tinted masking the driver's face. He was now just six feet away and the rear door swung open, but no one got out. He approached the door and peered in.

'Hi, Adam.' smiled Sash in a soft American accent. 'How are you?'

Adam's jaw almost hit the ground. *Oh my days, she's so hot!* Adam tried not to let on how nervous he felt. 'I'm okay.' He mustered.

'I'm Sash. Please don't be scared. I'm sure you've got a lot of questions. I'm here to explain everything. Can we go for a drive?'

Adam almost immediately leapt into the car, but he hesitated as he looked at the driver. He was an elderly man, who didn't seem to care what they were talking about. Sash noticed his apprehension.

'I mean, if we keep talking like this, we might draw attention to ourselves.'

Adam realised she had a point. Drug dealers and even prostitutes were common in the area after dark. Police presence was high, as was the local neighbourhood gossip circle. If any of his mum's friends saw him hanging around like this on the block, it'd be sure to get back to his mother. He looked around and then looked back at Sash sitting in the back. Her pretty face was all the convincing he needed. *How often am I gonna get a chance to sit in a car like this with a woman like that?* Adam lifted his shirt and removed the video game stuffed in his trousers before sitting down and closing the door behind him. Sash smiled and raised her eyebrow in curiosity as she glanced at the game.

'It's my excuse to get out of the house.' Adam admitted.

Sash nodded at the driver who immediately nodded back and began driving.

They both sat in silence as the car indicated and turned right onto the A13. Adam kept stealing glances at her. She was stunning. Her eyes were a beautiful shade of green and she had full red lips. Her blonde hair was slightly curled as it dropped just passed her shoulders. Her expensive looking bright red dress seemed tailored perfectly to her curves.

'Err...just so you know, I need to be back by-'

'11?' Sash interjected with a smile on her face. 'Yes, I know. That's why there's no time to waste.'

Adam sat back in stunned silence. He was strangely becoming accustomed to the fact that this woman knew everything about him. In a mysterious way, it was making him feel comfortable as if she had everything in control. She had a soft yet authoritative way about her that commanded obedience.

Adam continued to sit in silence and look out the window. He knew the roads well and could tell they were headed west. 'So are we going far?'

'Knightsbridge.' Sash replied.

'What's in Knightsbridge?'

'What isn't important, it's who.' She alluded. 'I'm taking you to meet a very important person.' She noticed that Adam was beginning to feel anxious and decided to be a little more open with him. She knew that anxiety was a possible trigger for his seizures and concluded that a little assurance would calm him. 'We've been watching you for over a year now Adam.'

Adam spun around and faced Sash. 'What?!"

'That's right. Around the time you had your first nightmare. Do you remember your first nightmare?'

'My nightmares...?' Adam didn't see that coming. There was no way she could have known about them.

'We know you have nightmares, Adam. It's one of the signs.' She explained casually.

'Signs?' Adam replied dumbfounded. 'Signs for what? And how do you know I have-'

'Adam it's not important how we know.' Sash interrupted. 'All you need to know is that you're not sick, and you're not dying of a brain tumour. We are on your side. I want to explain it all, but I can't here. You need to get the full picture, and that's where we're going. I'm taking you to see the full picture.' Although she spoke with the soft tone of a beautiful woman she commanded the authority of an army general. Adam glanced out of the window and noticed that they were already near Liverpool Street Station. He noticed that the driver was driving well over the speed limit. He glanced over and noticed Sash was wearing her seat belt. *Mama didn't raise no fool.* Adam thought, and reached behind and fastened his own seat belt. Sash noticed him doing so.

'Don't worry. Nick is a very good driver.' She reassured.

Adam looked at the driver as he calmly overtook another motorist. He clicked in his belt. 'I'm sure he is. But I don't know Nick as well as you do, and since you've got your belt on, I assume I'm not gonna hurt his feelings if I do the same.'

Sash laughed. 'You're funny. You remind me-' Sash stopped herself from completing her sentence.

'I remind you... of someone?' Adam pried wondering why Sash cut herself off like that.

'Nothing. Don't worry.' Sash turned and continued staring out of the window and admired the lights of the

Embankment as they approached London's iconic clock tower; Big Ben.

'You said I wasn't sick earlier.' Adam recalled. 'How can you say that for sure? I haven't got my test results back yet.'

'We know because we checked the hospital records. You'll be getting your results in the post tomorrow. The letter will say that the scan showed no abnormalities. They're going to ask you to come in for more tests, and they're going to chalk it up to a psychological issue.' Sash turned and looked at Adam. 'And they're wrong on all counts.'

'The hospital gave you all this information?' Adam asked in disbelief. 'Isn't it supposed to be confidential!?'

'Adam you don't realise it yet, but we're friends. We are on your side. We knew you weren't sick, but since you had the MRI scan we thought we'd take a peek at your results and make sure. We're quite resourceful. When you meet Belkin he'll explain everything.'

Adam assumed Sash was talking about hacking systems online to retrieve confidential patient information. It didn't seem farfetched these days for an outfit that clearly had financial resources at their disposal to hack such online databases.

'Who's Belkin?' He asked.

'Belkin. Well, he's our...' Sash wondered how to phrase it. The Fraction wasn't exactly one for titles and business cards. 'Let's just say he's the one in charge.'

For the rest of the journey, Adam sat and stared out the window. His mind was swimming with strange thoughts and questions. As the city zoomed by he realised that they were near Marble Arch. Knightsbridge was just on the other side of Hyde Park, which Adam could now see. Adam looked at his watch wondering what time it was. He pressed the button to illuminate the dial and glanced down in disbelief. It was only 8:32pm.

'Err... sorry, Sash.'

'Yes.'

'Do you have the time? I think my watch is running slow.'

'Your watch isn't slow.' Sash replied in complete confidence.

Adam laughed nervously. 'Yeah, it kinda is. It says here it's only 8:32pm, and I know I came out of the house at around ten-past, and there's no way we got to Knightsbridge in twenty minutes so it's defi-.'

'Adam, it is 8:32. Your watch isn't slow.'

'But we've been driving for over half an hour, how can it be-'

'Oh here it is, we've arrived.' The car suddenly came to a stop. 'I suggest you save your questions for Belkin.'

Adam looked outside and felt perplexed. 'Harrods?'

Sash unbuckled her seat belt and opened her door. Adam followed suit. She walked around the car and straight passed Adam. 'Follow me.' She ordered. He closed the door and the Mercedes sped away. Adam spun around and tried to keep up with her. *Dammit!* He looked back at the Mercedes as it turned the corner and disappeared. *The damn video game!* He crossed the busy road and chased Sash into the lobby of an expensive looking apartment block. Adam read the address;

10 Lancelot Place, London SW1

Wow, look at this place! Adam suddenly felt very conscious of his tatty jeans and t-shirt. Everything in the building was designed with grandeur. The floors were highly polished cream marble. The ceiling was decorated with beautiful strips of carved wood running in between the spotlights that Adam figured must have been a one-of-a-kind bespoke design by some snooty artist. Luxurious ivory leather sofas were placed in the lobby opposite the concierge desk where two men in suits were talking. The man and woman working behind the concierge desk looked smartly dressed and greeted them with a smile. Sash smiled back and headed straight for the elevators without saying a word. Adam gazed at the elevators in awe, they were a far cry from the ones back in his council block. The elevators were beautifully sleek with glass and chrome detailing. They stepped in and Sash inserted a key, the 8th-floor button suddenly illuminated blue and she pressed it. The doors swiftly closed and within mere moments opened again revealing the 8th floor. As they walked out Adam realised that this was no ordinary floor, there were no other apartments on this floor, just a short hallway about ten feet long with a door at the end of it. On the mahogany door were the characters "8F" engraved onto a silver plaque. It was the Penthouse Suite. An entire floor dedicated to one apartment, at the top of a building in Knightsbridge, one of the most expensive neighbourhoods in London. *Damn, if these guys are trying to make an impression, they're doing a heck of job.*

'Ready?' Sash asked Adam with a smile.

THE FRACTION

Sash tapped a card onto an electronic reader and the door clicked open. 'After you.' Sash said as she gestured towards the door.

Adam stepped forward and opened the door slowly. He entered the penthouse and took a few cautious steps inside and looked around. *Whoa, this place is cool.*

Sash gently closed the door and removed her black high heels placing them on the side. 'Adam.' She called out.

Adam was standing in the hallway soaking in the apartment. This was the nicest apartment he'd ever seen in real life. 'Yeah?' he replied in a semi-daze.

'Shoes.' She said as she pointed at his feet.

'Oh, sorry.' Adam stepped on the back of his grubby trainers without undoing the laces and stepped out of them. He noticed Sash had placed her shoes near the wall and placed his own beside hers.

Suddenly from around the corner, a chubby Indian man with long hair tied in a ponytail appeared with a huge smile on his face.

'Hey man, you're Adam right?' he beamed as he extended his hand.

'Yeah, are you... are you Belkin?' Adam asked as he shook hands.

The man exploded into a fit of laughter, unintentionally crushing Adam's hand in the process. Adam looked over at Sash and silently mouthed *"Who is this guy?!"*

'Ah man, I needed that. No dude, I'm Raja, but you can call me Raj. I'm the real brains of this outfit.' Raj covered the side of his face with his free hand and exaggerated a wink. 'I'm the man with the digital digits of power dude!' He beamed as he raised his hands and wiggled his fingers at Adam.

'Or as we like to call him,' Sash interjected. 'tech support.'

'Oh, is this what we're doing now?' Raj moaned. 'We're just insulting each other in front of guests? Is that what it's come down to?' Raj hated being referred to as tech support. He felt it undermined his abilities. 'If I'm tech support then Tony Stark is just a mechanic. I've got skills these guys can only dream of. Seriously, did you tell him Sash?'

Sash looked at him with a confused expression. 'And what skills are you referring to exactly?'

'You know...' He whispered. 'Anonymous...?'

Sash rolled her eyes. 'Raj, please spare him, the boy's barely walked through the door.'

'You've heard of them right?' Raj continued completely ignoring Sash. 'I was online one time doing my hacking thing' Raj paused. 'Sorry, can't give you the specifics, and suddenly my laptop gets hacked. I mean, MINE! I don't get hacked, I do the hacking! Anyhoo, it turns out it was Anonymous. Yeah, you heard, the world famous Anonymous. So like, they're pros, so I didn't feel too bad about getting hacked. They go around helping people, doing good stuff, so I let it slide. Anyway, they heard of my skills and wanted to recruit me to the cause.'

'Wow. That's pretty cool.' Adam nodded in appreciation.

'See!' Raj turned to Sash and yelled. 'Thank you!' He said as he took a bow. 'Anyway, they sent me some challenges to prove myself. You know, walk-in-the-park stuff really, and check this, they offered me silly money. I mean, change your life forever, cash-ola.'

Adam was impressed. He'd heard of Anonymous from television and the internet and always thought they were good people doing bad things to people who deserved it. 'So what happened?' Adam asked.

Raj's face dropped. 'She happened.' He said as he pointed at Sash. 'I mean, it's pretty hard to turn down a girl that looks like that right? But when she showed me what she could do, I realised this is some next level stuff.'

'Do?' Adam seemed confused and turned to look at Sash. 'What can you do?'

'That's enough Raj, thank you for your lovely introduction. But we have work to do tonight, and you know Adam doesn't have all night.'

'Shall we?' Sash gestured towards the recessed living room area of the apartment.

Adam was amazed at how beautiful the place was. It was like a dream, something a billionaire might own. Everything in the penthouse seemed elegantly designed, and it was fully kitted out.

'Is it okay to...' Adam felt he needed permission to sit on the luxurious looking sofas. Sash gave him a reassuring nod to proceed. Adam walked through the wide hallway and continued to admire the apartment in awe. 'You've got a pretty sweet pad here.' He remarked. The apartment was predominantly white, with splashes of vivid red and the odd bit of black and chrome. The furniture was high-end and most of it looked custom made. He walked through into the heart of the apartment and down a few steps into the recessed living room area. He stepped down into it and felt the thick pile of the white carpet engulf his toes.

'Take a seat,' offered Sash. Belkin will be with you in a moment.'

Adam sat on the large four seater white leather sofa closest to him. There were four in total, one sofa for each side of the recessed square. As he waited he looked around and admired the artwork on the walls. He noticed an imposing mahogany display shelf by the far wall. It was huge and took up the entire wall space beside the floor to ceiling glass windows. The display shelf was compartmentalised into twenty individual squares each one held an unusual vase, books, or a piece of art of some sort. Everything about it looked designer and very expensive.

'Adam,' a deep thunderous voice came from behind him. 'we meet at last.'

The voice took him by surprise. He stood up as he turned around, his heart pounding with nerves. *Finally, I get to meet Belkin.* He thought. He looked across the room and locked eyes with a tall black man taking confident strides towards him. He was sharply dressed wearing a single breasted white suit that seemed tailor-fitted. His sky blue shirt was unbuttoned at the top, and its collars were designer cut. Adam noticed that he was lean and athletically built. Adam was never good at guessing people's age, but if he had to guess he would've guessed that Belkin seemed like he was in his early forties, he didn't look old, but there was something very mature about the way he carried himself. He walked with effortless confidence. Adam's smile faded as he felt a haunting memory return. *Wait, is that him? Is that the stranger from the street!?*

'Err... do we know each other?' Adam asked.

'Possibly.' Belkin replied as he descended the steps and joined Adam. 'Please, sit down.' Belkin sat on the opposite end of the same sofa.

Adam slowly sat back down. 'You were there that night I had the seizure in the street.' Adam wasn't sure if he was the same man, but there was something about him that felt familiar.

'Seizure?' Belkin laughed heartedly. 'Is that what you think you had?'

'Yeah...' Adam replied suddenly feeling very conscious and unsure of himself. 'Well, I think it's a seizure, it was the first time I-'

'You didn't have a seizure, Adam.'

'But... you were there, you saw-'

'Can I ask you a question?' Belkin interrupted. 'Where were you rushing to that night?'

The questions threw Adam off. *Rushing? I wasn't rush-Oh!* He realised that Belkin was right. He had been rushing, rushing home to make his curfew.

'I had to be home by 11pm. I was worried I was going to be late and had to get home.'

'Did you wish you had more time to get home that night?'

'Well... yeah. I guess so.'

'Time is such a fickle thing. One must seize it. Savour it. We should all learn to live in the moment don't you think? And what is time if not a series of moments?' Belkin paused and stared at Adam. Adam sat there and wondered if he was meant to say something. 'Adam,' he continued. 'what do you know about your father?'

'My father?' Adam frowned. *Why is he asking about my father?* 'I... I don't really remember him. I was about three when he disappeared.' Adam felt uncomfortable talking about him. 'Why are you asking about my dad?' He asked.

'Joseph was a good man Adam. I loved him like a brother.'

Adam stared at Belkin in shock. 'Wait, what? You knew him?' Adam couldn't mask the stunned look on his face. 'How-'

'Do you know what he did for a living?' Belkin interrupted again.

'Um... yeah,' Adam racked his mind. He was caught off-guard, he couldn't remember the last time he'd heard his father's name in conversation, let alone what his occupation was. 'I think Mum said he was a Sales Manager for a telecoms company or something.' Adam recalled snippets of memories about his father. Brief discussions and conversations he had with his mother throughout his childhood. He could recall that she often said good things about him. How he was a successful company man who flew all over Europe making business deals. They were rich back then. He remembered seeing old photos of big houses and his mother and father posing in sports cars. He loved looking at those old photos. His favourite was one with his dad combing his hair in the mirror while Adam was in the crib behind him smiling. He often wondered if he actually remembered his father, or whether the photos had helped him create imaginary memories that started to become real over time. The one thing he did recall however was how as a child, he never understood why his mother would talk about good times gone by and cry. But now he understood. He learnt from a young age that it was only when things were gone that one truly realised their value, and that you should appreciate everything you have, no matter how trivial it seems today.

'Your dad was very good at what he did Adam, the best. But he wasn't a Sales Manager. He worked here, with us.'

The cogs in Adam's mind were turning at a hundred miles an hour. He had so many questions. He'd never met someone who knew his father outside the family before.

'We were best friends Adam. We went on many missions together.'

Adam's head was spinning. None of this was making any sense to him. This wasn't the image his mother had portrayed to him of his father. 'Missions?' Adam marvelled. 'Like...army missions? I think you guys have the wrong-'

'We were soldiers Adam, but not for the Army. We were soldiers for The Fraction. And your father was one of the best.'

'The Fraction?' Adam repeated as he stared at Belkin. 'What's The Fraction?'

'Adam, you need to know something about us.' Belkin stood up and began to walk around as he explained. Sash emerged from one of the rooms and joined them on one of the couches. Raj also appeared wearing a futuristic virtual reality headset that covered his eyes and ears. 'Everyone in this apartment is unique.' Belkin continued. 'Your father was unique too; special. He had a gift, as did his father before him, your grandfather, as do you.'

'A gift?'

'An ability. Belkin clarified. 'You can do things that no one else in the world can do. You are very special, and tonight you will learn what you are capable of.'

'Learn about what? What gift are you talking about?' Adam asked puzzled.

Belkin sat down close to Adam and stared straight into his eyes. 'The ability to manipulate time.' He whispered.

'The ability to what?!' Adam barked in disbelief. He'd heard Belkin's words as clear as a bell, but doubted that a man so serious would claim something so ridiculous. He looked around and suddenly he didn't feel comfortable with these people. *These guys are psychos. And they have me trapped here!* Adam felt a twinge of panic set in as he recalled the ridiculous amount of security to get into this apartment, making a dash for the door would get him nowhere. He had to play it cool.

Belkin didn't repeat himself. 'Your father didn't leave out of choice Adam, he loved you, your mother Sharon, and your sister Sidney, very much. He left to protect you.'

'Protect us?' Adam blurted. 'What, by abandoning us? By letting my mum raise us by herself? By not being there for us?' Adam realised he was getting emotional and he took a deep breath and calmed himself down. Raj heard the commotion and removed his headset and joined the rest of them on the sofas. To Adam, the topic of his father was a sensitive subject and he didn't like to talk to anyone about it. He had learned to suppress his anger and sadness in high school. Kids were harsh and unyielding back then. Parents evenings and sports days were the worst. His mind reeled back to all the taunts. *Where's your dad Adam? Don't you have a father Adam? How come your dad never comes to school? No Dad. does that mean you're a bastard, Adam?*

'You have to know that it was the hardest choice he had ever made. I know because I was there when he made it.' Belkin stood up again and walked to a bar area. 'We were unsure whether or not it had been genetically passed through to you or not.' Belkin said as he began pouring whisky into a glass tumbler. 'We knew about your night terrors, but that isn't conclusive evidence. But that seizure you had that night in the alleyway, that was the first true indication. We realised then you were a candidate, a strong one given your lineage.'

'Candidate?' Adam repeated. 'Candidate for what?'

'Think about this Adam; have you ever noticed that you only get seizures when your brain manipulates time? Or when you *wish* you could manipulate time?' Belkin dropped two cubes of ice into his glass and stirred. 'Drink?' he offered.

'No, I'm okay.' Adam replied still confused about Belkin's earlier statement. He tried to make sense of what he was alluding to. *My seizures only occur when my brain manipulates time?*

Belkin could see Adam was struggling to keep up. 'As children, we don't have a sense of time until it is taught to us. Time is irrelevant because all we know is the now, the present, the moment. But as we develop into adults, we realise the value of planning in order to manage our futures better.' Belkin walked back to the sofa Adam was sitting on and sat down as he placed the tumbler on the glass table next to him. 'You too are beginning to realise the value of time, but unlike the rest of us, when you want to control time, time actually listens. With the right training Adam, you can make time not only listen, but obey.'

'I can make time obey?' Adam had to repeat the words out loud just to make sure he didn't misunderstand what he was hearing.

'Let me start with explaining your night terrors.' Belkin paused as he took a sip of his whisky. 'At night, when we are in deep sleep our brain loses its sense of time, and our mind is transported into various realms of consciousness. Some we understand and some we don't. During this time your brain is manipulating time as it sees fit and consciously we're oblivious as to how it does it.' Belkin paused and took another sip of his drink. 'Have you ever gone to bed and slept for what felt like an hour only to realise it was already morning and eight or ten hours had gone by?'

'Yeah, all the time.' Adam admitted.

'Everyone does. It's a natural phenomenon that has scientists baffled. It's not just losing time however, it occurs the other way too, when you find it hard to fall into deep sleep and you're tossing and turning, watching the clock all night. Maybe you're excited or anxious about the next day. Doesn't the night just seem to drag on forever?

'Yeah, I've definitely had nights like that.' Adam replied hanging on to Belkin's every word, completely fascinated by the discussion.

'This manipulation of time is why you have seizures at night and typically during the deep sleep cycle in the middle of your unconscious state. Because of your unique gift Adam, your unconscious state and conscious state are at war with each other, fighting for control over time manipulation. The mental distress eventually peaks causing you to snap out of sleep state as if you had just awoken from a nightmare. When you're finally awake you assume you had a nightmare, because of your heightened brain activity and heart rate. But let me ask you this Adam, can you ever remember what happens in any of your night terrors?'

'No.' Adam whispered. Everything Belkin was saying about his night terrors made so much sense. He was describing exactly how he felt. He felt such a relief to finally meet someone who knew what he was going through.

'That's another indication. The fact that you can never remember what happens. Let me ask, do you ever find yourself in different places, unaware how you got there when you wake up from these night terrors?'

'Yeah,' Adam affirmed. 'I woke up like that just a couple of weeks ago.'

'Sometimes in this mental struggle the switch that paralyses your body in sleep gets disrupted because it can't detect whether you are conscious or unconscious, and your body moves unconsciously. Maybe you fall off your bed, break furniture, or even wake up in a completely different place. The stress and physical exertion can make you sweaty, even bruised or cut depending on how active you were.' Belkin watched Adam's eyes widen as he soaked in all the information and nodded incessantly in affirmation. 'I assume all this is all familiar to you?' he smiled.

'I suffer from all these things, but I'm sure other people have these seizures and sleep walk, what makes me so special?'

'What you experience are not seizures Adam, nor do you sleep walk in the traditional sense. They're manifestations of time control.' You, my friend, like your dad, are a Timestopper.'

'A Timestopper?' Adam gasped.

'Adam, I'm going to lay the cards on the table. We're a covert team of specialists with a simple mission passed down from our predecessors; to keep peace in the world as best we can.' Belkin paused to ensure Adam was taking it all in. 'That's what The Fraction does, and we want you to join us.'

Adam stood up, his mind was spinning and he needed some air. 'I don't know if I'm going to be much help to be honest.' He said as he began to pace up and down, clearly overwhelmed by it all. 'I need to go and speak to-'

'I'm afraid you can't speak to anyone about this Adam.' Belkin interrupted. 'It's one of the cons of being in a covert organisation.' Belkin looked over at Sash who had been quietly observing. 'Why don't we take a break? You look like you need a few moments to process all this, I know it can be overwhelming and there's really no way to sugar coat any of it.' Belkin waved Sash over. 'Sash, would you kindly show Adam around the place, maybe you can take him to the rooftop.' Belkin smiled as he turned back to Adam. 'The views from the roof are spectacular this time of night. Sash, do you mind?'

Sash walked over and stood beside Adam. 'Of course.' She smiled as she reached out and held Adam's hand. 'You're going to love this.'

Sash led Adam up the steps out of the living area and down the 2nd hallway that led to the other rooms in the apartment. To the left, there was a door that seemed slightly more reinforced than the others. 'This way.' Sash pressed down on the handle and she pushed the door open. The air was instantly warmer and Adam could tell that the air conditioning didn't reach to this section of the apartment. 'You okay?' Sash asked as she climbed the narrow flight of stairs to the roof.

'Yeah. Just, so much to take in.' Adam admitted.

Sash finally let go of Adam's hand at the top of the short flight of stairs. A thick metal door stood at the end of the stairway. Sash unbolted it from the top and bottom and twisted the door knob. The door swung open with a slight squeak. The warmth of the summer evening air engulfed him.

'After you'. She moved to the side and gestured out towards the roof.

Adam smiled and stepped past Sash and walked out onto the rooftop. *Oh my days.* Adam spun around and admired the 360-degree views of London. *This is just...wow.* The sun was still setting over the distant horizon in the west. The sky was still a vivid burnt orange, which blended into a bright yellow, and then rose into a deep purple until it fused with the midnight blue directly above. The cocktail of colours were truly breathtaking. *What an artist God is.* Adam admired. He always believed that his view of Canary Wharf was the best view in London, but his balcony faced east and never caught the splendour of a summer sunset over London. He realised now that he had been missing out. They walked across the grey concrete floor towards the edge of the rooftop where they leant on the metal safety barriers. The view of the city lights was spectacular, the yellows, reds and whites of the multitude of shops, cars, and streetlamps flooded the skyline. *Man, I love summer in London.* Directly in front of them was Harrods. Despite it being barely dusk its trademark year-round light display was already on, dominating the street with its brightness.

'Something, isn't it?' Sash admired. Been here a thousand times, but it never gets old.

Adam glanced back at her. Sash looked even more stunning in the evening glow. The light summer breeze wafted her hair. 'Yeah,' he agreed, 'summer in London-'

'No place like it.' Sash smiled as she finished off his sentence.

'Damn straight.' He smiled back. They stared at the sunset a while longer in silence until Adam finally decided to ask the question that had been burning in his mind the entire evening. 'So are you a Timestopper too?'

'No.' Sash smiled. 'My gift is very different. Until I was eighteen I had no idea I even had a gift. I was scared when I learned what I could do. But then Belkin found me. He found all of us. That's what he does, he finds people that need to be found. If he hadn't I would've been a mess, or maybe worse.' Sash broke eye contact and stared into the abyss as she seemed to recall a memory. 'He saved my life.' She said as she snapped herself out of her daze. 'I owe him everything.'

'So what's your ability?' Adam asked as he tried to mask his burning curiosity.

'Let me show you.' She beamed as she stood up right. 'Okay, choose any building you can see from here.'

'A building?' Adam repeated. 'What just...I mean... just point at a building?'

'Yes, just point at a building. Anyone you can see.'

Adam had no idea where this was going. 'Okay, well there's a huge building right here, there you go.' Adam pointed.

'Ah, I was hoping you wouldn't pick Harrods. The last time it took them four hours to re-open the store.'

'Why?' Adam wondered.

'You'll see. Okay, be silent for a moment I need some quiet.' Sash closed her eyes and raised her hands. As she raised her hands they began to spark. Tiny bolts of lightning emerged from her hands in all directions as if a small thunderstorm was brewing right there in her palms. Adam was mesmerised. He couldn't believe what he was seeing. He looked up to see if Sash was in pain or even aware of what was going on. But as he focussed on her face he realised that her eyes had narrowed into tiny slits of pure white light, her pupils had disappeared, and she looked as if she was possessed. A mixture of worry and wonder overwhelmed Adam as he unintentionally took a step back. The sparks from her hands grew brighter and larger. She seemed like she was in a trance. She didn't look like she was in pain despite the electricity bursting through her hands, she seemed comfortable and in complete control.

'Sash?' Adam called out over the crackling sparks. 'Sash, you okay?' But Sash didn't reply, instead, she motioned her hands towards the building. Suddenly as if someone had turned off the sun the rooftop plunged into darkness. Adam instantly turned his attention to the source of the blackout, but when he looked out to the street he realised that only the Harrods building had lost its power. The entire department store was plunged into darkness. No lights, no backup generators, not even an alarm. Just some faint distance screams from concerned shoppers and utter darkness. Adam looked back at Sash, her eyes had returned to normal and her hands had stopped sparking.

'Oh my days, Sash!' Adam gasped in astonishment. 'That was amazing!'

'Poor Harrods,' Sash said smugly. 'I guess it'll be another four-hours of protocol before they'll re-open.' Suddenly they heard Police sirens in the distance getting louder and louder. 'Guess that's them.' Sash glanced at her watch, 'What do you think, 90 seconds?' She asked rhetorically. 'Not bad London Met, not bad at all.' She jibed sarcastically.

'So you can control lights?' Adam asked. 'That's amazing.'

Sash rested against the barriers and peered down at the commotion in the streets she had just caused. 'Not just lights, I can control all electronic power. It's a developing strength. At first, I could only control my bedroom light. I remember laying there in my room one evening when I was seventeen and I was just looking at the bulb in my room. I felt a strange connection with it as if I had a remote control in my mind. So I visualised the remote in my mind and then tried to use it to switch the bulb off.' Sash laughed. 'The first time it happened I thought the bulb had blown, or a fuse had tripped. But I climbed onto my bed and took it out to check it, and of course, the bulb was fine. I placed the bulb back in and flicked the light switch a couple of times and the room lit up as if nothing had happened.' Sash paused for a moment, deep in thought. 'I practised and practised, for hours that night. I kept flicking that bulb on and off, on and off, until I could do it at will. I never breathed a word about what I could do to anyone. Not even my parents.'

'So all this explains the messages on my watch! Man, I thought people like you only existed in superhero movies.' Adam marvelled.

'If you're lucky enough to have an ability it's like any skill or muscle, the more you work on it, the stronger it becomes, and the better you become at controlling it. Shutting down buildings isn't hard now, and Belkin always tries to push us further.' She smiled to herself as she looked up at the sky. 'The things I can now do are unbelievable. Belkin's training regime is tailored to you, your ability and your potential and it's the hardest thing you'll ever do.' There was a slight grimace on her face as if she was recalling something unpleasant.

'Wha-what did he make you do?' Adam gulped.

'Whatever it took.' She replied curtly. 'But it was worth it.' She smiled as she stepped back and raised her hands letting off a few tiny sparks of electricity from her palms. 'Now I can even manipulate computers!' She exclaimed. 'Can you believe that?' She giggled. 'Just two weeks ago I copied and pasted a file from a hard disc to a USB stick without even touching the computer! Can you imagine the possibilities of developing an ability like that in this day and age?'

'Damn, that's crazy.' Adam paused as he considered the potential. 'Man, if you ever got online somehow you could do some serious damage.'

'I know. But great power, great responsibility and all that crap, right?' Sash joked.

'I was just about to say that,' Adam laughed. 'Damn Spiderman movies have made everyone a bloody philosopher these days.' They both burst into laughter. Adam turned and looked back at the street below and watched the hoards of people being ushered out of Harrods. 'Man, I didn't know you could get this many people in

Harrods, looks like about two thousand people down there right now.' He remarked. 'I kinda feel bad now, think I should've picked a smaller store.' He laughed.

'Ah don't feel bad, they'll be fine. Those rich bozos could do with a break from all that mindless materialism.' She turned and looked at Adam. 'In all seriousness, I know that I was born with these gifts for a purpose. A reason I have these abilities, a reason greater than myself...' She paused.

'What reason?' Adam wondered.

'When Belkin found me and told me about the prophecy I knew that it was my purpose. The reason I had these abilities. It just felt right. My heart and my gut both screamed "Yes!" I knew there and then that this was my calling... my destiny.'

Destiny. The word struck a chord with Adam. It resonated with him in a way he couldn't describe. 'What prophecy?' Adam wondered.

'I think Belkin will be better placed to explain that bit.' Sash replied with a smile. 'Shall we?' She gestured back towards the rooftop door.

Adam didn't press the issue and headed towards the door. Whatever they were involved with, he wanted in. He had always felt as though he was different inside like he didn't quite fit in with normal society, like he was destined for something else, something greater. They made their way back to the recessed living room area in the apartment. Adam looked around for Belkin, but the living room was empty. He could hear voices from the room on the far left. He stepped up out of the recessed area and walked towards the room the voices were coming from. He found Belkin and Raj inside. Belkin was stood behind Raj's computer chair and they were both staring at the computer monitor. Whatever it was it seemed important.

Belkin noticed Adam walking towards the room and silently raised his finger without looking away from the screen indicating that he needed a minute. Adam raised his hand apologetically and turned away to give them some privacy. He noticed Sash was sat down on one of the corner sofas and he walked over and took a seat beside her. He sat there in silence and tried to collect his thoughts about everything he'd witnessed so far. *What a crazy day.* He realised that despite walking into the headquarters of a secret organisation, meeting complete strangers who knew everything about him, and witnessing someone manipulate electricity at will- he was rather composed. *I must be in shock.* Suddenly Belkin appeared.

'So Adam, enjoy the view?' He grinned as he walked towards Adam and Sash.

'It's an amazing place you have here. I'd love to live in a pad like this someday.' Adam confessed.

'Well Adam, you never know...' Belkin alluded. 'But the best thing about this place is that it's private. It's a place we can think... and plan.'

'Plan? Oh, you mean for the prophecy.' Adam blurted. Belkin glanced over at Sash and Adam wondered if he'd said something he shouldn't have.

'Well, it looks like you've discussed a lot more than I expected in such a short amount of time. Tell me, how much has Sash told you so far?'

'Well, she actually hasn't said anything.' Adam admitted. 'She said you'd explain it better.'

Belkin let out a deep hearty laugh. 'Thank you Sash, for a moment I thought you'd stolen my opportunity to tell Adam the best part!'

'I wouldn't dream of it,' replied Sash. 'After all, you tell it so well.'

'I guess we all have our talents.' Belkin smirked as he took a seat beside Adam on the white sofa. He took a deep breath and paused for a moment staring down at the carpet. His playful jolly attitude quickly evaporated. He finally looked back at Adam with a serious expression and asked; 'Adam, what do you know about Doomsday?'

Adam contorted his face into a confused smile and searched Belkin's eyes to see if he was joking. Belkin stared back at Adam silent and deadly serious.

'Doomsday?' Adam laughed awkwardly as he looked around at Sash and Raj. He realised that no one else was amused and he quickly cleared his throat and took the question more seriously. 'You-You mean the end of the world?'

'Yes.' Belkin affirmed. 'What do you know about it?'

'Nothing really.' But then something he heard sparked in his mind. 'Oh wait, I did hear about on the news or something that some ancient Mexicans think it's going to occur this year. But-' Adam noticed Belkin immediately glancing over at Sash. Adam glanced at Sash and then back at Belkin. 'No...' he chuckled. 'No, this isn't about that thing everyone is talking about, is it? The 2012 thing? No, that's just a hoax right?'

'I'm afraid to say it is in fact, a very real possibility.' There was no humour in Belkin's face. 'December 21st 2012, will mark the beginning of the end for our species. The world will exist, but will be ravaged and undergo irreversible and severe climate change. The human species will not be able to adapt and we will perish.'

Adam was no longer smiling. 'Changes? What changes? You mean like global warming?'

'Global warming?' Sash chimed in. 'Unfortunately, it's not as subtle as global warming. This is something a lot more drastic and deadly.'

'Adam, look around you in the world today, what do you see?' Belkin asked rhetorically. 'Anytime you switch on the news you see mindless wars, innocent people dying across the world. Soldiers relentlessly fighting for a cause they don't even understand. The rich getting richer, the poor getting poorer, widespread corruption, people worshipping pop culture icons. These things have all been prophesised hundreds of years ago, they are the signs of doomsday.'

Adam couldn't refute anything that Belkin had said. War was something that was always on television, and these days it was never clear who the bad guys were. Power struggles between countries and terrorist activities were riddled with plausible conspiracy theories. America was always invading some middle-eastern country these days under the false banner of freedom, and wherever they went the Europeans weren't far behind. These nations were robbing the masses of their freedom under the false pretence of terror. Adam suddenly recalled a BBC segment he once watched about ex-servicemen returning from the war who couldn't deal with the psychological effects of what they had done and witnessed and ending their own lives. *Even those who survive, end up choosing to die*. Adam shuddered at the thought of what a man must go through to make him want to end his own life like that.

'Natural disasters, tsunamis, hurricanes, unparalleled earthquakes and volcanic eruptions,' Sash added. 'thousands of people dying all over the world just for being in the wrong place at the wrong time. Despite our advances in modern science we have more disease in the world today than at any other time in the world's existence, and millions more die. Adam, ask yourself; are these not also signs?'

Adam couldn't deny that natural disasters in the world were ever increasing. Adam recalled a headline he caught a glimpse of on the news on Boxing Day, 2004;

THE TSUNAMI IN BANDA ACHE IN THE INDIAN OCEAN. *DEATH TOLL REACHES OVER 174,000*.

As Sash spoke of the natural disasters his mind reeled to other disasters.

'Hurricane Katrina,' Sash continued. 'the Japan earthquake, the Haiti earthquake, all occurring in the past five years.'

'There's more Adam.' Belkin said calmly not wanting to overwhelm him. He sighed heavily and slowed down the pace. 'Adam, these diseases, natural disasters and wars have been foretold. We've been expecting them and they've occurred right on time, every time.'

'How?' Adam wondered. 'How do you know?'

'We have our ways of testing the theories to verify them. But you'd be surprised to know that we aren't the only ones privileged with this knowledge. This knowledge is freely available to anyone who wishes to seek it. The problem is that the government works hard to discredit the sources. But we know that the sources are reliable if you're able to decipher them. Millions know of the prophecies of Doomsday from the Bible, as well as the Quran and the Chinese I-Ching. By cross referencing these sources and using our unique gifts, we can not only become aware of what will be... we can influence it... change it.'

'I've heard of the other books, but what's the I-Ching?' Adam asked.

'It's an ancient book that the Chinese use to foretell the future.' Sash explained. 'The I-Ching literally translates to "the book of changes" and by using its Hexagram prediction methodology it has predicted numerous worldwide occurrences before they happen. It too has prophesied the end of the world in 2012.'

Adam sat there and tried to digest the information. *Could it all be just a big coincidence?*

'Our research doesn't solely depend on religious texts however.' Belkin assured. 'Modern day technology has predicted exactly the same thing. Have you ever heard of the Web Bot Project?'

Adam tried to recall, but the name didn't sound familiar. 'No. What's that?'

'The Web Bot project is a computer built to predict the future for stock trading, also known as futures trading. Stock brokers bet on whether they believe the price of commodities will rise or fall in the future based on trends. Commodities such as oil, gas, grain, gold, and things of that nature are all bet upon. The harvesting of many of these commodities is largely affected by the climate and weather. Therefore predicting what is likely to happen with it made financial sense to the traders. They invested millions in creating this computer to do just that.' Belkin watched Adam closely to ensure he was still following. 'Is this all making sense so far?' he asked.

'Yeah, I think.' Adam nodded. 'So these stock brokers created a computer to find out what the weather will be like in the future?'

'Exactly!' Belkin boomed. 'The computer takes everything relevant into account when making its predictions and it has been proven to be incredibly accurate. It predicted many significant world events. In August 2004 the Web Bot accurately predicted the Tsunami in Indonesia. It also predicted Hurricane Katrina in 2005. But the most alarming of all, is that it's predicted a significant global catastrophe in December 2012.'

'Catastrophe?' Adam whispered.

'But of all of these predictions Adam,' Sash chimed in. 'the most interesting is the prediction of the Mayans.'

'Who are the Mayans?' Adam wondered.

'The Mayans,' Sash continued. 'or Maya were and an ancient tribe of people native to South America. They were highly regarded for their mastery of astrology. The Mayans created a calendar of lunar eclipses and were obsessed with recording their calendar as accurately as possible. They went back thousands of years and charted their calendar plotting everything to make their future predictions as accurate as possible. Their lunar calendar was created between the 6th and 9th centuries, but even so, its predictive capability is on par with modern day technology.'

'It was so good in fact,' Belkin added. 'they were able to predict lunar eclipses hundreds of years in the future. Modern scientists discovered that their calculations were accurate to the nearest thirty-three seconds!'

'Whoa.' Adam marvelled.

'The power of this forecasting intelligence was considered godly to the Mayan people in those days, but today we know that they were just very good at astrology. But here's the most important part.' Belkin revealed. 'The Mayan calendar ends exactly on 21st December 2012, on a day that they refer to as Hoonaab-koo. It's the day that- according to their calculations- the earth is aligned exactly between the Sun and the Milky Way, an alignment that occurs only once every 25,800 years.

Sash reached out and held Adam's hand. 'The effect of this alignment is catastrophic.' She explained. 'We've run the geophysics data in our computer programmes and realised that if this was to happen the poles of the earth would shift and turn on their axis.' She let go of his hand and pointed up and down in front of his face to illustrate. 'Instead of the planet's poles pointing North and South,' she said as she slowly turned her hands horizontally. 'they'll point East and West, and it will happen almost instantly. Nothing would be able to adapt quick enough for the conditions, and the extreme weather change will wipe out every living creature on the planet.'

'Doomsday.' Belkin surmised. 'The end of every living thing on this planet. The end of the human race.' Belkin paused for a moment to allow Adam to gather his thoughts. 'Adam. Do you see the gravity of the issue? These incidents aren't coincidences, they are warnings.'

Adam slumped back on the sofa and just stared at a lamp across the room trying to digest everything he'd heard. He felt sick to his stomach. He turned and looked at Belkin. 'We're doomed.' He concluded. 'Why isn't the government doing something about this? We should tell them. We should tell everyone!' He declared.

'We're not doomed, not yet. The government can't help and going public isn't going to solve anything. The people can't stop this.' Belkin moved his face closer to Adam's and looked at him dead in the eyes. 'But you can.'

THE MAYANS

Deep in the heart of the Guatemalan jungle Ah Kin stepped back and observed the placement of the stones. Everything had to be perfect. He looked up at the black sky and read the glistening stars above. *It's almost time.* It was approaching midnight and it was still warm, the roaring fire blazing in front of him only added to the heat and he was sweating profusely beneath his thick ceremonial robes. Nacom walked towards the fire and added more logs to it.

'Chilan,' Ah Kin turned and faced his celestial advisor. 'is it time?' he asked. He had been waiting too long to risk jeopardising tonight's offering. The sacrifice had to be perfect for it to count. The entire mission would fail without the elder Gods' blessings.

'Patience brother, the moon is aligning.' The Chilan partially closed his eyes and continued to meditate. He visualised the high God Kinich Ahau himself coming down from the night sky to accept their offering as he continued reciting the holy scripture to invoke him. The Chilan hadn't performed a human offering before, but their Mayan ancestors had documented the ritual in great detail. Centuries ago it was common practice, but now it was considered barbaric by the few surviving Mayans who continued to practice the faith. The Chilan was honoured to be trusted to lead the prayer over tonight's offering.

Ah Kin walked over to the large circular stone block and ran his hand down the rope until it got to her ankle. She was weak now, her throat sore from the constant screaming and her wrists and ankles chafed raw. She was still squirming but inside she had all but given up. He watched her and wondered if she knew how important her soul was to this cause. How lucky she was to be chosen. That if she knew what he knew about her purpose perhaps she wouldn't feel this bad. He walked over to her and looked into her bulging terrified eyes. He wanted to reassure her but knew it was hopeless to do so. She looked up at him with a mixture of fear and anger. He placed his left hand on her forehead. 'You're a truly blessed child of the Sun God. May he accept our offering, and your-.'

'It's time brother.' The Chilan announced suddenly.

Ah Kin looked at the Chilan but only saw the whites of his eyes as he continued to chant in a trance like state. 'Brother Nacom,' Ah Kin called out as his heart began to race with excitement. 'let us begin.'

Nacom was sat leaning against a tree enjoying the brief respite from chopping and gathering firewood. With a grunt, he hoisted himself up. He was a large brute of a man, tall, and built like a wrestler. He was blessed with a natural strength and a high tolerance to pain. His understanding of his faith was limited to simply following orders from Ah Kin and doing what he was told. What Nacom lacked in intelligence he more than made up for in power and loyalty. He once had a short yet successful career as a professional Mexican wrestler before his manager sold him to Ah Kin. Ah Kin was kind to him and convinced him to pursue a more meaningful life by joining him and serving the gods. Ever since Nacom had served Ah Kin and Ah Kin vowed that in exchange his soul would enter a good place in the afterlife.

Nacom walked over to Ah Kin and lowered his head. Ah Kin crowned him with a large blue fan of feathers sewn together and attached to a decorated headband. Ah Kin proceeded to paint the holy symbols on his cheeks with the black soot of the fire. Nacom then walked to the Chilan who was still sat cross-legged on the floor and knelt before him. The Chilan's chanting grew louder and louder and he finally unfolded his arms and extended his hand and placed it upon

Nacom's chest. A strange sensation overcame Nacom and he felt his heart heating up. He grimaced as his heart felt hotter and hotter, he held his position until he couldn't take it any longer and he fell back and yelled in pain from the burning sensation in his chest. He took a few deep breaths and his chest cooled and he got back onto his feet and walked towards the huge flat stone block where the girl was tied.

The time had come, this is where his faith would be tested. He stood over her. Her teary eyes begging him to have mercy as she made a futile effort to squirm and break free. Nacom felt like he was no longer in control and he picked up the ceremonial blade. She saw the huge machete blade in his hand and her eyes bulged in fear. Her relentless screaming was starting to annoy him, and he tore off a piece of her white blouse and stuffed the rag into her mouth to silence her. She kicked and screamed but the ropes held fast. Her muffled cries were ignored as she begged him to let her go, to show mercy, to let her live. Nacom looked into her eyes and realised that this was the hardest thing he'd ever done in his life. He took a deep breath and reminded himself that this was what the gods wanted.

With everything now in place, Ah Kin raised his arms towards the sky and began reciting; 'Kinich Ahau, we stand before you humbly carrying out your decree. The great day of Hoonaab-koo will soon be upon us and we beg for your support. Accept our offering and permit our destinies to be fulfilled.' Ah Kin nodded towards Nacom and Nacom raised the machete high above his head and drove it directly into her stomach. Her eyes burst wide open and she let out a bloodcurdling shriek that the gag did very little to suppress. Her entire body convulsed violently and she pulled at the ropes in a final attempt to escape. Nacom knew that had to act fast. He used both hands and dragged the blade up to her chest, completely gutting her before sliding it back out. Blood gushed out of her torso and her body jerked even more violently. He knew that if he hesitated now he would lose his nerve to do what had to be done next. He immediately plunged his hand into her torso and pushed it up into her chest searching for her heart. Suddenly he felt the vibrations of her heart beating like a jackhammer and he tried to reach for it but something was blocking his access. Worried that the heart would give out too soon, he pushed his forearm in further and further, inch by inch until his arm had all but disappeared inside her. He finally felt her beating heart in his palm and clutched it firmly. He summoned every ounce of strength he had in his body and yelled as he yanked the organ out as hard as he could. The force was enough to expose the heart that was still connected to her arteries. With his free hand, he grabbed the machete and cut it away from her body. It was done. Nacom was exhausted, panting heavily, blood-soaked and gasping for breath, he was glad it was over. As he regained his senses he looked at the body and realised that the force had caused a number of other organs to fall to the ground, her intestines were now exposed and protruding out of her stomach, unrecognisable pieces of blood-soaked flesh were scattered everywhere. Dizzy from the adrenalin, he glanced down at his blood soaked hand, and he saw her heart. The Chilan suddenly appeared and gently took the heart from Nacom and placed it into the fire. The Chilan continued chanting over the fire and a strange purple smoke began to emerge from the heart. Ah Kin looked on and smiled, the smoke was a sign of acceptance. He'd done it. The Gods were pleased. Nothing could stop them now. He reached into the inside pocket of his robe and produced a long slim case. He opened it up carefully admiring its purple velvet trim. Inside, lying in its mould was a single slim metal skewer with a wooden handle. It was elaborately engraved with snakes and wild cats and was sharply tipped. With the skewer gripped firmly in his hand he plunged it into the roasted heart that lay atop the fire and raised it high over his head.

'Great lord! Upper God of gods.' Ah Kin called out. 'Accept our humble offering, bless our quest with success.'

The Chilan was waiting beside him with a silver platter engraved with numerous ancient Mayan symbols of snakes, panthers, birds of prey and a large sun etched into the centre of the dish. Ah Kin slid off the charred organ onto the plate. The Chilan raised the plate towards the moon and bowed his head. He rested the plate on the floor and sat down. Ah Kin and Nacom also sat around the plate to form a perfect triangle. Ah Kin looked at the steaming organ in the centre of the plate. 'Our spirits consume this offering. Bless us with the strength and cunning to be successful against our enemies.' And with that, he reached out and cut the heart with a knife into three equal pieces and handed them out. Ah Kin raised his piece of the heart to the moon in a silent toast to the gods and put the entire piece in his mouth and slowly began to chew.

THE TASK AHEAD

'So how exactly am I supposed to stop the world from ending?' Adam glanced at his watch, it was barely past 9:30pm. *This can't be right. It feels like I've been here for half the night!*

Belkin caught Adam looking confused about the time. 'Don't worry about the time anymore Adam. We like to think that we're the ones who tell time what time it is.' He chuckled. 'Why don't we go into the study, Raj has something that might help you understand it a bit better. Belkin gestured towards the room where Adam saw Belkin and Raj earlier. Adam got up and made his way over to the room. Sash followed closely behind.

'Adam, take a seat right here.' Belkin pulled out the white leather office chair behind the desk for him. Adam walked around the desk and sat down. Raj grabbed the wireless keyboard and started typing. A discreet projector hummed to life overhead. Sash walked over to the wall and flicked the lights off.

'Are we gonna watch a movie or something?' Adam wondered.

Raj moved the wireless mouse around and clicked a few icons on the screen that was now projected in front of him. 'Something like that.' he replied as he tapped a few more buttons on the keyboard. 'Alright guys, everyone sitting comfortably? And... action!' A bright blue light projected onto the screen. The image began moving and as it zoomed out Adam recognised the familiar shape of Africa. The camera kept zooming out until it displayed the entire planet Earth in magnificent detail as it rotated on its axis.

Suddenly a narrator began speaking. The sombre voice boomed through the speakers in the room. He felt like he was about to watch a BBC documentary.

'Geological research has suggested that the alignment between the Earth and the Milky way will be caused due to the Sun's annual cycle causing a slight wobble in the earth's axis as it spins, receding it backwards 1 degree every 72 years.'

The video showed the sun affecting the Earth in this way. It was clear that someone had spent a lot of effort and money in creating this video. The digital reconstruction of the events predicted was very lifelike.

'This effect is known as a precession. This precession has caused the earth to slowly align with the sun and the milky way during the December Solstice in 2012. If this occurs it will have a devastating impact on the North and South poles. In effect changing the magnetic fields across the earth and shifting the poles horizontally, causing them to face East and West instead of North to South.'

The image of the earth slowly rotated to its side and the polar ice caps melted and the countries that were previously situated around the equator moved to the North and South Poles. Belkin muted the video. 'As you can see Adam, this entire catastrophe occurs because of the alignment that only occurs once every 25,000 years. We need to stop that alignment happening. You don't know this yet, but you have the ability to do this.'

'But how can I stop an astronomical alignment?!' Adam argued.

'We will show you how. But we need you on board Adam. That means you'll need to stay with us. Here, full time.' Belkin paused to let the words sink in. 'There isn't much time and we must develop your ability exponentially to make you strong enough to do what it is the world needs you to do. And as you already know, we don't have much time.'

'And what exactly do you think I am gonna be able to do once you've made me strong enough?' Adam exclaimed.

Belkin switched on the light and walked over to the desk where Adam was sat. He rested his palms on the table top and leant over looking Adam straight in the eyes. 'Stop the world from rotating long enough for us to avoid the alignment.'

'Stop the world from *rotating?*' Adam repeated in disbelief. His mind suddenly recalled a scene from an old Superman movie he once watched where superman turned back time by flying at super speed around the earth in the opposite direction.

'I expected that you'd react this way.' Belkin stepped back and began examining something on the display cabinet. 'It seems impossible, but know this Adam; what modern science has uncovered about space and time is barely the tip of the iceberg.' Belkin turned and read Adam's facial expression and knew what his next question was going to be. 'You want to know how you're going do it right, how you're going to control the rotation?'

Adam nodded with his mouth ajar. 'Err... yeah.' he confessed.

'This isn't a joke Adam.' Belkin turned back to the cabinet and reached in retrieving two red glass chime balls and began rotating them in his palm. 'Remember your abilities are only useful to us if you're able to use them responsibly. Mastering the skill takes discipline and hard work. I will teach you how, but before I do, you must make a pact with me.' Belkin spun around and noticed how Adam was now sitting upright hanging on Belkin's every word. It was obvious from his body language that Adam was excited about being part of something so important. 'You must pledge your allegiance to this organisation and accept me as your commander. From here on you do nothing without my authorisation and you accept, without question, all of my orders. Do you understand?'

Adam took a moment to digest the conditions and he looked around at Raj and Sash who both maintained a solemn expression. *Damn, is this guy for real?*

'Adam, I wouldn't ask if this wasn't of up-most importance to our mission. After our mission, on the 22nd December, I will release you from this pact and you will be a free man to do as you wish.

Adam swivelled his chair towards Belkin and extended his hand without another thought. 'Agreed.'

'Good.' Belkin affirmed as he shook his hand and smiled. 'Welcome to The Fraction. Sash, please show Adam to his room.'

'My room?' Adam beamed.

'Yes, we all live here, this isn't a job where you simply clock in and out, we're all committed to saving the world and that means being on-call all the time.'

Sash walked over to the desk and extended her hand. Adam noticed that every time she smiled she seemed to get prettier. Adam blushed as he took her hand and she gestured towards the door with her head. 'Let's go champ.'

EMERALD EYES

Ah Kin waited until the Chilan came out of his meditative trance. 'Chilan, have you located the stone yet?' Ah Kin asked finally losing his patience. He knew that if their sacrifice was accepted then the Gods would have shown the Chilan where the sacred Mayan stone was located. The ancient stone held immense power and was the only threat to the mission. It had to be destroyed before The Fraction discovered it.

'The offering was truly a blessed one brother Ah Kin.' The Chilan finally replied. 'The gods are pleased and have shown the Chilan that the sacred stone is in Chichin Itza.'

Nacom breathed a sigh of relief as he heard the news. He knew Ah Kin was desperate to find it and was prepared to make as many human sacrifices as necessary to discover its location. Over the years Nacom had witnessed Ah Kin become more and more frustrated as every ancient scroll, etching, and book led to a dead end. It had been four years since they began searching and now time was running out. Ah Kin finally discovered an ancient locator spell that required a human sacrifice. It was a huge risk but calling on the upper gods for help was the last resort, and it seemed to have worked.

'Chichin Itza?!' Ah Kin boomed in frustration. 'Have we not scoured every inch of that land?' Ah Kin couldn't contain his fury. He stomped towards the Chilan and grabbed him by his robe. 'What else did you see?' he barked.

The Chilan seemed unfazed by Ah Kin's rage and allowed him to shake him like a ragdoll. 'There are others.'

He continued. 'A boy, with emerald eyes. He seeks the stone. He seeks to undo the prophecy.'

Ah Kin's anger dissipated and he felt a knot in his stomach. He let go of the Chilan's robe and took a step back. He realised that he had lost the advantage. The odds were now even and the search had become a race. He knew there was only one who could be plotting against him like this. *It seems that destiny wishes we cross paths again Belkin.*

'Nacom!' Ah Kin called. 'Gather the things and clear the area. We leave for Chichin Itza tonight.'

LIKE FATHER, LIKE SON

Adam found himself on the roof again, and this time, he was alone. He gazed out at the cityscape and looked at all the bright lights in the horizon. His brain tried to grasp what he was now involved in. He marvelled at how just this morning he had woken up worried about a brain tumour and now he was worried about saving the world. *What a difference a day makes.* He chuckled to himself as he shook his head in disbelief.

'Hey, you.'

Adam didn't need to turn around to know it was Sash, the soft twang of her American accent felt like music. 'Hey.' he replied.

'You ok?'

'Not really.' He joked.

'You've been up here a while, thought I'd check up and make sure you hadn't thrown yourself over.' She joked. Her smile had a strange way of instantly making him feel comfortable.

'Well, don't think I haven't thought about it.' Adam quipped.

'Belkin wants you to walk into this with your eyes open. So there's something else that you need to know.'

'Sure, throw it on me.' Adam said as he waved his palms in the air in mock defeat.

'There's no easy way to say this so I'm just going to say it.' She paused. 'Your dad worked with us, and was killed three years ago on a mission.' Sash watched Adam's smile disappear. 'He was working on Protocol 8F with us but went rogue and went against orders. He tried to do it all alone. He was a brave man. But on his last mission, his bravery wasn't enough. He was murdered in Mexico three years ago.'

'He's been alive all this time?' Adam gasped in shock as he felt his legs become weak.

'Yes, and it killed him knowing that his family thought he was dead. But he knew that it was the only way he could protect you. If you, your sister and your mum knew he was alive, you'd look for him or try and make contact. The risk of anything happening to you was too much for him to bear. Our enemies are smart and good at attacking our weaknesses; the people we love.'

'I can't believe it.' Adam whispered. 'All this time I...I thought he was dead.' He stepped back and leant against the rail for support. His mind flashed back to all the dreams he had as a kid imagining his dad as an angel in heaven watching over him. He felt deceived, betrayed.

'Adam, your father was a master of time manipulation, the best. He was able to do things with time that no one had ever seen before. He was a prodigy. It was not only his ability, but his skill in using his ability. Your father knew that you might one day inherit the power, just as he did from his father.'

'Wait, my grandfather was a Timestopper too?!' Adam blurted. His mind was spinning. Everything he thought he knew about his family came tumbling down like a house of cards.

'Yes, actually, your grandfather was only a teenager when he met Belkin. I'm not sure how they met, but I'm sure Belkin would be happy to tell you.'

Adam couldn't believe what he was hearing. 'Belkin... and my grandfather? Wait, how old is Belkin?'

'Old.' Sash replied. 'Very old. Think, Great-Great Grandfather old.'

Adam stood there in shock. 'Great-Great Grandfather old?' he repeated. 'The guy doesn't look a day over forty!'

'I'll get to that.' She dismissed. 'Your grandfather discovered an ancient Mayan ruby that enabled him to develop his powers of slowing time. It's a very powerful stone. Over time it became a part of him, and when your father was born he started showing the same abilities, only he didn't need the stone, a spark of its power was naturally inside of him.'

'My dad was born with the power in the stone?' Adam surmised.

'Exactly. Think of it this way; the stone is like an amplifier, and everyone who comes into contact with it develops a slightly different power. Once your pops had mastered his ability, he was very capable at manipulating time. He surpassed the abilities of your grandfather by leaps and bounds.'

'Whoa, I had no idea about any of this.' Adam admitted.

'Your father was smart. He knew that if the stone ever got into the wrong hands it could be dangerous. That's why he hid it.'

'He hid it?' Adam pondered for a moment. 'Do you know where it is?'

'We don't.' Sash admitted. She briefly paused and then looked back up at Adam. 'But we think you do.'

'I'm sorry love,' Adam laughed. 'but I honestly have no idea.'

'Isn't it possible to know something even if you think you don't Adam?' Sash watched his face frown in confusion. 'We don't have a lot of time to prepare you. It took your father years to develop his abilities to a point where he didn't need the stone anymore, and you only have a few months. But if we find it, it'd give you a huge boost in ability and you'll be able to stop the rotation of the earth just long enough to cause a misalignment and save us. Simple.' She smiled.

'But I've already told you, I don't know where this dumb rock is!' The more he discovered about the mission, the more it felt like suicide.

'We're going to work together and you're going to recall its location. But don't worry about that just yet. First things first, since you're now staying with us your mother and sister need to be informed.'

Adam had been so distracted by everything that he completely forgot about his curfew. 'Damn, what time is it?' He glanced at his watch: *21:52. Wait, what?!* Now, he was sure his watch was slow. 'Hey, do you have the correct time?'

'Sure, it's err... nine-fifty-two.'

'But how can that be?' Adam perplexed. 'It feels like I've been here for a lot longer than that.'

'Belkin figured you needed some extra time so he slowed things down a little, it's his thing, that's why he looks so young. His abilities work on a psychological level.'

'Man,' Adam gasped in wonder. 'who are you guys?'

'We're The Fraction.' Sash smiled.

∞

We have devised a cover to enable you to stay with us.' Belkin began as he sat on the dining table. 'Please Adam help yourself, you must be hungry.'

Adam gawked at all the delicious Turkish food laid out in front of him. It was beautifully presented in dinnerware that looked expensive. 'Yeah, thanks.' He said as he filled his plate with salad and pieces of grilled chicken.

'We will intercept your hospital letter tomorrow and send you a fake stating that you've got the all clear and that your problem was related to an allergic reaction to everyday painkillers. What painkillers do you take at home Adam?'

'Err,' Adam swallowed his food as fast as he could to reply. 'Paracetamol, Ibuprofen, I think Co-Codomol.'

'Good, that's what's causing it.' Belkin reasoned. 'Next, we will send you a secondary letter accepting your enlistment with the Royal Air Force as a cadet on a special cadet programme. You'll be expected to live in the barracks and your family will receive £5000 as a welcome gesture. We'll provide a telephone number for your mother to verify this if she wants.'

Adam thought it through for a moment. 'The RAF? Man, I've always wanted to be a fighter pilot.' He beamed.

'We know. It works because your family knows it's a lifelong dream of yours to be a pilot, so you have to have a realistic motive. We'll make it clear that this is training only and that there will be no field ops. The money will help your mother for a couple of months and thereafter we'll send her regular money on your behalf while you're with us as part of your salary.'

Adam looked down at his food and stopped eating. This was it, the moment his life was about to change... forever. They were good, they'd done their research and thought of everything. It felt right. Adam felt like he was doing a good thing, and financially supporting his mother was the cherry on top. The thought of making her proud made him smile. 'Okay,' he agreed. 'sounds good. Do I get to say goodbye?'

'We're going to drop you off tonight and you've got till next Monday morning.' Belkin explained.

'Monday?' He exclaimed. 'But that's less than a week?!'

'We know Adam. Like I said, we don't have much time. Once our mission is a success, you will have the rest of your life with your friends and family and we'll hand over your father's assets to you. And trust me they are substantial.'

'Yeah but six days?' Adam's murmured. His mind whizzed through all the things he had to do, the people he wanted to see. If things didn't work out, it could be the last time he'd ever see them. He thought about Sid, and mum, good old Zee, his gang... and Nikkita. He was going to miss her the most. *Just when I thought we were finally getting somewhere, typical.*

Adam glanced at his watch. *10:13pm.* 'I should probably be heading back.'

Sash wiped her face with her napkin and placed it on the table. 'I'm done. I'll take him.' Without another word, Sash stood up headed towards the front door and gathered her things. Adam could hear her putting her shoes on.

'Well, it was... an experience.' Adam grinned as he got to his feet.

Belkin also stood up and extended his hand. 'It's been a pleasure to finally meet you, Adam. You're everything I hoped you'd be.' Adam shook his hand and simply smiled back.

'We're leaving.' Sash declared to someone on the phone. 'Bring the car around.'

∞

The drive home was quiet, even quieter than the drive there. It felt like a lifetime had gone by since he'd been picked up from his flat. Everything felt different now. Sash was sitting beside him in the back. Her gaze was fixed firmly on her phone's screen. Adam didn't feel like talking much. He felt anxious but realised that he's anxiety wasn't coming from not knowing enough, it was coming from knowing too much.

Before long they arrived back in Stepney Green. The driver turned into the back roads that Adam was familiar with and finally parked in front of his council block. As Adam opened the door he realised that he didn't have any contact details.

'Hey, can I get your number?' Adam winced as he realised instantly that it sounded like a pick-up line. 'You know so I can call you on Monday.' He clarified.

Sash smiled. 'Just keep your phone on, we'll be in touch. We'll be here to pick you up at 10:00am sharp on Monday, don't be late.'

'Okay. See you then.' Adam stepped out of the car.

'Wait.' Sash called. 'Take this, it's an advance. Buy yourself some smart clothes, we have standards you know.' She smiled. 'And treat your friends and family. It'll be a while till you'll see them again.' Sash handed Adam an envelope that felt thick with cash. 'Oh and one more thing, drop into conversation with your mum that you've come across this RAF thing and you've applied for a spot online. There's a dummy website Raj created, the web address is written on the back of the envelope. All the contact details lead back to us. So feel free to let her call if she wants.'

Adam examined the back of the envelope. 'You guys are something else. And thanks for the money.' He was about to close the door and Sash stopped him again.

'Aren't you forgetting something?' Sash alluded with a smile as she waved his video game in her hand.

'Oh yeah, thanks. I'm all over the place right now.' He reached out and took the video game.

'Bye Adam.'

'Bye.' He saluted as he shut the car door and walked slowly towards the council block slipping the envelope and game down the front of his jeans.

RELIEF

'Oh my god Adam, wake up!'

'Huh?' Adam rubbed his eyes and sat up in his bed. He reached for his phone to check the time. It was 9:53am. 'Mum, it's so early.' Suddenly his eyes burst open. *The hospital letter!*

'Adam we got it! It's a letter from the hospital. I want you to open it with me. Come on, get up!' Adam emerged from his quilt and could now see that she was flapping a white envelope in her hands. It was marked and stamped from the hospital. Suddenly a wave of paranoia washed over him. *What if they didn't intercept the envelope and this is the real thing! Mum will never let me go to the RAF if it says I need more tests!* Adam tried to mask his concern. 'You ok Adam?'

'Yeah, I just hope it's good news.' Adam sat up, took the envelope, tore it open and pulled out the letter. It looked exactly like all the other letters from the hospital. Adam took a moment to skim through it to find the keywords. Relief overwhelmed him when he realised that the letter said exactly what Belkin said it would, it was giving him the all clear.

'Well?!' Sharon badgered.

'I'm fine mum, look read it for yourself.' Adam was relieved, relieved that The Fraction had come through on their word.

Sharon snatched the letter from his hand and began reading. 'Allergic to painkillers?' She frowned. 'Goodness, who would've thought?'

Adam was glad she was buying it. 'So, looks like it's good news mum.' He smiled.

Sharon hugged her son. *Allergic to painkillers, he's only allergic to pain killers!* She decided that tonight she'd pray extra long as relief washed over her. She had lost her husband and she wasn't ready to lose her son. She looked up in gratitude and thanked God silently for answering her prayers.

∞

It was around 3pm and Adam was feeling anxious. His mother had been on cloud nine since the all clear from the fake letter, but all Adam could think about was how to drop the RAF bombshell on her. He played the scenario in his mind over and over like a chess master planning his moves anticipating her every reaction and his subsequent counter argument. He decided that if there was ever a time to catch her while she was in a good mood it was now. He switched off the T.V. got up off the couch and went into his room. He reached into the back of his wardrobe and retrieved an old shoebox that contained his secret stash of knick-knacks. He took out the thick envelope Sash had given him and turned it over and read the web address on the back.

www.raf-cadet.mod.gov.uk

He wondered how hard it was to get a MOD web address. But he wasn't surprised that Raj had managed to obtain a domain specifically reserved for the British Ministry of Defence.

He opened up his laptop and typed in the web address. Instantly an official looking website popped onto his screen showing young cadets in smart blue RAF uniforms smiling and having the time of their lives. Adam clicked on the large icon that read *Recruiting Now* and was led to a new page that provided full details of the cadet programme. Their cadet eligibility specification described Adam perfectly and he met every requirement. He was even eligible for a £2,000 monthly grant over six months and a full qualification equivalent to an A-Level. *Oh my God, Mum's gonna love this!* The Fraction had thought of everything. Adam felt pumped, he was confident now. He grabbed his laptop, spun around and headed towards the kitchen.

'Mum, you gotta see this!' He wailed as he rushed in and sat down on the small circular dining table.

Sharon looked up as she adjusted the cooker's flame and took off her cooking apron. 'Just a sec hun.' She washed her hands and towelled them dry and sat down beside him. 'Okay, what is it?'

'Mum, you know how I've always wanted to join the RAF right?'

Sharon's smile instantly faded. The thought of her son joining the RAF and putting himself in danger tied a knot in the pit of her stomach. 'Adam, I don't think-'

'Mum, please.' Adam interrupted. 'Just take a look, it's just a cadet training school, they give you a full qualification and even pay you for going!' Adam turned the laptop towards her and allowed her to soak in the details from the website. Sharon took a few minutes to read through it and clicked on to the various tabs for more information. Adam tried his best to read her face, but he couldn't tell what she was thinking. 'Well?' He pestered.

'It's six-months Adam. You're going to stay away from us for six months?'

'Mum, I've thought about it, and I think it would be really good for me. I don't have a job and college is just a waste of two years. They pay for everything while I'm there so when I come back I'll have £12,000 to help with the bills and get my life started.'

Sharon looked at her son and a smile broke out on her face. 'Okay.' She beamed. 'If it's just training, I don't mind.'

'Okay?' Adam echoed in shock.

'I said you can go. But you have to call me every day.' She demanded.

Adam leapt up and gave his mother an uncharacteristic bear hug. 'Oh man, this is so awesome. I'm going to apply right now.' He clicked on to the *Apply Now* tab and scrolled through the dates. There were a number of dates that popped up but were all fully booked. There were only three dates available, one for Monday, one in November, and one in December. 'Mum, there's only three dates available.'

Sharon looked at the dates on the screen and frowned. 'Monday?! Uh-uh, no way. That's too soon!'

'Mum, I really don't want to waste the whole summer. I'll be done before Christmas if I leave next week. There's only one space left, someone must have dropped out, surely that's a sign mum!' He exclaimed.

Sharon saw the excitement on his face. It was so nice to see him finally enthusiastic about his future. 'Argh... fine!' She conceded begrudgingly. 'But I don't think they'll accept you this late, but apply for it, and let's see what happens.'

That was it. Adam had done it. 'Thanks mum, you're the best!' Adam said without taking his eyes off the screen. He quickly clicked *Apply Now* and continued to complete the online application form.

With the application form completed he finally clicked *Submit*, and received a confirmation screen thanking him for his application and letting him know that if successful he'd be notified within 24-hours.

∞

Adam didn't have much of an appetite that night. He went to his room and spent most of the night lying in his bed looking up at his ceiling. So much was going through his mind. He was going to move out in a few days, his friends, Nikkita, everyone at home would be left behind. It was such a strange feeling as if it wasn't really happening to him. He was so worried about getting things done that he didn't stop to consider whether he should be getting involved in the first place. It felt as if he was flung into the middle of some epic superhero movie where he was the star. But he felt like a fraud. *I'm a superhero with no bloody super powers.* Adam began to picture himself in a banana yellow spandex superhero outfit and chuckled to himself. *What a crazy, crazy world we live in.*

GOODBYES

It was Friday just after 4pm when Adam's phone starting ringing. He glanced down to see who it was and smiled. Adam answered the call. 'Yo, yo, yo!' He hollered.

'Whas-sappenin' bro!?' Adil replied.

'Nothing man, just jamming at home. What you sayin'?'

'Well we're all out in the park, sun's blazing and there are hunnies everywhere, you need to get over here dude.'

Adam stood up and walked to the window and took a look outside. The sun was high in the sky and there wasn't a cloud in sight. 'Cool, who else is out with you?'

'Everyone man.'

'Nikkita?'

'Course man, Nikkita, Tania, everyone, come out innit.'

'Alright safe, you guys on the hill or by the swings?'

'On the hill.'

'Safe, give me an hour.'

'An hour?! Bitch get your ass here now, we got this crazy weed here and it ain't gonna last an hour, you got thirty minutes max, or Zee's gonna kill it all.'

Adam laughed. 'Alright bro, bloody hell give me a minute, I need to get sorted. I'll be there soon.' Adam ended the call and wondered what he'd wear. He had to make sure that he looked decent since Nikkita was gonna be there.

'Mum! Just popping out to see Adil in the park!' He yelled from his bedroom door.

It was almost 5pm when Adam got to the park. In less than an hour, he had showered, ironed his t-shirt, and eaten a sandwich. But he didn't rush for the weed. It was the thought of seeing Nikkita that drove him. It felt as though he hadn't seen her in ages. As he strolled over to the hill he could see the gang sitting where they always sat, doing what they always did. He noticed Nikkita sitting on the hill next to Tania. Even from afar she looked beautiful. She was wearing her slim fitting blue jeans that accentuated her long slim legs, and a bright yellow vest top. As always she was bathing in the sun trying to top up her tan.

'Hey guys!'Adam bellowed as he approached the foot of the hill.

'Adam! Where you been buddy?' Zee walked over to him and gave him a big bear-hug almost lifting him off his feet. Adam squeezed back playfully.

'Sorry guys, I've had some crazy stuff happen lately and I'm glad you lot are all around I gotta tell you guys something.' Adil immediately glanced up in concern dreading what Adam might announce.

Adam sat down with the gang and explained everything that had happened to him over the past two weeks regarding the headaches, the night terrors, and the hospital appointments. He finally ended the story on a high note declaring the hospital had sent him a letter clarifying that it was a false alarm and that he was about to join the RAF as a cadet. He didn't breathe a word about The Fraction, or his quest to save the world to anyone, but he was aching to tell Adil and Nikkita the truth.

'Man, that's a messed up thing to have to go through just to realise you're allergic to paracetamol.' Zee huffed as he took a deep drag from the joint and passed it to him.

'Tell me about it.' Adam replied as he took the spliff. His head was already swimming in the hazy buzz of the cannabis. It felt good. Like a soothing blanket had been draped over his mind. He took a couple of drags and handed it to Adil.

Adil took a drag of the spliff. 'So does the RAF have any issues with you being allergic to painkillers?'

'They didn't ask on the application form, so I'm hoping it'll be fine.' Adam replied.

'Man, I can't believe you kept this on the low-low for so long. We don't even have enough time to arrange a proper goodbye.' Adil was trying his best hide his dismay. His best friend would be leaving so soon and for so long. A small part of him was annoyed that he was finding out with everybody else and wondered why Adam hadn't told him sooner. This was the type of information best friends were privy to before everyone else. But most of all he was just upset that his friend wasn't going to be close-by for a while.

Adam could sense Adil's tone. 'Bro, I would've told you sooner if I knew. I mean, I thought I had a brain tumour for sure. It was the only thing on my mind.' Adam chuckled as he realised the pun. 'No pun intended!' he smiled as the gang chuckled. 'I only found out that I was all clear two days ago, and the RAF only accepted my application this morning, so it's not really been that long since you guys found out. Everything's just happened so suddenly and I didn't wanna say anything 'til I knew for sure.' Adam kept glancing over at Nikkita, she'd been very quiet throughout, but she never took her eyes off him once. Her eyes seemed sad and disheartened. Adam wanted to walk over to her and hug her and just tell her everything. He wanted to take her with him, to stay with him at The Fraction's headquarters. But he knew that was impossible. *Heck, she doesn't even know I'm madly in love with her!* And then it hit him, he realised that he could actually die on this quest. If he failed the mission, the world and everything in it would be gone, and she would die never knowing how he truly felt about her. Worse yet, he'd never know whether she felt anything for him. *I gotta talk to her, but how do I get her alone?*

∞

Adam spent the next few hours hanging out with the guys, it was just past 8pm and throughout the evening he'd been thinking of a way to get Nikkita alone. He pulled out his phone and discreetly text Nikkita who was sitting just a few feet away.

Hey, can u come over to mine at 9? Need to tell u something, don't tell anyone pls. x

Almost instantly Nikkita's phone bleeped. She looked down and frowned in confusion as she read who it was sent by. Without a word she glanced up at him, but Adam turned away and began talking to Adil. Intrigued, she opened the message and read it. The corner of her mouth turned up as she suppressed a smile. She looked up and met his eyes and discreetly nodded. Adam smiled and looked away in subtle acknowledgement. He finally glanced at his watch, it almost 8:20pm and he got up and started to brush down his trousers with his hands.

'Listen up guys, I hate to call it a night so soon, but I gotta go.'

'Are you kidding me, Junior?' Zee ranted. 'It's your last day with us, we were gonna get some more weed and hit up central.' He got to his feet to talk him into staying.

'Sorry Zee, I gotta go bro, I don't have a lot of time with the family so I gotta be with them. It's my last weekend, and mum wants me to help her with a few things.' Adam knew that Zee appreciated how important the mother/ son bond was when there wasn't a father figure around. Shirking mother's command was the only thing that Zee wouldn't argue over.

'Man that's lame.' Zee looked towards Adil for support. 'Adil, tell him bro.'

Adil looked at Adam and knew something didn't quite add-up, there was more to this story but it was clear to Adil that whatever it was Adam was trying to keep it hidden. They always had an ability to communicate with the slightest of hints and knew when to support each other. It was their bro-code.

'Let him go Zee.' Adil conceded. 'I know Adam wouldn't leave unless it was important.' Adil walked over to Adam and extended his hand, they slapped palms and hugged. 'But you gotta promise to call once in a while, and if you're in the neighbourhood visiting don't leave without linking up first.'

'Course bruv.' Adam smiled as he hugged Adil. He knew he could always rely on his best friend to catch his drift and back him up.

Adam went around the group and hugged everyone goodbye and slowly walked back towards his flat.

OLD COMRADES

Nacom was getting tired. He'd been driving for five-hours without resting and despite initially enjoying the luxurious leather of the 7-Series BMW his back was now beginning to ache. But he didn't dare utter a word of his discomfort as he knew that such selfish thinking would displease Ah Kin.

Ah Kin was sat in the rear seat and noticed Nacom's eyes tiring with the strain of staring at the endless empty highway. He realised that they'd been driving for a considerable amount of time and Nacom hadn't taken a break. 'Nacom, how are you feeling?'

'I am fine brother Ah Kin.' Nacom said as he forced a smile and rubbed his eyes.

'You don't look fine, you must rest. How far are we from our destination?'

Nacom checked his watch. 'About six hours.'

'You won't make it that far. We'll drive to Campeche. I know members of the brotherhood there. We can reside with them until tomorrow before we continue our journey. Turn off at the next exit and find a nearby town.'

Nacom did his best to mask his relief. 'As you wish brother Ah Kin.'

Ah Kin was tired and hungry himself, but his focus wasn't on his appetite, it was on the stone. He felt compelled to attain it. It was his mission's single point of failure and he wasn't going to let down the brotherhood by being the weak link. Nothing could be left to chance. The end of the world was prophesied, and he was almost guaranteed to succeed *if* he had the stone. Joseph was his only threat, but he was now gone, but by hiding the stone he created a threat. If The Fraction recruited someone with similar powers and obtained it, Joseph's death would no longer be a victory. His mind recalled the words of the Chilan. *A boy with emerald eyes... who is the green eyed boy?*

Nacom turned off the highway and entered the historic city of Campeche. He had never visited Campeche before, but he'd heard a lot about it. Its rich history had made him proud to be a Mexican. The city was located off the Gulf coast of Mexico and it was known for its legendary pirate invasions and military wars. But now it seemed a far cry from the battle fortress it once was. Ah Kin glanced out of the window at the docile little town full of buildings painted in soft blue and pink pastel colours. The town's centre of attraction was a cathedral in the main square; the Catedral de Campeche. It was a grand cathedral with two large towers on either side. It dominated the main town square with its presence.

It was almost 9am when Nacom arrived at the cathedral and the town was alive with colour. Tourists were dotted around the cathedral taking pictures and arriving in hordes in the traditional old bus carriages. Nacom parked the car directly in front of the cathedral and switched off the engine. He got out and ran around to the rear to open the door for Ah Kin. Ah Kin stepped out of the car and breathed in the cool, fresh ocean air. The aroma of the nearby sea filled his nostrils. He paused for a moment as he stood at the foot of the building and admired its architecture. It was a beautiful building, with a grand design and dominant features. Ah Kin had been here before, almost fifteen years ago. But right now, all that felt like a vague dream he'd once had. It was strange how his associates from back then were still living in this town, patiently hoping for a new battle. *Soldiers are always soldiers, even when there is no war.* He swung open the large wooden door and walked in. He looked around to see whether much had changed since he last visited the magnificent cathedral and was pleased to see that it hadn't changed at all. Ah Kin noticed three men sat in the pews, their heads were bowed in prayer. Ah Kin recognised one of them immediately and calmly walked towards them. There were only a handful of other people in the cathedral, mostly tourists taking pictures. As Ah Kin approached them the two men sitting behind stood up and reached for their pistols in defence of the third who was still sat in silent prayer.

'I see you still need an entourage after all these years, Immanuel.' Ah Kin teased.

Immanuel turned his head and smiled. 'It's to keep dangerous Mayans like you at bay!' He jibed back as he rose to his feet and greeted Ah Kin with a hug.

'Ha! In that case, you're going to need a bigger entourage!' Ah Kin jibed back and they both burst into laughter. 'It's good to see you brother, have you been well?' Ah Kin asked.

'You're asking as if you don't already know.' Immanuel said as he nodded towards the Chilan. 'If I recall Ah Kin, you keep tabs on friends as well as your enemies. After all, how else would you know where to find me?'

'Your mind is still as sharp as ever old friend.' Ah Kin conceded.

'I hear you're here on business and I understand that you don't have much time.'

Ah Kin looked at his friend in admiration. *They don't make them like this anymore.* He missed the old days, the days of war between the faithful and the hypocrites. In those times Ah Kin would lead operations, and Immanuel led strategy, they made a formidable team. After ten long years of covert battle, it seemed the war had been won. Three years ago, on their final mission, they terminated the last and most powerful Timestopper; Joseph. He was the only one who could harness the power of the sacred stone and jeopardise the end-times prophecy. Defeated, the surviving hypocrites went into hiding.

'The hypocrites have returned Immanuel.' Ah Kin stated frankly. 'They have forged a new team, and we believe they have a new Timestopper.'

'Impossible!' Immanuel's voice boomed in the cathedral. He cleared his throat and composed himself. He realised that the conversation had to be continued elsewhere immediately.

Ah Kin could sense Immanuel's rage. The war was won, at great sacrifice, and the enemy was defeated, or so he thought. Immanuel recalled the announcement his leaders made: *Our trials on this earth are over, prepare for judgement, for now by the grace of the Gods the end of days is upon us.*

Immanuel was furious with himself and the complacency of his leaders. 'We should've gone after the survivors.' Immanuel whispered in anger. 'Now that incompetence has led to the birth of a new affront, and now we are the ones who were unprepared!' Immanuel looked around and noticed people staring. 'Ah Kin, let us discuss this matter in private.'

'That would be wise.' Ah Kin agreed.

'Your brothers are more than welcome to join us.' Immanuel gestured with open arms. 'I insist that while you are here you and your companions will stay with me, in my home.'

'That's very kind of you old friend, but we wish not to burden you, the war you signed up for is over. We have the resources to tackle this matter by ourselves.'

'Nonsense!' Immanuel boomed. 'I did not sign up for a war Ah Kin, I signed up for a cause, and it seems there is still work to be done to complete it. You will have my support until it is done. The Gods have favoured me by bringing you to my door. I will not turn my back on such a blessing.'

'You are a true brother Immanuel.' Ah Kin acknowledged.

Immanuel felt an old feeling stir within his gut. It was a feeling of purpose, of excitement. It was the anticipation of battle. 'Andrew, David; bring the car around.' Immanuel ordered as they began walking towards the exit. 'Ah Kin, I'd be honoured if you travelled with me.'

'Your hospitality knows no bounds brother.' Ah Kin turned to Nacom. 'Follow close behind. I'll be travelling with Immanuel.'

FRIEND ZONE

It was 9:16pm. Nikkita was anxious as she rode the lift to the top of the council estate. Like every council block in London it always smelled of stale urine and cleaning chemicals, but after all these years she'd grown used to it, and in a strange way had become accustomed to it.

The doors slid open and she stepped out and walked towards Adam's flat. She wondered what Adam wanted to tell her, what it was that he couldn't say in front of the others. Her imagination began running away with her as she imagined that maybe he'd confess to liking her. But she kept throwing the notion out of her mind. *Stop it Nikkita.* She looked at her reflection in the small pane of glass on his door and fixed her hair before she rang the doorbell. She pressed the bell and the door opened almost instantly.

'Hey, you.' Adam smiled. 'Took your time!'

'Sorry Adam, the guys thought I'd be hanging out late tonight and made it hard for me to leave when I told them I had to go. You know what Zee's like.' She said as she rolled her eyes.

'It's cool, come in.' Adam opened the door and stepped aside to let her through.

Nikkita walked in and noticed how quiet the house was. 'Where is everyone?'

'Oh, mum and Sid have gone to the shops, they're getting treats for my send off. I think I heard mum saying something about a cake!'

Nikkita laughed. 'Aw, that's so sweet. Your mum is the best. You know she's gonna miss the man around the house.'

'Tell me about it. She actually cried when I told her the RAF accepted me. But she's making the best of it, it feels like it's my birthday or something.' He chuckled.

'Well, I don't blame her. I mean, this is a big deal. You're going away to the RAF, I honestly can't believe it myself. You're gonna be living your dream.' Nikkita always knew how much the RAF meant to Adam. He often talked about it whenever they were high and talking about their dream jobs.

'Yeah, guess you're right.' Adam nodded. He was so used to lying now that a part of him actually wished he was joining the RAF. But he often reminded himself that his real job was far more exciting than some cadet school.

'Sheesh, I thought you'd be more excited about it than that!' Nikkita scoffed.

Adam realised that his tone sounded a little flat. 'No, no. I am excited, I mean, are you kidding? I'm joining the damn RAF! It's just I'm starting to realise that I'll be leaving everyone behind.' Adam opened the door to his bedroom to let her through. 'Hey want anything to drink? I think we've got some cola and, err... coconut water.'

Nikkita sat in her usual spot on the end of the bed. 'Coconut water? Ooh, how exotic.' She giggled.

'It's Sid, she bought a whole case of it half price from the market and we've been trying to drink 'em all before they expire!'

'Okay, that's like the worst sales pitch ever.' She giggled. 'No coconut water for me thanks.'

'Okay, suit yourself, but you're missing out.' He laughed.

Instead of his usual spot on the beanbag Adam perched himself on the other side of the bed. Nikkita's heart began to race, but she pretended not to notice. She could tell Adam was nervous about something and decided to break the tension. 'So, err...six months eh?' She blurted. 'Do you know if you'll be allowed to visit?'

Adam scooted back on the bed and rested his back against the wall and nervously played with his hands. 'No, I don't think they'll let me.' Adam's thoughts reeled back to the doomsday prophecy. 'If it all works out then I'll be back by Christmas. But that's only if I don't mess up.'

'What?' Nikkita replied in disbelief. 'It's a training camp. Just do what they say and you'll be fine. Even *you* are smart enough to follow orders.' She jibed.

'Yeah maybe.' Adam replied in an flat tone.

'Don't think like that. Hey, I'm joking, you're smart. You'll do well. I know it.' She said reassuringly.

But Adam wasn't thinking about the RAF. Every atom in his body was begging him to tell her the truth. He looked up at Nikkita and smiled. 'Thanks. You always know how to make me feel better.'

'So is this what all this is about?' Nikkita wondered.

'Actually no.' Adam confessed. 'Nikkita, I really need to tell you something.'

Nikkita's heart skipped a beat. There was something about the way he said it, and her imagination started running wild as she pre-empted what he was about to say. He finally looked up at her, and there was strange sincerity in his eyes that she'd never seen before. 'Yes...' She encouraged.

'I just don't want things to get awkward if I tell you though.'

Oh my God! This is it! Nikkita had dreamt of this moment. Over the years she had sent him so many signals but they were never reciprocated and she just assumed that perhaps he didn't like her that way. 'Don't be silly, nothing you can say will ever make things awkward between us Adam.'

Adam smiled awkwardly. He could sense that she was trying to make this easy for him. It made him feel confident. He took a deep breath and decided to tell her what he had been rehearsing in his head all evening. 'Do you remember that night at the funfair? We were climbing that locked gate after the park had closed with Zee.'

Nikkita knew exactly what he was talking about. It was the most embarrassing night of her life. She was wearing a long dress that night and half way up the gate she realised that it was a bad idea to have worn it. 'Yeah...' She blushed.

'Well, I was behind you and when you jumped off the other side your dress got caught and as you landed I... I kinda...well... I saw your bum.' He confessed.

'Oh my God, you didn't!' Nikkita turned a bright shade of pink. You perv!' She teased.

Adam laughed. 'I'm sorry hun. But you see that night I realised that I don't just see you as a friend. I've been kinda bottling it up since then. But I can't anymore I have to tell you how-'

'Adam!'

'Shoot! It's my mum!' Adam bolted off the bed like a burglar caught in the act of a robbery and ran out of the room. He ran towards the front door and saw Sid and his mum carrying huge bags of groceries.

'Come here and help me take these things to the kitchen love.'

'You guys are back already?'

Sharon paused as she looked around, and then looked back at Adam. Something about him was off. He was on edge about something. 'What's going on?' She pried. 'Is someone here?'

Adam was a fool to think that his mum wouldn't sense something. Nikkita had been over several times before, but tonight was different. 'It's just Nikkita mum, she's come over to say goodbye.'

'Oh splendid she can join us, it'll be like a goodbye party.' Sharon walked past Adam and into the kitchen. 'Nikkita!' Sharon bellowed. 'Come here and help us love!'

Nikkita came out of the room. 'Hello, Mrs Newton.'

'Come here sweetheart, glad you're here, you can help me get set up.'

'Mum...' Adam groaned.

'What? You two will have plenty of time to chit chat afterwards. Come on love grab those bags from Sid and put them on the table.'

Nikkita smiled. 'Sure thing.' she walked over to Sid and took the heavy bags from her and placed them on the dining table. She walked past Adam to get the rest of the things, but as she did, she discreetly brushed her chest against Adam's arm as she passed him in the narrow hallway. Adam blushed in embarrassment, his heart pounded so hard he thought it would burst out of his chest. He looked at her and she playfully smiled back. He tried his best to hide the smirk developing on his face as he realised she had got the message, and that she obviously liked him too.

∞

It was almost midnight and Adam was getting tired. His mum hadn't stopped nattering with Nikkita all night and he was beginning to lose his nerve about talking to her about his feelings. Adam had done his best to send hints to his mother that he wanted some privacy with Nikkita, but she was either unreceptive or simply ignoring them. Either way, this night was not going to plan. Adam decided that he needed a change of tact.

'Just gonna go check on something in my room.' He announced.

'What?' Sharon looked surprised. 'Where are you going? We're all here for you.'

'I know mum, I just need to go check on something.' He fibbed. He knew Nikkita would realise that it was a ploy for privacy and maybe she would find an excuse to follow him. Adam walked into his bedroom and sat on his beanbag. He left the door slightly ajar so Nikkita would feel comfortable to walk in if she managed to get away. He looked around and wondered how long it would take. He decided to distract himself and reached for his games controller and switched on the console. The game had barely loaded before there was a light knock on the door.

'Knock, knock... It's me.' Nikkita announced as she poked her head through.

She'd managed to get away quicker than he thought. 'Hey you, yeah, come in.'

'Scoot over.' She said as she sat on the small beanbag beside him. Adam moved over and she sat down, he instantly felt his heart rate rise. Although he was a little squashed he didn't dare move. Being close to her was all he wanted, even if it meant suffering a little.

'I thought mum was gonna keep you in there forever.' He joked.

'Yeah, she does like to talk.' She smiled. 'But she's sweet though, and loves you very much.'

'I know. I'm gonna miss her you know. Never been away from home more than a day before and now I'm going for half a year. Hey, do me a favour, can you pop by once in a while, just make sure Sid and mum are okay.'

'Yeah, of course, she's like an aunt to me. Besides, while you're gone being around here will remind me of you.' She paused for a moment. 'And then maybe I won't miss you as much.' A thin strand of hair fell in front of her face and she tucked it behind her ear. It was the simplest little thing, but there was something about the way she did that that made Adam's heart race. 'So weren't you going to tell me something?'

Adam blushed and instantly felt his face becoming red with embarrassment. He was ready to open up earlier, but now, with his mother in the next room he felt uneasy. 'Yeah, oh, it was nothing really. Just that I'm really gonna miss you.' Adam fibbed, hoping that she would let it go.

'What?!' She exclaimed. 'C'mon Adam you made it out to be something a bit more than that. You could've said that at the park.' Nikkita wasn't convinced, she was determined to get the truth out of him.

'Yeah but, you're special. I didn't just wanna say bye in the park like that.'

'Aw...' She replied. 'Special? That's so sweet.' Nikkita leant in and hugged him tightly.

Adam wasn't expecting a hug, but now locked in her embrace he couldn't let go. The smell of her sweet perfume was hypnotising, and her warm body felt perfect against his. A few moments passed and neither one loosened their grip. Adam closed his eyes, he would've happily stayed in her embrace for the rest of his life. Eventually, she let go and they faced each other, their faces just inches apart. Adam froze. *Kiss her!* His heart screamed. But he wasn't sure. There were signs, but he wasn't certain. *But what if I do and she freaks out? Don't be a coward, do it!* Uncertain, Adam pulled back and instantly regretted it as he saw the disappointment on Nikkita's face. *God, why isn't there a universal sign that lets people know when it's okay to kiss someone!*

Nikkita was confused. She'd made it so obvious to him. She wondered if she had misunderstood what he was trying to say earlier. She recalled how she brushed by him in the hallway and suddenly felt stupid and embarrassed. 'It's getting late. I should go.' She said as she got to her feet.

'Really?' Adam stood up and wished he could rewind the past two minutes and do everything differently. 'Ah, you should stay.'

'I can't, it's past midnight and I have to wake up really early tomorrow.'

Adam felt like he'd just missed out on the biggest moment of his life. He leant in to kiss her cheek, but they both moved their faces an inch too close and half his lips caught half of hers. Electric bolts ran all throughout his body, and his heart began racing. He pulled back and stared deep into her eyes. Fate had given him a second chance and this time he wasn't going to squander it. He cupped her face in his hands and gave her the deepest, most passionate kiss of his life.

DEADLY ALLIANCE

Despite his disdain for material things, Ah Kin couldn't help but admire the mansion Immanuel called home. It was a striking white cubed building situated on a vast amount of land high on the hills in an exclusive part of town. As the white Rolls Royce rolled through the front gate and up to the front of the house he noticed that the lower portion was predominantly made up of glass and was almost completely see-through, except for a few load bearing concrete beams supporting the upper levels. Two guards dressed in black combat gear and armed with machine guns were on patrol beside the front doors and swiftly surveyed the area as the car pulled in. Ah Kin was surprised by the level of security given the amount of time that had lapsed since the war.

'Are you still active Immanuel?' Ah Kin queried. 'Those look like soldiers from the Mexican SFB.'

Immanuel laughed. 'You're mistaken my friend, after the 2nd assassination attempt against me failed, the Secretary of Defence personally appointed GAFE agents for my protection. He even built them a residence here in on my land so they're always close by.'

GAFE agents were infamous within the Mexican military. A hand-picked special group of a hundred agents were selected from across the national military and trained to be the best of the best in anti-terrorism warfare. They received orders directly from the Mexican Secretary of Defence.

'GAFE? I'm impressed.' Ah Kin admitted. 'Are we expecting Anti-terrorist activity tonight by any chance?'

Immanuel laughed. 'Luck my friend follows the prepared.'

The driver stopped the car and opened Immanuel's door and then swiftly ran around to open Ah Kin's. As they walked towards the house the guards saluted and stood to attention.

'At ease gentlemen, my guest will be staying with us for a while. There is another car following behind with two others. You will see to it that they are given the same level of protection I'm given while they are here. Is that understood?'

'Yes, Sir!' They both yelled in unison.

Inside, the house was even more impressive. It was spotless and everything seemed lavish and expensive, yet it felt warm and inviting. The floor was solid walnut and gleamed as if it had been freshly waxed. The decor was elegant and had a Spanish feel to it. The living room was vast and lead to a dining area to the rear where a grand mahogany table was set for a party of eight. As Ah Kin glanced upwards he noticed a wide wrought iron spiral staircase that led to a catwalk on the upper floor overlooking the living room below.

'It's a spectacular home, Immanuel.' Ah Kin complimented. 'It must take Ivette a long time to maintain a palace such as this.'

Immanuel froze mid-stride. Ah Kin noticed that for the first time today, he had lost his smile. Ah Kin instantly realised that something must have happened to his wife. 'No...' He gasped. 'I'm so sorry Immanuel, I had no idea. What happened?'

'Three years next month.' Immanuel whispered. 'Those sons of-!' He paused, feeling overwhelmed by the memory. 'They thought it was me.' Immanuel closed his eyes as he summoned the strength to continue. 'It was a car bomb. They planted it while she was out shopping with Elsa.' Immanuel shook his head as he looked at Ah Kin with glazed eyes. 'They took my family from me Ah Kin...my beautiful wife and my innocent child.'

Ah Kin took a step closer to Immanuel and placed his hand on his shoulder. 'Did you find the ones responsible?'

'It took me a week. With the power I have at my disposal, it should've taken me a day, but the government is full of crooks!' He growled. 'But those responsible are now burning in hell where they belong.'

'Glad to hear it my friend.' Ah Kin suddenly realised why Immanuel had such high security. It was the least the Secretary of Defence could do given the sacrifices Immanuel had made for his country. Despite having so much, he'd actually lost everything. Ah Kin now understood why Immanuel was so eager to help him on his cause. His friend had nothing left to live for. For all his wealth, religion and power, underneath it all, he was a soldier without a purpose. Ah Kin knew in that moment that Immanuel was all in. He needed this. It would be a reason to wake up in the morning.

'My family is in a better place now.' Immanuel said humbly. 'And it's only a matter of time before we're all reunited once more. God has a plan for us and we have six months to ensure we do our bit to stop anyone from meddling with that.' He beamed, as his smile returned. 'Come, we have much to discuss, I need to know everything you know.' Immanuel looked over Ah Kin's shoulder and noticed that his companions were arriving. He turned around and began walking towards the dining table. 'But first, we dine!'

A NEW HOME

It was another sleepless night for Adam. There was so much going through his head that he found himself staring at the ceiling for most of the night. He must have fallen asleep at some point as he heard his mobile phone alarm chime. He groaned as he switched it off and rubbed his eyes. He looked at the time; *8:30am*. He then realised it was Monday. 'Damn!' He sprang out of his bed and flung open his empty suitcase and began emptying his wardrobe into it. He knew that Sash would be here at 10am sharp and he didn't want to be late on his first day on the job. Within fifteen minutes all his essential items were in his suitcase, he zipped the top and took a quick look around to see if there was anything he missed. Satisfied that everything he needed was in his suitcase he headed towards the bathroom to shower and get ready. As he brushed his teeth his thoughts trailed back to the night before and that passionate kiss with Nikkita. It was like a dream, his heart skipped a beat as the details of the memory came flooding back. He shook his head realising that thoughts of her right now would only distract him, and he had to focus. *One thing at a time, let's get this done and then I can daydream later.*

∞

It was 9:55am and Sash pulled the black Range Rover outside the block and peered upwards towards Adam's flat. She didn't see any movement and impatiently glanced towards Raj who was sat in the front passenger seat beside her.

'Relax.' Raj said. 'Give him a minute. He may never see his family again. Besides, what's the rush? I kinda like wearing this uniform. Do I look important?' Raj jested as he turned towards her and pulled a ridiculous face.

Despite her best efforts to remain professional Sash cracked a smile. 'Like a General, a General for the mentally insane.' She teased. She pulled down the visor and fixed her RAF hat and turned back to Raj. 'Is my hat straight?'

'It's fine.' He assured. 'Don't worry, they won't suspect a thing. We look so legit even I'm scared of us right now.'

Sash was on edge. She knew that if Adam's mother became suspicious it could compromise the mission before it even started. But more than that, she didn't want anything to go wrong because she truly believed Adam was the one, the answer, the missing piece. Belkin was a stickler for detail, leaving nothing to chance. Every moment of their interaction in the penthouse headquarters with Adam had been planned and pre-rehearsed. Every reaction was predicted and every possible outcome considered. Sash's demonstration on the rooftop, Belkin's speech, the computer presentation, it was all part of the plan. There were no second chances and there was no room for error. *If only Adam knew how important he was.*

'He's here.' Raj declared. 'Damn, he's bought the whole block out with him!'

Sash slapped the visor up and peered out the window and saw Adam struggling to get through the heavy security doors with a large suitcase. She noticed three women following him and recognised the first two as his mother and sister, but the third one was unfamiliar. Raj stepped out as Adam walked towards the car. Raj shook his hand in an official manner and took his suitcase and loaded it into the back. The women stood halfway down the path and were waving goodbye. Adam opened the rear door and waved back. His heart sank as the reality of the situation dawned on him, but just as he was about to get into the car Nikkita ran over and without a word threw herself into his arms and hugged him tightly.

'Don't forget to call.' She reminded as she kissed him on the cheek.

'I won't.' He promised. Adam climbed into the rear passenger seat and closed the door as Nikkita stepped back and soaked in his face for the last time.

'Wow, you guys really went all out, love the uniforms!' Adam exclaimed. 'Thought the real RAF had turned up for a minute!'

'Presentation, they say it's fifty percent of the marks.' He said as he turned and winked at Adam. The car pulled off and Adam waved until they turned the corner and his loved ones were out of sight.

'You okay champ?' Sash asked.

'Phew!' He gasped. 'Just glad that bit is over. I still can't believe this is all happening.' *This is so crazy!*

∞

Adam spent the journey wondering what lay in front of him now that he was part of The Fraction. He wondered whether he'd ever see his family and friends again. *What a mental month it's been.* He knew he was doing something good, but he felt he was a far cry from being a hero. He was just a sixteen-year-old kid who was way out of his depth.

It felt like they had barely been in the car twenty minutes but Sash was already turning into Knightsbridge. The car pulled into a side road and followed the building around where a gate opened and led them into an underground car park. He hadn't seen this part of the building before and he made a mental note of the street entrance in case he had to find it again. If there was one thing Adam was good at, it was directions. His trick was to turn around to see the location from the perspective of his return journey and take a mental picture of the landmarks.

The car parked up in a bay close to the lift. As Adam got out he looked around and noticed that the car park was like a car show. It was filled with exotic and expensive cars. He could've happily spent the entire day down here admiring the various Lamborghinis, Aston Martins and Ferraris.

'All these yours?' Adam joked to Raj as they exited the Range Rover.

Raj laughed. 'Don't be silly, we just own the ones against this wall.' He pointed towards a row of parked cars beside the Ranger Rover.

Adam's smile faded as he realised that Raj wasn't joking. 'What?!' He gasped. 'You mean that the Phantom, that GT Continental, the Lambo, and that Aston are all yours?!' He exclaimed.

'They're Belkin's.' Sash clarified as she walked towards the lifts. 'But we use them whenever we need to. He's not precious. Think of them as company cars.' She replied casually. 'Do you have a licence?'

Adam considered lying, but then thought better of it. 'Not yet.' He sighed. 'Too young, gotta take my test when I'm seventeen, but my birthday is only a few months away. I mean, I know how to drive. I've been driving since I was fourteen. I kinda taught myself after my uncle showed me how to use the pedals and the gears.'

'Fourteen?' Raj replied in shock. 'Man that's young!' The lift doors opened and the three of them stepped in. Sash stood closest to the buttons and inserted the key, the button for the penthouse lit up and she pressed it. The lift began ascending.

'Yeah, me and two of my mates decided to go buy a car when we were still at school. It was an old banger, a

Vauxhall Nova. It was in fairly decent condition for a three-hundred quid motor. We all chipped in a hundred quid each and bought it just before summer holidays. It made us the coolest kids in the school.'

'Man, that's so illegal, proper East London bad boys eh?' Raj chuckled.

'Yeah, but it didn't last long, one of the guys who chipped in had a younger brother who really wanted to drive it. One day he got hold of the keys without me knowing and he smashed it into a bloody parked car in a car park.'

'A parked car! In a car park?!' Raj roared with laughter. 'What a doofus!'

'Tell me about it! The idiot then calls me up and tells me that the car is somehow stuck in a ditch and he can't get it out. I just told him to leg it and leave the car there.'

'Damn, you must have been raging at him.'

'Yeah, I was. But the messed up thing was that the joker forgot his school bag in the boot of the car! The police crowbar'd the boot open and found all his personal details in it. They went straight to his house and that dumbass grassed us all up!'

'No way!' Raj exploded.

I was cacking myself when the police came to the flat.' The lift chimed as they reached the penthouse floor and the doors opened. Sash led the way as they stepped out and walked towards the door to the apartment.

'Damn, so what did the police say?'

'They tried to scare me with talks of jail and stuff but I simply told them that the guy they just spoke to wasn't a friend. I told them he picks on me at school and is trying to blame this on me, and that I had nothing to do with it.'

Raj was impressed with Adam's quick thinking. 'Did they buy it?'

'They had to, they had no evidence and the car was unregistered. I never heard from them again. But that didn't stop my mum from punishing me. There was this huge party I was supposed to go to that night which she banned me from. And when my uncle found out he shaved my head and my eyebrows off.'

'What?!' Raj choked. 'He shaved your damn eyebrows too?!'

'Mate, it took over a year for them to grow back. I looked like a freak. I was fourteen and had no hair on my head or face. All my mates at school thought I was dying of cancer!'

Sash turned around and looked Adam in sympathy and tried to suppress a smile. 'That's horrible.' She said as she looked at Raj who was also trying his best not to laugh. They both looked at each other trying to control themselves and they both burst into laughter.

'I'm sorry, I don't mean to laugh.' Sash apologise as she opened the door to the apartment.

Raj continued laughing as he walked in. 'Yeah, sorry dude.' He said as he wiped the water from his eyes. 'Saddest thing...' he chuckled. '...I've ever heard.' He said as he continued giggling.

'Yeah, yeah laugh at my pain.' Adam joked with a smile on his face. In truth it had been a tough year for him but he was glad he could laugh about it now.

They walked into the living room area and saw Belkin standing there to welcome them dressed casually in a white shirt and blue chinos.

'Well well, it's lovely to see everyone in such high spirits.' He beamed. 'It is indeed a day to celebrate. Today our team is complete. Welcome to The Fraction Adam.' He raised his arms openly. 'Our home is your home and nothing here is off limits to you.'

Adam instantly composed himself and cleared his throat. 'Thank you Belkin, I'm really glad to be here. I'm just a bit nervous, I know I've got a lot to learn. I'll do my best not to let you down.'

'I know you will Adam, but I don't want you to worry about any of that today. Today is not about business it's about getting to know us, and for us to get to know you. Work starts tomorrow, and every day from then on until the 21st of December as we agreed. Can you handle that?'

'Yes.' Adam assured. 'Yes, I can.' Adam looked around at his new home. It was a far cry from his tiny little flat back in East London. *I'm home.*

SACRIFICE: ACCEPTED

'You have a beautiful house, Sir.' Nacom said as he admired the dining room. His stomach was full to the point of bursting but wished he had more room as he stared at the delicious food that remained untouched on the dining table.

'We're all friends here Nacom, I prefer that you call me Immanuel. And yes, it was a labour of love building this place. Everything in here was built to my wife's impeccable taste.' Immanuel pointed to the spiral staircase that led to the catwalk above. 'That staircase there was her favourite. She had it designed from scratch. She was so fussy, everything had to be perfect. It drove me crazy at the time, but in the end, I have to admit, it turned out to be remarkable.' He sighed as he stared into the distance recalling fond memories. 'I guess that's what Ivette was... remarkable.'

A well-dressed butler appeared and gracefully approached the table and stood behind Immanuel. 'Excuse me Sir, but may I clear the table?'

'Yes, it looks like we're all done here.' He removed the napkin from his lap and placed it on his plate as he rose to his feet. 'Gentlemen, would you care to join me in my study, I'd like to show you all something.'

'Of course.' Ah Kin rose to his feet and Nacom and the Chilan followed suit.

'Jose, bring the cigars up once you're done here, and please see to it that we're not disturbed.'

The butler looked up and gave Immanuel a knowing smile. 'I'll be right up, Sir.'

Immanuel led the men up the spiral staircase onto the first floor. They walked across the catwalk overlooking the living room below. Immanuel turned right and placed his hands on a wall. He reached up and slid a hidden latch down. The wall parted revealing a hidden door, he pushed the door open and led the men up a hidden staircase until they arrived at a secret room at the top.

'Welcome to my study gentlemen.' Immanuel declared with pride.

Nacom looked around in awe. It reminded him of a NASA mission control room he once saw in a movie. It was dimly lit around the sides but was flooded with green light radiating from a wall of CCTV screens displaying every square inch of the building's interior and exterior perimeters. In the middle of the room, a large oak boardroom table surrounded by fine grain leather chairs occupied most of the floor space. The remaining walls were covered in large whiteboards, detailed maps of various countries, and satellite images of major capital cities across the world. Ah Kin walked towards a computer screen and noticed blueprints for weapon concepts, military equipment, and unique product ideas. He also noticed a large sketch pad with doodles and a few short poems scribbled across it.

Ah Kin glanced up at Immanuel and gestured towards the sketch pad. 'Keeping busy I see.' He teased.

'It's all works of a brilliant mind I assure you.' Immanuel grinned. 'Gentlemen please, take a seat.' The men sat on the oval-shaped boardroom table.

The Chilan looked around in silence, he hadn't said a word since he arrived but he was mesmerised by all the technology around him. Being raised in a tribal region of Mexico he had had little exposure to technology, but looking around the room a strange feeling overwhelmed him. He sensed a familiarity to this room. It felt like he'd been here before, in a vision. He knew that it was a sign from the gods that they were on the right path. He turned and stared at Immanuel, he knew this man was sent to them, he was the one who would help them exterminate the emerald eyed boy and retrieve the stone. A smirk grew across his face. *The sacrifice was indeed blessed.*

BOOK OF REVELATIONS

The past three weeks had been amazing. Adam enjoyed a lavish luxury lifestyle he'd only ever dreamt about before now. He was developing a strong friendship with Raj and they spent most of the time together cruising around in the exotic cars and shopping for new clothes. Adam would watch in awe as Raj would effortlessly hack various websites and access highly sensitive information to produce reports for Belkin. Sash wasn't around as much as Belkin and Raj. She was often out on jobs that Belkin would assign to her. Adam didn't know where she'd go, and she wouldn't talk about it when she'd return but he wished that she was around more, he enjoyed talking to her. She had an amazing perspective on the world and always saw the best in people.

Over the weeks Adam made a habit of staying in touch with friends and family. He made a special effort to make sure he spoke to Nikkita but Belkin's orders were not to call too often and Adam respected that. Sometimes he'd sit in his room and berate himself at how he took everyone he loved for granted. Not being able to speak to people when he wanted to made him miss them even more.

It was now the middle of August and although he was having a good time, he didn't feel that he was being very productive. He was learning things from Sash, Belkin, and Raj but nothing seemed directly related to developing his abilities. On most days, he'd completely forget that he was here for a special purpose. It mostly felt like he was on vacation, living all inclusive in an expensive hotel in a nice part of London. It was almost 6pm and Adam headed to his room to check his Facebook, but just as he sat down on his chair he heard a soft knock on the door.

'Come in!' Adam said swivelling around on his desk chair.

'I hope you're clothed.' Sash teased as she peeked through the door. 'Listen, Belkin asked me to give you this.' She walked in and handed him a thick and tatty brown leather-bound book. It looked old and some of the pages inside it were loose. It was bound by a simple string wrapped around it a few times and a red wax seal that was embossed with the word 'Newton'.

Adam took it and examined the seal. *Newton.* 'That's cool, same as my surname.' He noticed as he ran his thumb over the dried wax.

'Well, it would be. It's your father's.'

'Whoa, this is his diary?' He asked in giddy excitement. 'Belkin mentioned this ages ago. I totally forgot about it.'

'It was his wish that if anything was to happen to him it would be passed on to you, and only you. It's never been opened by anyone here. Not even Belkin's seen what's in it.'

'So you guys weren't even a tiny bit curious?' He quizzed sceptically. 'I mean, my dad died and you lost the stone. This could've told you where it was and you never even checked it?'

Sash gave him a stern look. 'Trust is a value we uphold here Adam.' She turned around and headed for the door. 'Your orders are to read this diary cover to cover and speak with Belkin in the morning. Play time is over Adam let's not forget why we're all here.'

Adam examined the thickness of the book. *Man, there is no way I'm gonna finish all this tonight!* But despite the arduous task before him, Adam was excited. It was his first real task he'd received since he got here and he didn't want to disappoint.

∞

It had just gone past midnight and Adam hadn't put the diary down once. His father's life was fascinating and he documented in vivid detail each and every adventure. He learnt how the war began and how the battle to save the world was being fought for years before he was ever born. His father had come close so many times but the Mayans were tricky, often using magic to assist them. Adam read how his grandfather was deceived by the Mayans who tricked him into parting with the stone. But their success was only short-lived as Adam's grandfather bravely sacrificed himself to retrieve the stone in a suicide quest to get it back to Belkin for safe keeping. The diary explained how Belkin recruited his father at the age of nineteen and trained him to develop his time stopping abilities so he could succeed where his father had failed. With the stone in hand, Adam's father developed his powers quickly and became the backbone of The Fraction successfully completing many missions.

The diary also described Joseph's personal life. Adam read about his father's marriage and how hard it was for him to part from his family once he realised that the Mayans were tracking them through magic. To Adam, it explained why they moved houses around East London so often early in his life. He read how his father missed his children and continued to financially support them discreetly by sending cheques in the mail for cash winnings from lottery draws that they never entered. Adam realised that despite his mother's lack of regular employment they always seemed to have more than enough to live on. He now knew his father had always been taking care of them. It all suddenly made sense.

Another hour or so had passed and Adam was lying in bed still feverishly reading through the entries in the diary. An unexpected knock on his door startled him. Adam grabbed a nearby pencil and bookmarked the page he was on. He was astonished to realise that he was almost two-thirds of the way through the thick book already. 'Come in!' He called out.

Sash walked in with a cup of coffee. She smiled as she glanced at the bookmarked diary. 'Wow! I'm impressed.' Sash beamed. 'Here, this is for you.' She placed the steaming cup on the bedside unit. 'It's coffee, it'll help keep you awake and help you finish.'

'Thanks, Sash. You know I'm so glad that my father decided to create this diary. There's so much that I would've never known about him had it not been for this book.' He picked up the book and placed it on his lap. 'You know, I think my father always knew I'd be here someday.'

Sash could sense something different about Adam. She felt he was beginning to realise his importance, how deep his family's legacy ran with The Fraction. 'You know, I think you might be right.' She affirmed with a smile. 'Anyway, you've still got plenty to get through. So I'm going to leave you to it. Remember you're meeting with Belkin in the office at nine tomorrow morning,' Sash said as she walked to the door. 'so try and get some sleep too.'

'Sure. Will do. G'night.'

The door had barely closed before he had the diary open in his lap again. He turned to the page he bookmarked and the pencil slid out. He picked up the mug of coffee and took a sip. *Wow, that's strong. Looks like I'm gonna finish this diary tonight after all!*

∞

It was almost 4am and Adam's bloodshot eyes were staring at the ceiling. He'd read every page of the diary and completed it cover to cover. He now lay in his bed terrified. His father had written pages and pages about the Mayan priests and their culture and religious practices. How they mercilessly killed and conducted gruesome sacrificial rituals to gain supernatural advantages using spirits known as Jinns to help them. He read about their prophecies and examined numerous sketches of pyramid structures, tombs, and ancient artefacts. Reading the diary had not only informed Adam about his purpose in his quest, it enabled him to connect with his father in a way that he never could in his real life. As he finished reading he realised that the deceased father's diary was a bittersweet gift. For the first time in his adult life he actually felt the absence of his father and he suddenly felt alone and vulnerable. *My father was amazing, and if he failed, what chance do I have?* The only thing that gave him solace was his new comrades. The soldiers he was now living with who were guiding him. He didn't believe in himself, but he believed in them. They would be his strength, his family, his hope. He clung to that warm feeling and closed his eyes. Exhausted, and with the diary resting by his pillow he fell asleep.

THE DREAM

Sofia jolted out of her sleep. Her breathing was shallow and her heart was pounding. She grabbed the notepad from the bedside unit and frantically began writing. It was a tip her mother gave to her when she was a just child. *The best way to remember your dreams honey is to keep a notepad by the bed and write it down as soon as you wake.* Most of Sofia's dreams contained clear messages, but sometimes they were metaphorical and only by writing down every last detail could they be interpreted accurately. She jotted down the colours she saw, the temperature she felt, the emotions she experienced, as well as everything she saw and heard. She'd been writing solidly for almost five minutes, only pausing to recall details of the dream. Satisfied she'd captured the entire dream, she clicked the pen shut and placed it back on the bedside unit. She flipped back to the first page of her entry and began reading. A sense of dread began brewing in her gut. The dream was a warning. She unplugged her mobile phone from its charger and called Belkin.

'Morning Sofia.' Belkin Answered. 'Pleasant dreams?'

'Belkin, we've got a problem.'

Belkin knew that Sofia wasn't usually the type to exaggerate a situation. If Sofia said that there was a problem Belkin would usually address it immediately. Sofia's premonitions were always accurate, provided they were interpreted correctly. The Fraction knew that if Sofia had a negative premonition only swift action could alter its course. 'I see.' Belkin acknowledged. 'Bring your notepad. I'm at headquarters.'

'I'll be there within an hour.' Sofia hung up the phone and flicked through her notepad again. *This is bad...*

Sofia parked up her silver Porsche in her usual space in the parking lot. It had only been a month since she'd been gone and already she felt like a stranger. She got into the elevator and inserted her key and pressed the button for the penthouse suite. As the elevator ascended she thought about all the emails that Raj had been sending her keeping her up to date with Adam, and she was looking forward to finally meeting him. She'd seen him in her dreams a few times and in a strange way felt like she already knew him.

Belkin heard the knock at the door but noticed that Raj was on his feet in a flash. 'I'll get it!' He boomed. Raj checked the surveillance monitors and his heart skipped a beat when he saw her face. Knowing that she was just on the other side of the door made him nervous and excited all at the same time. Raj never made it a secret that he found her attractive. She had beautiful Arabian features and was well proportioned with long dark brown hair. Her brown skin and wide hazel coloured eyes made Raj's heart race every time he looked at her. He had been putting out the signals since the first time they met. He knew Sofia didn't feel the same way, but that didn't stop him from trying. He took a deep breath and opened the door.

'Hey, gorgeous!' He beamed with his arms wide open.

'Hey, how you been?' Sofia smiled. She had to admit she missed Raj's cheekiness. She found him funny and cute but wasn't interested in anything other than friendship. She loved how regardless of what was happening in the world he always seemed jolly, and just being around him made her happy too.

Raj stepped forward and gave her a big hug and he suddenly remembered why she had left. He stepped back and put his hands on her shoulders. 'I'm so sorry about everything, did the funeral go okay?'

Sofia knew she'd have to talk about it sooner or later. He was a great listener, and when he wasn't goofing around he would give really good advice. But she didn't feel like going into all the details just yet. 'It was tough.' she admitted. 'But everything went smoothly. I just thought she'd live forever you know.' Sofia's voice cracked, she closed her eyes as she felt them well-up and took a deep breath to compose herself. 'We were all there for her, that's what she would've wanted.' Sofia felt her ability was often a curse rather than a gift. One of the hardest things about being born with precognitive abilities was seeing someone you cared about in a negative premonition.

∞

A month ago Sofia woke up from a nightmare that would rock her to her core. She witnessed her mother die suddenly in an accident back home in Egypt. She knew that there wasn't much time and spoke to Belkin immediately about leaving to be by her side before it happened. But she had lied, she didn't go to say goodbye at all. Her real motive was to try and stop it from happening. Despite her best efforts, the events unfolded exactly as she had dreamt they would. She arrived in Egypt with only a day's notice. She would always remember the look of joy on her mother's face when she met her at the arrivals lounge at Cairo International Airport. Sofia thought she'd brought the entire neighbourhood with her. They lived in a small home in Nasr city only twenty minutes away from the airport. As they drove to the house Sofia looked out the car window and recalled the memories she had as a child playing in those streets. The divorce between her mother and father was hard on Sofia. She was only nine years old when she was forced to live with her father. She always kept in touch with her mother and they spoke on the phone regularly. When she turned fifteen her father's work brought him to London and he moved to the UK with her and established a successful importing business. Sofia went to an English college and enjoyed the multiculturalism of British western society. She was fluent in English from a young age, and slowly lost her native accent over the years. She decided to pursue her childhood passion for dance and graduated from her performing arts course at nineteen. She was heavily influenced by the Bollywood movie industry and opened up a small dance studio teaching Bollywood dance and choreography. The studio soon became popular with locals and she held specialist classes for ladies wanting to burn calories in a fun way.

The success was, in Sofia's eyes, inevitable. It was almost all she would ever dream of, and she trusted her dreams. From early on she'd noticed that her dreams, good or bad, would always come true. She felt that her precognitive abilities grew stronger and stronger with time, and over the years her research into dream interpretation enabled her to analyse them better. Her dreams were God's gift to her.

At just twenty-two years of age, her father passed away from a sudden heart attack and she inherited his thriving importing business. Guilt-ridden that she neglected her father and blamed him for the divorce she sacrificed her love of dance and sold the studio in order to run her father's business. But she soon discovered that she was never cut out for the corporate world and despite her best efforts she felt that the meetings, policy issues, and financial reports overwhelmed her. After three years of persevering she decided that it would be best for the company if she sold her majority share to the remaining partners. She was now twenty-six and financially secure for the rest of her life.

Despite her wealth, she felt life was hollow, meaningless and without purpose. She travelled far and wide and spent time in India where she sought inner peace and self-enlightenment. Through her meditation and self reflection she realised that she'd been selfish and thus far had only been using her precognitive abilities for only her own benefit. She had the ability to help hundreds if not thousands of people and now she had the will to do so. She decided that that would be her new purpose.

Sofia returned to the UK and decided to search online to see if there were others like her, gifted people who wanted to give back. One evening, whilst chatting on one such online forum, she received a strange message.

Hi there, I'm Raj :-)

Hi Raj, I'm Sofia nice to meet you.

My organisation does a lot of good for people and we think you could really make a difference if you joined us.

That sounds interesting, tell me more.

Well, we don't exactly do Job Descriptions, but how about I arrange an interview for you with the boss?

∞

Belkin walked over to Sofia and took her hand in his own. 'We're glad to have you back Sofia. How are you?'

'I'm better.' She assured.

'The Fraction is your family too, whatever you need, just let me know.'

'I know, and thanks.' She said as she cleared her throat. 'I've got something to tell you.'

'Yes, I believe you had a dream that needs analysing. Shall we?' Belkin gestured towards the office. Sofia nodded and began walking towards the room. 'Raj, Sofia and I are going to need some time to analyse this dream's message. Unless it's urgent, please see to it that we're not interrupted.'

'You guys go do your thing, I'm gonna be here working on those statistics you wanted.'

'Good. Those reports still on schedule for tomorrow?' Belkin queried.

'Will be done by tonight mate.' Raj replied with a cheeky wink.

Belkin smirked and turned to follow Sofia into the office, closing the door behind him. Once inside he sat down on the leather chair and leant forward on the desk. 'So Sofia, let's talk.'

'It's hazy now.' Sofia admitted. 'But I wrote it all down. Wait...let me get my notepad out.' She opened up her Prada handbag and pulled out her A5 sized notepad. She flicked through the pages until she got to the last entry and handed it over to Belkin.

I was walking down a sandy road that seemed deserted. It was warm and the sun was high in the clear blue sky. Looking around it felt like I was somewhere in South America, (Columbia/ Mexico). The houses built on the street were small and painted in soft pastel colours; aqua, pink and yellow as if they were from the 1950's. I was in a small town but there were no cars or people, and the roads were silent. I was alone except for a large Rottweiler that I noticed about a hundred yards away slowly trotting towards me. The dog felt important. As if it was the authority in the area. The Rottweiler was large and muscular, it had a short thick black hair and a black collar around its neck, the collar had sharp metal spikes. I felt the dog knew me. As if it was a person. Maybe a spirit, or a manifestation of someone who was watching me. It terrified me.

I glanced over and I saw Belkin, Sash and Adam. There was someone else too. A girl. She was glowing so brightly I couldn't see her face. Belkin was playing chess and looked disappointed. Adam was standing on a bridge and crying and Sash had her face down a well. The dog was still watching me and was now watching everyone else too. Its mouth was open and drooling. It barked loudly and it almost deafened me. I was scared and I ran, but it chased me. It caught me and jumped on me and as it tried to bite me it lost its teeth.

'That's all of it?' Belkin asked.

Sofia took a deep breath and looked up at Belkin. Retelling her nightmares was never a pleasant experience for her. Belkin sat in silence looking at the floor as he ran through the details of the dream in his head. He finally looked up at Sofia and decided to get her opinion before he offered his own. 'What do you make of all this?'

Sofia stood up and walked towards a white board on the far wall of the study and grabbed a marker. 'Well, I have noticed a few things. Firstly, the dog is usually a symbol of friendship,' she began writing key words on the board. 'but the colour black signifies secrecy and deception. The dog was old but strong, perhaps it's someone who's either old with power or someone younger who has power.'

'You just said 'his',' Belkin interjected, 'are we ruling out females?'

'Absolutely, there was nothing feminine about this dog.' Sofia turned back towards the whiteboard and added *'Male'* before she continued. 'The location seemed like the only thing that was clear about this whole dream. Whatever is going to happen isn't going to happen anywhere near London. It felt like I was somewhere foreign, like I said, South America is my bet and considering everything we know about the Mayans I'm putting money on Mexico.'

'What do you make of what we were all doing? Chess, a bridge, the well, the dog attack, and the glowing girl?'

'None of them are good signs Belkin.' Sofia confessed. 'I'm seriously worried about initiating Protocol 8F, maybe we should reconsider-'

'No.' Belkin interrupted. 'We are the world's only hope Sofia. If we do nothing, we all die anyway. The Fraction doesn't back out of its missions out of fear of failure. Ever.'

TRAINING DAY

Adam yawned and took a long stretch. His eyes suddenly popped open as he bolted up and remembered that he was supposed to meet Belkin at 9am. His eyes darted towards the small clock on his desk which read 10:33am. *Oh, snap!* He shot out of bed and opened his bedroom door. He jogged into the living room area and noticed no one was around. He headed for the office and saw Raj squinting at the computer monitor in front of him.

Raj looked up and noticed the panic in Adam's face. He smiled and looked back at his monitor. 'Morning, sleepyhead.'

'Dude, I'm so late, do you know where Belkin is? Adam asked completely flustered. 'I was supposed to meet him here at nine.'

'Relax British Rail, he's gone to meet someone.'

'British Rail?' Adam frowned in confusion.

'Yeah.' Raj snapped his fingers and pointed at Adam. 'You're always late right?' He chuckled. 'Anyway, he wants you to meet him at this address at 2pm sharp.' Raj handed Adam a torn piece of paper. Adam felt somewhat relieved as he walked over to Raj and grabbed the note. Still half asleep, his eyes struggled to focus on the small writing.

'Unit 32a, The Old Brickworks, Wembley.'

Adam felt confused. *This wasn't the plan.* 'Raj, tell me straight, was he mad about it?'

'C'mon man, who wouldn't get mad being stood up by a sixteen-year-old?' Adam wasn't sure what that meant, but by now he was used to Raj's strange style of conversation. 'But Sash covered for you bro, she told him you were reading War and Peace last night so he didn't go completely bananas over it. But if you don't get there at 2pm sharp,' he said as he pointed at the note Adam was holding. 'you might as well just slap Belkin across his face and call his mother a hippo.'

Adam interpreted Raj's words and extracted the general gist of them. His feelings from last night re-surfaced, bringing back Adam's insecurities and fears of loneliness. He remembered his father's words and how The Fraction felt like a family to him. It made him feel even worse for letting Belkin down. His only saving grace was that Belkin was aware that he'd been up working all night.

'Okay, yeah, 2pm plenty of time.' Adam looked at the address again. *Wembley.* 'This is west London. Do you know where exactly this is?'

'Yup.'

Adam looked at Raj expectantly and realised that Raj wasn't going to say anything else. 'Well?'

'Dude, what am I, Google Maps? I'm busy here. I've got money to make, and hearts to break. Laptop is in your room, I suggest you use it.'

Adam shook his head but couldn't help but smile. 'You're a joker Raj. I'm gonna go get sorted and leave.' Adam turned and headed for the bathroom to freshen up. Something in the pit of his stomach was telling him that today was gonna be a challenge.

∞

Adam was sat in the living room area with his laptop researching the route on Google Maps. It had just passed noon and he was feeling a lot better. The shower and change of clothes helped, but knowing that he wasn't late anymore was the biggest relief. He was able to locate Wembley easily enough and before long Adam found where he was supposed to meet Belkin. The map dropped a pin in a large area that seemed to be part of an industrial estate. *Weird place to have a meeting.*

'Hey Raj!' Adam called out.

'Yo?' He yelled back.

'Do you know if this place is on an industrial estate? This map isn't too clear and I don't want to end up in the wrong place man.'

Raj finished his sandwich and walked over to the sink to wash his hands. 'Yeah, it is. One sec.' He walked over as he dried his hands and peered at the screen over Adam's shoulder. 'Yeah, that's the place.'

'Man there ain't a single registered business here man, what is this place? You been here before right? Something doesn't feel right man.'

'Dude, why you acting like such a big girl's blouse? What's the matter? Come, tell uncle Raj.' Raj walked around sarcastically and took a seat beside Adam.

'Shut up man.' Adam smirked.

'No seriously man,' Raj's tone switched. 'what's up with you, you were super chilled the past few weeks, and now it's time for action and suddenly you're sounding like the biggest pussy known to man.'

'It's just...' Adam took a deep breath and let out a sigh. 'What if I can't do it, man? What if I'm not strong enough to stop all this crap from happening? My dad was way stronger than me, and not even he-' Adam stopped himself from completing the sentence.

'Listen here hero.' Raj said as he locked eyes with Adam. 'Belkin isn't some fool. Do you know how important that guy is? What he's worth? Who he knows? And out of everyone in the world, he chose you to save us. All of us.' Adam turned away unconvinced. 'Look at me,' Raj demanded. Adam turned back and hesitantly met his gaze. 'You're a nice bloke but honestly, I don't know what the hell he sees in your skinny arse, but you owe it to him to at least try. Give it your best. We're all depending on you man. Your dad was a gangster, and if you have even a little bit of your dad in you, I know you won't let us down.'

Adam smiled. It was the strangest pep talk he'd ever heard. But somehow it did the trick. 'You're right...' He sighed.

'I know I'm right, now quit being a pussy and go handle yo business.'

'Fine.' Adam huffed. 'Can you at least tell me what the meeting with Belkin is about today?' Adam asked as Raj got up and walked back towards the breakfast bar.

'We all have our unique abilities, right? We all need a safe place to develop them. You know, really bring them out. Make them better, more powerful.' Raj unwrapped a Snickers bar and took a bite. 'It can get messy.' He said as he chewed. 'Don't want you wrecking the place.'

Why would I wreck the place? Adam thought.

∞

It was 12:34 and Adam flipped down the laptop and went to grab his things and head over to the address. He grabbed his set of apartment keys that he now kept on a metal fob that he hooked into the belt loop of his jeans and grabbed his phone and wallet. *Phone, keys, wallet. Check.*

'Hey Raj, I'm heading out what car should I take?'

Raj exploded with laughter. 'Hang on Lewis Hamilton, you think you're ready to drive one of our cars? I don't think so. You can take the moped.'

'What? Come on dude!' He pleaded. 'You've got Gumball 2000 going on downstairs and you want me to use the thing our pizzas get delivered on? At least drop me off.'

'I wish I could dude.' Raj said sympathetically. 'But orders are orders. You gotta make your own way. The moped will get you there faster and you're legally allowed to drive it. Tell you what; if you save the world from ending, I'll let you drive the Lambo. But for now, catch!' Raj tossed him the keys to the moped from across the living room.

Adam realised that arguing was futile. He sighed as he looked at the keys in his palm. *Even the keys are ugly.* He slipped a thin jacket and grabbed the helmet as he turned towards the door to leave the apartment. *This sucks.*

∞

The ride hadn't been bad at all. In fact, Adam was looking at the positives as he weaved through the traffic on the moped. *Maybe the moped was the best vehicle for the job.* He managed to arrive ten minutes early but couldn't find the industrial estate anywhere. He parked up and took out his smart phone and searched its GPS application for the building. It was showing that it was close by but his position on the map kept changing, which confused him. Adam rode around the block and finally found a large open gate that led to the old industrial estate. Once inside Adam hopped off the moped and walked towards the building. It was a tall abandoned office block five stories high. It looked as if it had been built a long time ago and was in poor condition. Half of the windows had been boarded up and the paint work was worn and had crumbled off in many places.

As he approached the front door he noticed an intercom switch. It only had a single button on it which he pressed. To his surprise, the button worked and buzzed loudly, after a short pause he heard the speaker make a ringing sound as if it was calling a phone. The ringing stopped and a familiar voice crackled out the speaker.

'Hello Adam.' Belkin greeted. 'Welcome to your training day. Inside this building are your challenges. You must complete them all to be successful. Your first challenge is to find a way into this building and make your way up to the 5th floor. You have fifteen minutes exactly, and your time starts now.'

The phone line went dead and Adam found himself stood there totally confused and dumbfounded. 'Err... Hello? Belkin?' He pressed the button again, but this time, the speaker just rang and rang and then the line went dead. *What the damn? What am I supposed to do, break in?* Adam took a few steps back to analyse the building. Most of the windows on the ground floor were double glazed and seemed locked. He walked up to the ground floor row of windows and cupped his hands around his face as he peered inside. It was dark, but he could just make out the shapes of old office furniture and dust cloths over the bookshelves. The place looked completely deserted. He tried opening the windows and discovered that they were locked from the inside. He banged on the windows a few times to see if he could nudge the lock open, but the locking mechanism seemed to be the only thing that still worked in this derelict building. He realised that he was getting nowhere and he was wasting time. He had to think it through. He stepped back to reassess the situation. *I'll check the rest of the windows and if nothing is open I'll go around the back of the building to see if there's another way of getting in.* Adam looked around and noticed a pile of large rocks and planks of old timber near a skip just a few meters away lying by the side of the building. *And I guess if all else fails.*

Adam swiftly went around checking all the windows and to his disappointment, they were all locked from the inside. He walked around the side of the building but realised that the windows here were way too high for him to reach. He ran around to the back of the building and discovered that at the far end there was one window that was unlocked and had been left slightly ajar, it was on the first floor and Adam estimated that it couldn't have been more than thirteen feet high. *I can make that. I just need something to climb on.* Adam went back around to the skip near the front of the building and gathered as much junk wood that he could. He ran around with the wood in his arms and arranged it so that it leant against the wall directly underneath the window. *Gotta hurry!* Adam frantically checked his watch. *Damn it!* He realised that it was useless to check his watch now as he didn't make a note of the time when Belkin started the countdown. Panic was setting in. *Okay, just keep a calm head and do this quickly.* He checked the wooden planks for stability and he took a few steps back. At full speed he charged towards the unstable wooden structure and leapt on top of it. He was just able to get a boost up before the entire wooden structure beneath him collapsed under his weight. He stretched out and barely managed to get his fingertips on to the window ledge. With both his hands now firmly gripped on the window ledge he hung there against the wall thirteen feet high and paused to catch his breath. He could feel his grip slipping and he looked over at the wall to his right. He swung his leg over towards it and just about managed to hook his foot onto the top of the wall. With his foot now firmly planted on the wall he was able to free up one of his hands to fully pull open the window. He took a deep breath and used his entire body to propel himself up and made an all or nothing lunge through the open window thrusting his arms through and grabbing hold of the windowsill on the inside. He felt the sharp window frame dig into his arms but he didn't dare let go. The sheer adrenalin coursing through his body somewhat numbed the pain yet he screamed in agony as he used all his power to pull himself up. His body was now through the window and inside the building and he collapsed in a heap as he fell onto the floor. He lay there for a moment to catch his breath but then remembered the clock was still ticking. He sprung to his feet and shook his arms trying his best to ignore the burning ache as the pain kicked in. Adam knew that he didn't have much time and ran down the hallway and found the elevator. He pressed the button and although the light on the button lit up he couldn't hear the elevator working. He stood there repeatedly pressing the button, and still there was no response. Frustrated and anxious of the time, he followed the fire exit signs and found the stairs on the far side of the building. He pushed opened the emergency door and found a concrete staircase. He ran towards it and stared up at the seemingly endless flights of stairs. *Urgh. No gym for me tonight.* He took a deep breath and started sprinting up as fast as he could.

At last, he saw the sign he was waiting for *5th Floor*. He barged open the door and noticed an arrow printed on a piece of paper stuck on the wall. He anxiously followed it down the hall until he saw another one pointing towards an office door. He quickly opened the door expecting to see Belkin or Sash, or someone who would explain what the hell was going on. Instead, he opened the door and saw a large red LED timer counting down. '12...11...10...9...' Adam realised that this was the timer Belkin had set. He bolted towards the device at the far end of the room and found the "Stop" button at the top and slammed his palm down on it with just three seconds to spare. He panted hard to catch his breath. His lungs were burning and he collapsed beside the device. He took a closer look and noticed that the timer was connected with electrical cables to something on the table. It looked like a big bunch of old brown tubes wrapped together, he was about to pick it up and he suddenly froze in horror. 'Oh my God... Dynamite?' Adam slowly stepped back, but then noticed a sealed envelope lying on the table next to the timer. He tentatively reached for it being careful not to touch anything else. He flipped it over and there, in thick black felt tip was a simple command scribed on its front.

ADAM, READ ME.

Adam tore open the envelope and took out the note, he checked to ensure that there was nothing else in the envelope before throwing it on the floor. He unfolded the note inside and read it slowly.

Congratulations Adam, if you are reading this you have succeeded in your first challenge. Yes, that Dynamite is real and I'm glad you took the deadline I gave you seriously. I knew you would.

Unfortunately, this building is now your fortress. The stairs you took have now been sealed and the only way out of this building is through the elevators that will take you down one level at a time after you successfully complete each challenge. These challenges are dangerous and are not for our amusement, they are to train you and prepare you for the Protocol 8F. If you are careless, you could die in here. You have been warned.

'These guys can't be serious!' He gulped as he continued reading.

These challenges are designed to enable you to access the abilities I know you have. We want you to succeed, but if you fail, it is safer that you fail here than in the field where others will be at risk. You will have no access to the outside world while you are in training and we have jammed the signal to your mobile phone to ensure this.

If there was ever a time to believe in yourself Adam, this is it. We're counting on you. You have until midnight to make it out of this building. We will be waiting. - Belkin.

Adam read the letter five more times before the reality of the situation finally sunk in. *I'm trapped. This is hell. I'm actually in hell.* Adam looked at his watch. It was now 2:30pm. *I've got nine and a half hours. Surely I can get out of here in nine and a half hours! Right?* Adam considered how close he was to getting blown up with the first deadline and he decided not to waste any more time. He walked back into the hallway. He looked around to see if there were any more clues as to what he should do next and suddenly he heard the elevator whirring to life. *Ding.* The elevator opened in the hallway. He slowly crept towards it and looked to see if anyone was in there. Seeing it was completely empty a feeling of embarrassment washed over him. *This is stupid.* Suddenly he recalled Raj's words. *Raj was right, I need to man up. I'm never going to make it out if I act like a pussy.* For the first time in his life, Adam felt like he was truly thrown in a life threatening position and he was surprised to discover that he wasn't completely freaking out. *I mean, I've already diffused a time bomb, right? How bad can the rest of these challenges be?* Adam stepped into the elevator, the button 4 was already selected, and the doors began to close. *Here goes nothing.*

THE RIDDLE

The steel doors of the old elevator slowly opened. The first thing that Adam noticed on the 4th floor was another piece of paper stuck on the wall, the words Mental Agility were written in big letters and it had an arrow pointing towards a smaller piece of paper that was stuck on the wall beside it.

Adam slowly walked out of the elevator and looked around, seeing that the coast was clear he walked closer to the smaller note and read the text;

Answer the riddle to proceed.

Adam read the note twice to make sure he wasn't missing something. *Hmm... Answer a riddle. I can do that.* He followed the arrows on the walls pointing towards an open office door. He tentatively walked inside. Covering the entire right-hand wall written in red paint was the riddle.

*I CERTAINLY NOT WAS, AM FOREVER TO BE,
NONE HAS EVER SEEN ME, NOR EVER WILL,
AND YET I AM THE ASSURANCE OF ALL
I AM A FLICKER OF HOPE IF AT PRESENT YOU FALL.
WHAT AM I?*

Adam stood in front of the wall for a while and noticed that the more he read the riddle the more confused he became. *Okay, this is a lot harder than I thought.* He dusted off a chair from a nearby desk and rolled it in front of the wall and sat down. He repeated the words over and over again. *"I certainly not was, am forever to be?"* What does that mean? Is it something that doesn't actually exist in the past? He read the second line. *"None has ever seen me, nor ever will."* So this is not a physical object, maybe another sense other than sight, maybe a sound, or a feeling? His mind was spinning in confusion. *"And yet I am the assurance of all".* Assurance... assurance. I have no idea what that means. He paused and read the final line slowly. *"I am a flicker of hope if at present you fall."* I know it's not a physical thing, so that must be a metaphor. So falling can be related to being hurt, or in pain. Or, it could be falling in love? Is the answer love? Wait it can't be love, the first line wouldn't make sense. I am always to be. Some people are in love. No, this is something no one has.

∞

Adam sat there for almost forty-five minutes and stared at the riddle, still unsure as to what the answer was. He got off his seat and decided that he was focussing too hard and only confusing himself further. He needed a break. He walked around the office and decided to distract himself. There wasn't much to look at, but he kept himself distracted by opening up drawers and filing cabinets that looked like they'd been abandoned for years. He wondered if he might even find a clue somewhere.

Another hour had passed and despite his frantic searching, he still found nothing. He even tried meditating to see if the answer would come to him through his subconscious, but nothing seemed to fit. *This is hopeless. I can't even get passed the first challenge.* Adam thought to himself. Feeling deflated Adam began reflecting on his day so far. From having such a nice time over the past few weeks today was a reality check. He checked his arms to see if there were any marks left over from his earlier stunt through the window. *I can't believe what a day I've had today. Guess either way it will be all over tomorrow. Either I'll be-* Adam stopped. His eyes almost popped out of his head in excitement as the revelation dawned upon him. He ran back to the wall and re-read the riddle. 'Oh my god... I've got it!' He read the words out loudly and clearly again, assuming that someone would hear him. 'I certainly not was, am forever to be, none has ever seen me, nor ever will, and yet I am the assurance of all, I am a flicker of hope if at present you fall. What am I?' *I've got it!*

'Tomorrow!' Adam cried out. 'The answer is 'tomorrow!'

Adam waited, but there was nothing. He was certain he was right but his stomach was churning with anticipation. *Nothing's happening.* He re-read the riddle. *Wait, did I get it wrong?* Suddenly he heard the familiar sound of the elevator. *Ding.*

That simple sound filled Adam's heart with joy. 'Thank the lord!' Adam prayed. 'I did it! I was right!' Adam ran into the elevator and stood there patiently waiting for the doors to close. He felt proud of his achievement. *Tomorrow, eh?* He sighed. *Tomorrow...*

The elevator doors began to close and it descended down to the 3rd floor. Adam checked his watch. It was 4:33pm. *I've still got time. Doing okay.*

The elevator stopped and the doors slid open. *Ding.* Instantly a feeling of dread washed over him. His heart suddenly skipped a beat, and then pounded violently as he read the words on the piece of paper stuck to the wall in front of him;

FEAR MASTERY

HIDDEN AGENDAS

The plan was good, it was better than good. It was perfect. Ah Kin and the men around him had devised a simple and effective way of achieving their aim. It was a strategy as old as time itself; divide and conquer.

'Remember Ah Kin,' said Immanuel, 'the plan relies on us getting the boy. The stone is not our primary objective.' Immanuel felt he had to reiterate the point to Ah Kin. 'Is that clear Ah Kin?' The stone is a distraction. It's a lost cause, the boy will be easier to find. The mission is to kill the boy.' Immanuel knew that the stone would amplify the powers of anyone who possessed it and that his old friend always felt drawn to its power and was keen to possess it for himself.

Ah Kin felt a slight twinge of embarrassment. It had been a long time since he was spoken to in such a patronising tone. Ah Kin bit his tongue. Anyone other than Immanuel would've been severely punished for such insolence. But the accusation Immanuel was alluding to was not without merit. They'd spoken years ago about the powers of the stone and how, if they had possession of it, would benefit their cause. But Ah Kin had to agree that Immanuel was right, the boy was the primary objective. If they succeeded there, God's plan would be unstoppable. The world would end and the stone would be unnecessary. *But oh the power I would wield, even for the briefest of moments...a God on earth.* 'Brother Immanuel, I agree wholeheartedly. The boy is the primary objective.' He lied.

∞

Ah Kin watched people sleeping as he sat on the plane headed for London, the lights had been turned off in the first class cabin and everyone but Immanuel seemed to be asleep. Ah Kin reclined the spacious leather seat and tried his best to relax but the mission was playing on his mind. He felt bitter that he was travelling away from the stone that he knew was hidden in Mexico. But Immanuel was clear that exterminating the boy was more important. Ah Kin began wondering where he lost his control of his quest. He wondered whether bringing Immanuel on board was a smart move. His resources and strategic input were useful, but he forgot how narrow-minded Immanuel was sometimes. It was often hard to argue with him because his logic was usually sound, but Ah Kin knew that not everything in this realm operated on logic alone. To Ah Kin some mysteries were worth the risk.

The Chilan was ordered to perform a locator spell to locate the boy, but Ah Kin didn't need it. He knew that a boy with such powers could only be the son of Joseph, and therefore had to be located in the United Kingdom. It was obvious that London would be the best place to start searching. However, the Chilan did make one new discovery, a name; Adam, Adam Newton. Ah Kin believed that you could tell a lot about a person by their name. The weight of it, the way it vibrated on the tongue, the way it sounded. Ah Kin began conjuring up images of Adam in his mind. He felt he was beginning to understand him, his strengths, and his weaknesses. He knew that this boy would be useful. He was the key to finding the lost stone and killing him would be a mistake. Ah Kin glanced over at Immanuel who sat in his seat just a few feet away and began to feel contempt in his heart towards him. *Only a fool would give up this opportunity to locate the ancient Mayan stone. Immanuel will need convincing.*

CRANEFLY

Adam didn't want to leave the elevator. He knew that whatever lay ahead would not be a pleasant experience. He looked at his watch and took a deep breath and stepped out slowly. The lift instantly closed behind him.

This was different, this time, he could hear something after the lift had closed. It was a strange sound of movement, like scurrying and chirping. It was coming from an office down the hall and he slowly made his way to it. The office door was closed but the sounds were definitely coming from within the office to his right. He grabbed the doorknob and took a deep breath. *Here we go.* He opened the office door and in front of him was a large see-through Perspex box. The box was about four feet high, about four feet wide and was open from the top. It was almost completely full with dark brown thick fur. But the fur seemed to be moving. Adam froze in shock as he suddenly realised what he was actually looking at. It wasn't fur at all. The box was full of giant rats; hundreds of them. *No... freaking... way!*

He slowly edged closer to the Perspex box and noticed a piece of paper stuck on the outside. He moved in closer to read it.

Inside this box is a key. Find it and open the safe next to the filing cabinet, in the safe you will find a password. Simply state the password to proceed to the next level.

Adam ripped off the note and read it a few more times hoping that he had misread something. *Inside this box is a key! Are you kidding me?!* Adam tossed the note aside. He looked at the filing cabinet resting against the wall to the far end of the room. In it, he saw a shoebox sized safe. He walked over to the safe and tried to pull it open praying that by some miracle they had forgotten to lock it. *Damn.* The safe was locked tight. *C'mon Adam, they're not that stupid.* He walked back to the box and watched the rats scurrying around, all clambering on top of each other, irritated, and trying to find a way out of their enclosure. *They look angry.*

Adam looked at the box to see if he could see a key, he searched all around the sides and over the top, nothing. *Oh man, knowing my luck it's stuck somewhere at the bottom.* He knew what he was meant to do, and he knew that someone had thought this through to ensure he had to go inside the box and retrieve the key. There was no other way around it. He tried tipping the huge box over, but the box wouldn't budge. He cast his mind towards the safe. *The password is in there.* He examined the keyhole, but he had no idea how to pick a lock. He looked around for a small pin or piece of metal to pick it with but despite searching every drawer and desk there was nothing he could use. He tried removing the safe, but it was bolted into the filing cabinet, which was bolted to the wall. He kicked the safe a few times, but the metal safe was too sturdy to be opened with brute force. There really was only one option and he sighed as he turned around to face the Perspex box of horror. *Fear mastery my ass, this is just pure evil!*

Adam slumped down against the filing cabinet and watched the rats scurry around in a crazed frenzy inside the box. *I can't do this.* Suddenly he was reminded of a time when he was nine years old and petrified of a Craneflies, or Daddy-Longlegs as he used to call them. He always hated the end of summer when these wretched insects would appear out of nowhere and find their way into the house. The way they hovered and bounced from wall to wall terrified him. They moved like insect-ghosts and seemed to have no fear of humans. *Well, I'm sure that these things are probably more scared of you than you are of them. You're a big boy now Adam, and you need to face your fears.* The voice of his mother was ringing in his head. But it was his mother's new partner who helped him get over his fears of Craneflies. After many years of having their mother to themselves, Adam and his sister realised that they were never going to replace the companionship she needed from a partner. His father had been gone for years and she had finally met someone new. Adam wasn't sure how he felt about Alan, but he seemed nice and always bought them chocolate covered coconut sweets whenever he would come over. To this day, ten years later, the sight of those chocolate covered coconut sweets still made him think back to those days with Alan. He remembered that night clearly; the night he killed his first Cranefly.

∞

It was dusk and the sun had just set. It was late September and three Craneflies found their way into the dining room of the old house where they used to live before they moved into the flat. Despite his mother preparing his favourite dish for him Adam couldn't eat, his eyes darted from one Cranefly to the other wondering which one was going to lunge itself on to him first.

'Adam forget those things and eat your food.' His mother ordered.

'Ma please.' Little Adam begged, as he continued to watch them like a hawk. 'Please let me eat in the other room.'

'Finish your food right now young man, don't worry they can't hurt you.'

But the food was the last thing on Adam's mind. He didn't want to disobey his mother, but his fear of these dreadful things was crippling.

Noticing that Adam's mother was not having any effect on him Alan intervened. 'Okay Adam,' He said. 'you and me, we're going to kill these things.'

The thought of actively hunting these creatures terrified little Adam. 'No, it's okay. I'll just eat my food quickly.'

'No Adam, these things are harmless, and you can't be afraid forever.' Alan looked at Sharon and Sidney. 'You two go into the other room and finish your food. We're going to take care of these Craneflies once and for all.'

Adam looked at his mother for support, but to his surprise, she got up and left the table. 'Come on Sid, we're going to the other room.'

Adam's heart started pounding. He didn't want to do this. He was petrified. *Why do I have to stick around and kill these damned things? Sid is just as scared of them as I am, why doesn't she have to stick around and kill them?* The dining room door was now closed as his mother and sister left the room. Alan went to the kitchen door and closed that door too. He took off his slipper and handed it to Adam. 'Right Adam, now hold this like this.' Alan helped Adam grip the slipper from its heel. Alan's slipper felt gigantic in Adam's tiny hands. 'Now Adam, pick which one you want to kill first.'

Adam instantly spotted one he'd had his eyes on for a while. It was hovering against the wall above the door, high up close to the ceiling. 'That one.' He pointed.

Without another word Alan lifted Adam up by his waist right towards it. Adam wasn't ready, and he resisted the urge to scream as he was hoisted up and now face-to-face with the scary insect as it bobbled around the ceiling.

'Now, Adam! Hit it!' Alan yelled.

Adam began smacking the slipper against the wall over and over again. He had no idea where the Cranefly was.

'Okay Adam stop, stop, stop.' Alan instructed.

Adam opened his eyes and looked back towards the wall. There was nothing there.

'You missed it, but it's flying down.' Alan quickly lowered Adam back down.

Adam could now see that the Cranefly was still alive but seemed wounded. It wasn't as bouncy as before and was struggling to fly. He could see it resting on the red carpet in front of him.

'Now, Adam!' Alan yelled.

Adam raised the slipper over his head and with all his might smacked the slipper on top of it. Adam breathed a sigh of relief. He looked at the floor and there was nothing there. For a moment, he was worried that he had missed it, but he then checked the bottom of the slipper, and there it was, as flat as a pancake, its twisted twiggy legs and wings sticking out like thin splinters on the rubber sole of the slipper. Adam looked at Alan and Alan smiled back.

'You did it!' Now take this,' Alan peeled off the insect by the tip of its wing and placed it into Adam's bare hand. 'and go show it to your mum.'

Adam carefully took the creature and held it with his fingertips, it wasn't as scary now. He examined it carefully and realised that the way it moved was what frightened him, and now that it wasn't moving it seemed harmless. It was dead, and he had killed it. He was stronger than it was. The fear was only in his mind. He walked into the living room where his mum was sitting and he showed her his achievement. He felt nothing short of a warrior bringing home a slain beast, a beast that had terrified the city. His mother put aside her plate and walked over to him and without a single word gave him a big hug. In that moment, for the first time in his life, he felt brave.

∞

Now here he was, feeling nine years old again facing a new fear. He drew strength from his past and tried to remind himself that he was a giant in comparison to these little things. *They're probably more scared of you than you are of them.* Adam took a deep breath and blew out sharply. He checked his watch, he had been procrastinating for the past thirty minutes, and nothing had changed, except the fact that he had less and less time to do what he knew he had to do. He pulled over a chair and stood on to it. He placed his hands on the rim of the huge box and tried to shake it again hoping to get some movement on it, but it was rock solid. He slowly raised his leg over the side and looked on at the frenzy of activity going on beneath. The stench was overpowering. Adam turned his face and breathed through his mouth, it smelled like rotting flesh that had been left in the sun for weeks. Adam covered his nose with his shirt and looked back into the box. He noticed that most of the rats were facing towards the centre of the box and trying to dig to the bottom as if they were digging for something. He wondered if they knew what was about to happen and didn't want to be the rats that got trampled on the top. Some rats were jumping across each other, and a few were trying to escape the box and were jumping against the sides. Adam backed off and took his leg back out. He got off the chair and decided to tuck his jeans into his socks. He tucked his shoelaces into his trainers and got back onto the chair. He gently lowered his foot into the middle of the pack of rats and tried to move them out the way. He nudged one and it barely moved. The shirt over his nose was doing little to mask the pungent odour and was only getting in his way, so he slid it back down. The smell was so bad he could feel his stomach turn and felt a sour taste in his mouth, he thought he was about to vomit in disgust. He turned his head again and took a few breaths of cleaner smelling air and decided to go for it. His foot was now hovering just inches from the giant pile of rats that were now sniffing his trainers in curiosity. He lowered his foot further and put some of his body weight down on top of the pile. The rats didn't like it and burst into a frenzy dashing around so fast he couldn't tell the rats apart anymore, it just looked like a moving mass of brown fur. Undeterred, he shifted more and more of his body weight on top of the rats until his entire weight was on the pile and he quickly began sinking down. He flung over his other leg and distributed the weight as best he could. The rats were now chewing up his jeans and trainers and he felt like he was standing in quicksand that smelled like rotting skunks. He slowly sank deeper as the rats beneath him moved out of the way to avoid being crushed. His feet had disappeared under the mass and he was shin deep but he had suddenly ground to a halt. He felt scratches and bites and knew he couldn't just stand here, he had to do something. He had to get his hands involved and dig through to the bottom. At this point, he calculated that if the key was at the bottom, he would be waist deep in these rats and be forced to use his hands to fish for the key and there would be a strong chance that he'd have to lower his face down to them. The thought sickened him. Then, suddenly, something happened. A switch he never knew existed flicked inside him. He became angry, filled with rage. He was sick of being scared. He had had enough of this. He let out a loud scream. 'Aaaarghh!' And he ploughed his hands into the pile of rats like a mad man. He didn't care anymore. His face twisted into something demonic as sheer determination burst through him. He shovelled the rats aside ferociously yelling and screaming as he did. Rats were being thrown everywhere, he didn't care where they landed; he was getting this key. Now halfway buried and his feet close to the bottom he continued shovelling the rats like they were stuffed toys. The rats were now all over him, his back and legs were covered but he couldn't care less, he didn't feel them anymore. He ploughed deeper and deeper until he finally realised what these rats were digging towards. His fingers touched something strange and cold. He grabbed it and pulled it as hard as he could and winced in disgust as he saw a sheep's leg almost completely stripped of meat. It smelled horrid and rats were still clung to it as he threw it out of the box. He could finally feel that he was now standing on the bottom of the box and shifted his feet around to stabilise his footing. The rats were acting differently now, there were fewer in the middle where he stood and most were clambering around the sides trying to get out. He was waist deep in the rats and he was less frightened of them now than when he was outside the box. He took a few sharp breaths and bent over and started shovelling the rats again with his hands, tossing them over his head and out of the box. His heart filled with joy as he finally saw the clear Perspex bottom of the box. He began scouring the base to find anything that resembled a key. He searched and searched but couldn't see anything. He kept tossing the rats out and checked the area where he was standing. But he still couldn't find anything. He shifted his search to the right and checked the corners, but still no key. He decided to turn around and check behind him. He had been shifting the rats to this side of the box and the pile behind him was now huge. Like a diver, he thrust his arms into the pile and shovelled the rats out as quickly as he could. As the area cleared he began digging down, suddenly in the bottom left corner he saw a metal chain. He almost cried with happiness. *I found it!* He picked it up and noticed that it had been chewed through. *Damn it! Where's the rest of it?* With fresh hope and the finish line in his sights he dug even more ferociously than before, and then he saw it, another tiny glistening piece of metal. He grabbed it and pulled on it but it seemed stuck. He tugged hard and it gave way and there, dangling on the end of twelve inches of a metal chain was the key. 'Yes!' Adam yelled out in delight. He grabbed the sides of the box and quickly hoisted himself up stepping on the remaining pile of rats for support. He rested his foot on the rim of the box and hopped over landing on the floor. He could feel rats everywhere and he shook himself wildly as he realised rats were still clinging on to him. A number of large rats flew off and quickly scurried away. Adam took off his clothes and brushed off his entire body. Remarkably besides a few minor scratches, he was completely fine. He shook his clothes which were now in tatters, and in some parts, completely chewed through before putting them back on. He took a long look at the key at the end of the chain, he closed his eyes and he held his prize tightly. He simultaneously laughed and sobbed in joy and collapsed to his knees as he stared at the Perspex box of horror still standing there before him. He felt like he'd just won a war.

He stood up and walked over to the safe and inserted the key. He felt exhausted, but his adrenalin was still pumping through his veins. He turned the key and the lock clicked open. He turned the handle and opened the safe. It was completely empty except for a single small brown envelope. He took out the envelope and opened it. Inside was a small piece of paper and he stood in stunned silence as he silently read the note.

The password is: Cranefly.

THE NEXT LEVEL

Adam stood there just staring at the piece of paper. *Cranefly.* All the horror he'd just been through temporarily evaporated from his mind. *How did they know about that?* Adam deduced that nothing this relevant was just coincidence.

'Cranefly!' He shouted. 'The password is Cranefly!' He waited for something to happen. Suddenly he heard the sound of success. The elevator sprang back to life. *Ding.* Adam walked back towards the hallway and towards the elevator. As he was about to leave the room he looked back at the huge box of rats still scrambling around. He couldn't believe that just moments ago he was rummaging around in that hell pit. Looking back on it now, he felt a sense of accomplishment. He let the moment soak in. As he knew that one day he'd draw strength from what he accomplished here today. It wasn't just the rats he conquered, he'd conquered his fear. *Fear Mastery.*

The elevators slid closed and Adam looked at his G-Shock watch. It read 5:48pm. *Almost 6pm. I've got 2 floors left. I can make it out at midnight. I've got plenty of time.* Adam instantly wished that he could un-think that last thought. He didn't want to jinx himself. *Be positive, you can do this.* The elevator stopped at floor 2. *Ding.* The doors slid open. He looked at the wall and there was another A4 sheet of paper.

TIME MASTERY

Adam stepped out of the elevator but then heard a click, *SWOOSH.* He turned his head and something dark bolted towards him. It was so fast he could barely see it. It hit his shoulder spinning him and knocking him to the ground. His shoulder burned in agony as he felt something wet on his shirt. *Oh my God, that's blood! I'm hit!*

FLASE PROPHECY

Ah Kin felt a wave of memories flood back as he exited the taxi and took his first steps on London's streets. Despite coming to London many times before, he hadn't visited Camden Town before and he wasn't sure if he loved it or despised it. Immanuel had a safe house here and the taxi dropped them off directly outside. Immanuel unlocked the front door of the large terraced house. The door opened up to a narrow hallway and directly in front of them were the stairs leading to the upper floors of the house. The house was beautifully furnished with sofas, rugs and expensive paintings yet it was deprived of soul and felt hollow as if no one ever lived in it.

'Well gentlemen, this is it, get acquainted with the place. We'll be operating from here while we're in London.' Immanuel informed.

'I see you enjoy luxury living regardless of where you happen to be.' Ah Kin strolled into the living room and then spun around to Immanuel with a smirk on his face. 'This will do nicely my friend.'

The group unpacked and was getting settled. Ah Kin decided that this was the perfect time to revise the plan with Immanuel.

'Immanuel, do you have a moment.' Ah Kin asked as he gestured towards the kitchen.

'Of course.' Immanuel replied as he folded the newspaper and walked through into the kitchen. Ah Kin closed the door behind him.

'I'm afraid there's bad news.' Ah Kin informed.

'Bad news? What kind of bad news?'

'The Chilan has had a vision and unfortunately his prophecies are never wrong.'

'Of course,' Immanuel agreed. 'He is a Chilan after all, what did he see?'

'If we kill the boy here, we will fail.' Ah Kin informed.

'What?!' Immanuel spat in shock.

'Like I said, the Chilan is never wrong. We must instead devise a plan to sacrifice him on the stone altar at the top of the Kukulkan pyramid and I think I have an idea. But there's more…'

'More? This is outrageous!' Immanuel said as he banged his fist on the table. 'What else can there be?'

'In the prophecy the Chilan saw that while the sacrifice was being made I held the Mayan stone in my hand… I'm afraid, it seems, killing the boy won't be enough, he must first help us locate it.'

'This has thrown out the entire strategy!' Immanuel boomed. He barged out of the kitchen. 'Chilan! Chilan!' He yelled.

The Chilan slowly descended the stairs. He glanced at Ah Kin who followed closely behind Immanuel.

'Is all this true?' Immanuel boomed. 'Your vision; we must sacrifice Adam on the altar of Kukulkan with the stone?'

The Chilan remained quiet.

'Well? Answer me?!' Immanuel bellowed restraining himself as best he could.

The Chilan calmly peered over Immanuel's shoulder and glanced at Ah Kin again. Ah Kin remained silent and simply stared back at him vehemently. He finally looked back into Immanuel's eyes and slowly nodded his head.

'Dammit!' Immanuel huffed. 'So what are we going to do now? Everything is ruined.'

'Not quite,' Ah Kin alluded. 'I have a plan. But first, we need a powerful locator spell. We need to make a sacrifice.'

AN IMPOSSIBLE TASK

Adam grabbed his right shoulder and winced in pain. *Was that an arrow?* There was blood running down his arm and his jacket and shirt were torn through. The hallway on this floor was set up like a shooting range, and he was the target.

Thirty feet down the hallway was a partition wall that had a two-foot square hole cut out in the middle of it. As Adam peered through the hole he noticed it was completely pitch black. Behind him was another partitioned wall with a square exactly the same size and he was stuck in the middle. There were no doors leading to any offices on this floor, and he felt like he was trapped in the barrel of a loaded gun. *Man, you have got to be kidding me. What the heck am I supposed to do here?* He looked around for clues and noticed a white case in the corner behind him that had an envelope stuck on it. He crawled towards it keeping his head out of the line of fire. He tore open the envelope first, to ensure there were no nasty surprises in the case.

Congratulations on completing your Fear Mastery challenge. We know that must have been hard for you. But this challenge is infinitely more dangerous. These arrows travel at over 350 feet per second. To succeed you must believe in yourself the way we believe in you. To move on to the next level you simply need to catch one arrow and read out the password that is scribed onto it. There are only 5 arrows in the chamber. The case contains food, water and medical supplies as we anticipate a few close calls and don't want you to bleed out should the worst occur.

Good luck.

Belkin

Adam laughed out loud as he re-read the challenge. 'Simply?' He cried out hysterically. 'I *simply* need to catch a speedin' freakin' arrow aimed at my head!?' Adam grabbed the case and crawled to the side and rested against the wall. He opened the case and rummaged through it. Inside it was a tuna sandwich and a bottle of water, along with some basic First Aid supplies; A few large plasters, wound dressings, safety pins, scissors, cleaning wipes and antiseptic cream. He took the supplies out and slowly took off his jacket and shirt and began patching up his shoulder.

Adam checked his watch and realised that he had the best part of six hours to go and desperately needed to take a break. His head was feeling woozy and he decided that this would be a good time to just sit for a moment and recharge. He ripped the cling film off the sandwich and took a big bite. He sipped the water to help wash it down. Despite his hunger all he wanted to do right now was sleep. He felt physically and emotionally drained. He checked his wound and noticed that the bleeding was now contained. He took another sip of water before re-capping the bottle. He looked down the hallway. *How am I supposed to catch something so dangerous travelling so fast? Five arrows... well four now.* He started to think of ways he could minimise the risk of being hit again. His eyes felt heavy. *I shouldn't sleep.* But the very mention of sleep only made him feel even drowsier. His blinking slowed and he slowly closed his eyes. *Okay, well maybe just a quick power nap.*

∞

Adam woke up confused. For a moment, he had no idea where he was. Then suddenly everything came flooding back and he realised that he was still stuck in the office block from hell. *Oh snap, how long have I been out?* He checked his watch and it read 8:36pm. *Damn! How did I just lose two hours!* Adam had completely forgotten about his challenge and was about to stand straight up in the line of fire, but at the last moment, he saw the strange hole in the wall in front of him and remembered where he was and ducked down. *Damn, that was close!* He crouched back down and checked on his shoulder. It was sore but the bleeding had completely stopped. He went to put his shirt back on but then had an idea. He picked up his shirt and waved it in the line of fire hoping to trigger an arrow, but nothing happened. He slowly leant forwards and waved it again; nothing. *Is there a person back there or is this thing hooked up to a sensor?*

'Hello!' Adam called out towards the black hole. 'Anyone there?' He waited for a response but quickly realised that he probably wasn't going to get one. Adam spread his shirt open and dangled it in the line of fire making sure his arms were out of range. Adam heard it. *Click. Swoosh.* A black arrow bolted out of the hole at full speed. Adam could only jerk in shock as the arrow torpedoed through his shirt at an incredible velocity and disappeared into the black abyss behind him. Adam examined the hole in his shirt. *It's too fast.* He conceded. *I can't do it.* He crawled back to the note and read it again to see if there was a hint, a clue, anything that alluded to overcoming this task. He carefully examined every word of the note, but he found nothing. *Two arrows wasted. Only 3 left. C'mon Adam, think!*

He had a new plan. Adam knelt down ensuring his head was out of sight and slowly raised his arms. He soon realised that clapping his hands above his head to catch the arrow wouldn't work as well as he wanted since his shoulder was so badly wounded. *This is a bad idea.* He got his arms into range and waited for the sound. As he knelt there with his arms up he felt completely vulnerable. He waved his arms to try and trigger the sensor but he got no response. He tentatively raised his head ensuring he could get out of the way quickly if he heard something; still nothing. His neck was now at full stretch as he knelt there with his arms waving around, but still no arrow. He slowly got into a low squat on his feet and tentatively raised himself up. He was almost completely upright when he finally heard it. *CLICK. SWOOSH.* The arrow darted out and Adam instantly crouched down keeping his arms outstretched above him. He tried to watch the arrow shoot towards him but his instincts forced him to shut his eyes and he barely got a glimpse of it, he clapped his hands as fast as he could. *Aargh!* He winced as he gripped his shoulder. He'd missed it, and he knew his timing had been way off. *I need to clap faster. I can do this! Three down, just two left!*

Adam re-positioned himself in the squat position and raised his arms for a second attempt. He slowly raised himself like before and waved his arms frantically. *CLICK. SWOOSH.* An arrow bolted out, he clapped his hands instantly and the arrow clipped his forearm as it flew past. 'Aaargh!' Adam shrieked in pain. He collapsed on the ground and held his forearm out. 'Dammit!' He yelled. This time, he was cut deep. For a moment Adam saw no blood, just thick layers of skin and fat completely split apart leaving a gaping wound. Then, as if someone had opened a tap, bright red blood gushed freely. 'This is impossible!' He screamed in frustration. He crawled back to the case and tore off more dressings and patched his forearm up as tightly as he could. 'Why are you doing this to me?' Adam cried out. He felt rage brew within him and wasn't sure if he was angry at The Fraction, or himself. He simultaneously began laughing in hysteria and crying out of despair. *I'm going insane.* He sat there for another twelve minutes contemplating his situation as he nursed his forearm. *How did I get myself into this mess? What am I doing here? I'm not the one they're looking for.* 'I can't do this!' He yelled. 'Do you hear me? I'm done, I want to leave!' Adam slumped over and sobbed at the helplessness of his situation. In his heart, he knew they wouldn't just let him quit and walk out of here. Adam checked his watch. It now read 9:02pm. But now even the midnight deadline felt pointless. *I can't pass this challenge... I've failed either way.*

To succeed you must believe in yourself. Adam read the line from the note again and again, and he began to realise that throughout this challenge he hadn't truly believed in himself. *I've taken the safest option every time, I've been a coward.* He began wondering if that was the key to unlocking his abilities, his faith in his power. *A person who truly believes doesn't play it safe. They go all in!* The spark of inspiration ignited in Adam's heart. It was an inexplicable feeling of pure certainty. *The arrows travel through time, and I can control time, so I must be able to control the arrows.* Adam read the note and reminded himself that he had to believe in himself the way The Fraction believed in him. *I'm going to catch the next arrow and get into that lift and move down to the final floor. I will not fail here.* Adam began to visualise his victory. He checked the time. It was now 9:34pm. *I've wasted enough time here – let's do this!* With stone cold determination on his face, he rose to his feet staying close to the wall and shuffled along to his shirt lying on the ground and put it back on. He rolled up his sleeves and stepped directly into the line of fire.

Adam stared into the darkness of the square hole directly in front of him. He drew strength from everything he had overcome thus far and the unwavering belief The Fraction had in him. This black hole was now his ultimate challenge. He faced it head on as if he was having a shoot out at high noon. His face was blank and expressionless, unfazed by the imminent danger that lay before him. He stood there waiting for the imminent click of the trigger but realised that he'd been standing in the firing line longer than usual. There was usually only a two-second delay, but it had been at least five seconds since he'd stepped in front of it. *Wait, am I doing it?* He wondered. *Am I slowing time?* But as soon as the thought crossed his mind Adam heard it. *Click!* This time, there was a noticeable delay between the click of the trigger and the sound of the arrow bolting towards him. Adam's senses were on full alert. He felt aware of everything around him but his energy was solely focussed on the space between him and the black square in front of him. He took a deep breath. *Swoosh.* The arrow bolted out towards him at 350 feet per second aimed directly for his head. Adam saw it clearly and instinctively raised his hands towards it. *'Stop.'* He said as he breathed out calmly. What happened next was something Adam could not explain. He witnessed something completely supernatural and unearthly. His palms created an orb shaped field of purple energy that enveloped the arrow and dramatically slowed it down as if it were passing through thick purple liquid. The more Adam concentrated on the arrow slowing, the slower it became. But the arrow was still creeping towards his face. With grit and determination, he focused even harder, taking deep breaths and breathing out sharply again and again until finally the arrow completely ground to a halt. Adam couldn't believe his eyes. Right there, frozen in midair was the arrow surrounded by the orb of purple energy he had somehow created. Adam tentatively lowered his hands and walked around the side examining the miracle before him. He slowly raised his hand and reached inside the purple sphere of energy and plucked it straight out as if the arrow had been hanging on a wall. As his focus shifted from the orb to the arrow, the orb exploded in a harmless flash of white light. He raised his prize high above his head, but then immediately crashed to the floor and held his head as a severe migraine suddenly overwhelmed him. He dropped the arrow as he rubbed the temples of his head and tried to shake off the feeling. *Aargh!* Adam took some deep breaths and slowly felt himself recover. He finally collapsed against the wall and looked down at the arrow lying by his feet. He picked it up and once again held it above his head. 'I did it...' he gasped. 'I-' He suddenly noticed the word that was scribed on the side of the arrow. 'Perseverance.' He whispered.

Ding. The doors of the elevator slid opened.

DIRTY TACTICS

Nacom walked past the lift and ascended the stairs slowly to the 3rd floor. His faith and loyalty to Ah Kin had never been in question, but today he wondered if the gods would forgive him for the innocent blood he'd shed. As he got to the 3rd floor he double checked the address on the piece of paper in his hand.

Flat 12, 3rd Floor

He walked across the flats looking at the numbers on the doors and began wondering how the magic worked. How the Chilan used the souls of those two poor tourists today. The kidnapping went smoothly on the side streets of busy Camden. The Chloroform soaked rag did the trick pretty quick. They dumped the women in the car and snuck them back to the house easily enough, but Nacom wondered if completely draining them of their blood while they were still alive was necessary. The sacrifices felt less religious to Nacom this time. It felt dirty, it felt like murder. The Chilan was able to summon the spirits and cast a powerful locator spell that pinpointed exactly where Adam's energies were strongest. Nacom disliked witnessing the Chilan's possession rituals. He didn't like being around him when the spirits were speaking with him, his face would contort and his eyes would roll up in into his head, it reminded Nacom of a scene from horror movie he once watched as a child.

The Chilan described the building, floor and door number with utmost detail in Kekchi, an ancient language only spoken by a handful of people in the world today. Ah Kin scribbled the translation onto the piece of paper that he now held in his hand.

Nacom finally arrived at a green door with a silver metal '12' screwed into it. He had no idea where Immanuel had found this postal worker's uniform from, and he hoped it was convincing enough. He just needed someone to open the door, the rest he could handle. The only thing he worried about was the noise, the quieter the better, he didn't want neighbours reporting the commotion to the police. He shifted the fake package to his other hand as he felt for his knife to ensure it was still there. Nacom took a deep breath and then loudly knocked the metal letterbox.

∞

Nikkita walked over to Sharon with a cup of tea and a small plate of chocolate digestives.

'Ooh, thank you dear' said Sharon. 'Now quick, take a seat, I love this show.'

Nikkita smiled, she loved spending time with Adam's mum and being around the house while he was gone made her feel closer to him. Suddenly she heard a loud knock on the door.

'I don't believe it, who would come over at a time like this?' Sharon said with her eyes still glued to the TV.

'I'll go see.' Nikkita offered.

'No, it's ok dear, I'll go. They're only going to do contestant introductions for the first ten minutes anyway.'

KNOCK, KNOCK, KNOCK.

'Okay, okay!' Sharon shouted. 'Keep your pants on.' Sharon left the room and walked down the hallway to the front door. She peered through the peephole in the door and saw a postman with a parcel in his hands. 'Yes?'

'Package for Adam Newton Ma'am. I need a signature.'

Sharon groaned. *Adam and those bloody auction sites.* 'Ok, just a minute.' Sharon removed the chain and unlocked the door. 'That's a lovely accent you have.' She said as she pulled open the door and stood in the doorway. 'Where is it from?'

'Mexico Ma'am.' Nacom replied as his eyes darted side to side to ensure the coast was clear.

Sharon looked at her thin dainty wristwatch and noticed it had just passed 7pm. 'I didn't know you delivery guys worked this late.'

'Last stop Ma'am.' The man gave an awkward smile. 'Is Mr Newton here?'

'No, I'll sign for it, I'm his mother.' Sharon raised her hands to accept the parcel. The postal officer hesitated for a moment and then handed her the parcel. 'Oh, it's rather light for such a large-'

Suddenly the man charged towards her grabbing her arm. The shock threw her off balance, she wanted to scream but her voice escaped her and the parcel fell out of her hands. His other hand was raised above his head and he was holding something shiny, she realised it was a knife just as it came crashing down. She took a deep breath to scream, but the scream never made it out as she felt the blade ram straight into her throat. The force knocked her to the ground and everything went black.

OUT OF THE FYING PAN...

Adam stood in the lift with the arrow gripped in his hand. He looked at his wristwatch, it was 11:14pm. *Wait what?* Adam was sure that the time was wrong. *It was 9:30 about fifteen minutes ago!* Adam wondered if whatever he did upstairs may have affected how time had lapsed, or that it may have fried his watch's electronics somehow. He watched the digital display for a while, but the seconds were ascending as usual. *Hmm...it doesn't seem broken.* He raised his fingers to his temples again. *Damn headache won't go away.* He gently rubbed his temples again. *Ding.* The lift doors slid open and Adam calmly took a step forward, as he looked up he was shocked to see an angry looking man standing in front of him.

'Aaargh!' The man yelled and grabbed Adam by his shirt and threw him out of the lift and into the hallway. The arrow flew out of Adam's hand as he landed hard on the floor on his wounded arm.

'Wait!' Adam yelled. 'Wait... what's going on?!'

The man didn't say a word. He looked furious. The man slowly walked towards Adam as he scrambled back down the hallway. Just then Adam glimpsed the words on the A4 sheet of paper stuck on the wall and once again sheer terror gripped his heart as he read the note;

COMBAT MASTERY

INTRUSION

Nikkita heard a loud noise and quickly got to her feet. *Something's wrong.* She tiptoed towards the living room door and gently pushed it open. Suddenly a man jumped out from behind the door and wrapped his huge hands around her mouth. He spun her around like a rag doll and raised the knife to her throat.

'Don't make a sound.' He ordered.

She was terrified and stood there frozen with shock at what was happening. The man forced her back into the living room, the TV was still on but she couldn't hear it anymore.

'Sit down and shut up.' He instructed.

She didn't dare disobey. She sat back down where she was sitting just a few moments ago about to enjoy her tea and biscuits. 'What do you want?' She whispered as she sobbed in fear.

'I told you to shut up!' He replied angrily.

He kept the large knife pointed towards her as she sat there and he reached for his mobile phone. 'Who else lives here?' She wanted to lie and tell him that Sharon's husband was going to be home soon, but the fear of his presence crippled her. She decided not to tell him about Sidney who was still out with friends and not due back till later. 'No one... no one else.'

'Where's Adam?' He demanded.

Nikkita stared back confused. *He's after Adam?* Whoever he was, he wasn't just some random burglar. 'He's not here, he's joined the military.' She hoped that the fact that Adam was part of the military would frighten him off. But when she said that, he seemed more confused than afraid. He pressed a few buttons on his phone and held it up to his ear.

'What's your name and how do you know these people?'

'Nikkita, I'm just a neighbour.'

His call connected. 'It's me. The mother is here and a girl called Nikkita.' He paused as the other party spoke. 'No, no one else.' another pause. He lowered the phone after a few moments and looked at her again. 'Where's Sidney?'

What? How does he know so much? 'She doesn't live here anymore.' She lied.

He raised the phone back to his ear. 'It's only the two of them.' Pause. 'Okay, got it. I'm on my way.'

He ended the call and put his phone back into his pocket. 'Get up, you're coming with me.' He grabbed her by the hair and led her towards the front door. He pointed the blade into the small of her back. 'Do anything stupid and I'll drive this straight into your back.' She nodded in acknowledgement, tears streaming down her face. He opened the door and she saw a paramedic standing at the front door of the flat. For a brief moment, Nikkita felt saved and overwhelmed with relief. But her relief was short-lived as she noticed something odd about him.

'The other one is in the bathroom on the left.' Nacom said to Immanuel who was dressed in a paramedic's uniform. Nikkita watched as he began unfolding a wheelchair. Her heart sank as she realised that they were all in this together. Nacom frog marched her down the stairs and across the green towards a silver van parked with its engine running. He slid open the rear door and threw her into the back.

'Please, you have the wrong person. I won't say a word, just let me go.' Nikkita begged.

Nacom followed her into the back of the van and closed the door. He produced cable ties and tied her wrists behind her back and threw a black cotton sack over her head. 'If you scream, I'll put a rag in your throat. You won't like that.' Nacom threatened.

Nikkita's world was plunged into darkness as she heard the man leave and slam the door behind him. 'Help me, God.' She cried.

THE FIGHT

Adam scrambled back as he saw the angry man slowly stride towards him. 'Why are you fighting me?' He yelled in fear.

The man didn't answer. His face seemed twisted with anger. His eyes were bloodshot and transfixed on him like a wolf staring at his next meal. Adam managed to get to his feet and kept his distance.

'I'm part of The Fraction.' Adam explained. 'Do you know Belkin? He's a friend of mine.' But the tall muscular demon in front of him didn't seem to care. He just kept walking towards him. His dirty white vest was stretched to its limit as it struggled to contain the bulging muscles beneath. In one swift motion, he lifted Adam up with arms that resembled tree trunks and slammed him against the wall before unleashing a flurry of gut punches that floored Adam once again.

There was no reasoning with this beast. He was here to kill him. Panic took over and a burst of adrenalin shot through Adam's heart and he scurried away on the floor. The beast was in no rush, he knew there was no escape from this level. There was nowhere to run, nowhere to hide. Adam managed to get fifteen yards away and got to his feet. His stomach ached and his shoulder was bleeding again. He tried to focus as he did upstairs but the threat in front of him was too distracting. He couldn't concentrate. The man was once again within arm's reach. Adam mustered all his energy and let out a loud cry and punched the man in the face as hard as he could. The punch struck the man clean on the jaw, but judging by the man's reaction, it hurt Adam's hand more than it hurt him. The beast rubbed his chin and to Adam's horror, he smiled. Then suddenly his face twisted and he let out a beastly cry and pulled his arm back to punch Adam on the side of the head. Adam saw the blow coming but there was little he could do to avoid it. At the last moment, he raised his arm to block the punch but the force was so immense he almost broke his forearm defending himself from it. The blow knocked Adam back but surprisingly he managed to keep upright. Managing to withstand the brutal punch Adam felt a sudden sense of courage. The man pulled his arm back again to deliver another crushing blow and Adam closed his eyes and fell on one knee and raised his hand up. 'Stop!' he boomed.

Adam heard his voice echo in the deafening silence as he waited for the impact of the punch, but it never came. Adam tentatively opened his eyes praying that somehow the man had come to his senses. But what he saw was far stranger. The beast was suspended in time mid-punch. The twisted grimace on his face was frozen. Even the sweat dripping off his head was suddenly motionless.

Adam slowly got to his feet, and just stared at the man stuck in a transparent purple orb that completely encapsulated him. As Adam stared at him he realised that the man wasn't completely motionless anymore, the orb was weakening. He was moving, but incredibly slowly. Adam walked around to the side and watched the man as he moved millimetre by millimetre. This was his chance. He punched the man in the face as hard as he could. The man barely moved but Adam knew that he had hurt him. It was like punching a wax manikin. His face was hard but Adam knew that there was only one way out of here, and that was by putting a stop to this man.

Adam took a deep breath and stood in front of him and delivered a combination of brutal punches and kicks letting out all his frustration and rage. He kept beating and beating him. His hands were now in agony, but Adam had never felt more alive. He stopped to catch his breath and the man's face was now beginning to show signs of Adam's punishment. His broken nose slowly began bleeding and the beast's face began displaying signs of the assault. But Adam knew he was still conscious and he was starting to move faster. *The orb is weakening.* Adam closed his eyes and raised his hands towards the man again and tried to recall the feelings and emotions he felt that enabled him to generate the orb of energy. 'Stop!' he yelled again. But it was no use, he realised that the power he had was linked to his emotional state somehow. He assumed it was his fear, and he conjured up scary images. He started thinking about Freddy Kruger and how scared he felt of the popular horror movie character as a child. He opened his eyes and realised that nothing was happening and the man was starting to move faster and faster as the effects of the orb were wearing off. Soon, the purple sphere had almost completely evaporated. *I can practice summoning time orbs later.* He ran back towards the elevator and looked around on the floor. *Found it!* He picked up the arrow he'd dropped earlier and ran back towards the man who now looked both shocked and confused and was almost back to full speed. Adam took a deep breath and plunged the arrow into the beast's neck just as the effects of the purple time orb wore off. The giant man's eyes bulged in their sockets as he wrapped his hand around his throat. Even in his last few moments, he tried to grab Adam but the blood was flowing out of his throat too rapidly and he clutched his neck, gargling on his blood as he came crashing down like a demolished building. Adam stood over him and took in the gory reality of what he'd done. He didn't know whether he felt pride or disgust as he stood over the motionless titan he had defeated.

Suddenly the elevator chimed to life. *Ding.* The sound snapped Adam out of his trance. He looked at his wristwatch as he entered it to go down to the ground floor. Adam could've sworn that this fight only lasted six or seven-minutes but his watch read 11:51pm. He ran into the elevator and repeatedly tapped the ground floor button. Somehow every time he used his powers, time was skipping forward, and right now he needed every second of every minute if he was going to get out of this building before midnight. His crippling migraine returned accompanied with a nosebleed this time. He knew that his powers were taking a toll on him and he prayed he didn't need to use his new found ability on the final floor.

TAKEN

Nikkita felt suffocated with the sack over her head. It was pitch black and her panicked breathing wasn't helping. She'd been sitting in the back of the van for hours. She was clueless as to where they were going, or what they wanted with her. She tried to listen out for clues as to who these people were, but they didn't speak much, and when they did it was in a different language, she wasn't certain, but sounded a lot like Spanish.

Suddenly the van pulled up and she heard the doors open. 'We're here.' Nacom announced. 'I'm going to remove the sack. You know what I'm capable of, so if you scream or run or do anything stupid, I will cut you. Do you understand?'

Nikkita nodded her head. She had seen enough to know that this wasn't an idle threat. Throughout the entire journey she had been scheming of ways that she would escape, but now given the opportunity, fear took over. She convinced herself that the only way she'd get out of this alive is to play along and wait for a better opportunity.

'Good.' Nacom whipped off the sack and he waved the knife in her face. 'Don't forget.'

'Okay, I got it.' Nikkita said as she closed her eyes and turned away from the sight of the shimmering blade.

Nacom exited the car and looked around to ensure the coast was clear on the busy Camden streets. The tourists seemed distracted with their own conversations to take any notice of the hostage situation. The van was parked right in front of Immanuel's safe house. Nacom marched her into the house and Nikkita decided it'd be best not to protest. He walked her straight upstairs and led her to a large bedroom. She hesitated for a moment, but Nacom pushed her inside and she noticed two other men standing there. One of whom she recognised as the paramedic she saw back at the flat.

'Good evening.' The taller man greeted. 'We're pleasantly surprised to have you join us. Please, take a seat.' He gestured towards the single chair near the table.

Nikkita sat down, looking around praying that someone would tell her why she was brought here. She wanted to explain to someone in charge that they had the wrong person, she was no one, and her family wouldn't be able to raise much of a ransom. 'Sir, I think you have the wrong-'

'We,' the man interrupted. 'have exactly who we were meant to have.' He declared authoritatively. 'Allow me to introduce myself, I am Ah Kin, and I believe you've already met my friend Immanuel. We're here on a sacred quest to carry out the gods' will, and you my dear, have been chosen by the gods to help us.'

EXIT STRATEGY

Adam arrived at the ground floor and he felt anxious. Time was slipping through his fingers. He exited the elevator and was met with dead silence on the ground floor. On the sheet of paper in front of him was a simple order; *Exit the building.* Adam sighed in relief. *Finally!* Adam scanned the ceilings and found an exit sign and followed it. It led to a set of heavy wooden doors that were locked shut. *You've got to be kidding me!* He tried opening the windows but they were all double glazed and locked. It was now 11:55pm and Adam began panicking as he kicked and barged the solid wooden doors with all his might. The doors barely moved. *What the heck man!* Adam looked around at the furniture and wondered if he could use something as a battering ram. But nothing seemed suitable. *Dammit!* He checked his watch again. 11:56pm. His mind cycled through his options and suddenly he had a brain wave. He ran back into the lift and pressed the button for the 5th floor. The doors closed and the elevator began moving. *Yes!* As the floor numbers ascended, each number reminded Adam of the horrors he'd overcome. *Worst day ever.* The elevator stopped at the 5th floor. *Ding.* The doors slid open and he ran into the office and carefully picked up the dynamite-rigged bomb, complete with the attached clock. He carefully walked back to the elevator with the device cradled in his arms and pressed the 'G' button to head back to the ground floor. It illuminated and the doors slid shut and the elevator began its slow descent. *C'mon, c'mon, c'mon!*

The doors finally opened on the ground floor and Adam briskly walked towards the locked wooden doors. He checked his watch and it read 11:59pm. *C'mon!* Adam placed the bomb near the doors and slapped the button. Immediately the clock began counting down. He ran back into the hallway, curled into a ball behind the wall, closed his eyes and pushed his fingers into his ears.

KA-BOOOOM!!

The blast was tremendous and sent a shockwave through the entire ground floor. Adam's ears chimed with a loud ringing sound that he couldn't shake off. He peeked around the corner and saw the huge gaping hole where the doors once stood. Thick grey smoke billowed across the hallway. Adam ran through the smoke and debris and leapt over the rubble of the collapsed wall and out into freedom. *I'm outside! I made it!* He checked his wristwatch, 00:00am. He jogged into the car park area outside the building and turned around to look back at the destroyed office block from hell. A small fire burned inside as he dusted himself off.

'Now that's what I call an exit.'

Adam spun around and wondered if he'd merely imagined the soft, sweet familiar voice coming from behind him. 'Sash!' he exclaimed as he saw her standing there. He ran to her and gave her a big hug. 'I'm so glad to see you. I-' Adam didn't know where to start and felt himself get choked up in overwhelming emotion.

'You did me proud.' She said as she patted his back. 'Welcome to The Fraction.'

Adam remained locked in her embrace for a few moments until he finally gathered himself and turned around to look at the devastation he'd caused. 'Did Belkin put you through all that too?' He wondered.

'Similar, but not exactly.' She admitted as she stared at the diminishing fire within the building. 'We all have our unique gifts and Belkin pushes us all differently. What you can do, only you can do. What I can do, only I can do. That's what makes us so valuable.'

Sash held Adam as he limped towards the car and sat down. His clothes were filthy and blood-soaked and every part of him ached in pain. 'I killed a man.' Adam admitted as he sat in the car riddled with guilt.

'No you didn't' Sash replied calmly. 'That was Ali. He can take care of himself. He's one of us. He's unique too, he can regenerate, a super healer. He's practically invincible. He died three times to complete his training day. He'll be conscious again soon and it'll be like nothing ever happened. We've got a clean-up team heading over right now. They'll take care of him. He's actually a really nice guy once you get to know him.' Adam just stared at Sash in stunned silence. She opened the car door and helped him in. She climbed into the driver's seat and turned the ignition. 'Belkin wants to see you for a full debrief, let's get back to headquarters.'

A GUT FEELING

The next three months had been relentless for Adam. Having survived the training day Adam was subjected to immense levels of physical, mental and spiritual training. Each day was harder than the last, and by the end of each week he felt different; better, smarter, evolved. His body was now in excellent shape, and he was starting to see the benefits of the diet and exercise regime Ali was putting him through. Sofia had taught Adam some amazing meditative techniques that were improving his concentration and his ability to control his energies. He learned that it wasn't his emotions that controlled his abilities to create time trapping orbs; it was his spiritual and mental energies.

By the end of his third week, Adam was able to create small, beach ball sized time orbs at will. Initially, his nosebleeds were a worrying side effect, but with Sofia's help, they had reduced significantly. Belkin referred to the nosebleeds as Bloodletting and apparently they were an important part of the process and quite common in Timestoppers. That's what they called him; a Timestopper. But he didn't quite feel worthy of the title yet. His abilities were only effective in small isolated spaces, and the orbs would often disappear within twenty or thirty seconds. On his best day he created a time orb the size of a small car. He was only able to hold it for eight seconds. The energy that it took to manifest a time orb that large was immense. His legs buckled and he would have collapsed onto the floor had Sash not caught him.

By the second month of his training Sash, Sofia and Ali were allowing Adam to design his own training sessions. They had helped him build the foundations for his growth, and it was now up to him to push his boundaries further and further. Adam realised that he was pushing himself hard. He had become disciplined and learned to listen to his body and spirit. Easing off where necessary, and pressing harder whenever he could. Ali taught him useful healing techniques and his overall endurance, strength and recovery were suddenly developing by leaps and bounds.

Every night just before bed Adam would retire to his room and read his father's diary. Having rushed through it once already, he decided to start it again, from the beginning, this time savouring his father's words to get to know him through the text. He researched about the Mayans and Raj helped him download digital books on ancient Mexican civilisations. The more he delved into it, the more fascinated he became. He learned about their magic, their astrology, their rituals and beliefs, and most importantly, their prophecies.

∞

Adam walked into his room after another exhausting training session and collapsed onto his bed. His heart had been aching to speak to his mother and Nikkita for weeks, but Belkin's orders were strict. Since his training day, his phone calls were extremely limited. He lay there remembering fun days with his friends and Nikkita and his heart began to sink. He hadn't spoken to anyone in over a month and he knew that his mum was probably worried sick. He knew that whenever he did eventually speak to her, he'd have to listen to at least ten minutes of verbal abuse for not calling sooner. He continued sending letters home once a week making up stories about the RAF cadet school, and he usually received letters back. But as he lay there doing the math, he realised that she hadn't written back in over two weeks. *Maybe she's just busy, it must be hard to write regularly when you've got a normal life to live.* But deep in Adam's heart, he wasn't buying it. He knew his mother would go out of her way to stay in touch. *Maybe the letters got lost in the post. What if they've been sent to the real RAF!*

But Adam knew that Belkin had his ways of intercepting mail, so it was unlikely. The theories all whizzed around in his head but none of them really sat well with him. He suddenly got a bad feeling in his gut and he felt he had to call her. He had to hear her voice to make sure she was okay.

∞

The next morning after training with Ali, Adam showered, got dressed and walked towards the office where Belkin usually spent the day. As he approached the door he heard strange whispering inside the room. It was loud enough to hear from outside with the door closed, but not quite loud enough to comprehend what was being said. Adam stood there for a moment listening and wondering whether or not he should knock and interrupt. As Adam concentrated he realised that whoever was speaking, wasn't speaking in English. Adam turned around and noticed that the rest of the team were all accounted for. Raj and Sofia were having breakfast in the lounge, Ali was still in the shower, and Sash was on her laptop. *Does Belkin have a guest in there?* Adam decided to knock. The whispering stopped immediately. 'Belkin?' Adam called. 'It's me, Adam.'

After a few moments of silence, Belkin finally replied. 'Come in.'

Adam opened the door and saw Belkin sitting cross-legged on a yoga mat on the floor and seemed to be meditating. He looked like himself but something seemed different about him. Adam looked around and was surprised to discover that he was completely alone.

'Err... sorry to interrupt you, Belkin.' Adam apologised as he looked around. 'I just wanted to talk to you about something, but you look busy so I'll just come back later.'

Belkin's eyes fluttered as he blinked repeatedly. 'No, it's fine.' Belkin assured.

Adam stood there frozen in shock as he noticed Belkin's eyes change colour a few times. Belkin blinked a few more times and his eyes fluttered back to their normal shade of dark brown. The transitions were so brief that Adam convinced himself that he had probably just imagined it.

Belkin rose from his mat and perched himself on the desk beside Adam. 'What's bothering you?'

'Nothing, it's just that I've not had a letter from my mum in a while and she's usually really punctual with things like that. I'm a little worried I guess. I just wanted to talk to her to make sure she's okay.' Adam stared at Belkin to gauge his reaction. 'Is that cool?'

Belkin looked at Adam and he seemed disappointed. 'Adam, I need you focussed on our mission. I don't want you distracted with family matters at this crucial time. That was our deal, remember? We're in the middle of December, you've made huge strides in your training but you're not done. You don't need distractions from home setting you back.'

'I know Belkin. But please, just two minutes, I won't even ask her about anything, I just want to hear her voice and know she's ok. I've got a weird feeling.' Adam couldn't understand how speaking to his family would hinder his training but he decided not to push Belkin too much on the matter. Belkin had been right about everything else up until this point, and Adam trusted his judgement. But no matter how hard Adam tried, he just couldn't shake off the strange feeling he had. He had to call home.

Belkin looked at him deep in his eyes for a moment as Adam stood there uncomfortably. 'Okay.' He finally said.

'Okay?!' Adam repeated ecstatically.

'I see that this is something you won't be able to let go of and thus if I were to refuse, your mind will be just as distracted, if not more so. So yes, go ahead, ease your mind.'

'Thanks, Belkin I-'

'One short call.' Belkin interrupted. 'You snuck away from RAF training and managed to get to a phone. Tell her you won't be able to do so again, and tell her to stick to sending letters.'

'One-off call, stick to letters. Got it.' Adam summarized excitedly.

Belkin put his arm around Adam's shoulders and walked him back into the lounge area. 'Raj. Get Adam a secure line patched through to his mother's house. Two-minutes, not a second longer. We don't want to risk anyone tracing us back to this safe house. Our enemies are smart, and we can't take any risks.'

'You got it big man!' Raj said as he picked up his bowl of cereal and began walking towards the electrical storage room. 'This way E.T.'

Adam frowned. *E.T?* The penny dropped and he finally got the joke. 'Ha-ha, very funny.' Adam remarked sarcastically as he rolled his eyes.

Adam followed Raj into the storage room and looked back at Belkin with a thankful smile. Belkin acknowledged it and smiled back before turning around and heading back into his office.

Adam hadn't been in the storage room before. It was dark and filled with spare cables and monitors. As Adam turned the corner he realised that the room was a lot larger than it first looked and housed a host of strange looking gadgets, gizmos and pieces of expensive looking technology. 'Whoa! Cool gear.' Adam said as he marvelled at all the tech.

'Yeah pretty sweet eh?' Raj began pressing some buttons on a strange looking electronic device with a phone receiver on it. 'This stuff's worth millions. I've been working with tech all my life and even I was stumped with half this stuff.' Raj looked up some numbers in a file nearby, pressed a few more buttons and then lifted the receiver. 'Here you go, it's ringing. You have exactly one hundred and twenty seconds from when the call is connected.'

Adam quickly grabbed the handset and put it to his ear. It rang and rang. But no one was answering. Adam checked the time on his watch and wondered if he'd called at a time when his mother and Sidney were likely to be out. He was just about to give up when he heard a slightly longer pause than usual between rings, followed by a slight change in the ringtone as if the call was being diverted. He held the phone to his ear with intrigue. *That's weird.* He'd called home hundreds of times and had never heard this before. Suddenly the call connected. But there was dead silence on the other end.

'Hello?' Adam said into the receiver. 'Hellooo? Mum?' Adam could tell someone was listening but no one was speaking. The call timer began counting down. 'Hello! Can you hear me?' Adam looked at Raj in confusion. Concerned, Raj picked up a set of headphones from the table and connected them to the device to listen in. Suddenly a man in a thick Mexican accent responded.

'Is this Adam?' The voice croaked.

'Who is this?' asked Adam. Raj stared at Adam wide-eyed as he listened in to the call.

'We have your mother and your girlfriend. We know who you are, and the unholy alliance you have made. Surrender yourself to us now and we will not harm them.'

'Who are you? Where is my mum?!' Adam shouted down the phone. Raj looked at Adam and silently mouthed the word "Mayans". He looked at the timer. There wasn't much time left before the call could be traced.

'If you want to walk on the straight path, and redeem your soul you can meet us at Talacre Gardens next to Kentish Town tube station at 10pm tonight. Come alone. If you're not alone, or if you do anything stupid, we will kill them both.'

'Okay, okay! Talacre Gardens.' Adam repeated. He looked at Raj who was pointing at his wrist indicating there wasn't much time left. 'Wait! What do you look like? How will I know who to speak to?'

'You'll know.' *Click.* The phone went dead.

'I'm sorry dude.' Raj apologised. 'If I left it on for even a second longer they could've triangulated our location.'

'What the hell!' Adam gasped. 'They've got my mum... and my...my girlfriend?' *Nikkita.* Adam got to his feet. 'I need to speak to Belkin.' He charged out the room and walked straight past Sash and Sofia who had overheard the panicked yelling and were standing by the door.

Sash reached out to Adam as he walked passed. 'Adam, what's wrong? Is everything ok?' She said as he pushed past.

'No, nothing's okay. I need to speak to Belkin, now!' He brushed past her without stopping and headed straight for Belkin's office.

Adam wrapped loudly on the office door. 'Belkin!' Adam boomed. 'Belkin, we've got a problem!' Adam didn't wait for a response. He turned the door knob and barged into the room. Belkin was rolling up the cuffs of his salmon pink linen shirt. 'I'm sorry, I know you're changing, but we've got a huge problem.' Adam said frantically.

Belkin turned to face Adam he could tell something was wrong. 'What's the matter?' He asked. 'What happened at home?'

'The Mayans!' Adam blurted as he began to pace up and down. 'They were at my house, I just called home and they said they have my mum. They've kidnapped her. I think they have my friend Nikkita too. I'm really worried. I don't know what to do.'

Belkin stared at the ground as he thought, his eyes darting around trying to figure out how this could have happened. He finally looked up at Adam. 'A Chilan.' He whispered.

'What's a Chilan?' Adam asked.

'Not what, who.' Belkin clarified as he finished rolling up his cuffs. 'A Chilan is a clairvoyant that the leader of the Mayans; Ah Kin, must have used to locate your mother. There's no other way they could have found her.'

'A clairvoyant?' Adam echoed in disbelief.

'But The Chilans have been extinct for-' Belkin stopped as he interrupted his own thoughts. 'They've been in London for a while, days, maybe even weeks.'

'They've had my mother for weeks!?' Adam exclaimed.

'But how...' Belkin walked past Adam and into the lounge area where the rest of the team were stood listening in to the conversation. 'Sash, how could they have found his family?

'My guess is that they performed a sacrifice to the gods right here in London.' Sash hypothesised.

'Sacrifice?' Adam fretted.

'Not of your family Adam. Most probably some other poor soul.' Sash explained. 'Only a human sacrifice can summon the energies required to locate someone in such a densely populated place. They must have found your home, where your energies are strongest.'

'These guys can do that?' Adam marvelled in shock. 'What are they demons?'

'More like ancient warlocks.' Sash explained. 'The Mayans use a Chilan, a master of black magic. Magic that uses blood sacrifices, usually animal blood, but in extreme cases human. The sacrifices and rituals are for their gods who seem to grant them visions of clairvoyance and other unseen knowledge.'

As Adam stood there listening to Sash his mind recalled reading about these practices in his father's Diary. 'Wait, I read about this in my father's diary. I thought the Chilan was dead.' Adam said. 'I read that my father killed the Chilan when he was in Mexico years ago. He wrote about it.'

'Your father has killed many Chilans.' Belkin recounted. 'Until now, I thought he'd killed them all. But Chilan is not a name, it's a special title given to a Mayan who is trained, and a seasoned practitioner of black magic. A Chilan must perform various spells before a group of elder priests will approve his status as a Chilan. Once approved, he gives up his birth name to be known only as Chilan.

'The name Chilan in English literally means Oracle.' Sash chimed in.

'Oracle...' Adam echoed in wonder.

'What exactly did they say to you over the phone?' Belkin asked.

'They said that they wanted to meet at Talacre Gardens? I have no idea where that is but they said it's somewhere close to Kentish Town tube station.'

'Anything else?'

'They said I had to be there alone at 10pm tonight. They said if I wasn't alone, they'd kill them.'

Belkin sat down on the sofa as he contemplated the next move. He knew that this was a trap. If they agreed to their demands, The Fraction would lose Adam. If they didn't the Mayans would certainly kill his family and Adam would mentally spiral out of control rendering him useless for the mission.

'Why do they want him so badly?' Sofia turned to Belkin and asked.

But Belkin was deep in thought and didn't hear the question.

'They think he can find the Mayan stone his father hid.' Sash intervened. 'Ah Kin, their leader, is hell bent on possessing it. I've seen the way it amplifies powers. In the hands of a person like Ah Kin, he would wield almost God-like abilities.'

Belkin sat down deep in his own thoughts continuing to strategise the next move. The game had tilted, the Mayans wanted Adam and now they had the perfect leverage to tease him out. He felt foolish not to foresee that they would use a Chilan and target his family. But it didn't matter right now, he had to play the hand he was dealt. Belkin stood up and walked away from the group and stood facing the window looking out into the city below. 'Adam, if you go tonight they will take you. They will want to kill you. Your only leverage is that you can help them find the stone. But once you find it, they'll probably kill you. That is what you face if you decide to save your loved ones.'

'Is there another way?' Adam wondered.

'Yes. You stay with us, continue with our plans. You call their bluff and we all pray your family remains unharmed.'

Adam took a deep breath. He felt upset his loved ones had been dragged into this. 'You never told me that my family would be in danger Belkin.' Adam responded angrily. 'If you told me that my mum could be in danger I would've never had agreed to any of this.'

Belkin spun around and faced him. 'Adam, you are the last Timestopper. Your mother, your girlfriend, your sister and everyone else in the world would be guaranteed death on December 21st if you didn't agree to this mission. You have given us all a chance to live. If we lose you, we've lost everything. So I'm going to ask you again; Are you sure you want to go tonight?'

Adam took another deep breath and calmed himself down. Belkin's words reminded him that his family would have been doomed anyway. He was here to save everyone, and this was the time to step up to the plate and be the hero.

'I'll tell them I can get them the stone, I'll play along. I'll do whatever it takes, and then wait for my chance to escape.'

'Ah Kin has been searching for the stone for years.' Sash intervened. 'As long as he believes you can get it for him he won't kill you. And he's certain you know where it is.'

'But I don't.' Adam admitted.

'Yes, we know that, but he doesn't.' Sash explained. 'You may be able to convince him to exchange yourself for your mother and your friend. And then wait for your chance to escape.

'It's a risky.' Belkin confessed.

'I'll do it.' Adam knew there wasn't much chance of success, but it was better than nothing, he had to try.

Belkin walked over to Adam and placed his hands on his shoulders. 'Adam before you get carried away, you must know that this plan is riddled with hazards. Not only will you be walking straight into the arms of a very powerful enemy, you will be out of our protection. His only weakness is his lust for the stone. It is the only thing that will stop him from killing you. Your ability to find it for him is your only bargaining chip. If he feels at any point you can't locate it for him he'll kill you.'

Adam didn't take Belkin's warnings lightly, but he had already made up his mind. 'If I do save the world, it'd be a hollow victory to live in it without my mum and Nikkita... I'm ready Belkin, I can do this.'

THE DARKSIDE

The black Range Rover stopped a few hundred meters before the park. It was coming up to 9:45pm and Adam's heart was pounding. Now that he was here, he felt anxious. Doubts kept creeping into his mind and he silenced them away by reminding himself why he was doing this. Don't be a pussy.

Belkin turned around from the front passenger seat to look back at Adam. 'Remember what I told you, Adam. We can't plan for every situation, so if you get stuck, go with your instincts. Your father always trusted his, and you would be wise to do so too.'

Adam nodded. He felt like he was venturing into an ocean full of sea monsters in nothing but a row boat. He took a deep breath. *Instincts.*

'Do you remember how to activate the beacon?' Raj asked as he looked back at Adam from the rear view mirror.

Adam looked down at his white G-Shock watch. 'Yes. Top button twice and lower button three times.'

Raj had programmed Adam's watch with a distress signal that was directly linked to a frequency that Sash could pick up with her electrokinesis from up to five-miles away.

Adam turned to Sash who was sat in the back with him. 'Should we practice one last time, make sure you can still pick up the signal?' He asked nervously.

'Adam, stop worrying. It works. If anything, my senses are only getting better at picking up the signal. But use it in an emergency only okay?' Sash tried to mask her concern for

Adam's safety. In her heart, she knew that this was a suicide mission. But Adam was adamant, and there was no talking him out of it. The only thing she could do was be supportive. Belkin reminded her that forcing Adam to stay would only create more problems. 'Just be careful out there, and don't play around with your watch, we won't know if a signal you send is a mistake or not, and you can't undo it, so if you press the sequence, and I pick it up we're coming to get you whether you like it or not. Got it?'

Adam nodded. He knew that the signal wasn't going to save his life if he was in any immediate danger, but it made him feel better that there was a way to connect back to The Fraction if he had to. 'I Got it.'

'Okay, you set?' Belkin asked. 'It's time.'

'Wish me luck guys.' Adam replied as he took a deep breath and psyched himself up.

Sash leant in and kissed him on his cheek. 'Good luck Timestopper. Go get your family back.'

'Thanks.' Adam blushed.

'Yeah, good luck bud.' Raj chimed in. 'I would kiss you too, but as you can see I'm all buckled in over here.' He winked.

Adam got out of the car and slowly started walking towards the park. It was pitch black and the street lamps did little to illuminate the roads. The cold December winds were beginning to bite. Adam blew into his cupped palms and rubbed his hands together before putting them into his jacket's pockets. He stood in front of the park's entrance and he looked around for someone who might fit his preconceived notion of an evil Mayan bad guy. But as he scanned the park he didn't see anyone at all. He walked through the open gates and slowly into the middle of the park where he'd have a better view of the surroundings. It was a small residential park set around large expensive looking townhouses. Down the path, just a hundred feet away he noticed a bench. He checked his watch. It was now exactly 10pm and there was still no sign of anyone. He decided to walk over to the bench and wait there. Just as he arrived at it, he heard rustling coming from the bush behind him. He quickly turned around.

'Who's there?' His voice cracked, and Adam quickly cleared his throat. He began walking towards the bush. 'Who's there?' He repeated in a more authoritative tone.

'No one is back there.' Came a voice from behind him.

Adam spun back around and to his shock he found a man sitting on the bench. What the- How did he... The tall man was dressed completely in black. He wore a long black raincoat, black shoes, and a black Fedora hat. Initially the man didn't look Mexican and reminded Adam of American gangsters of the 1920's.

'You're brave.' He whispered.

Adam stood in front of him with his fists clenched, heart thumping and adrenalin coursing through his veins. 'You have my mother and my friend, and I'm here to offer you a deal to get them back.' Adam had been practising that line all day and felt quite pleased with the way he seemed to have delivered it.

'A deal?' He sniggered. 'What do you have that I could want?' The man asked with intrigue.

'I'm only going to speak about that with Ah Kin.' Adam said in his most confident voice.

'Oh really? And what could you possibly have that Ah Kin would be interested in?'

The conversational exchange seemed to be amusing to the tall man and Adam suddenly felt like he wasn't being taken seriously. 'Look, I've told you already. Take me to Ah Kin and I'll tell him myself.'

The man stood up and took a few steps towards Adam, towering over him. He removed his hat and performed an elaborate bow. 'Ah Kin, at your service.'

With his hat off Adam could clearly see his face. The man looked old. The thick skin on his face was deeply wrinkled and had a brownish tint to it. He looked like a Native American as if someone had dressed up an Apache in a suit and hat. He had big ears, and a large nose covered in pockmarks. His lips were thin and drooped down at the sides. Adam noticed a tattoo marking near his neck. The man smiled and Adam noticed his discoloured crooked teeth. Adam had a hard time believing that this old decrepit man was such a threat to Belkin. *I think even I could take this guy in a fight.*

'How do I know you're really Ah Kin?' Adam asked sceptically.

'Well young man, you don't have much choice, do you? And since I'm the only one here why don't you just tell me what it is that you have to offer.'

Adam had barely been around this man for five minutes and he was already fed up with him. 'Okay fine. You want the stone. My dad was the one who hid it and only I can find it. I will find it for you if you promise to let my Mum and Nikkita go. That's the deal.'

Ah Kin laughed loudly. He wasn't expecting Adam to willingly offer his services to find the stone. He was making it so easy. *The boy actually wants to find the stone for me. It's a sign from the Gods!* Ah Kin began considering the possibility of an elaborate trap set up by The Fraction and his expression suddenly became serious as he contemplated the potential threat. He couldn't be sure if it was a trap or not, but he did know that the boy was sincere about keeping his loved ones safe. He knew that Adam would never do anything stupid if his mother was at risk. Ah Kin smiled as he realised that he would always be holding the trump card.

'You have a deal.' Ah Kin agreed as he extended his hand for Adam to shake.

Adam looked at the hand, he felt like he was about to make a deal with the devil. He took a deep breath and shook it. But as he did so, the strangest thing happened. Adam felt a sense of peace, a sensation of comfort washed over him. It was the complete opposite of what he was expecting to feel. He couldn't deny it. There was something about Ah Kin that felt... noble.

FREE SLAVES

It was the start of her third week held up at the safe house and Nikkita was getting used to sleeping on the springy mattress on the floor. Her captors rarely spoke English in the house and she felt she was going half way mad cycling through anyone who ever held a grudge against her or her family who would have wanted to kidnap her. Nothing made sense. There was no obvious reason for her abduction and they weren't asking anyone for a ransom. Physically her captors were taking adequate care of her. But it was the lack of communication that felt like the real prison.

Her room was decorated minimally with old reclaimed furniture dotted around. She hadn't heard or seen Sharon since she'd been here and feared the worst for her. Strangely, since that horrific day her captors hadn't been abusive to her, in fact, they barely acknowledged her at all. Her room consisted of a wardrobe, a mattress and a door that led to a small private bathroom, which was stocked with basic hygiene supplies. The room faced the back of the house and was always kept locked. The only human interaction she'd have was when one of the men would come and deliver food to her. If it wasn't for the TV she would've gone insane.

Every day Nikkita schemed of ways to escape but her plans were always foiled. On the first night, she considered jumping from the window, only to find that the windows were bolted shut and the toughed glass was unbreakable. It created so much commotion they barged straight in and took away anything that could be used to break the glass. A week later she tried faking a sickness so she could make a run for it out of the door, but despite three days of incessant wailing, no one came to her aid. The men just delivered her food as always and locked the door. She realised that her suffering had no effect on them. *They couldn't care less if I lived or died.* Her final attempt was a few days ago when she hid behind the door and tried to ambush the man who delivered her food. The door opened and she jumped out at him. Her strength was no match for his and he swatted her away like a fly. He pushed her back and she flew across the room like a discarded garment. He wasn't even angry about it, he just grunted and closed the door. She cried that night. She was finally broken, there was no way out.

Today was another day, and it began exactly the same as the rest. Nikkita woke up after another terrible night's sleep on the cheap mattress and slowly walked towards the bathroom. Freshened up, she took her time getting changed into the baggy sportswear her kidnappers had provided and switched on the T.V. She glanced at the jam sandwich and bottle of water they had sent up to her sitting on a tray by the door and she felt sick at the thought of eating it. *Every day it's the same damn sandwich.* The afternoon trudged by slowly and the TV kept her occupied for most of it.

Day became night and she continued to watch T.V. until she became sleepy and began to prepare for bed. But then suddenly she heard loud voices downstairs. The men were speaking louder than usual and she was almost certain they were speaking in English. She pressed her ear up against the door and tried her best to listen in and make out the words. But despite her best efforts, she couldn't understand what was being said. The door was too thick and they were too far. But then she heard footsteps. Someone was coming up to her, something was different. Her heart began to race. She checked the time and realised that no one ever came to her room this late. Suddenly a feeling of dread washed over her. She began to step away from the door. Someone was coming for her. She heard the footsteps get louder and louder as the person ascended the stairs and approached her room. The footsteps stopped just outside her door and then there was silence. She crept back towards the door to see if she could hear what was happening on the other side. Suddenly the thick metal key slammed into the deadbolt and the sudden noise made her jump. She watched as the handle moved and the door finally swung open. Of all the faces in the world, this was the last she'd ever expected to see. She burst into tears and ran towards him and held him tightly. 'Oh, Adam!' She cried.

Adam held Nikkita tightly. He was relieved to see her safe and unharmed. 'Did they hurt you?' He asked.

Nikkita didn't reply. Her voice had disappeared as she sobbed silently, relieved to be saved from her imprisonment. She simply shook her head and kept her face buried in his chest. She noticed that he physically felt different. His body was bulkier and more muscular. She leant back and looked at him to ensure that she hadn't made a mistake and that she wasn't embracing some complete stranger. She looked into his eyes and had no doubt that it was him. His vivid green eyes were unmistakable. 'Get me out of here Adam. Please.'

Adam let go and turned around to face the men behind him standing outside the bedroom door. 'Where's my mother?' He demanded.

The men exchanged looks and the shorter man stepped forward. 'As you know, you have a deal with Ah Kin.' Immanuel reminded. 'You will help us find the stone and we will return your mother. For now, we will give you Nikkita in good faith, but I'm afraid you will only see your mother once the stone is with us.'

Nikkita stared at Adam in disbelief. 'You made a deal with these people?' She hissed.

Adam noticed the disgust in her voice. 'It was the only way to save you both.' He explained. 'They want something and they think I can find it for them; a stone. It's complicated. I promise I'll explain everything to you later.'

Adam turned back to the men. 'Fine. But if you've harmed her in anyway the deal is off.'

Ah Kin ascended the stairs and joined Nacom and Immanuel. 'Despite the lies The Fraction has told you, you will find that we are not liars, and we keep our word.' Ah Kin gestured towards Nikkita. 'We are reasonable people, just ask your friend here. Considering she's our detainee, has she not been well provided for?'

Adam looked at Nikkita and couldn't dispute the fact that she seemed physically well for a three-week hostage and her living arrangements seemed decent, all things considering. 'Okay fine. But from now on, she stays with me.'

'Agreed.' Ah Kin grinned. 'In fact, you both can stay right here.'

Nikkita looked at Adam in shock. 'We're staying here!?' She gasped.

'I'm sorry Nikkita.' Adam replied remorsefully. 'It's part of the deal. They were going to kill you unless I helped them find the stone.

Nikkita's elation evaporated. She tried to force herself to look at the positives of the situation and be grateful that Adam was here. But she felt overwhelmed with sadness knowing that she would remain a prisoner here and that her family would still have no idea where she was. *They are probably worried sick.* Deflated, she walked back towards the mattress and sat down to process it all in her mind.

'If we're going to stay here we're going to need some things.' Adam demanded. 'You can leave this door open too. I'm not leaving without my mum, so don't worry about us trying to escape.'

'Make a list of your needs and we'll see what we can do in the morning.' Ah Kin acknowledged. 'We will no longer lock this door. You are free to roam the house as you wish.

Your mother is not being held here. Try to escape and you'll never see her again.' Ah Kin spun around and walked back down the stairs. Nacom and Immanuel followed behind.

Adam closed the door and walked back towards Nikkita. 'Hey, look, it's not for long. I need to play along for now. I've got a plan, and friends who can help us, we're not alone. We'll both be back home soon, trust me.'

Nikkita tried to stay positive and muster a smile as she looked up at Adam. She was about to say something reaffirming like 'Sure.' or 'Okay', but she knew her voice would crack and he'd sense the sadness so she stayed quiet and just nodded. He looked at her and it broke his heart that she was so unhappy. He bent down and kissed her on the cheek. 'I'll get you home in one-piece, I promise.'

She looked up at him and he could just make out the tiniest glimmer of hope in her eyes. 'I know.' She replied.

∞

Early the next morning Adam had been summoned by Ah Kin, and he now found himself lying down on the living room floor with the Chilan sat cross-legged beside him with his hands hovering above his abdomen and chest. He felt cold as he lay there shirtless with his bare chest exposed waiting for something the happen. The Chilan was in deep meditation and had an unsettling expression across his face. As Adam looked up at him all he saw were the whites of his eyes. Smoke wisped out of the incense burning nearby and filled the room with an earthy, sweet scent. Almost ten minutes had passed in complete silence and Adam started feeling stupid laying there. He began wondering whether or not the Chilan actually had any real powers at all. He lay there and his mind recalled an interview he once watched of a reporter who showed a so-called psychic a photograph of a young girl who had supposedly disappeared many years ago. The psychic went into horrific detail describing how the young girl died a gruesome death many years ago. The reporter then explained that the photograph was in fact just an old picture of herself as a child and that she had never been abducted, let alone murdered. It was car crash T.V. at its best. The psychic was left gobsmacked and was exposed on national television as a fraud and stormed off the set. Since then, Adam never really trusted anyone who claimed to be psychic. But as Adam lay there he began feeling a strange sensation creeping up his neck. Not on his skin externally, but internally just below his head. It felt like a wave of overwhelming calm as if he'd been drugged with a powerful sedative. The wave crept up slowly, climbing up and was now at the base of his head. Suddenly the wave of overwhelming euphoria crashed down over his brain and Adam's eyes rolled back into his head. Everything went black.

Adam woke up in a strange place. He was standing in the corner of a child's room. It looked familiar but he couldn't quite place it. It looked like an old photograph he'd once seen. The decor was dated and although the things around him looked old, they also looked new, like polished items in a charity shop.

Adam was standing in the corner and noticed that he wasn't alone in the room. On the other side against the large window of the bedroom was a crib and a cute chubby baby boy was holding on to the wooden side rail as he stood there trying to balance on his own two feet. Adam was about to walk towards the baby but suddenly the bedroom door opened and startled him. He froze as he watched a man in his early-twenties walk into the room. He recognised the man instantly. He looked just like the old photos his mother had shown him; it was his father, Joseph.

As Adam stood there he realised that he was living through a memory. This was his old house, and he was standing in his old room. *Why am I in my own memory as a third person?* Adam concluded that this must be a dream. But for some reason, no one could see him in this dream. He was like a ghost. He watched his father lift the baby out of the cot and cradled him in his arms as he sat on the rocking chair. It was strange for Adam to see himself as an infant in what felt like real life. It was like being in a virtual reality home movie. He stood there watching his doting father smiling, tickling and playing with the baby. Then suddenly his father looked up at the ceiling and said 'Pay attention now, this is why you're here.'

Adam froze. *Is he talking to me?*

Without any further explanation, his father turned back towards the baby and began singing a lullaby that Adam had long forgotten.

> *'In far off lands where many people go,*
> *Is a place of hope where a power is stow,*
> *A dangerous place, where people will die,*
> *But not you my son, for your father am I.*
> *Twenty-Six-Eighty-Eight-five.*
>
> *Hands make the sacred bird chirp its song,*
> *To the South is buried the treasure you long,*
> *The warmth of the stones will bleed you my son,*
> *Call for help if there's nowhere to run.'*

Adam listened carefully and tried to make sense of the cryptic verses. The lullaby wasn't familiar at all, but he knew it was related to the stone somehow. It was a clue. *This is why I'm here!* The room started to get dim, darkness began to spread everywhere, but just before the room disappeared completely his father stopped rocking his chair and looked at Adam dead in the eyes. Adam's heart skipped a beat. *Can he see me?* Adam tried to say something but words wouldn't come out.

'I'm with you son, always.' His father reassured as the room vanished into a black hole. Adam felt his consciousness returning. He opened his eyes and he was back on the living room floor with Ah Kin grinning over him.

'You've done well Adam.' Ah Kin said with a smirk across his face.

Adam rubbed his eyes. 'How long have I been asleep?' he asked.

'Just over three hours,' replied Ah Kin 'but it's been a productive use of time. We now know where the stone is, and we know that you are our key.'

SURVEILLANCE

The walkie-talkie crackled to life 'What's the status report?' Belkin asked.

'It's quiet. Not much I can see from here.' Sash replied as she lowered the binoculars. 'We need to get ears inside Belkin.'

'Sash we don't have time to bug the house. Anything you can do?'

'Maybe.' She paused and thought it through. 'I'm gonna try something.' Sash lowered the walkie-talkie down and sat upright in the car. She placed her fingertips to her temples and tried to focus on visualising the electronic pulses emanating from the building. Each electronic object had a vivid individual colour. Her consciousness became like a high-frequency scanner, picking up electric energy signatures of everything around her. She focussed specifically on the house Adam was being held in, and drowned out the rest of the electronic noise around her. Now inside the house, she began silencing the louder electronic energies emitted from appliances and electronic objects and tried to tap into the tiny mental electronic pulses emitted by the human brain.

Just then the walkie-talkie crackled back to life. 'What's going on?' Belkin asked. 'There's a strange interference on this line.'

The sound broke her concentration. 'It's just me Belkin. I'm trying to tap into Adam's mental electronic energy.' Sash explained. 'The brain is constantly firing off little electronic pulses to send signals. Recently I've been able to see their signatures. If I can just tap into Adam's electronic signature I might be able to communicate with him telepathically.'

'Outstanding!' Belkin boomed. 'I had no idea you were capable of such a feat. I'll leave you in peace. Notify me as soon as you make contact. I want him to know we're close.'

THE LULLABY

Adam sat up and tried to make sense of what he'd just experienced. Now that he was fully awake he knew that it wasn't just a dream. In truth, he wasn't sure what it was. Despite only hearing the lullaby once he couldn't get its verses out of his head. They circulated in his mind over and over again like the chorus of a catchy pop song.

'That's all for now.' Ah Kin said as he dismissed Adam.

'Wait, what was that?' Adam turned and asked the Chilan. 'What did you do to me?' He snapped as he rubbed the back of his neck still feeling the after effects of the tingling sensation on the back of his head. But the Chilan just stared at him blankly.

'You relived a memory.' Ah Kin explained. 'A memory you didn't even know you had. A memory buried deep in your subconscious. A memory your father clearly expected you to access someday.'

'Wait, how do you know I saw my father?' Adam perplexed.

'You were sleep talking.' Immanuel interjected. 'It's part of the process. Everyone sleep talks through these things, it's the only way we can trust the process. You didn't think we'd simply rely on you telling us everything we needed to know did you?'

'I... I... I would have.' Adam stammered.

'Well fortunately for us we don't need to rely solely on your honest nature.' Immanuel smirked.

'The lullaby is a clue.' Ah Kin explained. 'Every verse hints at something. We already know that the numbers are coordinates.'

'Coordinates? How can you be so sure?' Adam wondered.

'Let's just say, we know this location well.' Immanuel hinted.

'And the rest of the verses?' Adam inquired.

'We have our theories.' Ah Kin alluded. 'But we're going to test them out in the field, so to speak.'

'But I might be able to help you if-'

'I think you've done enough for now.' Ah Kin interrupted. 'Nikkita will be wondering where you've got to, perhaps you should go up and keep her company.'

Adam looked at Immanuel and then back at Ah Kin and realised that they weren't prepared to share any more about what they knew. He left the room and headed up the stairs back towards the bedroom. Suddenly, just as Adam reached the top of the stairs he felt the strangest feeling. He felt as if Sash were standing right behind him. He turned around, but there was no one there. 'Hello?' He whispered in an empty landing. There was no response, but Adam could feel Sash's presence as if she were a ghost haunting him. Suddenly Adam heard something in his mind. Like a clear thought, but in someone else's voice.

Hi, Adam.

'Sash? Is that... is that you?' Adam muttered quietly in disbelief.

I can't believe this worked! I have no idea how I'm doing this Adam, but I've somehow managed to tap into your minds electro-neuro signature.

'What! That's crazy. You're a telepath now?!' Adam whispered.

I guess so. My abilities are developing so fast that even I'm struggling to keep up with what I'm capable of. Wait, try thinking instead of speaking. I wanna see if I can pick up on your thoughts.'

Adam cleared his mind. *Err... Hello.*

Wait, did you just think "Hello"?

Yeah, I did. Adam thought back.

This is amazing. The colours are different when you think something compared to when you say something. I can see them, they're beautiful.

Sash, I gotta tell you something very important. These guys, they just put me in a weird voodoo trance and made me relive some old memory of when I was a baby, my dad was there and he was singing this lullaby to me.

Whoa, whoa, slow down... your father was singing you lullaby... what lullaby? Do you remember how it went?

Are you kidding? I can't get it out of my head!

'Hey, you!' Nacom yelled from the ground floor. 'Why are you just standing there?'

'Oh, err... just um, just looking for the bathroom.' Adam improvised.

'First door on your right.' Nacom replied with a suspicious look on his face.

'Oh, thanks.' Adam waved awkwardly. He opened the bathroom door and locked it behind him.

Sorry, Sash.... you still there?

I'm here. I've got a pen, tell me how the lullaby went.

Okay it goes like this; In far off lands where many people go, Is a place of hope where a power is stow, A dangerous place, where people will die, But not you my son, for your father am I. Twenty-Six-Eighty-Eight-five. Hands make the sacred bird chirp its song, To the South is buried the treasure you long, The warmth of the stones will bleed you my son, Call for help if there's nowhere to run.

Got it. It definitely sounds like your father's style. Did the Mayans give you any clues as to what it means?

Not really. They're not telling me anything, the only thing they've mentioned is that the numbers are coordinates.

Wait, I can look it up. Sash unlocked her phone and typed in the coordinates into her world maps application. *Got it... hmm... I thought so. I mean, where else would it be?* Sash sighed.

Where is it? Where's the stone?

Mexico Adam, they're going to take you to Chichin Itza.

They're taking me to Mexico? But I don't even have a passport!

These guys are resourceful Adam. Immanuel was a top Government official, arranging the paperwork to bring you into his home country won't be an issue for him. Just do what they say. We'll be close behind you.

Glad to hear it to be honest.

Is there any news on your mother and Nikkita? Are they okay?

Nikkita's here, but they said that they're keeping mum elsewhere and I won't see her until I get them the stone. What do you think? Can I trust them Sash?

What choice do you have? The only silver lining in all this is that Chichin Itza is where you need to be anyway. Your father was a smart man. You need to obtain the stone to amplify your powers and stop time at the top of the Kukulkan pyramid.

Kukulkan pyramid? How will I know which one is the Kukulkan pyramid?

It's the biggest one there. Trust me you can't miss it.

You guys are gonna be there too, right?

Of course Adam, we're right behind you, every step of the way. We've not developed you over all this time just to abandon you now.

'Adam?' Nikkita called from the hallway before gently knocking on the door. 'Everything okay?'

Sash, I gotta go.

I'll be in touch later Adam. Good luck, you're doing great.

Adam unlocked the bathroom door and pulled it open. 'Sorry, had to take a breather, that crazy witch séance down there took it out of me.'

'They're asking for you downstairs. Do you know what's going on?'

Adam forced a reassuring smile as he walked out of the bathroom and embraced her tightly. He finally let go and looked her in the eyes. 'They want me to go with them to Mexico and find the stone my dad hid. They think only I can get to it, and they kidnapped you and mum so I wouldn't refuse.'

'I thought you said your dad was...'

'Yeah he died, but on a mission just a few years ago, turns out he was working with The Fraction all along.

'Oh that group of friends of yours you mentioned last night?' Nikkita asked.

'Yeah.'

'Wow. This is all just so crazy.'

'You have no idea.' Adam alluded. 'Hey, when's the last time you saw my mum, do you know if she's okay?'

'Sorry Adam, I haven't seen your mum since that evening they took us. The big guy downstairs, Nacom, he came to your flat. I was there with her and she answered the door, but I haven't seen her since then. They took her somewhere. I don't know where.'

The response was unsettling to Adam and he was starting to fear the worst. He had no idea where she was and whether or not she was okay.

Adam and Nikkita walked downstairs into the living room together. Ah Kin and Immanuel stood there with passports in his hands. 'You're going to need these. We're going to Mexico, there's a flight that leaves from Heathrow tomorrow.'

'Why does Nikkita have to come? She's been through enough already.' Adam protested.

Nikkita held his hand. 'No Adam, I'll go with you, it's okay. I want to help.'

'Nikkita, I don't want you caught up in all of this anymore, if anything were to happen to you...'

'Listen Adam.' Nikkita asserted. 'Your mum is like family to me. I-'

'If you're both quite done!' Ah Kin finally interrupted. 'The point is moot, the girl stays. Once we get the stone you'll both be free to go, but until then you're both in this together.'

'And what about my mum?' Adam demanded. 'How do I know she's okay?'

'We don't harm our hostages.' Ah Kin assured. 'Like I told you last night, just look at Nikkita, she's proof isn't she?'

∞

Sash held the mobile to her ear as she started the car. After a few rings, it connected.

'I hope you have good news.' Belkin said as he answered the call.

'Something strange happened Belkin. I connected... I connected with Adam telepathically!'

'Excellent.' Belkin beamed.

'I've never done that before. I could hear his thoughts as clear as a bell from a block away. And it was two-way. He could speak to me and I could speak to him, completely telepathically.'

'How is he? What did he report?'

'He told me that they put him in some kind of trance, he saw a vision of his father telling him a lullaby as a baby.'

'A lullaby...?' Belkin repeated.

'Yeah, I've written it all down. There are numbers here that look like coordinates. I entered them into my GPS and guess what?'

'I don't need to guess Sash.' Belkin replied. 'Chichin Itza.'

'How did you know?' Sash wondered.

'I had a hunch the stone was hidden there. It's where I would have hidden it. I ruled it out since Joseph hadn't been on any missions in that area. I shouldn't have underestimated that man.' Belkin paused. 'But this is good, we can use this. I need to see the verses in that lullaby, and I need you to find out when they're leaving. How soon will you be back here at HQ?'

'Already en route, I'll be there in fifteen.' Sash hung up the phone and sped through the London traffic towards Knightsbridge.

MEXICO

Adam tried his best to sleep throughout the flight, but it had been a long seven-hour journey. The pilot finally made an announcement that they would be landing in twenty minutes. Adam was sat next to Nikkita and they held hands as the plane made its final descent.

They were all dressed in casual clothes and tried to draw little attention to themselves as they headed through passport control. Adam's heart was pounding as he approached the front of the queue. He was certain his fake passport would be spotted. The official gestured him over and he walked towards the desk. The man took his passport without saying a word. He analysed the picture for what felt like an eternity to Adam. He looked at Adam up and down and finally scanned the passport into the computer.

'What's the purpose of your visit?' The official asked in a stern tone.

'Holiday.' Adam replied as confidently as he could. He recalled the brief that Ah Kin had given him during the flight should he be questioned.

'Where will you be staying?'

'Err... the Ryu Cancun hotel.'

'Ryu?' There's no hotel here by the name of 'Ryu.

Adam felt a surge of panic run through his body and wracked his brain. 'Sorry, I meant Riu, Riu Cancun.' Adam chuckled nervously.

The official didn't seem impressed. He clicked a few buttons on the computer's keyboard and finally stamped Adam's passport and handed it back to him.

'Have a good holiday Mr Lambert. Next!'

A wave of relief washed over Adam. 'Thanks.' He smiled.

Adam walked towards the baggage claim exit and found Nikkita standing next to Ah Kin and Immanuel.

'Everything okay?' asked Immanuel.

'Yeah, he asked a few questions, but it's cool, no drama.' Adam replied with a huge sigh of relief. *This is it, I'm in Mexico!*

MEXICAN PYRAMIDS

The following day Belkin, Sash, Raj and Sofia landed in Cancun International Airport. Ali was ordered to remain back at HQ in case Raj needed anything from any of the hard drives from the computers in the office. The team were sat on the seats in the baggage reclaim as Raj stood by the carousel waiting for his forth suitcase.

'Hey, Mariah Carey are you sure you didn't forget anything?' Sash joked.

'Ha-ha, very funny.' Raj replied sarcastically. 'For your information, I've barely brought any personal items. All this is important tech I need to keep The Fraction running smoothly. Do you have any idea how hard it was to arrange a trip to South America so suddenly for all your jokers?' Raj turned back towards the carousel. 'Ah, here it comes, the last piece.' Raj reached out and grabbed the silver hard shelled suitcase.

'Anything else?' asked Belkin.

'No, that's everything.' Raj hoisted the suitcase onto the overloaded trolley as they began walking towards the exit. 'Yeah don't all rush to help me or anything!' Raj complained as he struggled to balance the mountain of luggage on the trolley.

'Mexico is a big place Belkin, how are we going to find Adam?' Sofia wondered.

'We're going to Chichin Itza.' Belkin replied. 'Sash made communication with Adam a few days ago. We know that's where they're headed.'

'Mmm... did someone say Chicken Pizza?' Raj called out from behind the pile of suitcases he was pushing.

'No silly,' Sash chuckled. 'He said Chichin Itza!' Sash turned back to Sofia. 'It's an ancient sacred Mayan heritage site. It's where the Mexican's built their pyramids.'

'I had no idea the ancient Mexican's built Pyramids too?' Sofia admitted. 'Did the Egyptian empire come this far out?'

'No, the Mayan pyramids aren't related to the ones the ancient Egyptians built.' Sash explained. 'The Egyptian pyramids were tombs with temples attached, whereas the Mayan pyramids were more like public temples, they were places of rituals and celebrations. Although the shape is the same, their architecture has differences.'

'Impressive, I learn something new every day.' Sofia beamed. 'It's amazing that civilisations so far apart would create such similar structures. I mean, of all the shapes in the world, what was it about pyramids?'

'It's quite fascinating really.' Sash continued. 'Some historians have even claimed extraterrestrial involvement. But it's all just speculation.'

'Damn, dirty aliens!' Raj yelled from behind as he shook his fist comically.

The team exited the airport and stood by the roadside. Belkin approached a man who handed him a key and gestured towards the Range Rover he was standing beside. Belkin turned back towards the group. 'Load up and get in. This is us.'

With the luggage loaded up and the group sat in the car. Belkin pulled off and headed towards their apartment in Chichin Itza.

'I'm still thinking about what you said earlier.' Sofia said as she turned towards Sash who was sat beside her in the back of the car. 'I mean, I know all about the Egyptian pyramids, and the wonder that they are, but for another ancient civilisation to also have them. You wonder where they got their technology from. It's got to be alien right?'

'Possibly.' Sash reasoned. 'But the ancient Mayans were very smart people. They created complicated calendars mapped out using astrological reference points that made their calendars highly accurate. Their mathematics and understanding of astrology was considered highly advanced for its time.'

'Sash, have you tried connecting with Adam again?' Belkin looked through the rear view mirror and asked.

'Yes, every chance I get, but I'm not getting anything. We must still be too far apart from each another. Maybe they're already in Chichin Itza. Or maybe they've gone somewhere else.'

Belkin reflected silently for a moment. He checked his watch again. 'Try again once we get closer.'

QUIET REFLECTION

It was the end of their first night in Cancun and the beach area in front of the hotel was almost deserted. It was a remarkably warm night considering it was December and Adam made the most of it as he watched the waves crash against the shore. He watched Nikkita as she walked along the beach in the surf under the moonlight. He felt emasculated realising that he'd failed to rescue her from the predicament she was in. He had surrendered himself to save her and his mother, and here he was half way across the world having saved neither of them. His heart sank as he wondered how he was going to get out of this situation and be the hero The Fraction thought he was. He felt as though he was spiralling into depression. He decided to take a deep breath and stay positive by counting his blessings. *No, I should be grateful.* He sat there and began thinking about things he should be grateful for. *I'm still alive... I have my time stopping abilities... I have... Nikkita.* He sighed as he watched her slowly walking back over to him. Her small shorts accentuated her long slender legs as they glistened in the moonlight. *She's so beautiful.*

'We should get back.' He called out as she approached.

'I think that's what he's coming over to tell us too.' She said as she pointed behind Adam. Adam turned his head around to take a look at what she was pointing at and he realised Nacom was walking towards them.

'Ah, Kin wants you both back in your room. We're leaving for Chichin Itza early in the morning. Get up, let's go.' He ordered.

THE HIDDEN MESSAGE

With the team fully briefed and up to speed on all the details of Protocol 8F, Belkin asked Raj to project the lullaby on to the wall.

'For those of you who knew Joseph, you will know that this isn't just some random lullaby.' Belkin explained.

'He sang this to Adam as a baby?' Raj remarked. 'It's dark man, I'm surprised he didn't grow up to become a serial killer!'

'Raj behave, this is serious.' Sash scolded.

'Now let's analyse these verses to see what we can find.' Belkin started with reading out the first half of the lullaby. 'In far off lands where many people go, is a place of hope where a power is stow, a dangerous place, where people will die, but not you my son, for your father am I. Twenty-Six-Eighty-Eight-five.'

'Okay, so let's start with what we know, the coordinates 20.6-88.5 lead here, to Chichin Itza. Sash hasn't been able to pick up Adam's electro-neurological signature telepathically so we're assuming he's not here yet.'

'My range is improving.' Sash informed. 'I'm up to a range of around three-clicks. As soon as he arrives I'll know it.'

'My guess is that they're going to wait for tomorrow to arrive.' Sofia hypothesised. 'The morning of the 21st. From what you told us earlier Belkin, I think they'll seek the stone tomorrow and whether they find it or not, they'll want to be here to witness the apocalypse themselves at midnight.'

'Your reasoning is logical.' Belkin concurred.

'So what's with the third line?' asked Raj. 'A dangerous place, where people will die? This place looks pretty tame to me, who's going to die around a tourist spot like this?'

'Are we sure it was 'will die' and not 'have died'?' Sofia asked. 'From what I researched about this place, long ago people held ritual sacrifices at this Kukulkan pyramid, but no one dies here anymore.'

'No, he definitely said will,' Sash confirmed. '...people will die.'

'Great.' Raj sniggered. 'Thank God I'm tech support. Good luck you lot!'

'Such an ass.' Sash huffed as she rolled her eyes.

'We're seasoned field ops professionals people. Everything we do in the field is life or death.' Belkin reminded. 'It's a deterrent for others, not us. The important thing is that whatever the risks are, they won't affect Adam.'

'Ah yeah.' Raj agreed. 'Look, it says; but not you my son, for your father am I... pssh' Raj whinged. 'Alright for some, eh?'

'Adam's safety is paramount.' Belkin reminded. 'Joseph knew this, so whatever dangers loom in this mission, the lullaby suggests that they shouldn't be hazardous to Adam. But we can't become complacent and take that for granted.' Belkin nodded at Raj, and Raj tapped on the keyboard to display the second half of the lullaby. Belkin began reading. 'Hands make the sacred bird chirp its song, to the South is buried the treasure you long, the warmth of the stones will bleed you my son, call for help if there's nowhere to run.'

'Hands make the sacred bird chirp its song.' Belkin repeated. 'I think I know where we need to be. Raj, pull up the overhead site map for Chichin Itza.'

Raj pressed a few buttons on the laptop and a birds-eye-view of the area popped up. It detailed the pyramids, ruins and temples in the area with their sizes to scale and proximity to each other. Belkin pointed to a large pyramid near the centre.

'This is the pyramid of Kukulcan also known as The Castle pyramid. It has a unique feature in that if you clap your hands from a specific location outside it, you get an echo of a bird chirping.'

'What?' Raj gasped in disbelief. 'That's so cool. What a real bird?'

'No.' Belkin clarified. 'It's a unique acoustic illusion. No one really knows how they achieved it. But I've heard it myself. It's quite remarkable. If you stand here, on this spot and clap,' Belkin pointed to a spot about fifty yards from the base of the pyramid. 'you can hear a bird chirp back to each clap.'

'So to the South is buried the treasure you long.' Sash added. 'South of that would be... The Temple of the Warriors.' She pointed. 'The stone is in the Temple of the Warriors!'

Belkin faced the map and reviewed it thoroughly. Sash was right. Just south of the bird chirping location lay the Temple of the Warriors. 'Sash I think you might be right.'

'But what about the rest of the lullaby?' Sofia wondered. 'The warmth of the stones will bleed you my son?'

'I believe that only once we're at the Temple of the Warriors tomorrow will we understand what the rest of this lullaby means. That particular verse seems specific to Adam.'

'I've been searching all day.' Raj chimed in. 'So far the research has pulled up nothing about warm or hot stones in this area. It's a mystery, folks.

'We will have to do some investigating.' Belkin instructed.

'Would the Mayans know?' Sofia asked.

'Possibly.' Belkin considered. 'Why, what are you getting at?'

'Well if we get there tomorrow morning before they do and spy on them, we can let them lead the way. If they crack the code we can then follow them and see where they lead us. We know where to find them; The Temple of Warriors. We just need to get there early and stake out the site.'

'It's a good plan.' Sash beamed.

'I like it.' Belkin agreed. 'Okay, listen up here's how we're going to play this...'

THE SECRET OF THE TEMPLE

Ah Kin led the group towards The Temple of Warriors early the next day. The ancient temple was in ruins. The white stones that would have once shone brightly were now a dirty ivory and covered in moss from centuries of neglect. A hundred stone columns twelve feet high that once supported the ceiling of the temple protruded from the floor at the base of the temple. The temple looked like an incomplete pyramid. The structure was over a hundred feet high and situated at the top of its steep steps was a partially demolished temple room. Ah Kin led the group through the columns at the base of the temple searching for any clues as to a secret entrance.

'Keep an eye out for anything unusual.' Ah Kin ordered to the group.

'This whole place is unusual!' Nikkita sniggered as she looked at Adam.

'The warmth of the stones...' Immanuel recalled. 'The lullaby said something about the warmth of the stones. Everyone spread out and feel the stones as you pass them.'

The group dispersed and began feeling the stones that made up the temple's base. Despite the Mexican sun shining brightly, to Adam they all felt cool to the touch. As Adam walked around he reflected on the lullaby, a feeling in his gut made him want to explore the area behind the temple. Ah Kin noticed Adam disappearing around the corner and decided to follow him. Adam felt the stones around the corner of the temple and despite the rear wall being in complete shade, it felt slightly warmer to the touch than the stones out front in the sun. He had a feeling he was on the right track. He kept walking and finally reached the far left corner at the rear of the temple. The stone wall was unusually warm back here as if it were being heated from the inside somehow. The stone layout at the rear of the temple was different from the front. It wasn't made up of smaller stones stacked on top of each other. It was made up of larger stone blocks, some up to six feet tall. But in the far left corner, the stones became small again, some as small as bricks. It was inconsistent with the rest of the rear of the building and seemed unusual. Adam placed his hands on the smaller stones here and realised that they were almost hot to the touch.

'Find anything interesting Adam?' Ah Kin boomed as he suddenly emerged out of the corner. Adam almost jumped out of his skin. He didn't notice that Ah Kin had been following him.

'Err, not sure.' Adam confessed. 'The stones are really warm back here but I can't find any sign of an entrance.'

Ah Kin walked around Adam to take a better look at the wall. 'Wait a second...' Ah Kin touched a few stones and seemed to have noticed something. He stepped back, and then stepped back again, his eyes transfixed on the wall the entire time. He took a third step back and then smiled. 'Immanuel!' He yelled. 'Get back here with the rest of them!'

Adam tried his best to see what it was that Ah Kin had noticed but he didn't notice anything unusual about this part of the wall other than the fact that the stones used here were smaller. Immanuel and the rest of the group rushed around the corner and joined them.

'What have you seen?' Immanuel asked excitedly.

'Come and see for yourself.' Ah Kin said as he gestured him to stand where he was stood. Immanuel positioned himself next to Ah Kin. 'Do you see it?' Ah Kin asked with a grin across his face.

'Good lord... that's amazing.' Immanuel marvelled.

Nikkita wondered what all the fuss was about and out of curiosity walked to where Immanuel and Ah Kin were stood. She gasped as she realised that the small stones on this wall created an elaborate image of a nine-foot high coiled snake. It was so subtle that unless someone was looking for it, the pattern would have gone completely unnoticed. 'Adam, come see this.'

Adam joined Nikkita and marvelled at the image. 'Whoa. That's cool.'

'Chilan! Chilan, do you see it?' Ah Kin exclaimed.

The Chilan stood next to Ah Kin and took a few slow steps towards the image all the while reciting something under his breath. He stopped directly in front of the image and raised his hand and placed it on top of the stones that formed the snakes head. His chanting became louder and louder as he started moving his body and jerking his head strangely as if he was being possessed. Adam was so fixated on the Chilan that he didn't notice the image of the snake had begun to change colour. Within just a few moments the image began to glow bright red and looked like it was scorching hot. Suddenly and without warning the Chilan grabbed Adam's arm and in one swift motion drew out a blade and sliced open Adam's palm. Adam yelled in pain and instinctively pulled his hand back. But Ah Kin grabbed him from behind and forced his bleeding hand onto the burning hot image of the snake's head.

'AAARGH!' Adam screamed in pain.

Almost immediately the entire structure of the snake began crumbling inwards. Dust and debris fell everywhere as a large hole appeared in the back of the temple. The Chilan and Ah Kin pulled Adam back to safety as the stones collapsed.

'What the hell!' Adam yelled at them in anger.

'Apologies Adam.' Ah Kin said half-heartedly. 'You must really blame your father. He locked the entrance with blood. Only a blood descendant would have been able to break the lock and open it.'

'Seriously?' Adam scowled. 'I mean, I don't mind if you need my blood but a bit of warning would be nice.' Adam moaned as he blew on to his seared palm.

Nikkita ran towards him to tend to his hand. 'Show me.' Nikkita said as she gently wiped his hand. 'Wait it's not bleeding.' She noticed.

'The heat sealed the wound.' Ah Kin explained. 'He'll be fine. After all, we wouldn't jeopardise his safety, especially now that we're so close.' Ah Kin grinned.

'I'm okay.' Adam assured her. 'Just in shock, my hand's fine. Thanks.' He smiled. He looked at the gaping hole in the back of the temple and noticed now that there was a lot of warmth radiating from within it. As he looked around at the group he realised everyone was staring into the black void.

'Inside, go!' Ah Kin commanded as he nudged Adam towards the dark void. Adam let out a deep sigh and crept towards the opening. He peered inside, as he held his hand that was still stinging from the burn. Noticing that there wasn't any immediate danger he raised his leg over the edge of the hole and placed one foot inside. It was dark and unusually warm. He couldn't see anything but he felt safe now that he was completely inside. He turned on the light on his watch and the bright turquoise light illuminated his surroundings. He suddenly noticed the LED display on his watch had a message on it.

Don't worry, we're close.

His heart pounded with anxiety hoping no one else had seen the message. He quickly pressed a button and the message disappeared. He turned around and faced the rest of the group. 'It's fine. I'm not dead, see. All you chickens can come in now.' He teased as he flashed his watch's light again and illuminated the walls inside. He realised that a couple old fire torches were placed on the wall. He lifted them off the sconces bolted to the inside of the wall and held them up. 'So, who's got a lighter?'

ALL IN

Hidden in plain sight Belkin, Sash and Sofia stood by the pyramid of Kukulcan dressed in hats and sunglasses and blended in with all the other tourists. But their attention wasn't on the striking pyramid, it was further to the south, and they took turns in peering over at the Temple of Warriors for signs of Adam or Ah Kin.

'I've just spotted Adam.' Sash announced discreetly. 'He's there walking around the back of the temple.' Sash glanced around casually and then faced Belkin to give him an opportunity to look behind her.

'We've got to keep a low profile, but we need to keep eyes on him.' Belkin said as he watched Ah Kin follow Adam to the back of the temple.

'What about those trees?' Sofia suggested. 'We can find cover there at the edge of the forest and keep an eye on them. It's discreet and the view will probably be better.'

Belkin surveyed the area and realised that it was their only choice. The trees would provide the best cover, keeping them out of sight whilst having a clear view of Adam. He looked back at Sofia and nodded. 'Agreed, let's go.'

∞

In the darkness of the forest's canopy, they walked through the trees until they got a clear vision of Adam and the others. Belkin noticed the Chilan chanting.

'What are they doing?' Sofia asked.

'Looking for an entrance.' Belkin replied. 'Stay down.'

They watched as the events unfolded and Adam entered the hole in the temple.

'What are you doing Sash?' Belkin asked as he noticed Sash press her fingers to her temples.

'Transmitting a message.' Sash explained. 'It's too risky to make two-way communication right now. I'm sending Adam a message on his watch. I want him to know we're here.'

They waited until the group had all disappeared inside the temple. Belkin finally stood up straight from behind the tree. He looked at Sash and Sofia. 'Are you both ready for this?' Belkin asked. 'It's going to be dangerous in there.'

'I've been waiting for this day for years Belkin.' Sash reminded. 'I'm not backing out now.'

'Sofia, you?'

'I'm part of The Fraction too aren't I?' Sofia smiled. 'Let's do this.'

...INTO THE VOLCANO

Adam held the torch above his head. Its fire was burning bright as he led the group through the dark passageway. Nikkita walked closely by him and locked her arm in his as they both crept gingerly into the unknown. They turned a corner and the passageway was engulfed in darkness. They could barely see six-feet ahead at any one time and Adam had no idea what might lie ahead.

'Stop!' Ah Kin ordered suddenly. He seemed to be focussing on something on the wall beside them. Immanuel, who was at the back, walked past the Chilan and Nacom and stood beside Ah Kin to see what had caught his attention. They exchanged glances and both began to grin. Adam turned and looked at the wall. It was covered in strange engravings. Like symbols or hieroglyphics.

'This is it. We're here!' Immanuel exclaimed giddily. He walked towards Adam. 'Well done my boy! You've done it!' Adam felt a strange hollow sense of accomplishment. 'All these markings are ancient hieroglyphs, they're warnings. We must tread carefully. No sudden moves everyone. This place is filled with danger. This must be where the stone was first discovered.' Immanuel marvelled.

Ah Kin grinned. It seemed that Immanuel was finally as excited to witness the stone's power as much as he was. 'Lead us to the stone boy.' He commanded. 'I know it's here. I can feel it.'

Adam continued walking and the path started descending steeply. Every step he took he felt the air around him get hotter, the flame of the torch above his head only making the heat all the more unbearable. 'Why is it so hot down here?' He turned to Ah Kin and asked.

'Legend has it that this temple was built on top of a volcano. It hasn't erupted in thousands of years, but it held spiritual significance to our Mayan warrior ancestors who offered sacrifices into it for blessings in battle.'

'So let me get this straight.' Adam gasped. 'We're walking down into a volcano?!'

'Well technically son, none of this should exist.' Immanuel chimed in. 'These secret tunnels, aren't part of the temple above. These tunnels were considered myth, folklore!'

'Your father was a smart man.' Ah Kin admitted. 'Not only was he aware of this place, he navigated its depths and hid the stone here before casting a blood spell on its entrance. It seems there's more to your father than you or I know. Too bad he was fighting for the wrong side.'

Adam felt a pinch in his heart. 'Maybe he was smart enough to realise where the right side really was!' He retorted.

'You have no idea...' Ah Kin muttered.

'No idea about what?' Adam asked unsure about what Ah Kin meant by that. But Ah Kin just ignored him and didn't continue the conversation any further.

The stone corridor came to an abrupt end and they were now all stood in a large square room with stone walls all around them. Everything from the ceilings to the floor was just hollowed out parts of the volcano that had been excavated and hand chiselled thousands of years ago.

'We seem to have come to a dead end.' Immanuel remarked.

Adam and Nikkita looked around. He was right. They were in a simple box shaped room about thirty-feet squared. Other than the light provided by the two torches held by Adam and Nacom the room was completely dark.

Nikkita turned to Adam. 'Did we miss a turn somewhere?'

'No.' Immanuel replied. 'The Mayans were never going to make it easy to get to their treasure.'

'Wait... treasure?' Nacom replied with a sound of excitement in his voice. 'I like the sound of that.'

'What treasure?' Adam wondered. 'You mean the stone, right?'

'Well,' Immanuel began. 'we weren't sure if your father hid the stone in the ancient Mayan Catacombs.'

'What's a Catacomb?' Nikkita asked.

'It's an ancient underground cemetery.' Ah Kin replied. 'And only the best of the Mayan leaders, astrologers and sorcerers were buried there.'

'That's right.' Immanuel continued. 'The ancient scriptures say that at the brink of their extinction before the Spanish invaded around five-hundred years ago the elders gathered up the cities wealth, which was mainly gold, silver and gems, and buried it within the sacred volcano.'

'And no one went looking for it?' Adam asked.

'Well, how could they?' Immanuel reasoned. 'The maps and riddles the Mayans used to document this place were only discovered thirty years ago by an archaeologist from New Zealand. He deciphered the text, broke the code, and discovered that the treasure was buried here.'

'So if he knew, why didn't he come after it?' Nikkita asked.

'He did.' Immanuel continued. 'But after he came to explore the area and found no volcano or sign of treasure he published his findings in a book and portrayed the whole thing as a myth. He said that the Mayans were symbolic people and hypothesised that the volcano and treasure were a metaphor.'

'So is there treasure or not?' Nacom moaned, clearly confused.

'In his book, he translates the code, and when you translate it, it reads. 'The wealth of the Mayans went down the volcano.' Not buried, or hidden. They use the word *down* suggesting they sacrificed it to their Gods by throwing it into the volcano's lava.'

'Do you think it's a metaphor? Nikkita quizzed. 'Or do you think it could still be down here?'

'Until this morning I didn't even believe these catacombs existed. Now I'm open to any eventuality.'

'I hope it does exist.' Nacom grinned.

'If the history lessons are over,' Ah Kin jibed. 'may we please find a way out of this room? Nacom, Chilan, I want you both to use the torches and find a way out of here, there must be a hidden passage here somewhere. Shine a light on the walls and work your way around. See what you can find.'

Adam handed over the torch to the Chilan who followed Nacom's lead and began scouring the walls of the room for anything that looked unusual.

It had been ten minutes and Nacom and the Chilan still hadn't come up with anything. It seemed that the room was just a room. No lever, no hidden buttons, just a dead end. Adam sat down on the floor and examined his palm trying to test how well it'd healed by stretching it open. 'Ouch.' Despite the burn sealing the gash, it was still raw and painful. He began to get a strange feeling. It felt as though he'd been here before and felt a sense of Déjà Vu. Suddenly a familiar voice chimed in his head.

How you holding up champ?

Adam sat there wide-eyed and in stunned silence. Instinctively he glanced around to make sure no one else heard the voice. He immediately relaxed once he recognised that it was Sash, and that she was communicating telepathically. He tried not to act excited at the sound of her voice.

Thank God. Where are you guys?

We're right behind you. You left a big gaping hole in the temple we had to patch up, didn't want Tourists following us down here now did we?

I'm so glad to hear your voice. How far down the tunnels are you?

We're about sixty feet behind. We can see the light from your torches. We're holding back till you move ahead. But you guys aren't moving anymore. What's the holdup?

That's the problem, we can't move, we've checked every corner of this room, it's a dead end.

Dead end? Wait, a sec.

Adam felt the disconnection with Sash inside his mind. *Man, that's such a weird feeling.* He sat in silence for about six-minutes watching the others look for clues before Sash re-connected.

Adam, you there?

Hey! Adam replied in his mind hoping for some good news.

Belkin's just found something, you need to tell Ah Kin to retrace his steps, there's a hidden lever back here in the passage towards us. They need to send someone back here to yank it. But it can't be you Adam, we have no idea what this thing does, so it's probably best for you to stay there. Got it?

Yeah. Okay.

I mean it Adam, anyone but you.

Alright, alright, I get it. I'll stay put.

The connection went dead and Adam felt in control of his brain again. Adam looked around to see if anyone had noticed his telepathic conversation, but everyone just seemed busy looking for a way out. He casually stood up and walked to Nikkita who was standing by the entrance. He put his arms around her and gave her a reassuring hug. 'You okay?'

Nikkita looked into his eyes and smiled. 'Yeah, I'm okay.' She assured enjoying the unexpected affection.

'Hey.' Adam said as he turned to look at Immanuel. 'Maybe someone should check back up the way we came in. Maybe there's something we missed before coming into this place.'

'Good thinking young man.' Immanuel praised. 'Nacom, go back up the passage and take a look.' He ordered.

'And take Nikkita with you.' Ah Kin added.

Adam's heart skipped a beat. 'Why does she need to go?' Adam protested as he tried to hide the concern in his voice.

'She goes. You stay.' Ah Kin looked at Nacom and waved his hand.

Nacom walked over to her and gestured her towards the passageway. 'After you Miss.' He grinned.

Adam didn't know what to do. He stood there in a daze as he watched them leave. His mind whizzing as he tried to think of a way to keep her by his side without letting on that he knew something they didn't. He realised that any further protest would raise suspicion. He looked at her as she walked away with Nacom. Just as she left the room she turned back and gave Adam a reassuring look and silently mouthed *It's okay.*

Adam watched them ascend the narrow tunnel slowly checking the walls as they did. He turned his back and found a dark corner and began praying. *Please God...keep her safe.* For once he was glad it was dark, no one could see him worrying.

Ah Kin had been quietly observing Adam for a while now. Something was not quite right. Sending the girl was insurance, he knew Adam was up to something but he knew he wouldn't do anything stupid if she was at risk.

Adam tried to connect with Sash. He wanted to inform her that Nikkita was with Nacom and see if she could give him any advice, but he couldn't connect.

'I've found something!' Nacom's voice bellowed back from about thirty feet up the passage. 'It's a lever. I think it's connected to the room. I'm going to pull it to see what happens.'

Ah Kin darted to the entrance and shouted back. 'Wait don't-'

But it was too late. The earth shook underfoot and dust started falling from the ceiling. The room was moving. Adam stood up quickly and almost lost his footing as he clung on to the wall and noticed that the entire room was sinking down. The opening to the passage was slowly disappearing into the ceiling, as the room descended like a giant elevator going down to the floor beneath.

'Hey! What's going on?!' Nacom yelled.

Then Adam heard Nikkita scream. 'We have to stop this!' Adam yelled at Immanuel over the thunderous noise.

Immanuel rushed to the shrinking passageway entrance. 'Pull the lever back up!' He yelled.

Large stone chips were crumbling off the ceiling and the walls as the room continued to descend. The passage entrance was now half the size of what it was when they first walked through it. Suddenly a new faint orange light illuminated the room and Adam noticed that a new exit was emerging below. It was an opening to a lower level. He could now see half of the original passage entrance above and half the new exit below. 'Run Nikkita!' he shouted through cupped palms. 'Run!'

Nacom pushed Nikkita aside as he darted towards the disappearing gap. Nikkita fell to the floor and banged her skull hard against the wall. She screamed in pain as she grabbed her head. She looked up and watched Nacom toss the torch and sprint back towards the room. He slid across the floor and fell through the gap and collapsed in a heap back into the room. She saw that the entrance was closing fast and the passage she was in was also crumbling, she had to move now. Adrenalin surged through her veins and she jumped to her feet. She ran as fast as she could as she dodged the large sharp rocks falling in her path from above her. The earth was shaking violently and she struggled to keep her balance as she ran towards the room. She was close now, only a few yards away, but the large entrance to the room was now barely a two-foot tall gap from the floor. *I gotta make it!* She dived and threw herself to the ground thrusting her arms through the gap.

Adam saw her arms poke through. It was tight, but she could make it. 'Crawl through! He yelled. 'Quickly, c'mon!' Everyone was staring up and watching as Nikkita used her arms to scoot forwards and push her head through. The ceiling mercilessly continued to descend down on her. The gap was now barely a foot tall. Her chest was through as she shuffled on her stomach as fast as she could. Adam reached up and grabbed her hands and pulled, she was now through to her stomach and then suddenly she stopped. She was wedged around the waist and her hips wouldn't slide through.

'I'm stuck!' She gasped as she looked into Adam's eyes.

'Push!' Adam yelled. 'Don't give up!'

Nikkita looked down at Adam one final time. 'I'm sorry.' She sobbed with a smile across her face. Suddenly she let out a bone chilling shriek so loud that it temporarily muted the thunderous noise of the room descending. It was a sound that would haunt Adam for the rest of his life. He then heard something snap loudly and her lifeless body fell limp. The room ground to a halt as her dead torso wedged itself in the small cavity.

'NO!' Adam screamed. 'No, Nikkita wake up!' He let go of her hands and reached for her face lifting it in his palms. 'Get up!' He looked up to the ceiling and screamed 'AAARGH!' Adam couldn't contain his grief, he felt as if he was about to explode. 'AAARGH!' He yelled again.

'Calm him.' Ah Kin ordered Nacom.

Nacom grabbed Adam to restrain him and calm him down. But Adam kicked and bucked like a wild horse. Despite the orange light now filling the room, his vision was going dark and everything was fading to black. He couldn't stop screaming 'AAARGH!' Suddenly, as clear as a bell he heard a voice in his head. It was a man's voice. A voice that was familiar but he couldn't quite place. *You know what to* do. *You have to focus!* Immediately Adam stopped screaming. He panted hard as he struggled to control his breathing. His eyes were closed and blood started dripping from his nose. Suddenly everything became completely dead silent. He opened his eyes and his vision was misty, there was a mist of purple plasma all around him. It engulfed the entire room. Adam realised that Nacom was frozen and was no longer holding him down. He slipped out of his grip and looked around. Everything around him was now perfectly still. Everyone in the room was frozen solid and they all looked like wax mannequins. The room had stopped moving, and everything was silent. *I've stopped time.*

Adam staggered back. His rage subsided as he looked around in awe at what he had done. The entire room was engulfed in electrically charged purple plasma. It was the biggest time orb he'd ever created and it had frozen everything in the room. Adam slowly raised his hands, he had no idea what he was doing but instincts were taking over. He visualised time as a reel of wire in his palms and began slowly reeling the wire back. He saw tiny sparks of purple electricity dance in his hands and forearms. In ultra slow motion the events that took place just moments before repeated themselves, but this time in reverse. He saw a ghostly image of himself standing next to Nikkita pulling her hands. He reeled back faster, and faster and faster and as he did so he saw everything rewind. Nacom disappeared back up through the passageway entrance that was now growing back to its original size as the room started to reset itself. The more Adam reeled back the weaker he was beginning to feel. He was quickly becoming physically drained and a pounding headache almost debilitated him completely. Nevertheless, he persisted and continued to reel back further and further. He could barely stand now and he noticed that he'd reversed time to the point where Nikkita was about to walk out of the room with Nacom. *Just a bit further.* His head felt like it was going to explode, the focus, attention and mental effort this process took was enormously demanding. Finally just as he felt he was about to pass out he stopped. A ghostly shadow of himself was sat by the far wall looking at his cut palm. He walked towards it and instinctively he knew exactly what he had to do. He sat down into his own ghostly apparition and replicated the exact posture.

Like being suddenly awoken from a daydream Adam was back in the room. The migraine had disappeared and his breathing was back to normal. *Ouch.* The familiar sting in his palm brought back an indescribably vivid sense of déjà vu. Right on cue Sash came through telepathically.

How you holding up Champ?

TAKE: TWO

Hi, Sash.
I see you're getting used to these conversations, it almost sounds like you were expecting me!

Listen Sash, I know you are wondering why we've stopped, it's because we can't move ahead. This room seems like a dead-end, but it's actually an elevator and we can't find the lever.

Wait, how-

Look I can't explain right now. But you need to do me a favour. You need to throw a lever located about thirty feet away from the entrance of this room. Be discreet. I'll make sure no one comes out there in the next few minutes. We're going to drop down. This entire room will drop down. You need to follow us down afterwards.

Wait, what are you talking about, slow down.

Adam took a deep breath. Sash this may sound crazy but I think I just turned back time. I've been through this with you already. Our first plan didn't work out too well and Nikkita died. You must pull the lever so we all go down together otherwise... otherwise Ah Kin will send her out again. Once we're down try pulling the lever back up, get into this room and it will take you down too. It's just like a big elevator. Just make sure you get to it quickly when it's your turn, it doesn't give you a lot of time and it starts moving straight away.

Adam, I need to talk to Belkin about all this. Sit tight, I'll reconnect in a moment.

Adam's mind went silent. He looked around and noticed that Immanuel had also begun searching the walls for hidden clues. *C'mon, c'mon...* Adam sat there nervously praying for Sash to reconnect before someone decided to search back down the passage and jeopardise his plan.

Adam.

Yes, yes I'm here.

Belkin trusts you. We'll do it your way. Keep them out of the tunnel and we'll find this lever.

A sigh of relief washed over Adam. *Thanks Sash, and don't worry. I'll keep them here.*

Adam felt Sash disconnect with him. He stood up and pretended to investigate the walls. He pretended to find something interesting. 'Hey Nikkita, come check this out.' Nikkita walked towards him. 'What do you make of these marks?' Nikkita stood by him and examined the wall. The Chilan was close by and the light from his torch softly illuminated her face. Adam just stared at her, soaking her in. In the dim flicker of the torch fire she looked even more beautiful. Her hair fell to one side and was tucked in behind her ear on the side closest to him. He gazed at her soft cheek as he resisted the urge to lean in and kiss it. He couldn't take his eyes off her. Suddenly he recalled her blood-curdling shriek as her back snapped and it instantly jolted him out of his lustful gaze.

Nikkita sighed in disappointment. 'No, I don't think that's anything.'

Ah Kin began walking towards them 'What is it?' He asked as his curiosity got the better of him.

'Just these markings.' Adam replied as he continued to fake interest.

'Bring that torch here.' Ah Kin ordered the Chilan. With the light now illuminating the wall, it was obvious that there was nothing remarkable about this section of the wall. 'It's nothing. Just chisel marks caused by sculpting and excavation.' He huffed, annoyed to have wasted his time.

Just then a familiar sensation began again. A thunderous noise boomed as the earth began to shake underfoot and dust started falling from the ceiling as the room started descending. Nikkita screamed in fright and clung on to Adam.

'Don't worry.' Adam reassured calmly. 'Just stay close.' This time, Adam was ready. 'Nikkita, sit down!' he yelled over the noise.

'Are you crazy? This place is falling apart! Let's get out of here!' She yelled back as she headed towards the passage entrance.

'No! Trust me!' He pulled her back and stared into her eyes. 'Trust me.'

Nikkita felt confused. *How is he so calm?* She watched as Adam sat back down on the floor, a picture of tranquillity amidst the chaos ensuing around them. Despite her trust in him, her survival instincts overpowered her and her body refused to sit down with him. Suddenly a violent shudder shook the ground and she fell on her knees. Adam grabbed her and pulled her close. Feeling more stable on her knees she looked around and realised that the walls seemed to be moving upwards. This whole room is moving down!

Ah Kin propped himself up onto his hands and knees, he noticed a new orange light illuminating the room and he noticed Adam sitting remarkably calmly on the other side of the room. Something about his demeanour and reaction to this didn't feel right. Ah Kin wondered if Adam was somehow familiar with this place, expecting this somehow. The orange light began to fill the room, and the room became brighter. Ah Kin noticed the light was flooding in from a second doorway that was emerging from the floor below. The entrance they first came through was now high above them and slowly disappearing into the ceiling.

As the room slowly came to a standstill Adam felt something scratching his back. The room was pretty well lit now and he noticed that a small five-inch gap appeared as the room reached its finally resting point. He realised that the gap ran across the bottom of all the walls. *Hmm, didn't notice that last time.* He slowly got to his feet but then felt that odd scratching on his lower back again, and now his leg was itchy too. He reached around to scratch his back and felt something weird. *What the heck!* Something moved on to his hand. He pulled his hand away quickly and instinctively flicked his arm violently and sent something the size and weight of a baseball hurtling off. It bounced off the wall and scurried off. Adam instantly recognised what it was. The way it crawled was unmistakable. He'd seen plenty of tiny versions of this creature in his bathtub back in London, but this one was huge, and hairy.

'Adam your leg!' Nikkita shrieked.

He looked down, and there, clinging to his shin, was another huge black hairy spider. His heart froze. Without a moment's thought, he kicked his leg in the air as hard as he could and unknowingly flung the creature directly at Nacom. The Tarantula hit Nacom square in the face, bounced off and swiftly crawled away.

'What was that?!' Nacom yelled as he frantically wiped his face.

'The Burrowing Red Kneed Tarantula.' Immanuel clarified as he watched the spider scurry off into the darkness.

'Oh my god!' Nikkita cried. 'I hate spiders!' A strange faint sound began to fill the silence around them. Suddenly, out of the gaps in the walls, thousands of spiders scurried out, blanketing the ground as they poured in.

'Run!' Nacom screamed.

They scrambled through the new doorway that emerged below and into a narrow rocky passageway. The surface of the walls here was sharp and rocky and they all did their best to avoid being scratched as they shuffled through as fast as they could out of the room. Adam was running near the front of the group with Nikkita close beside him gripping his hand as they ran through the narrow rocky passage. After about twenty yards down the passageway Immanuel, who led the group, tripped on something and he stumbled, narrowly avoiding falling flat on his face.

'Damn it!' He yelled as he looked down noticing a snapped trip wire. He stopped quickly and turned to warn the rest but it was too late. A loud cracking sound boomed in the narrow passageway and the floor began collapsing behind them. Nacom was at the back of the group and was stamping on the spiders as he ran. But suddenly, just three feet behind him the floor broke away and crumbled into a void beneath. It was breaking away too quickly and the group was blocking the narrow passage in front of him. There was nowhere he could go.

'Aaargh!' Nacom yelled as the floor crumbled beneath his feet and he plummeted into the darkness. The Chilan fell next, followed quickly by Ah Kin.

Adam turned around and watched Ah Kin disappear into the ground. There was no time, he barely had a moment to think. 'Hold on!' He yelled at Nikkita.

Suddenly the floor disappeared beneath her feet and she fell, her hand still clasped tightly in his, dragging him down with her. For a moment Adam felt completely weightless as he fell into the darkness. The dust got into his eyes and blinded him as he kept his eyes tightly shut. He landed awkwardly on his legs after the shortfall but he avoided any real injury.

'Are you okay?' He yelled at Nikkita over the thunderous racket. Dust billowed everywhere and she coughed uncontrollably as she nodded back with her eyes still closed wafting away the dust. Just as Adam was about to get to his feet and check on the others a small rock fell from above and struck him on the back of his head. Everything went black.

A DIFFERENT PATH

Belkin, Sofia and Sash watched the room descend and its entrance disappear. The route ahead was now blocked but they realised that something was different in the passageway. Just a few feet away the wall moved revealing a small opening. Sash tried pulling the lever back up hoping the room would ascend back up, but it was jammed.

'Give me a hand with this.' She asked Belkin. They both pulled up as hard as they could on the thick iron lever almost bending it in the process. But it was stuck fast and wouldn't budge.

'Guess there's no other choice.' Sash huffed as she nodded towards the small gap in the wall.

Sofia analysed the gap. 'Are you sure this will take us to the same place Adam went?' She asked with obvious concern in her voice. The gap that appeared was dark, barely four feet tall and just three feet wide.

'Like I said,' Sash reiterated. 'there's no other choice.'

Belkin walked over to examine the end of the passageway where the entrance of the room once was. 'Sash is right. We're not getting through here and that lever isn't bringing that room back up. That path is our only route.'

Sash noticed Sofia beginning to hyperventilate and took her hands in her own. 'Hey, don't worry.' She comforted. 'Just stick close to me, you'll be fine.'

Belkin squatted down to examine the opening, it was dark and visibility was poor. 'We're going to have to crawl.'

He pointed out. He got onto his hands and knees and led them into the narrow darkness. 'Let's not procrastinate any longer.'

THE CINVAT BRIDGE

Hey!... Hey! The voice was familiar. Adam was floating in darkness searching to find where the sound was coming from. *Wait. I know that voice.*

'Hey! Hey! Wake up! Adam, can you hear me?' Adam was immediately dragged out of his warm cocoon of dark peace and opened his eyes to a shooting pain in his head.

'Aaargh.' He winced. 'My head.' He looked up and his eyes focussed on Nikkita as she hovered over him.

'Hey, are you okay?' Nikkita asked again. Her forehead was cut and two thin streaks of blood ran down her face.

'Oh my God, you're bleeding.' Adam noticed as he sat up momentarily forgetting about his own pain. 'Are *you* okay?'

'I'm fine,' Nikkita smiled happy to see Adam wasn't seriously injured. She wiped her brow. 'it's just a small cut. You've been out for a couple of minutes, you had me worried.' Adam looked around and the whole group was shaken up. Everyone was bloodied and bruised and was dusting themselves off. He looked up and noticed that they had fallen about ten-feet or so. It was the debris, dust, and falling rocks that did most of the damage.

'Well, at least the spiders are gone.' Nacom remarked as he stared up at the broken path above. 'Hate spiders.'

'We're committed now.' Immanuel conceded as he too stared up at the broken pathway above. 'We can't go out the way we came in. We're in this till the end, and we are going to have to find a new way out.'

'Wow, it's even hotter than before.' Adam remarked as he flapped his t-shirt.

'Yeah, and while you were passed out, we realised why.' Nikkita replied. 'Check it out.' She pointed to the side and Adam noticed that they were on a rocky pathway that dropped off completely on one side. Adam slowly stood up and gasped in awe as he looked around at his surroundings for the first time. About a hundred feet beneath them ran rivers of boiling hot lava. The orange and yellow bubbling streams of molten rock illuminated the giant cavern they were in.

'W-w-we're... we're in an underground... volcano.' Adam stammered in shock.

The path they were on was barely a few yards wide and ended in a sheer drop straight into the bubbling river of magma beneath.

'Are you sure the stone is down *here*?' Adam perplexed as he considered the notion of someone hiding anything in such a volatile and dangerous place.

'Look at this place,' Ah Kin beamed with his arms spread wide. 'is there a more fitting place to hide the most powerful object in the world?'

'This place looks like hell.' Nacom whispered.

Ah Kin led the group down the path deep into the volcanic cavern. The heat was intense and taking a toll on all of them. At some sections the path narrowed drastically and was barely a few feet wide. Adam precariously followed the path and kept his feet away from the crumbling edges. Every step was carefully placed as he used his arms to balance himself across. They stopped as they approached what appeared to be a forty-foot wide gap in the trail. Adam had seen it coming a while back and assumed Ah Kin had a plan, or maybe he'd seen a route from up front that Adam missed.

But as they stood there at the precipice of the gulf he realised there was no alternative route. There was no way across to the other side.

'You have got to be joking.' Nacom wailed as he surveyed the hopeless scenario before him. 'All this way and now we get stuck here!'

Ah Kin ignored him and continued to walk until he reached the edge of the broken path.

'Careful Ah Kin.' Immanuel called out.

Ah Kin crouched down and dusted off the edge of the path. There, on the floor etched directly onto the stone, were ancient Mayan hieroglyphs. *Cinvat*.

'So, what now?' Adam huffed.

'Cinvat Bridge.' Ah Kin whispered. He stood up and turned to Immanuel. 'Cinvat Bridge!' He cried out loud.

'No...' Immanuel gasped in shock. 'No, it's a myth. It's not a real thing.'

'I didn't think so either my friend, but here, see for yourself! Ah Kin beamed as he motioned towards the etchings on the floor.

Immanuel marched towards the edge of the path and glanced down. 'It can't be.' He said as he marvelled at the symbols etched on the floor. 'It's... it's true.' He chuckled. 'It exists!' He exclaimed as he exploded into a hysterical laughter.

The Chilan walked past Adam and Nikkita without saying a word and joined the others on the edge of the path. He crouched down to review the markings for himself. Satisfied, he finally stood up and turned to face Ah Kin and nodded slowly.

'So, why exactly are we all happy about this?' Adam asked completely perplexed.

'We must cross here.' Ah Kin declared.

Adam frowned in confusion as he glanced at Nikkita. He took another look at the vast gap between the two sides and the flowing lava that ran beneath. He looked back at Ah Kin none the wiser. 'What we gonna do, fly across?' He sniggered.

Ah Kin didn't seem amused. 'Only our deeds can carry us across now.' He replied.

'Our deeds?' Adam scoffed. 'How are our deeds going to help us cross? I mean, you may not have noticed but there is nothing here. This Cinvat Bridge of yours has gone. It's probably eroded over the centuries and collapsed from all the heat down here.'

Suddenly the Chilan began chanting and a dark smoke began to swarm around him. The Chilan chanted louder and faster and the smoke became thicker and thicker and it began to take form. The smoke was now dense, almost solid as it manifested into what looked like a creature made of black fire hovering in the air. The creature extended its misshapen arm out towards the Chilan and he took hold of it. The Chilan then walked to the very tip of the path and without breaking his stride stepped onto thin air.

Adam and the rest of the group watched in stunned silence as the Chilan continued to walk calmly, chanting as he did, across the invisible bridge above the fiery river of lava beneath as he held the hand of the black demon.

'What is that thing?' Nikkita whispered.

But Adam didn't hear her. He was mesmerized as he continued to watch as the Chilan made it all the way to the other side unscathed. He stopped chanting and the dark fiery demon spun back into a black smoke and vanished.

'How did he just do that?' Adam gasped in utter shock.

'It's the Cinvat Bridge.' Immanuel explained. 'I have only ever heard legends of it, but here it is right in front of me.' Immanuel stared at the Chilan who was now sat cross-legged on the other side patiently waiting for the others. 'Legend says that it's your deeds that manifest themselves into creatures. If you have been a selfish, self-serving person having achieved nothing for yourself or others your guide will be weak and you will fall. But if you've been noble and good, upright and honourable your guide will be strong, solid and guide you across with ease. Of course, the guide can come in any form. Everyone's guide is unique.'

'Wait, so what you're saying is that if you're evil' Nikkita interjected. 'You won't be able to cross?'

'Actually, evil is almost always only a matter of perspective. Someone you consider evil might be considered by someone else as a hero.'

'So who decides who's worthy and who's not?' Adam asked.

'Did you see how the Chilan crossed just now with his guide?'

'Yeah.' Adam and Nikkita both replied in unison.

'Well, the Chilan has done things that most laws would have him locked up for. He's killed and hurt many people. But his intentions have always been noble, he's doing what he's always felt has been right according to his beliefs. He's dedicated his life to his gods and his guide is drawing strength from that faith. In his own way, he's been completely selfless, obedient and honourable.'

'So what you're saying,' Adam surmised as he tried wrapping his head around the concept. 'is that if you're devoted to whatever you believe in, you'll be okay?'

'Exactly.' Immanuel confirmed.

'Even if what you believe in seems crazy to everyone else?' Adam quizzed.

'Yes.'

'Okay, I think I get it.' Nikkita nodded. 'You only need to worry about falling if you've not believed in anything, or have just lived for yourself and been selfish.'

'Precisely.' Immanuel affirmed.

'But what if you're neither good nor bad?' Nikkita asked. 'What if you're just a normal average person who doesn't really believe in anything?

'Those people my dear, are the ones who need to worry the most.' He warned.

Nacom, having paid no attention to Immanuel's guidance rushed to the edge of the bridge. He reasoned that whatever magic just took the Chilan across would be used up if he didn't act fast. There was no way he was being left for last. As he stood on the precipice waiting for something to manifest he looked down in terror at the bubbling lake of lava below. He gulped hard and began to pray to the gods for help. Suddenly a yellow mist began to appear and the faint outline of a young boy appeared in front of him. The boy was transparent like a ghost and stared at Nacom silently. Its empty eyes somehow peered into Nacom's soul. Nacom felt reassured seeing that something had manifested for him and he reached out but the boy's extended arm was too short. He reached out again extending his arm fully but his hand couldn't quite reach the boy's. He realised that he had to leap out and grab it. Nacom turned around and looked at Ah Kin for advice.

'Go.' Ah Kin stated flatly. 'He's your guide. He'll catch you.'

Nacom looked back at the ghostly boy. He gulped hard and drew a deep breath. He took a few steps back and then yelled as he ran and leapt into the air towards the apparition. The ghostly boy reached out and was just able to grab Nacom's arm in time. Nacom dangled helplessly in thin air as the boy slowly began trudging to the other side, struggling to carry his weight.

'C'mon!' Nacom yelled at the ghostly boy as he glared down at the gushing river of lava beneath. 'C'mon you weakling move it!' But the more he kicked and flailed the more the ghostly apparition weakened. Nacom was now dangling by his arm over the middle of the gap and the young boy was barely visible. 'No!' Nacom screamed as he realised how faint the apparition was becoming. Suddenly the boy's faint outline spun away and disappeared. 'No!' Nacom yelled as he tumbled down and splashed into the burning hot lava. '**AAAARRGGHHH!**' Nacom screamed as he flapped his arms frantically in the molten river splashing orange and yellow molten rock everywhere. His face peeled from his skull as his body charred in the heat. Nikkita spun around and buried her head into Adam's chest. She closed her eyes tight and covered her ears with her palms to drown out the screaming. Suddenly it went quiet. Nikkita slowly released her palms and looked up at Adam.

'I can't do this.' She whimpered as tears ran down her face.

Adam held her tight. He looked down in horror as he watched Nacom's lifeless torso drift with the current until it finally sank into the fiery river and disappeared.

Immanuel gulped hard, he turned to look at the rest of the group. 'So who's next?'

Adam looked at Nikkita. Her face said it all. It was obvious she was petrified. 'I can't do this Adam. I don't really believe in anything. I'm gonna fall. I know it.'

Ah Kin turned towards Adam. 'My magic will summon a guide strong enough to transport two others with me. You and Immanuel are coming with me.'

'But what about Nikkita?' Adam argued. 'If you think I'm doing anything for you if you leave her behind you can forget it!' He protested.

'Immanuel, can you summon magic?' Ah Kin asked.

'Never have never will.' Immanuel declared. 'You know I don't practice any of that stuff Ah Kin. If you want me on that side, you'll need to take me with you.'

'It appears we've reached a stalemate.' Ah Kin conceded.

'Take Nikkita.' Adam commanded. 'The three of you should go. I can make it by myself.'

'Wait Adam, are you crazy?!' Nikkita blurted. 'How are you going to get across? You don't know magic!'

'I have to trust my father.' Adam explained. 'He sent me here. He wouldn't have if he didn't think I could cross this thing. I can do it.'

'This is crazy! I'm not going without you.' Nikkita argued.

'Go. I'll see what kinda guide I get, and if it looks weak, I'll just find another way across.'

'Another way?! Adam what other way? There's no way you-'

'Hey.' Adam interrupted in a stern tone before taking a deep breath and calming himself down again. 'Please...just go. You'll see. Trust me.'

Nikkita stared into Adam's eyes. She wanted to trust him, but her heart was telling her to stay.

'Go. Now!' He insisted as he physically spun her around and marched her towards Ah Kin. 'Take Nikkita, I can make it across myself.'

'How valiant you are.' Ah Kin smirked. 'Surely a man of your morals will conjure up a beast of a guide and cross with ease.'

Adam watched as Nikkita begrudgingly stood beside Ah Kin and Immanuel at the edge of the broken bridge. Ah Kin tilted his head back and his eyes rolled back into his head. He began chanting in the same ancient language the Chilan was chanting in earlier. Ah Kin's recitation grew louder and louder as a thick cloud of green smoke manifested and began to take form. It was larger than any of the other apparitions Adam had seen and it grew and grew until it solidified into a ghostly boat. At the base of the boat stood the ghostly shape of a man holding a long rowing oar. Ah Kin was the first to step into the boat. Nikkita observed that he was sitting comfortably and it gave her the confidence to follow him into the ghostly vessel. Despite her reservations, the boat felt solid, although the sensation was unsettling. It was like sitting on a solid cloud. Immanuel swiftly joined them and the boat began to slowly glide across the air over the volcanic gulf. Nikkita did her best not to look down. Instead, she fixed her gaze back at Adam feeling terrible for leaving him behind.

As they approached the other side Ah Kin got to his feet and prepared to disembark. The boat pulled up gently as it reached the other side. Ah Kin stood up and was the first to step out onto the bridge, but as soon as he was on solid ground the apparition spun into smoke and the spell that kept the boat solid was broken. Nikkita and Immanuel leapt towards the edge of the bridge at the last moment but neither of them made it over. Nikkita held on to the sharp rocky edge of the bridge as she dangled perilously over the river of lava beneath. Immanuel was clinging on to a small crack in the cliff face by his fingertips.

'Help!' Nikkita screamed.

'I can't hold on!' Immanuel yelled.

Ah Kin threw himself to the ground and stretched out his arms over the edge. Nikkita grabbed hold and tried to pull herself up but she didn't have the strength to lift her body. Immanuel grabbed Ah Kin's other arm. But the weight was too much for Ah Kin and he began sliding over the edge himself. 'Wait Immanuel, you're too heavy!' He yelled. 'You're dragging me with you!' He cried.

'I'm not dying here Ah Kin!' He yelled back. 'Pull me up!'

The Chilan stood up and grabbed on to Ah Kin's legs. Ah Kin dug the toes of his shoes into the floor in an attempt to anchor himself, but his shoes didn't grip. 'I'm slipping you fool! Let go or we'll all die!'

But despite Ah Kin's demands Immanuel held on tightly. It was over, Ah Kin could feel it. He would die here today. They all would. He began to slide across the threshold and wondered how the Gods would judge his actions and deeds. *I was so close.* His torso was now completely dangling over the edge and suddenly Immanuel jerked his body in a final attempt to pull himself up. The force pulled Ah Kin over the edge and they all screamed in horror as they hurtled down into the bubbling river of lava below.

'**NO!**' Adam cried as he watched them fall. He instinctively stretched out his hand towards them and he instantly sent a powerful shockwave of purple energy that pulsed throughout the entire underground cavern. The energy froze everything in time and Adam gasped in awe as he witnessed the three of them suspended, froze in mid-air. The stream of lava stopped running, and the cavern fell deadly silent. Once again Adam could feel the thread of time in his hands as he began winding his hands backwards. His palms crackled with sparks of electricity. Right before his eyes time rewound itself and Ah Kin rose back up with

Nikkita and Immanuel until they were all dangling off the side of the rock-face again. Adam continued rewinding. His nose started to bleed as the strain of his power began to take its toll. He watched in reverse as Ah Kin was about to get off the boat but he kept rewinding time. He wasn't going to take any chances. The ghostly boat slowly drifted back towards him returning to his side of the bridge. His nose now bleeding profusely, but he persisted. He watched Immanuel get back off the boat followed by Nikkita and Ah Kin. He finally stopped rewinding time when he saw a shadow of himself talking to Nikkita persuading her to go with Ah Kin. He had to get into alignment with his own ghostly outline quickly, the headache was excruciating and he knew it'd all go away once he realigned himself. He stepped into his figure and copied his pose. Suddenly another pulse of light blinded the cavern and when it cleared he heard Nikkita's voice.

'Another way?! Adam what other way? There's no way you-'

'Hey.' Adam interrupted for the second time. 'Please...just go. You'll see.'

Nikkita stared into Adam's eyes just as she had done the first time.

'Go.' He insisted. This time, he pulled her in and tenderly kissed her on the lips. 'Just make sure you get off first.' He whispered.

'What?' She whispered back with a confused look in her eyes.

Adam spun her around and marched her towards Ah Kin. 'Take Nikkita, I can make it across myself.'

'How valiant you are.' Ah Kin smirked. 'Surely a man of your morals will conjure up a beast of a guide and cross with ease.'

'We'll see.' Adam replied.

Once again Ah Kin cast his magic spell and the boat appeared. But this time, the ghostly figure rowing the boat was staring directly at Adam. The three of them boarded the boat, and just before the ghostly figure began to row, it subtly nodded at Adam.

'Hey!' Adam called out as they began to set off. 'Just let Nikkita off first on the other side, this magic looks like it's only connected with you Ah Kin. If you get off they might fall.' A look of bewilderment was slapped across Ah Kin's face as he realised that he hadn't considered such an eventuality.

'Good thinking boy!' Immanuel replied with a hearty laugh. 'First Nikkita and then me, I'm not taking any chances either Ah Kin.'

Ah Kin sat quietly and watched Adam with curious suspicion. *How could this imbecile...?* But Ah Kin hushed his mind. *I'm on to you, boy...*

Before long the boat reached the other side and all three of them stood up. This time, Nikkita got off first, followed by Immanuel and then Ah Kin. As soon as Ah Kin stepped off the boat, the boat vanished and he realised that Adam was right. The magic was linked and they would have plummeted to their deaths had they not have disembarked first. Ah Kin darted his sight back at Adam. He looked overwhelmed with relief once he saw that they had all crossed safely. *He knew...* Ah Kin nodded. *He knew...*

THE MAYAN PUZZLE

Belkin, Sash and Sofia crawled through the small path they discovered and were led into a vast, dimly lit cavern. There was a large stone tablet on the wall about six-feet tall and five-feet wide. Within the large stone tablet there was a five-by-five grid of smaller stone tiles. Each tile had a different symbol etched on to it.

Sash walked over to the huge tablet. 'What do you think it is?' She asked Belkin.

Belkin stepped closer and shone his torch over the tablet. 'It says something. I know this language. The symbols are definitely ancient Mayan, but...' He paused.

'But what?' Sash wondered.

'The words,' He replied. 'they don't make any sense. The order is wrong.'

'Hey, guys!' Sofia called out from the other side of the room. 'Come check this out.'

Sash and Belkin walked over to where she was standing. 'Look, can you see that door, right up there? I've taken a look around and it's the only exit in this place. Maybe that's where we have to go.'

The gigantic door was suspended on the wall about thirty-feet high. Sash noticed that it was elaborately decorated with engravings and markings that shimmered like gold. 'Wow, was that made for giants?'

'It's beautiful though, right?' Sofia admired.

'But how are we going to get up there?!' Sash wondered.

'I think I might be onto a solution for that.' Belkin declared. He ran back to the tablet and shone the light on it and noticed a slide mechanism behind the stone tiles. 'Just as I thought, these stone tiles move. See this gap?' Belkin pointed to a blank space to the bottom right of the tablet. 'It's intentionally left blank in order for us to be able to...wait...' Belkin paused. He was done thinking. He knew what he had to do. 'Someone come and take this torch from me.' He ordered.

Sofia and Sash ran back to the tablet. Sofia took the torch from Belkin and kept the light shining on the symbols.

'What are you gonna do?' Sash asked.

Belkin didn't reply. His attention was transfixed on the tablet. He slowly raised his hand and touched the symbol above the empty space. 'Golden.' He read.

He tried to pull the symbol down into the blank space but the panel was jammed. He pulled harder and the piece suddenly slammed into the blank space causing a loud bang as the tiles slammed into each other

'Whoa!' Sofia yelled as she jumped in shock.

'It moves.' Belkin muttered. 'I knew it! Right, now we have to make sense of this. 'Sofia, your notepad please.'

Sofia swung her rucksack off her shoulder, pulled out the notepad and handed it to Belkin. He unclipped the pen and started translating the words. There were twenty-five tiles in total arranged in a five-by-five grid. Belkin's eyes darted from the notebook to the tablet and back, over and over again.

He'd been sketching, writing and rearranging symbols for almost fifteen minutes until he finally stopped and clicked the pen shut. He'd successfully translated the message and rearranged the words correctly. But his success was bittersweet as he read the translated text from the tablet.

'What is it, Belkin?' Sash asked, hoping that it wasn't as bad as it seemed.

'It's... nothing.' Belkin lied.

'Belkin,' Sofia interjected. 'If we're in some sort of trouble, you need to tell us. Don't keep us in the dark.' She could tell that Belkin seemed troubled by something.

Belkin let out a deep sigh. 'Well, there's good news and there's bad news.' He admitted.

'What's the good news?' Sofia asked. 'Good news first.'

'The words in front of us are arranged incorrectly and I've translated them and have successfully rearranged them in the correct order. Once that happens it should somehow lead us through that big door over there.' He pointed.

'And the bad news?' Sash wondered.

'Well maybe if I just read the translation out to you.' Belkin opened up the notebook and began to recite.

'The people of the tongue,
reach the Golden door.
The gods test the believers,
with their greatest fears.
Only the believers succeed.'

The group stood there in stunned silence for a few moments after Belkin had finished.

'Do you believe in all this Belkin?' Sash asked. 'Is this a warning for us now, or was this meant for the people who first created this place?'

'I don't know Sash. This tablet is ancient, constructed thousands of years ago, it could be nothing. But on the other hand, when it comes to supernatural phenomena anything is possible.

'So what are our options, Belkin?' Sofia asked.

'The way I see it, there are only two options.' Belkin surmised. 'Option one is that we turn back. Wait for them outside the temple and ambush them. But we'll have to hope that Ah Kin doesn't kill Adam and Nikkita the moment he possesses the stone.'

'And option two?' Sash asked.

'We solve this tablet's riddle and press on and take the risk. We find the stone and save Adam and Nikkita so that he can complete the mission and stop the alignment.'

'I'm not leaving him.' Sash declared. 'I'm sorry, but we have a very important person trawling through this hell hole with a very dangerous enemy. The only reassurance he has is that we're in here right behind him. So I vote to press on.'

'Sofia?' Belkin quizzed.

'I'm with Sash. In for a penny, in for a pound.' She smiled.

'I guess it's unanimous.' Belkin smiled. He approached the tablet and started sliding the symbols left and right, up and down. He began slamming the tiles around faster and faster, trying to figure out how to rearrange the symbols into the correct order. He worked on correctly arranging the top-left corner and worked his way down to the bottom right.

Ten minutes passed and he was finally about to slam the last symbol into place. 'Brace yourselves!' He slid the last symbol into its correct position and then stepped back. But nothing happened. Sofia and Sash looked at each other.

'Are you sure you got the order right?' Sash asked.

'I don't understand.' Belkin confessed as he checked the notepad again. 'It's perfect. All the symbols are where they should be.'

'Wait, what about this bit.' Sofia pointed out. She noticed that one of the last tiles on the bottom was blank and it seemed to fit perfectly into the final gap. She stood next to it and pushed it up hard until it slammed into place and completed the tablet. 'There.' She said as she dusted her hands clean.

Suddenly the room began to shake. Everything in the vast cavern felt like it was moving. A thunderous crack boomed from the wall beneath the giant golden door. The wall beneath the door began to move and protrude out in levels forming steps leading up to the door above. They stepped back as the steps clanged out to reveal themselves forming an opulent and extravagant stairway towards the equally opulent and extravagant door. Eventually, the entire mechanism stopped and the room became silent again.

Sash stood at the foot of the golden steps and looked up at the grand door. *Hang in there Champ.*

THE CROSSING

Adam stood as close to the edge as he dared. He waited for something to appear but nothing seemed to be happening. *Why isn't anything happening?* Adam shuffled a little closer and his toes were now poking over the edge. All he saw was the river of lava flowing below. Even this far up its heat was roasting him. After a couple of minutes, he realised that nothing was coming for him. He suddenly recalled what Immanuel told him when the Chilan was crossing. *Our deeds create our guides.*

'Nothing's happening!' Adam yelled across the bridge to the others. He began looking for other ways he could get across.

Ah Kin was worried that this might happen. He cursed himself for taking the girl. He thought he'd use her as leverage but she was useless if he wasn't able to make it across. 'Think Adam!' Ah Kin yelled back. 'What did your father tell you about this place?!'

'This place?' Adam yelled back. 'Nothing! He told me noth-' Adam stopped. Was that true, did his father give him absolutely no clues, no guidance in this situation? Adam's mind recalled the lullaby his father sang to him. It had brought him this far, maybe there was something he was missing. He recited it in his mind and analysed each word, each verse, but nothing seemed to jump out at him. *Hang on a minute.* He repeated the last two verses of the lullaby to himself slowly in a low whisper. 'The warmth of the stones will bleed you my son, call for help if there's nowhere to run.' He wondered if this was what his father meant. *It must be! I can't go forward I can't go back, I've got nowhere to go...*

nowhere to run. Adam took a deep breath and screamed out at the top of his lungs 'Joseph!' He yelled. He took another deep breath and cupped his hands around his mouth. 'Joseph!' He yelled out again. He felt silly yelling out his deceased father's name into the vast cavern but he couldn't think of anything else. He took a final deep inhalation and yelled again 'Joseph!' He coughed as he felt his throat become sore. He looked around in hopeful anticipation but still nothing happened. He fell to his knees dejected.

Nikkita's heart broke seeing Adam defeated and on his knees. She began to feel guilty for leaving him behind, and felt powerless to help him. Nikkita also fell to her knees. She never really believed in God, but after everything she'd seen today she came to the realisation that there had to be a creator. She closed her eyes and began to pray; *God, I believe in you. I really do. You are the all-powerful. Please help Adam. Only you can save us now.*

A single tear ran down her cheek and splashed to the rocky floor. But just as it did, something miraculous occurred. The splash instantly transformed into a tiny bead of pure white light and it began to grow. It grew rapidly and it began forming into what looked like a handrail made of pure white light. Ah Kin, Immanuel and the Chilan stepped back and watched on as the structure continued to grow and form a path and then another handrail on the other side.

Immanuel gasped in awe. *The Cinvat bridge!*

The light expanded and grew and it was growing back towards the other side, back towards Adam. It became more and more elaborate in design as it weaved itself into an architectural marvel. It was now half way across and the intricacies of its details began forming, its elegant handrail, the parapet, its short towers, all made out of the same beautiful and translucent white light that shone like crystal.

Adam looked on in utter disbelief as he saw the most beautiful and extravagant display of magic he'd ever witnessed. The bridge had now reached his side and had completed its formation. Adam stepped onto it and looked down at the bridge's base. Its arches beneath were suspended in mid-air, but while he stood on its surface it seemed as solid as white stone. *Is this a dream?* He touched the handrail, almost expecting it to disappear once he did. But it felt firm and solid in his hand.

Ah Kin and Immanuel stood there in silence, marvelling at the spectacle. Ah Kin knew that this was not the work of any guide. He knew that this intervention must have been divine. 'Angels...' He whispered. Ah Kin extended his hand to touch the bridge, but his hand passed straight through it as if it were merely a hallucination. Immanuel saw what Ah Kin was trying to do and witnessed his hand pass straight through. He reached out himself and his hand too passed straight through. Neither of them could touch it.

'It's for Adam.' Nikkita said as she stood up smiling. Her face wet with tears of joy. 'God did this for him.' She beamed.

Adam slowly began walking across marvelling at the bridge's beauty as he did. *I'm walking on a ghost bridge made of light! This is so awesome!* He chuckled to himself in disbelief. As he crossed he could see the river of lava beneath him but he felt no heat from it. In complete contrast, a cool breeze wafted over him as he walked across and a subtle fragrance of sweet musk filled his nostrils providing a sense of inner refreshment that he couldn't quite describe. He approached the end of the bridge and took his final step off. He turned around and the bridge burst into millions of individual atoms of light and dispersed up into the air.

'How awesome was that!' He exploded, as he turned back to face the group with a huge wide grin.

Nikkita ran over to him and threw herself into his arms. 'You moron!' She cried. 'I thought you'd be stuck there forever!'

Adam embraced her tightly. 'Sorry I took so long. You know me... I like to make an entrance.' He bragged.

Ah Kin felt a pang of envy and didn't want to give Adam the satisfaction of basking in his glory. 'If you're both quite done!' He huffed. He turned around and walked passed Immanuel and the Chilan to continue down the path that led to a large crack in the wall ahead of them.

Immanuel walked up to Adam and smiled. 'That was some powerful guide there sonny.' He confessed. 'Truth be told,' he continued. 'I've never seen anything like it.' He rested his hand on his shoulder. 'There's definitely something about you kid.' With that, he turned around and followed Ah Kin and the Chilan through the gap in the wall.

Adam smiled and for the first time felt he had the confidence to do what he was here to do. *I'm gonna save the world.* He walked over to Nikkita and put his arm around her shoulders. 'Thank you.' He whispered as he looked up.

A PERSONAL TOUCH

As they ascended the golden steps, Sofia marvelled at the size of the door. She approximated that it must have been at least twenty-feet tall. As they arrived at the top of the steps they noticed that a wheel mechanism, similar to that of a vault, kept the door locked. Belkin began pulling it and felt the internal bolt slide. With the door unlocked Sash and Sofia pulled the door's handle with all their strength and the door crept open just wide enough for Sofia and Sash to slip through. Belkin let go of the wheel and dashed through the gap just as the door swung shut. The wheel spun back and the door locked itself once again.

'Well, there was no way back now.' Belkin observed as he walked into the room. 'So, what is this place?' He wondered as he began to look around. Sofia and Sash were unusually quiet. He spun around and realised that they had both disappeared and he was completely alone. His eyes darted around the room. 'Sash?' He called out. But there was no response. 'Sofia!?'

The only sound echoing in the room was the sound of his own footsteps. He descended a set of steps in front of him and entered a brightly lit circular space below. It was wide, about forty-feet in diameter and looked like a shallow pool that had been drained of its water. The round recessed area had a strange pattern on the floor. *Where are they?* He spun back around and looked back at the giant door from which they'd entered. It was still there, its presence dominating the room and its golden gleam shimmered in the darker outskirts of the room. He suddenly felt like something was watching him. He felt someone's eyes on the back of his head and a strange presence. He spun around and gasped in shock to find an idol of a Mayan God suddenly situated in the middle of the circular area. It looked like it hadn't been moved in thousands of years. *Where did that come from?!* The room around him began to go dark, only the recessed circular area where he stood was now lit. He was drawn towards the statue. From the corner of his eye, he saw something move from behind it. 'Who's there?' Belkin shouted. 'Show yourself!' He slowly approached the idol and clenched his fists tightly, ready for anything.

∞

Sash was relieved once Belkin dashed through the door. Keeping that door open took all her strength, but she was glad they had all made it. She turned to survey the room they were now in. There were steps leading down to a circular area below and the area was brighter than the rest of the room. 'Hey guys you know-.' But she froze in shock as she turned back and realised that no one was there. Confused, Sash scanned the area. 'Guys?' She yelled out. 'This isn't funny.' But she knew better than to think that Belkin and Sofia would play games with her at a time like this. 'Ah, what the hell?' She muttered. But she knew that the Temple of Warriors held secrets. She had done her research, known about the Gods and the sacrifices they demanded, the tests they imposed. But knowing it and living it were two different things. No amount of research could have prepared her for what she was feeling right now as she took cautious steps down into the circular area of the room. Sash descended the steps and began to look around to see where all this light was coming from. She glanced up and it felt like she was staring into the sun. She winced and looked back down. 'Ah!' She jumped. She froze in terror as she gazed upon the face of a strange looking stone idol. *That was not there a second ago!* She immediately recognised the idol as a depiction of the Mayan god Ah Puch. She racked her brain. *Ah Puch, Ah Puch, what is he the god of?* Suddenly she recalled reading about him and her heart began pounding like a drum. *Oh no... Ah Puch, God of the underworld.* She whimpered.

Sofia walked slowly towards the large stone idol. Her friends had disappeared and she was left alone in the room with a strange stone statue that had suddenly appeared out of thin air in front of her. The idol was made of a dark grey stone and had menacing red eyes that seemed to radiate with a dull red light. It was dusty and old as if it had been untouched for thousands of years. Its face was intimidating and its gaping mouth seemed to want to suck the soul straight out of her. On top of its head, its crown was detailed in gold with a jaguar carved into the middle of it. Above that, a large bird of prey stood proudly with wings spread wide. The statue's arms were bent at the elbows with open palms. One palm faced down and the other faced up. It wore a large necklace with a human shaped skull hanging on it like a pendant. *What the heck is this thing?* She wondered. She took a few steps towards the idol but then stopped dead in her tracks. A strange echoing noise began to resonate from within it which grew louder and louder. A black smoke began swirling around the idol and it grew thicker and thicker and began taking form. Sofia stepped back but a strange mix of fear and curiosity overcame her and her legs felt like tree trunks rooted into the floor. The smoke grew thicker and thicker and she could now see the outline of a giant man forming. As he solidified Sofia guessed that he must have been nine-feet tall. He draped a black cloak over his shoulders and wore a large black hat that covered most of his face. The smoke dispersed and now only the man remained. Sofia couldn't take her eyes off him, she finally mustered the strength to take a step back, and as she did so she noticed that he had no feet, he was hovering a few inches off the ground, his legs just faded into flickering black smoke. The echoing stopped and the apparition slowly glided towards her.

'Stop.' She ordered. 'Who are you?'

The ghostly figure stopped, it was still a few yards away. He tilted his head to the side and a horrible whispering sound emanated from him that seemed to surround her. 'You know me, Sofia.' He hissed.

Sofia grimaced at the sound of his voice. He sounded like the devil himself. 'I don't know you!' She exclaimed. 'What do you want from me?' She asked. The demonic apparition seemed to find her anxiety amusing.

'You *do* know me, Sofia,' he hissed back. 'I am the reason you can do the things you do.'

'Do what?' She barked back. 'What can I do?'

'Your dreams Sofia, I am the reason you can see the future.'

Sofia froze and stared at him in stunned silence.

'Listen to my voice Sofia, isn't it familiar to you? Isn't this the voice that recites you your dreams every morning as you write them down? Listen to my voice Sofia. Listen... to... my... voice.'

Sofia felt her knees go weak. Now that she thought about it, its voice did feel familiar. It was the voice she heard during her nightmares. She recognised it now. she knew this voice and the realisation paralysed her in fear. The sound of his voice flooded back memories of terrifying and vividly realistic nightmares she'd had.

'Yes.' He hissed. 'That's right, you know me don't you. Did you think you could just take and take without ever paying me back for the gifts I've shared with you?' He raised his arms out towards her and the loose sleeves of his cloak began twitching. Sofia wanted to run, but her feet failed her. He had her under his spell. She couldn't move. She stared at his baggy sleeves with dread wondering what he was about to do. She noticed something falling out of his sleeves and onto the floor. They were tiny pinkish-white things, and at first, she couldn't quite make out what they were. But they became thicker and larger, and now some were black and some were brown, all falling onto the floor in slimy clumps. Instantly her wonder turned into disgust and horror as she watched hundreds and hundreds of slimy mealworms, giant centipedes, spiders and beetles spew out of his sleeves in an endless stream.

Sofia collapsed back in horror and noticed the slime had reached her feet and the mound of bugs was slowly crawling towards her. The slime began to spread all over her as if it had a life of its own. She couldn't escape it. She screamed at the top of her lungs. But it didn't do any good. The slime became extremely sticky and stuck her to the ground pinning her down. The bugs were now beginning to creep all over her. Hundreds of them started crawling all over her body and getting into her clothes and hair. She screamed louder. 'Help me!' She cried again and again. She shrieked so loud that her throat felt like it was on fire. The demon lowered his hands and started cackling with laughter, revelling in her torment. The slime and bugs had completely coated her body, she shook her head to keep her face clear, but it was no use, she was overcome and her fate was sealed, the slime finally crept over her face. Everything went black as she closed her eyes.

As Sofia lay there in darkness her subconscious mind came alive. In that moment of complete despair when all hope was lost, she decided to accept her fate and give up. She lay there, unmoving, waiting for the sweet release of death. But then something strange happened. With her eyes closed and in utter darkness she saw a tiny white dot. *Is this it? Is this what happens?* She wondered in the vast emptiness of her mind. The light grew brighter and larger and she realised that something bright was coming closer. As it neared it began to take a human shape. There was something very familiar about this person. It was a woman. When she finally recognised her, she felt her heart skip a beat. *Mother!* The sight of her mother looking so radiant and beautiful brought her to tears and she began to weep in her dream like state.

'How are you, Sofia?' Her mother's angelic form replied in an eerie echoing voice. She appeared dressed in two pieces of white unstitched cloth wrapped around her. She radiated with a beautiful green aura.

'I'm better now that you're here.' Sofia admitted. 'I'm ready to go with you mother. Are you here to take me?' Sofia looked around and discovered that she was no longer in the room under the bugs. The slime and insects had all disappeared. Everything was feeling better now, she looked around and she realised that she was on top of a building and it felt warm and familiar. 'Where are we?' She asked as she looked around.

'We're where you want us to be honey. Somewhere you feel comfortable.' Her mother's spirit echoed back. 'I didn't bring you here Sofia, you brought me here. And I'm not here to take you anywhere either. You see my darling, you've always been the one in control.' She smiled. 'You...' She pointed. And with that, the spirit of her deceased mother began drifting back and fading into the black horizon from where it came.

'No! Mother! Don't go.' Sofia reached out with her hand and tried to move, but she was paralysed. Her surroundings began fading to black as she fell back into the dark abyss. 'I need you!' She cried as the light turned back into a small dot. But just before the tiny dot of light disappeared, a final message came echoing back in her mother's voice.

'Fear is a choice honey... Choose courage instead.'

With those final words reverberating in her mind she suddenly snapped back to reality and realised that she was suffocating under the thick slime. She assumed that she must have passed out. Now that she was conscious she tried to open her eyes but realised she couldn't since her face was still buried beneath all the insects. She shook her face frantically and cleared some insects out of the way.

'You don't scare me!' She yelled. Instantly some of the slime dispersed off her face. She could see now and noticed that she was buried beneath thousands of horrid creatures still crawling all over her. She wiggled her hand free and reached out to grab the scariest creature she could see. A giant hairy tarantula the size of a baseball mitt was crawling slowly over the other insects. Without hesitating, she picked it up and pulled it close to her face. She stared at its face for a moment and smiled. She leant up and bit the spider's head off and spat it out. 'I'm the boss!' She yelled. 'Who wants to be eaten next?' She screamed. Everything instantly disappeared and she found herself lying there, completely bug-free and clean. All the slime that had covered her body and stained her clothes had suddenly disappeared without a trace. She got to her feet and stared at the tall man directly in his face. Suddenly it all made sense to her.

'You can't scare me anymore.' She declared. 'In fact, you haven't moved an inch since I first told you to stop, have you?' Her confidence began to grow the more she thought about it. 'In fact, I control *you* don't I?' She asserted as she took a step closer to him. The demon just stood there quietly as if he'd transformed into a waxworks dummy. 'Go on, say something.' She dared. He didn't speak. She took a few more steps towards him until she finally got right next to him and extended her index finger out and prodded him. The giant dark figure was as light as paper and fell back like a giant statue made of hollow glass and shattered into thousands of pieces. She watched the fragments disappear up into the air. She turned and looked on the floor and realised the room was back to normal and the stone idol of the Mayan God had reappeared, but something was different about it now. The statue's eyes were no longer pulsating with a red glow, and suddenly it no longer looked as menacing as it first did.

∞

Belkin was calm as he approached the idol, he knew that this would be a test, he recognised Ah Puch, the Mayan God of the Underworld instantly. He knew there was no escape from whatever was about to happen. He began to prepare himself mentally with each step, his senses on full alert. He was now in the recessed circular area and about ten feet away from the idol but he stopped in his tracks as he spotted something emerging from behind it. The figure of a man stepped into the light and Belkin's eyes widened in shock. 'Joseph?' He gasped.

Joseph stepped out from behind the idol holding an unsheathed Japanese Samurai sword in his hand dressed in full Samurai battle armour.

'Joseph! Is that you? It can't be... you're dead!' Belkin exclaimed, ignoring the intense way Joseph was staring at him. 'I'm here with your son, Adam. We must...'

'Shut up Belkin!' Joseph interrupted. 'Do you have any idea, any idea whatsoever the sacrifices I made for you?'

'Joseph, what are you-'

'Did I say you could speak?!' Joseph scolded as he interrupted Belkin again. 'That's all you do Belkin, talk, talk, talk. How many innocent people have you *talked* into killing themselves for your precious mission Belkin? How many?!'

'Joseph, I-'

'Do you know how long I've been down here waiting for you Belkin? Joseph pointed his sword at Belkin as he continued. 'I've almost lost my mind down here thanks to you. Have you ever felt that Belkin? What it feels like, to lose your mind?'

Belkin felt confused. *Could he have survived?* But something was off about Joseph. This person before him looked like Joseph, his voice sounded like Joseph's, but it didn't feel like Joseph.

'Who are you?' Belkin demanded, now with a more assertive tone. 'What have you done with Joseph?'

Suddenly and without warning, Joseph lunged towards him swinging his sword skilfully at Belkin's head. Belkin ducked and side stepped the attacks with similar poise before finally jumping back to stay out of range. Belkin and Joseph were both competent in numerous martial arts but Belkin knew that being unarmed against Joseph was a huge disadvantage. They knew each other's strengths and weaknesses as intimately as they knew their own.

'You fool.' Joseph continued. 'Don't you get it? This is the effect you have on people if they're lucky enough to survive after you've thrown them into the pits of hell. Look what you've turned me into Belkin!' He said as he smacked his chest with his hand. 'But now you've got nowhere to hide. Now, old friend you can't talk your way out of this. You will pay for your mistakes!' Joseph burst into a full sprint towards Belkin with the sword pointed straight at him. '**AAARGH!**' He screamed.

The blade came slicing down through the air with full force. Belkin saw it coming and sidestepped. Despite his speed Joseph's physical stance always made him predictable. Joseph swung again and again and again. Belkin dashed back, ducked and sidestepped as quickly as he could but the final swing brushed his shirt slicing clean through. Belkin recoiled back clutching his chest and winced as the cut began to bleed.

Joseph charged again, this time, holding the sword high above his head, but it was a distraction. At the last moment, he surprised Belkin with a leg sweep that knocked him off balance. Joseph then dashed forward with a swift elbow to the head knocking Belkin flat on the ground.

Belkin rolled back to safety and got back to his feet. He held his head and shook off the pain. *This can't be Joseph...His style is... different.*

That realisation was all the confirmation Belkin needed. *He's not Joseph.* Belkin dusted himself off and stood up taking a deep breath channelling his inner energies and positioned himself into a Wing Chun fighting stance keeping his front hand tightly fisted and his back palm open. *This is going to end, right here... right now.*

Joseph bolted towards Belkin again swiping the sword angrily, left-right, up-down, the blade moved so fast that it was almost impossible to dodge. But Belkin remained calm, he looked at Joseph's foot positioning, weight distribution, shoulder movements and made calculations in split seconds to accurately estimate his next evasive manoeuvre. He knew that for him to stand a chance he had to disarm him. Finally, after the sixth swing, Belkin saw his chance, a brief window of opportunity. Belkin grabbed his sword-wielding arm and twisted it sharply. The sword flew out of Joseph's limp hand and spun in the air. Belkin roundhouse kicked the sword out of the circular arena into the black abyss that surrounded them. Belkin then dashed in and unleashed a flurry of quick punches and elbows ending with a brutal kick that landed on Joseph's face that sent him flying backwards landing hard on the ground.

'ARGH!' He wailed. 'How dare you strike me!' Joseph screamed in anger. 'I was always loyal to you. You were like a brother to me... and you... you let me down.'

The words swelled up buried emotions within Belkin and he was once again unsure as to whether or not this person was an imposter. 'You understood the risks, Joseph.' Belkin maintained. 'You put our entire operation at risk by going rogue. This was supposed to be our mission. You bailed on us. Do you think I wanted to get your son involved in all this?'

'My son?!' Joseph snarled. 'How dare you put my son in danger!' He barked.

Belkin could see his rage boiling up again. 'Joseph, we trained him, he's smart, and gifted like you. We're watching over him every step of the way.'

'Watching over him?' Joseph chuckled. 'More lies. Look around, you're down here with me, so how exactly are you watching over him right now?'

'I've taught him to protect himself, Joseph.' Belkin replied. 'The same way I taught you.'

'He's a child Belkin! Ah Kin could've killed him by now.' Joseph snapped back.

But Belkin didn't reply. He just looked at Joseph in stunned shock. The game was up. Now Belkin was certain this wasn't Joseph. 'Who said he was with Ah Kin right now Joseph?'

Joseph stopped. He looked down and began chuckling. His laughter became more and more hysterical and he suddenly looked up laughing uncontrollably. Something was different about his face now, it was his eyes. From bright blue, they'd transformed into pitch black. 'No more games.' Joseph bellowed in an unfamiliar evil growl. He removed his samurai helmet and revealed a twisted, ugly version of Joseph's face that was grinning disturbingly. He lunged at Belkin with combinations of punches and kicks that Belkin dodged, blocked and evaded. The blows kept raining down and Belkin continued to evade them as best he could but now the occasional kick and punch began to land as Belkin struggled to keep up with Joseph's speed. Suddenly Belkin was struck hard in the jaw by an uppercut he didn't see coming. It hit him with such force it levitated him off the ground and he collapsed on the floor in a heap. There was no respite. Joseph immediately dashed forwards to finish him off, but Belkin kicked Joseph's legs and skilfully used the momentum to get back to his feet.

As Belkin stood there panting hard for breath he began reflecting and realised why he had been hesitating all this time. In his heart of hearts, he had always felt responsible for Joseph's death. He sought out Adam after he learned of Joseph's demise not only to continue the mission, but to also provide his soul with a sense of peace by stepping in as Adam's father figure, a guardian. But now, facing his emotional demon he realised that he had to let go of the guilt he felt for his friend's death. *I made mistakes, but I didn't want this.* Belkin felt responsible because his friend died under his leadership, but missions were dangerous, the risks came with the territory.

'You were my best friend Joseph!' Belkin finally said as he caught his breath. 'You died... But I did not kill you!'

Joseph got to his feet and stood up uncomfortably on his damaged legs. But now Belkin was ready for him. This was his opportunity to make amends with his soul. This creature before him wasn't Joseph, it was his own demon; his guilt. Belkin always hoped to find the strength to face this demon someday but he never realised he'd have to literally battle it.

Belkin stood in his Wing Chun fighting stance with a sense of peace. It felt like a huge weight had been lifted off his shoulders. 'Goodbye old friend.' He focussed on Joseph's eyes. It helped remind him that he wasn't really fighting his fallen comrade.

Belkin bolted towards Joseph who seemed caught off guard by the attack. Belkin pulled his arm back and tightened his fist. 'Aaargh!' He yelled as he jumped into the air bringing his fist crashing down. But he hit nothing but thin air. Belkin was stunned that he had missed. He spun around looking for his opponent but the demon had disappeared. Belkin suddenly felt a new presence behind him and yelled as he spun around with his fists up ready to attack, but he froze in shock as he saw the Mayan stone idol Ah Puch staring back at him blankly.

'It's over.' Belkin sighed in relief as he lowered his arms. 'It's over.'

∞

Sash knew that the idol had something to do with everyone's disappearance and decided to examine the Mayan god up close. The way it was looking at her made her feel uncomfortable. Its red glowing eyes seemed to follow her around no matter where she stood. She noticed the stone was carved to show the god wearing earrings that looked like the heads of two tribal warriors. Sash didn't believe much in the powers of the ancient Mayan gods. As far as she was concerned this statue had about as much supernatural ability as any other rock back up on the surface. She touched the face and noticed that it was wet to the touch. She checked the statue and realised that a small stream of water had started dripping slowly from its red eyes. Fascinated by what she was seeing she rubbed the statue's eye harder to find the source of the water. In doing so the eye crumbled under her fingertips and a high pressured jet of water burst out hitting her in the chest and knocking her to the ground. Before she even knew what was going on the second eye exploded and a second jet burst over her head. She scrambled away and headed straight for the steps to get out of the low circular area and on to higher ground. But as she tried to flee she was knocked to the ground again, this time by an invisible force-field that seemed to surround the area. What the hell? Winded, and nursing a slight concussion she looked around and noticed the water was pooling and filling up the area very quickly. She realised that the force-field that surrounded her was not only stopping her from escaping but it was also stopping the water from spreading. Before long the water had reached her knees. *It's a trap!*

She banged her fists hard against the force field and noticed that whenever she did so, a blue light flashed and quickly dissipated. *This force-field is electronically charged!* She realised that this was her ticket out of here. The water level was now approaching her chest. She swam around looking for a dry place where she could stand and use her electrokinetic abilities and attack the force-field, but everything, including the idol, was now submerged. Using her electrical abilities while she swam in the water could be fatal. *Think Sash, think!*

She wracked her mind to think of a painless solution but she was quickly running out of time. She swam around wondering what to do and was now treading water completely off the ground. *I've got to try. I've got no other choice!* She took a deep breath and dove down to the ground in an attempt to crack a hole in the base. She placed her palms on the force-field and surged the electricity at her command into her hands and blasted it. The electrical burst electrified the entire pool of water and zapped her with an intense shock sending her body into a spasm. Her body went into a seizure and she quickly pulled her hands back. She quickly swam back to the top of the dome and coughed, gasping for air. She was now treading water twenty-feet off the floor. Undeterred she swam back over to the force field and punched the invisible barrier again and again, but other than creating bright blue flashes her blows had no effect. *What am I supposed to do?* She wept.

Sash took a few deep breaths and tried to rationalise her situation and think it through. She figured that by keeping her hands out of the water she could reduce the intensity of any unintentional self-electrocution. She raised her hands and felt for the force field, once her hand touched it the force field began to glow blue. She let out a small zap with her hands out of the water, she winced in pain but the shock was bearable. She wondered if she had damaged it, but since it was invisible she couldn't tell. She zapped it again, this time, harder. The residual aftershock she felt was stronger too and she grimaced as the pain coursed through her nerves. She zapped again, and again, and again. The shocks travelled through every nerve in her body. She felt like she was being stabbed by thousands of tiny needles. In utter frustration, she harnessed her electrical energy in her fist and struck the force field with an electrically charged punch. A thin blue crack made of blue light appeared permanently etched onto the force field. It was the sign she was waiting for. *It cracked!*

By now the dome was now almost completely filled with water. She looked up at the way it was shaped. It's like a giant snow-globe! She realised that there was no time to waste. The crack swiftly became submerged too as the water levels rose higher and higher. She realised that she had to keep attacking this particular weak spot. She took a deep breath and dipped under the water and aimed at the crack again. She harnessed her electrical charge again and punched it in the same place. Submerged again, the pain was excruciating but seeing the crack become larger filled her heart with elation. She punched the crack again, the crack got even larger and other smaller cracks began branching. But the pain of electrocuting herself again and again, coupled with having to hold her breath was almost unbearable. She needed air and looked up and noticed how quickly the water had risen. She swam all the way to the top of the dome and took a few precious breaths. She knew she was close. *I can do this!*

She took a final deep breath and dove back down to the crack, now clearly visible as its fractures glowed brightly. She channelled her energy back into her fist and punched the crack again. A small blue chunk of matter broke off and created a tiny hole and allowed water to start trickling out on the other side. The crack grew even larger and was now about three feet across littered with numerous minor fractures. However, each electroshock punch she swung sent her body into an uncontrollable convulsion, each feeling worse than the last. She realised that she was trapped in her own worst nightmare. Her energy was almost completely depleted and once again her lungs were gasping for air. She glanced up and realised that she wouldn't make it back up in time for another breath. This was it, her last chance. She channelled all her remaining power into her fist. Her fist began to spark and glow and she let out a fierce punch and blasted out every ounce of electrical energy she had. The blast catapulted her back and she lost complete consciousness. The crack grew a full meter but remarkably remained intact. Sash's limp unconscious body let out the oxygen her lungs had been holding and her body convulsed one last time as she floated lifelessly in her watery tomb.

A TERRIBLE LOSS

As Sofia discovered her rucksack on the floor she walked over to pick it up and suddenly saw Belkin appear out of the corner of her eye.

'Goodness me!' She exclaimed as she jumped in fright. 'Where did you guys go? I-'

But Belkin walked right past her without a word. 'Sash!' He yelled out.

Sofia spun around and saw Sash lying on the floor soaking wet.

In a flash, Belkin was hovering over her and realised she wasn't breathing. 'She's been drowned!' Belkin cried. He breathed into her mouth and began performing CPR. He pumped on her chest. 'Come on Sash, don't do this.' He blew into her lungs again. 'Breath... C'mon!' But there was no sign of life. Sash's body just lay there, motionless. He repeated the CPR procedure a third time, this time pounding her chest over her heart. 'Live!' He yelled with each blow. 'Live!'

Sofia started sobbing. She knew her friend was gone. She could feel that she wasn't coming back. 'Stop, Belkin.' Sofia finally mustered. But Belkin wouldn't stop. He became more and more vigorous pounding on her chest again and again. 'Belkin, stop!' She cried out. 'Please... She's gone!'

Belkin refused to give up. 'Live, Sash, live!' He continued yelling as he blew into her mouth and began pounding again.

Sofia couldn't take it any longer and she lunged at Belkin and tackled him off her lifeless body. 'She's gone, Belkin.' She sobbed. 'She's gone.'

Belkin let out a frustrated roar. '**AAARGH**!' His cry echoed in the large room. He looked at the stone idol standing there just a few meters away. He was sickened by the sight of it. 'This is your fault! He yelled at it as he rose to his feet.

'What are you doing?' Sofia wept.

But Belkin ignored her. Filled with rage he toppled the idol over. It fell off its pedestal and smashed on the ground shattering into several pieces. Belkin then grabbed its head and smashed it on the floor. He felt somewhat vindicated, panting hard as he began to cool off. Venting his frustration on the idol responsible for his friend's death brought a brief moment of comfort to him. But as the idol fell he noticed that it had been resting on a pressure pad that began to ascend. Suddenly a noise boomed and shook the room and Belkin and Sofia watched as a wall rose up in the far corner revealing a hidden passage.

Sofia and Belkin looked at each other as they watched the wall rise. 'There's a pressure pad underneath.' Sofia pointed out. 'Help me move the pedestal.'

Belkin and Sofia pushed the heavy stone pedestal the idol had been resting on to the side and the pressure pad rose further. The room shook once more as the hidden passage became larger allowing them just enough space to be able to walk through it.

Belkin turned back around and looked at Sash's body lying on the ground. He walked over to her and wiped his hand over her face to gently close her open eyelids. 'I'll ask for you in the next life.' He whispered and he kissed her forehead before gently resting her head down and walking towards the doorway in the wall.

Sofia wiped the tears from her face and knelt down over Sash's body. She gently brushed aside the wet hair from her face and held her hand. 'From God you came, and to God you will return.' She slowly rose to her feet and wiped away her tears before following Belkin through the hidden doorway.

THE MAYAN STONE

Ah Kin led the group through the narrow tunnels in the walls. There was only one path and he was certain it had to lead somewhere. The group continued to walk through the walls until they finally arrived at an opening. The group exited into a large dark room but found themselves suspended high up on a wooden platform.

'Ah Kin look!' Immanuel yelled as he pointed down towards the floor.

Thirty feet below Ah Kin gazed in awe as he feasted his eyes on his prize. The stone looked like a huge uncut red ruby the size of a baseball and seemed to be floating in mid-air surrounded by a strange golden disc that was hovering around it. 'I see it!' He beamed. 'By the gods, I see it!' Ah Kin bellowed in delight.

The group all stepped out onto the old creaky wooden platform. Adam walked to the edge and held on to the wooden handrail as he peered down to get a better look at the stone. *All this hell for this stupid rock.* But as he stared at the hovering gem, he had to admit that it looked impressive. The light it emitted seemed to pulsate unlike any precious stone he'd ever seen before.

Suddenly a thunderous shaking began and light started pouring in from the far end of the room.

'Did someone touch something?' Ah Kin barked.

Everyone shook their heads as they continued to witness the wall on the far end of the room rising up revealing a new passageway. Suddenly it stopped.

'That was weird.' Nikkita remarked.

Moments later the shaking began again and the wall rose up higher. The shaking became so fierce that it started to unsettle the wooden structure they stood upon and they all grabbed on to something to steady themselves.

'Quick, get back!' Immanuel panicked. 'Off the platform! Get back into the wall!' They all clambered back into the wall as quickly as they could, but Ah Kin remained. He was less worried about the platform collapsing and more intrigued by the way the wall was moving on the far end of the room. The more he looked on, the more curious he became. *Maybe this is our way out.* He pondered.

'Everyone be silent!' Ah Kin commanded the rest of the group behind him. He could hear muffled voices coming from the distant passageway that had just emerged in the wall. He took a few steps back and crouched down to be sure he wouldn't be spotted. Suddenly a man stepped out of the wall, shortly followed by a woman. *Belkin.* Ah Kin grinned. *We meet at last.*

FACE-TO-FACE

Belkin entered the huge room and marvelled at its vastness. The room was about the size of a football field and straight through the middle of it, a wide aisle led to an altar at the far end. Belkin noticed something red glowing in the distance.

'What is this place?' Sofia wondered as she glanced around. She saw large golden fire cauldrons on either side of the aisle leading all the way down to the altar at the far end and also noticed something red glowing in the distance. 'Hey, do you see that?'

'I do.' Belkin affirmed. 'Hand me the fire starter.'

Sofia rummaged through the rucksack and handed Belkin the flint and striker. Belkin unscrewed the device and walked over to the cauldron closest to him. Just beneath, he noticed some dark resin. He struck the rod piece with the metal striker to create a spark. The fire didn't catch. He struck it again, and this time, the resin burst into flames and Belkin and Sofia jumped back as they watched the flame run down the aisle lighting dozens of golden cauldrons down the aisle. With the cavernous room now fully lit Belkin could see that they were, in fact, standing in the lost temple itself.

'This is it!' Belkin exclaimed. 'We've found the lost temple! That red glow must be...' Belkin drifted off as he caught a glimpse of a number of legendary ancient Mayan relics and artefacts thought to be lost in time forever scattered all over the temple.

'Whoa...will you look at that!' Sofia marvelled as she glanced around at the vast quantities of gold idols adorned with rubies, emeralds and diamonds. Everything in the temple seemed to be made of precious metals and gems; the statues, the ancient tablets, even the large vases scattered around overflowed with priceless ancient gold coins and jewellery.

'We've found it.' Belkin gasped. 'I don't believe it... It's the lost treasure of Montezuma!'

∞

They've been following us. Ah Kin seethed. He turned to Adam. 'You led them here didn't you?!' He accused in an angry whisper.

'What? No way!' Adam fibbed. 'I've been with you the whole time!'

Ah Kin thought through his options. He realised that by being stuck on this suspended platform they were at a significant disadvantage. Ah Kin peered down and realised that there was no obvious route of getting down. A jump from this height would easily result in broken legs, or worse. Although they were closer, in a straight race Belkin would get to the stone first.

'We must get to it before they do.' Ah Kin growled.

Immanuel pondered for a moment. 'Why not let them get the stone for us?' He suggested. 'After all, we have the Timestopper and his precious girlfriend.' He reminded. 'Don't *we* have the upper hand here?'

∞

Belkin and Sofia slowly made their way down the aisle towards the red glowing stone. It was magnificent. The last time Belkin had seen it was when he glimpsed at it briefly decades ago when Joseph's father, Solomon, disappeared with it. It was a lot larger than Belkin remembered it to be. *We've got to it first!* He thought in disbelief. He couldn't believe his luck. But as he neared the stone he began wondering if this was a trap. If Ah Kin and his men were hiding somewhere waiting to ambush them. As the possibility crossed his mind, he paused and started to examine his surroundings. Just then a voice boomed from above them.

'Looking for someone Belkin?' Ah Kin mocked.

I knew it! Belkin's eyes immediately shot up to where the voice was coming from. He saw Ah Kin, Immanuel and the Chilan holding Adam and Nikkita with knives at their throats.

'Leave them alone!' Belkin boomed back.

'Of course we will, right after you lower us down.' Ah Kin demanded as he pointed towards a large wooden pulley system that controlled the platform.

'Alright! Alright!' Belkin yelled with his hands raised. 'I'll bring you down. Just don't harm them!'

'What are you doing?' Sofia whispered to him as she followed him towards the wooden pulley.

'I have no idea,' he confessed. 'but Adam is in danger and there's nothing I can do for him down here. If he wants the stone, we'll exchange it for Adam and Nikkita.' He whispered back.

'But won't the stone amplify Ah Kin's powers?' She whispered. 'He'll be a greater threat to us with it!'

'Do you have a better idea?' Belkin scolded quietly. 'Because if you do, I'd love to hear it!'

Sofia silently considered the various possibilities. She had a bad feeling about this. *There must be another way.*

Belkin was now at the pulley and started heaving it, the initial jerk of the platform almost made everyone fall to their knees, and the Chilan's blade nipped Nikkita's throat and she shrieked in pain. The cut was small but blood began streaming from her neck.

Belkin stopped turning the wheel and glared up in anger. 'Hey!' he growled.

'That little cut was your fault, Belkin!' Ah Kin reported back. 'Gently does it now.' He smirked as he waved Belkin to continue.

Belkin huffed in frustration as he continued to turn the wheel lowering the platform as smoothly as he could.

'Nikkita, are you okay?' Adam asked.

Nikkita took a deep breath. 'I'm okay... it's nothing.' She reassured.

'Thank you, Belkin.' Ah Kin sniggered as the platform approached the ground. 'Without your help, we would have been stuck up there forever.'

The platform was still twelve feet from the ground and Belkin suddenly stopped.

'What are you doing?' Ah Kin growled. 'We're not down yet!'

'Let's just say it's insurance.' Belkin replied. He walked over to the stone. It was hovering celestially surrounded by a golden disc etched with Mayan hieroglyphics. Belkin reached out to grab it.

'Wait!' Ah Kin shouted. 'If you touch that stone it could kill you!'

Belkin had heard of legends about this stone. That it would amplify the bearer's powers almost infinitely. A telepath would become a teleporter, a trickster would become a powerful sorcerer, and someone with reasonable combat training, should, according to Belkin's logic, become a lethal assassin.

'There's only one way to find out!' Belkin retorted. He reached out with his palm outstretched, his eyes wide marvelling at its magnificence. Even before touching it he could feel the energy radiating from within it. He was now just inches away from finally holding the stone in his hand. He closed his eyes and prepared for whatever was about to come next.

But then, just as he was about to touch it he was yanked back with immense force. He lost his balance and fell to the ground. Belkin looked up and saw Sofia towering over him standing by the stone.

'I've already lost Sash Belkin!' She cried. 'I'm not going to lose you too.' And with that, she plunged her hand through the disc and grabbed the stone. The stone burst into a whirlwind of light around her, spinning faster and faster all over her body. The physical stone had disappeared and the light spinning around her started flowing through her body, starting at her feet and passing up through her entire body until it reached her head. She began to levitate as she convulsed and her body contorted as if she was in unimaginable pain. Finally, the light radiated up to her head and suddenly everything went silent. Sofia hovered in the air like a celestial being. As the winds settled Belkin noticed how her clothes had been torn, her skin ravaged, and her hair wild and windswept.

Terrified of what Sofia had transformed into Belkin slowly backed away as he rose to his feet. Sofia turned towards Ah Kin and his men and tilted her head slightly. Instantly Ah Kin, Immanuel and the Chilan collapsed screaming in agony. They were holding their heads as they wailed on the floor in pain. Their eyes were shut tight and they seemed terrified. They began scrambling away as if they were being attacked by something in their minds. Sofia continued staring up towards them and a red light began swirling softly around her.

Belkin realised that this was their opportunity. He ran over to the lowered platform and looked up at Adam and Nikkita. 'Jump!' He yelled.

Adam looked at the men doubled over in pain. They all seemed to be petrified in their own way. The Chilan was screaming, Ah Kin was holding his head frozen in terror and Immanuel was curled into a foetal position and crying loudly.

'I'll lower you down first.' Adam said as he turned to Nikkita. 'Get over the ledge and climb down as much as you can, hold my arm and I'll lower you, Belkin will catch you once I let go.'

Nikkita was scared, it looked like a long way down but she knew this was their opportunity. Belkin was already standing at the bottom of the platform ready to receive her. She lowered herself down and held on to Adam's arm as he dangled it over the side of the platform.

'I've got her, let her go!' Belkin instructed.

'You ready?' Adam confirmed as he stared into Nikkita's eyes.

'Yes.' Nikkita nodded.

Adam let go and she fell directly into Belkin's arms. He put her aside and made sure she was okay to stand before he turned back to Adam. 'Okay, your turn, let's go, quickly!'

Adam turned around and positioned himself to follow suit. But as he did so, he began to hear a loud stomping sound that shook the entire platform. He turned around and saw that Immanuel was now on his feet and jumping up and down stomping hard on the floor, screaming in agony with his eyes still shut tight as if he were having some kind of hyper-realistic nightmare. Before Adam had a chance to react, he heard a loud crack. The ropes keeping the platform up snapped and instantly the entire platform came crashing down.

Adam dove off the platform falling onto Belkin just before the platform crashed onto the jagged rocks beneath. The old brittle wood shattered into hundreds of sharp stakes.

Adam and Belkin dusted themselves off as they got to their feet. 'Now that was close.' Adam laughed nervously.

Belkin bolted towards Sofia and grabbed the rock from the floor and placed it back into Sofia's palm. The rock immediately began absorbing the red energy and Sofia slowly lowered back to the ground. Her eyes changed back to their natural shade and she collapsed to the floor. A small whirlwind formed around the stone and soon all the energy flowed back into it transforming the rock back into a beautiful red gem once again. At the same time, the cries of agony from Ah Kin and his men subsided and all became silent. Belkin rummaged through the rucksack and found a handkerchief which he used to wrap the stone in being extra careful not to touch it before placing it gently into the rucksack and then slinging it over his shoulder. He went back to Sofia and carefully raised her head into his lap.

'Hey, Sofia.' He called as he gently slapped her cheeks to wake her up from her semi-unconscious state.

'Wha-what happened?' Sofia groaned. She looked at Belkin's face and she suddenly recalled everything that had occurred. 'Belkin, the stone, it took over. I couldn't... I couldn't control it.' She admitted apologetically.

'You're stupid for taking such a big risk, Sofia.' Belkin sighed. 'But I'm really glad you did.' He smiled. 'Come on, we need to hurry, we don't have much time. Can you walk?'

'I think so.' Sofia nodded.

Belkin helped her up and they started walking back towards the passageway they had entered from. As they walked back Belkin turned around frequently to ensure no one was following them. Suddenly in the distance, Belkin saw a figure standing up from the rubble dusting himself off. *Ah Kin.* 'Quickly guys, let's move!' he ordered.

∞

The group was now at the passageway entrance and Belkin turned around again. Ah Kin was slowly walking towards them wielding a knife in his hand. It was clear by the way he moved that he was injured, but he was determined not to let them get away so easily. Belkin peered through the passageway and noticed that Adam and Nikkita were almost through to the other side.

'Adam!' Belkin shouted through the narrow passageway.

'Yeah?!' Adam shouted back.

'When you get into that room there's a low circular area!'

'Okay...?!'

'There's a pressure pad sticking out the ground. I need you to stand on it. Run go!' Belkin turned around again. Despite Ah Kin's injuries, he was making up good ground and was beginning to walk faster.

Adam ran into the room. He spun around and saw the huge golden door. *Whoa.* He looked around and instantly recognised the area that Belkin was talking about. He jumped down into the circular area and then saw something he wasn't expecting. Lying there on the floor was Sash's body. *What? Oh my God! No!* Adam immediately ran over to her. 'Sash! Wake up Sash!' He yelled as he shook her gently. 'Get up!'

Sofia was struggling to keep up as Belkin began rushing her through the passageway.

'Belkin!' Adam yelled back. 'Come quick, something's happened to Sash!'

Belkin cursed himself. In all the commotion he hadn't had a chance to explain to Adam that Sash hadn't made it. He didn't want Adam to find out like this, he knew how close they'd become over the past few months. 'Adam, I'm sorry. I know!' Belkin yelled as he shuffled with Sofia through the wall. 'I'll explain everything, but right now I need you to get to that pressure pad! Ah Kin is right on our tail, we can't let him get through!'

Adam slowly backed away from the body, but couldn't take his eyes off her. He looked around and then saw the pressure pad protruding from the ground. 'This?' He shouted back. 'You want me to step onto this thing?' He noticed the broken pieces of stone on the floor and guessed it was once a statue of some sort. *What the hell happened here?* He wondered.

'Yes, do it now!' Belkin shouted back impatiently as he watched Ah Kin now jogging painfully towards them.

Adam jumped on the pressure pad and slowly the wall began closing. Nikkita stood at the passageway entrance urging Belkin and Sofia through. *C'mon!*

Ah Kin watched the passageway slowly begin to shrink and he began running towards them ignoring the pain shooting through his legs. Belkin and Sofia were now almost through to the other side.

Ah Kin was now at the passageway and he clambered in as quickly as he could. With the ceiling slowly closing down on him from above, he shimmied through frantically and could see Belkin and Sofia on the far end. He was making good ground on them but the ceiling was closing down on him too fast. He was a third of the way through but he paused. He judged the distance in front of him and then looked at the distance behind. *I'm not going to make it.* 'Curse you!' He howled, as he turned back around and shuffled back the way he came. By the time he reached the exit the ceiling was so low he was crawling on his hands and knees and he leapt out just in time before the wall closed in narrowly escaping being crushed.

Belkin and Sofia slowly hobbled over to Adam who was sat on the pressure pad with his head in his hands staring at Sash's drenched lifeless body in utter dismay.

Sofia sat down and rested on the steps beside Nikkita. They both watched as Belkin walked over to Adam to offer him some comfort.

'What happened man?' Adam finally asked without taking his eyes off her. 'How can she be dead?'

'I honestly don't know.' Belkin admitted. 'We came in through that door.' Belkin pointed to the huge golden door that Adam had been admiring earlier. 'But once we got inside this room somehow we all disappeared to each other. We were all still here, but alone... with that thing.' Belkin pointed towards the shattered pieces of stone on the floor. 'It messed with our heads. I don't know how, but it took the fears in our minds and made them real.' Belkin kicked the pieces of stone. 'Sofia and I pulled through, but once we got back to reality, we saw Sash lying here soaking wet. She'd drowned somehow. I tried to revive her... but... it was too late.'

'This is it.' Sofia suddenly realised. 'This is what my dream meant! I knew it was a bad omen.'

'Dream?' Adam frowned. 'What dream?'

'I had a dream the night before we met Adam. I was facing a vicious dog. Belkin was playing chess and he seemed upset. You were there too!'

'I was?' Adam said curiously.

'You were on a bridge. It looked like it was made of light. It looked like you were crying.'

Adam and Nikkita just stared at each other. 'That's crazy...' Adam remarked. 'A bridge of light is what just saved me a little while ago. It helped me cross this huge gap in the path. It was like... err... cinbat, cinkap or something-'

'The Cinvat?' Belkin offered.

'Yeah! That's the one. It was out of this world man! It just appeared out of nowhere! Hey, wait... was Sash in your dream?' He wondered.

'She was.' Sofia whispered. 'Her head... it was down a well... she wasn't moving.' She recalled sadly.

Adam stared at the ceiling as he held back his tears. *No one even knew how she died... she drowned all alone.* He imagined what she must have gone through and it broke his heart. *She was always there for me, and in her time of need, no one was there for her.*

'I can bring her back.' Adam claimed. 'I've done it before.'

'What?!' Belkin exclaimed. 'When?'

'When we were stuck in that first room and you were following us. I communicated with Sash and told her to throw this lever. You remember that?'

'I do.' Belkin replied with intrigue.

'Well, I did that because, things went wrong the first time around and, well we lost someone.' Adam sheepishly admitted as he inadvertently glanced towards Nikkita.

'Who?' Belkin quizzed.

'Yes Adam,' Nikkita said as she stood up in surprise. 'Who?'

'Well, Nikkita,' Adam confessed. 'It was you.' Adam watched Nikkita's face turn pale.

'Wait, what?' Nikkita replied with astonishment. 'I...I died?'

'Yeah... you see the first time around, Ah Kin sent *you* out with Nacom. You both found the lever and pulled it, but as the room started dropping down, you didn't get back in time and you got stuck trying to get through and you... well... you got squished.' Adam smiled awkwardly as he tried to soften the blow.

'I got... squished?' Nikkita reiterated in shock.

'Yes, and losing you was...' Adam chose his words carefully as he tried to downplay his grief. '...it was hard on me... I couldn't take it.'

'So then how did you bring me back?' Nikkita wondered.

'Well, I'm not really sure, I was just so mad. I went crazy and then I saw all this bright energy, everything suddenly stopped and I could just feel this cable in my hands. When I reeled it backwards, everything just... reversed.'

'That's amazing.' Sofia gasped.

'To restart time I had to re-enter my ghost.

'You're ghost?!' Nikkita frowned.

'I'm not explaining it very well... it's really hard to explain. Not exactly my ghost. It's more like a shadow of the original me.' Adam could see that they weren't following. 'Look it doesn't matter how I do it, I just know that I can do it.'

'So you have to re-enter your ghost to restart time?' Belkin clarified.

'Yeah.' Adam replied.

'So how are you going to save Sash when you weren't here in the first place? Your ghost would be elsewhere.'

Adam hadn't thought it through. Belkin's argument made complete sense. Adam's ghostly shadow would have been elsewhere during Sash's death. Adam suddenly realised the limitations of his ability.

'But...but I have to try Belkin!' Adam argued. 'We have the stone now, maybe-'

'You can't play God Adam!' Belkin interrupted in frustration. 'Time stopping isn't a game. You've already over exerted yourself at least once today, and it sounds like the biggest time warp you've ever done.' Belkin took a deep breath to compose himself. 'Your powers can't save her now, but you can save the rest of the planet. I need you to focus on the mission Adam. The mission is bigger than any one of us... it's the greater good.'

Adam lowered his head as he conceded that Belkin was right. Saving the world was more important, and if Sash were here right now that's what she would've wanted him to focus on.

'We need to get out of here and get on top of Kukulkan pyramid as soon as we can. It'll be midnight in less than two-hours.' He reminded as he tapped his watch. 'We can still do this if we work together.'

'Agreed.' Adam finally looked up and said with steely determination. He turned and looked back at Sash's body. *I'm gonna do this for you Sash, I'm gonna make you proud.*

A GOD'S DECREE

Ah Kin scrambled out of the gap just in time and narrowly avoided being crushed. His body was badly bruised and his back was in agony. He huffed in frustration as he turned around and walked back to the collapsed platform to assess the situation of his colleagues.

The Chilan wasn't moving. His eyes were bloodshot and rolled halfway up his head as he lay there with a wooden stake protruding from his chest. It was well known that most Chilans suffered traumatic and violent deaths. It was the price they paid for the magic they wielded.

'Ah Kin...' Immanuel croaked.

Ah Kin noticed a bloody hand emerge from the debris. Immanuel was buried under a number of timber planks. Ah Kin hoisted them off as quickly as his battered body would allow. He finally uncovered Immanuel's mangled body. His legs were twisted unnaturally and a broken shin bone was protruding from one of his legs.

'I don't think I'm going to make it old friend.' He whispered. 'I think I've punctured a lung.'

'Nonsense Immanuel, I won't-' Ah Kin stopped as he noticed Immanuel's skull partially fractured and bleeding profusely.

'Yeah, thought so.' Immanuel concluded reading Ah Kin's facial expression as he watched him examine his head. 'I won't be able to get out of here, and since you aren't much of a paramedic I think I'll make peace with my maker now. Put me out of my misery Ah Kin. Please.'

Ah Kin stood up over Immanuel. 'You're not going to get out of this that easily Immanuel. You and I have unfinished business.' And with that Ah Kin raised his arms and began chanting an ancient Mayan spell. Immanuel knew what Ah Kin was doing, he was conjuring healing magic. Ah Kin's voice grew louder and louder as he repeated the phrase again and again. A strange wind began whipping around him. Ah Kin could feel the power of the magic in his hands, and within mere moments they began to glow yellow. The light in his hands grew brighter and brighter until he finally shouted the chant one last time. 'MATSU-KOKI, HUWARIDA, ICHIMAE!' He waved his arms to break free of the wind around him and forcefully slammed his left palm down on Immanuel's forehead. Immanuel went into a shock-like state as his body began to spasm and convulse. Ah Kin then placed his right palm down on Immanuel's chest directly over his heart. Immanuel's body shuddered so hard that at times he seemed to levitate. His body continued to jitter and shake from head to toe but Ah Kin maintained his position and kept pressing down as hard as he could keeping the bright yellow energy channelled into his body.

Suddenly Immanuel stopped convulsing and his body became still and limp. Ah Kin brushed himself off as he slowly got to his feet. He watched the yellow glow become dimmer and dimmer and as it did so he could see the light dispersing throughout Immanuel's body. Immanuel shone in the yellow hue as if he were a statue made of gold. Ah Kin reached down to Immanuel's leg and tore his trousers to take a better look at the broken leg. The magic was working, his wounds were looking better already.

'Sleep well comrade.' He whispered to his unconscious friend. 'When you wake and have recuperated, come find me.' He looked around and realised that he was the last man standing. *I will sacrifice my soul a hundred times over before I let a mere mortal alter what the Gods have decreed.*

Ah Kin walked over to the altar and picked up the circular disc made of gold that had once surrounded the

Mayan stone. With the golden disc gripped in his hand he knelt down. He raised his arms up waving them slowly in a rhythmic circular motion as if he was drawing a symbol in the air and he began chanting again. A strong gust of wind blasted over him, but it didn't distract Ah Kin, he continued chanting with his eyes shut tight. He chanted louder and louder over the howling winds, waving his arms in the same motion over and over. Just at the right time Ah Kin drew his knife and sliced open his palm. He clenched his fist and allowed the blood to spread across the ancient golden disc. He smeared his bloody hand across his closed eyes and continued to chant intensely. He suddenly burst open his eyes, his dark brown eyes were replaced by a pair of red, glowing embers. He moved as if he were in slow-motion through the chaotic wind as he scanned the area around him. He scanned the room to the left and then to the right, then suddenly he saw what he was looking for. Through his enchanted vision, he was able to spot a hidden passageway in a wall that seemed to lead straight up back to the surface. He stood up and in the trance-like state began walking towards it. The subservient wind followed him blasting away everything in his path. Being otherwise completely undetectable to the naked eye, Ah Kin could see the hidden passageway beaming like a beacon through his temporarily improved sight.

The magic was fading. Ah Kin knew spells of this magnitude didn't last long. He had to move quickly. He placed his blood soaked palm onto the stone wall and with his fingers he traced the outline of the bright door he saw in his mind. '**Zot'z**'. He whispered.

Instantly the wall exploded and like a protective force-field the turbulent wind blew away any fragments that would have otherwise harmed him. The hidden passage revealed a stony stairway that led straight up into the starry night above. Ah Kin finally stopped chanting and let go of the magic. The wind instantly calmed and quickly died out. Everything became silent again. He blinked a few times as he snapped out of his trance and the red glow in his eyes disappeared. Instantly the fatigue overwhelmed him and he fell to his knees, the strain of the magic exhausted him and all the pain of his prior injuries returned with a vengeance. He groaned as he got back to his feet motivated by one simple thought. He looked up at the night sky above. *I'm coming for you Adam.*

ESCAPE

Belkin, Sofia, Adam and Nikkita worked together to carefully return the heavy stone pedestal back on top of the pressure pad. They piled on the broken pieces of the stone idol on top of the pedestal to add enough weight to stop the wall from rising back up.

'There, like it never happened.' Adam remarked sarcastically as he stepped back and looked at the destroyed Mayan god of the underworld.

Sofia sat down for a moment to rest her legs. Having barely recovered from her previous ordeal, moving the heavy stones around in the heat had completely drained her. As she went to pick up the rucksack she noticed something strange. The bag was bulging as the stone inside was pushing against the inside of the bag. 'That's weird.' Sofia said as she inspected the bag from the outside. She picked it but noticed that however she held it the stone stayed true to the direction it was pointing in, as if it were a compass. 'Belkin, come check this out!' Sofia exclaimed as she continued to play around with the direction of the rucksack.

'What is it?' He asked as he dusted his hands.

'It's the stone.' Sofia pointed out. 'It's doing something... weird.'

Nikkita also noticed Sofia playing around with the rucksack and joined the group as they all gathered around watching the strange phenomena.

'Watch this.' Sofia said as she rotated the rucksack around. Regardless of which way she held it the stone always seemed to point west.

'It's being attracted to something.' Belkin concluded. He took the rucksack from Sofia opened the canvas flap and carefully gripped the stone with the handkerchief. With the stone in hand, he could feel that it was being pulled by some kind of invisible force. He slowly unwrapped it and opened his palm to let it loose. Instantly it shot away and smashed into the western wall.

The stone had set itself perfectly into the centre of the wall and suddenly the circular carvings within the wall began to come alive. The etchings somehow began to appear to glow red and rotate. The large triangle shapes unexpectedly collapsed into each other and a section of the wall began to rise.

'Seems as though we've found our exit.' Belkin smiled. But almost as soon as he had said it, the wall stopped rising.

'Uh-oh. I think you've just jinxed it, Belkin.' Nikkita teased.

Belkin squinted towards the wall. 'It seems to be stuck on something.' All of a sudden a terrible blast resonated through the room. It sounded as though a giant boulder had smashed into a wrecking ball and the entire room began trembling.

'It's an earthquake!' Adam yelled as he tried to steady himself.

'We need to get out of here, now!' Belkin exclaimed as he looked up at the ceiling.

The group ran towards the opening in the western wall. Belkin turned to take one last look at Sash's body. *I'll see you soon Sash.* With that, Belkin swung the rucksack over his shoulder and ran to catch up with the rest of the group. He looked up and noticed rocks from the ceiling were breaking off and beginning to smash onto the ground around him. 'Watch your heads!' He screamed to the others over the thunderous crashes as they fell and exploded on the stone floor.

Adam watched boulders the size of small cars break away and come tumbling down shattering into hundreds of pieces just yards away. He leapt around and dodged the debris as he sprinted towards the small opening in the western wall. A deafening crack boomed through the cavernous room, shortly followed by a crash that resembled the sound of a cluster-bomb exploding behind them. Everyone turned around and witnessed dozens of boulders all falling at once over the recessed area where the stone idol was. *Sash.* Adam gasped. But he took comfort in knowing she was already long gone.

They continued running and finally made it to the opening narrowly avoiding the crushing boulders falling from the sky. Sofia and Nikkita crawled through the small three-foot tall gap, followed closely by Adam.

'Belkin!' Adam shouted, 'Come on! We're all through!'

'Stay there!' Belkin yelled back. He swung the rucksack off his shoulders and whipped out the handkerchief and started prying the Mayan stone out the wall.

'What are you doing?!' Adam screamed through the gap.

'I'm getting the stone out, our mission will be over without it!' He yelled back.

'No!' Adam screamed, 'Leave it! You'll die in there!'

But Belkin couldn't leave without it. Rocks began crashing from the ceiling at a faster rate. He kept glancing up and darting out of the way to avoid being struck. He finally managed to get his fingertips gripped on to it.

'I've got it!' He beamed. 'I just need to...' Belkin grunted loudly as he used all his might to pull the stone from the wall. Suddenly it popped out and Belkin fell back. Adam watched Belkin fall down as the wall came crashing down trapping him inside.

'No... **NO**!' Adam screamed as he banged on the wall.

There was no time to waste. Adam instinctively started feeling a tingling in the back of his head as if his body knew what it had to do. He shut his eyes tight and began to focus. Beads of blood began dripping from his nose again as he began shaking. Purple electric plumes of plasma suddenly burst out of his body and then the moment he had been waiting for; silence. He opened his eyes and everyone was still. Nothing was moving, Nikkita was frozen and looking at him wide-eyed marvelling at the spectacle of her friend emitting purple electricity from his hands. He rose to his feet and using his hands he began making the same winding motion he made earlier. His hands began sparking with electricity and the wall began rising again. As the gap in the wall rose back up Adam saw his own ghostly shadow crawl backwards. He continued reversing time until he saw his former self on the other side again. He slid back through the gap and stopped winding time just as Nikkita and Sofia were safely through and his ghostly shadow was about to join them. This time, he wasn't leaving without Belkin. He stood into his ghostly shadow again. Instantly the room burst into full motion and sound. It felt as though he'd suddenly pressed play on his MP3 player forgetting he'd left it on full volume. He cupped his hands around his ears in shock. The thunderous boulders, once again, continued to crash around him.

'Come on Adam!' Nikkita yelled to Adam through the other side.

'I'm waiting for Belkin!' He yelled back through the chaos. Adam turned around and ran back towards Belkin who was still jogging to catch up with them. 'What the hell are you doing?' Belkin bellowed at him. 'Get across,' He waved. 'I'll be fine!'

Adam ran back and caught up with him. 'You can't take the stone out without me. If you remove it the wall will collapse and you'll be stuck on this side!' Adam yelled back as they both ran towards the western wall.

Belkin stared at him with a puzzled expression. 'Wait... how did you...?' Adam didn't respond but Belkin understood. 'We've done this before! You've come back to save me!' Belkin couldn't shake the eerie feeling that suddenly washed over him. *Did I die?* The notion of this being his second chance overwhelmed him and he instinctively stopped running unable to shake the paradox from his mind.

Adam spun around and noticed Belkin fall back. Suddenly a huge boulder broke off the ceiling and was headed straight for Belkin. Adam quickly ran back to him and dove into him tackling him out of the way at the last possible moment.

'I'm sorry.... I- I-...' Belkin stammered in shock.

'Apologise later!' Adam exclaimed as he helped him back to his feet. 'Come on!'

They finally reached the western wall. 'Okay, you go ahead, I'll grab the stone.' Adam instructed.

Belkin looked into Adam's eyes and discovered a new side to him. He suddenly saw a confident and capable young man. He was no longer a trainee. Belkin held his shoulders and nodded. 'Be swift about it.' He ordered. He dropped to his knees and crawled through the gap.

Adam was now alone and the red stone was glowing brightly in the wall. He almost touched it with his bare hands before he remembered that he needed the handkerchief. *Dammit, I need...*

'The rucksack!' He yelled to the others. Belkin had forgotten to hand it to him and he quickly swung it off his shoulders and threw it through the gap. Adam grabbed it but then noticed a large boulder tumbling down right above him. He dove out of the way narrowly missing it as it smashed in the spot he'd just been standing in. *Damn, that was close!* He stood back up and scanned the ceiling quickly for any other hazards. Seeing there was no immediate danger he rummaged through the rucksack and retrieved the handkerchief.

'Hurry, Adam!' Nikkita yelled from the other side.

The stone was wedged tight into the wall. He used all his strength but it barely moved. The handkerchief made things even more cumbersome, but he finally got a little purchase on it on one side and gave it a ferocious yank almost ripping his fingernails off in the process. He could feel it was looser now, and with one more tug, it would be free.

Suddenly from the other side of the wall, Adam heard Sofia's voice. 'Adam look out!' She shrieked.

Adam panicked and instinctively looked upwards. A huge boulder the size of a garden shed came tumbling down from the ceiling directly on top of Adam. There was no time. Adam froze. He couldn't focus. He couldn't think. He just watched it hurtling down towards him. He let go of the stone and the handkerchief fell to the ground. As he closed his eyes awaiting the impact he was transported back to his nursery and saw his father singing him the lullaby. *Call for help if there's nowhere to run.*

'Help me.' He whispered. Instantly the stone shot out of the wall and embedded itself in Adam's palm snapping him out of his trance. Adam cowered down and braced for impact but suddenly everything went silent.

Am I dead? Adam wondered. He took a deep breath and opened his eyes and realised that everything looked different. He looked around at his surroundings. Everything was frozen in time, but this time, it all looked strange. There was a thick grey fog and everything was in black and white. When he moved it felt as though he was moving through water. He opened his palm and there in his hand was the stone. But it too looked different. In a black and white world it was the only thing that was still in colour. It wasn't glowing anymore it just looked like a plain red stone in a black and white portrait. Adam felt acutely aware of everything around him, every small detail. He felt aware of his consciousness in a way he'd never experienced before. He felt connected with everything around him, but at the same time, he felt disconnected from himself and his ego. He felt as though he'd finally awoken and that this had been the real truth of consciousness all along, this was the truth of existence. He could feel his mind sending messages to his body and nervous system. But not only could he feel them, he could control them, manipulate them. He raised his left hand in front of his face and it was glowing red, by simply sending the command to his mind he sent the red energy up his arm, across his chest, into his other arm and the energy began emanating from his right hand as well. Red sparks crackled as he flexed and moved his fingers. As he looked up he noticed the mammoth boulder barely three-feet above his head suspended in mid-air. As he concentrated on it, he noticed something strange. The boulder began altering in its physical composition. The more he stared the more he noticed the minute particles that the boulder was formed of, as if he were looking at it through the lens of a microscope. He felt a strange sense of connection with it as if it were part of him somehow. He raised his hand towards it and the rock began to glow red. He watched as individual particles and atoms within the huge boulder began vibrating. Adam began winding time in his hands, but this time, he wound it forwards, and the boulder gently lowered down over him. However, instead of crushing him, it simply passed through him, its vibrating atoms parting around him, allowing his body to cut through it like a fish through water. *This is amazing.* He waved his arms through it and its atoms dispersed as if it were a cloud.

Adam looked back into his palm and realised that the mysterious Mayan stone had given him some kind of amplified ability to manipulate physical things. With this realisation, Adam analysed the wall before him that had been slammed shut ever since the stone bolted out of it. As he focussed he could see the molecular makeup of the tiniest particles of the wall in vivid colourful detail in the otherwise black and white background. As he continued to focus he began to see human forms and realised he was seeing the outlines of Belkin, Sofia and Nikkita on the other side as if he was looking through a colourful x-ray machine. He pressed his glowing hand against the wall and the particles simply moved aside allowing his hand to push through. To Adam, it looked as if he was pressing his hand gently through multi-coloured jelly. He continued pressing until his arm was through the wall. Without any further hesitation, he took a few steps straight through and emerged on the other side with Belkin, Nikkita and Sofia. But he could only see them on a strange atomic level. He could see more than just their bones, he could see their hearts, their vital organs, even their brains glowing and firing electronic signals throughout their nervous system. *It's so... it's so...beautiful.* He admired as he watched the internal workings of the human nervous system.

With a heavy heart, he realised that he couldn't stay in this beautiful dimension forever. He looked at the stone in his hand and with a deep sigh he dropped it. A bright flash blinded him and he instantly felt woozy and fell onto his hands and knees and vomited. The sudden pain in his head was excruciating.

'AAARGH!' He cried.

Adam! Can you hear me? Adam could just make out the fuzzy image of Belkin kneeling beside him. *Say something Adam!* Adam tried to respond but the picture was getting worse. Everything went dark.

When Adam woke up he realised that he was moving. He was still feeling nauseous and he found himself swaying from side to side facing the floor. He quickly discovered he was being carried over Belkin's shoulder. 'Urgh...' He groaned as he felt his head spin.

Belkin heard Adam groan and stopped. 'He's coming around.' He informed. Sofia and Nikkita stopped and turned around and watched as Belkin gently lowered Adam down to his feet.

'How long have I been out for?' Adam wondered.

'Not too long. How are you feeling?'

Adam stood on wobbly legs holding his head. The pain has subsided somewhat but there was a lingering throbbing in his head that he couldn't completely shake off. 'Better... ish.'

'That was quite a light show back there.' Nikkita chimed. 'And I had no idea you could walk through walls!' She exclaimed.

The memory of everything that occurred came flooding back to Adam. Then suddenly he remembered that he'd dropped the stone. He instinctively patted himself down. 'The stone! I dropped it, did you see it?' Adam fretted. 'Back there when I-'

'Don't worry Adam.' Belkin assured. 'We've got it. It's in my jacket pocket. It's wrapped it in a rag. We all need to be careful not to touch it with our bare hands. Its power is remarkable, now you know why Ah Kin wants it so badly.'

'I've never felt anything like it.' Adam confessed. 'I can now understand why my father went to such crazy lengths to hide it.'

'What happened back there?' Nikkita asked.

'I don't really know... I... I was about to be crushed and then I heard... wait- Sofia!' He recalled. 'You saved me. You told me to look out! How did you know I was in danger?'

'I just.... saw it.' Sofia admitted. 'I can't describe how, but it felt like a small part of the stone's power was still inside me and I saw a huge boulder about to crush you in a vision. It was so instant and real I felt compelled to scream out and warn you.'

Adam recalled the feeling he felt while he was under its influence. A residual feeling of connection with his surroundings was still with him and he could relate to what Sofia was saying. It felt like the reality he was now in was lacking a vital dimension. A dimension he had only experienced with the stone. Everything around him felt fake and hollow. He suddenly felt the allure of the stone. Its power was addictive. With it in his hands he felt invincible. But it was all encompassing, overwhelming. He stumbled as he started to walk and Nikkita caught him before he fell over.

'Here, give me your arm.' Nikkita urged. 'Lean on me. Belkin can probably do with a break.' A cute reassuring smile appeared on her face as she helped him.

Adam stared at her in awe as she swung his arm over her shoulders. He couldn't believe how lucky he was to have her. She had shown such strength through everything they had gone through, and even now she was there to support him. 'You're amazing.' He whispered to her.

Adam turned around and realised the wall he passed through was nowhere to be seen. 'Hey where are we? Where's that wall I came through?'

'Back through that gap.' Sofia replied. 'It's about ten-minutes behind us.'

Adam turned to look but all he saw was a narrow crack in the wall. 'Did we come through that?' He asked, perplexed.

'Yup.' Nikkita confirmed. 'We were hoping you'd wake up, but you didn't so Belkin carried you through it. It was hard work.'

Adam felt embarrassed. 'Sorry Belkin.'

'Don't apologise Adam.' Belkin replied puffing a little more than usual. 'Time and again, you've proven yourself today. There's just one last thing left for you to do.' Belkin turned and continued walking. 'So let's get you out of here and get it done.'

A RACE TO THE TOP

Ah Kin didn't waste any time. He knew that every minute was precious. He was furious. Despite coming so close to obtaining it, the stone had slipped out of his grasp. There was only one thing on his mind now, to ensure The Fraction failed. *The gods will prevail.*

He was already half way up the Kukulkan pyramid, the largest pyramid in Chichin Itza. He peered towards the skies as he climbed. The clouds were gathered in an angry storm. A flash of lighting followed by the faint rumble of distant thunder boomed. *Hoonaab-koo. The Hour is approaching.*

Ah Kin had to get to the top before The Fraction. He was positive that they wouldn't escape the Temple of Warriors in time, but he had to be sure. *Why can't they understand?* He pondered. *This world is just an illusion. We should be begging for our trials of this world to end, but these fools can't see past their own noses!* He took another painful step up and buckled. He was now on his hands and knees but he continued to clamber to the top as quickly as he could.

The temple at the top of the pyramid was now finally in sight.

A COSTLY MISTAKE

The darkness was almost absolute as Adam, Belkin, Nikkita and Sofia emerged from a hidden trap door in the middle of the forest. Belkin looked up and heard a crack of thunder.

'A storm is approaching.' He announced. 'It's a sign. Our time is running out.'

Adam glanced up. It was the strangest storm he'd ever seen. It only seemed to be circulating directly above the huge pyramid. It reminded Adam of a horror movie he'd once seen where the gates of hell were being opened for the first time. A flash of lightning shone across the sky and lit up the huge pyramid situated about a hundred yards away.

Adam was tired. The climb out of the Temple of Warriors below had exhausted him and his heart was pounding erratically. He felt like everything he'd gone through today was now suddenly all catching up with him. He took a deep breath in through his nose and released it slowly out through his mouth a few times. It was a simple recuperative technique Ali had taught him during one of their training sessions.

'How are you feeling?' Belkin inquired noticing Adam's heavy breathing.

Despite feeling drained and exhausted he met Belkin eye-to-eye and nodded in determination. 'I'm good... I'm good.'

'You've got heart, Adam. But you're going to need more than that right now.' Belkin reached into his pocket and pulled out a small syringe with orange liquid inside it. 'This is a temporary booster shot.' Belkin explained. 'This will give you immense energy for about 20-25 minutes.'

'Err... I'm not good with needles.' He confessed. 'What if I just try stopping time to get a head start?'

'Conserve your energy, Adam. You can't stop time over such a big area without the stone. You need to get up there.' He pointed.

'Okay, okay.' Adam panted. 'Go ahead, jab me. I'm ready.'

Belkin approached him as he pulled off the protective guard and exposed the syringe's needle. It was the largest injection Adam had ever seen. He turned his head towards the pyramid and focussed on his goal. He scanned the pyramid for any traces of Ah Kin but couldn't spot anything unusual on the dark steps of the pyramid. Suddenly a bright flash of lighting and a huge crack of thunder blasted through the sky. The rain suddenly began hammering down.

Belkin pulled Adam close and whispered into his ear. 'We're counting on you, Adam. Go save the world.' Then, without any warning, Belkin jammed the syringe into Adam's leg and pushed down on the plunger. Adam winced in pain as the thick needle pierced his jeans and penetrated into his thigh muscle. The pain quickly subsided and was instantly replaced with a colossal surge of adrenalin. Adam felt his heart pound in his chest, his mind became fully alert and his body exploded with energy. He let out a beastly scream into the sky and immediately burst into a full sprint towards the pyramid. Like a flash, he was gone, headed towards the giant pyramid.

∞

Within moments Adam was at the base of the pyramid and scaling the steps ferociously.

Belkin, Sofia and Nikkita emerged from the forest and watched him climb.

'Wow. Look at him go!' Nikkita exclaimed.

'He's like a man possessed!' Sofia glared.

Belkin noticed Nikkita shivering in the cold rain. 'Here, take my jacket.' He offered as he removed his brown leather biker jacket and handed it to her.

'Thanks.' Nikkita smiled in appreciation as she slipped it on. It was warm and provided instant relief from the pouring rain. She buried her hands into the pockets and felt something inside one of them. She suddenly realised what it was and instantly her heart sank with dread.

Belkin glanced over and noticed her expression change. 'What's the matter Nikkita?'

Nikkita felt like she'd lost the ability to speak. Then slowly she took out her left hand from the jacket's pocket and held up the stone wrapped in the rag. 'Wasn't Adam supposed to take this with him?!'

Belkin stared wide-eyed at the wrapped up stone Nikkita held out. He couldn't believe he'd been so absent-minded. He grabbed the wrapped stone from Nikkita and ran towards the pyramid. He cupped his hands and shouted as hard as he could '**ADAAAM!**'

Adam was already close to the top of the pyramid and all he could hear was the crashing thunder and the torrential rain. He had no idea Belkin was screaming his name down below.

'What are we going to do?' Sofia fretted.

Belkin shook his head as he thought through his options. He knew that without the stone Adam wouldn't be powerful enough to create a large enough time warp. 'I'll run this up to him.' Belkin concluded wishing he'd had another syringe to boost his own energy.

'You're exhausted Belkin.' Nikkita pointed out. 'Your legs still haven't fully recovered from carrying Adam all that way. You won't be able to get up there quick enough.' She paused in thought. 'I'll go.' She finally declared.

Sofia and Belkin both looked at her in astonishment.

'I'm stronger than I look.' She assured. 'I was captain of the girls' netball team in school, and I've completed Shaun T's sixty-day Insanity workout. I can make it!' She said with determination.

'But Nikkita, if Ah Kin is up there already, you could be in serious-.'

'I'm your best shot, Belkin.' She pointed out. 'You're exhausted, and Sofia still hasn't recovered from touching the stone. Right now I've got the freshest legs.' She walked up to Belkin with her palm open. 'I can do this.'

Belkin didn't like it, but Nikkita was right. There was no other option, she was the best bet. Time was ticking and he had to make a decision fast. 'Go!' Belkin finally agreed. 'But be swift about it...go now... run!' He yelled as he planted the wrapped-up stone into her open palm.

Nikkita felt nervous adrenaline course through her veins. *This is it!* She took a deep breath and spun around and began sprinting towards the pyramid with the stone tightly gripped in her hand. *I'm coming baby.*

∞

The final level of the pyramid was a tall stone block and Adam used the last bit of his energy to pull himself up on top of it. He lay there panting hard gasping for air. The adrenaline was still coursing through his body, but his muscles were screaming in agony. He knew Ah Kin could be up here so despite his exhaustion he cautiously stood up and scanned the area.

The temple room was a small twenty-foot square room made of stone at the top of the pyramid that contained a number of small partition walls inside it. There were two entrances to the temple; one from the north and the other directly opposite from the south. The cracks of lightning and thunder became more frequent and the rain continued to pour relentlessly. The noise from the storm echoed in the room loudly. The acoustics were strange and it almost seemed like the thunder was booming inside the temple itself. The occasional flash of lightning lit up the otherwise pitch black room. He tentatively glanced around and checked the room. He finally breathed a sigh of relief when he didn't see any sign of Ah Kin or anyone else already up here. He positioned himself at the northern opening of the temple room and reached into his pocket to retrieve the stone, but it wasn't there. Panic set in. 'No. No. No!' He whispered to himself. He patted down his other pockets. *Oh my God, did I drop it?* He wondered. His mind traced back his steps and he recalled the conversation he had with Belkin just after he'd regained consciousness; *'Don't worry Adam. It's in my pocket...'*

Damn it! Adam peered down and wondered how long it'd take for him to run back and retrieve it. But as he glanced down he saw a figure in the dark bounding up the steps of the pyramid. *Is that... Ah Kin?* Suddenly he heard something creep up behind him. Startled, he immediately spun around. He gasped as he saw Ah Kin towering over him wielding a large piece of wood above his head. Before Adam had a chance to react, the log came crashing down. Adam raised his arm to block the attack but it did little to defend the blow. The force and weight of the log crashed on his arm and knocked his head. Adam collapsed to the floor. Ah Kin noticed that Adam was still conscious and he grunted loudly as he struggled to raise the large log back up for a second swipe. Adam noticed his window of opportunity and used the precious few moments to gather himself. He was weak but he used every ounce of energy in his body and focussed on stopping time. He raised his hands but nothing happened. Ah Kin now had the log back over his head.

Adam forced his eyes shut. **'STOP!'** He screamed. Suddenly everything went quiet. A few moments passed and Adam cautiously opened his eyes. He saw the familiar purple plasma appear all around the temple room and it seemed to have trapped Ah Kin. But it hadn't completely frozen him. Ah Kin was still bringing down the log, albeit now in ultra slow motion. The time warp was weak, he felt something wet running down his mouth and chin. He stood up and wiped his face. It was blood. Instantly his head felt like it was going to explode and he stumbled to the side as a sharp shooting pain pierced through his brain. He fell to his knees and the time warp that Ah Kin was trapped in burst and Ah Kin was free.

The log came crashing down onto an empty floor. Ah Kin looked around and found Adam curled up in a heap on the side. He was dumbfounded as to how Adam had teleported out of harm's way. But Ah Kin didn't care anymore. *No more games, boy.* He walked over to Adam who lay there unconscious, blood flowing from his nose and ears. *Hoonaab-koo. The will of the Gods* Ah Kin smiled.

∞

Adam awoke and found himself staring at the ceiling of the stone temple. His head was still pounding. As he looked around he discovered he was lying on the large dusty stone altar situated in the middle of the temple. He tried to reach for his head to soothe it but discovered his hands were tied. *What the-!*

Adam noticed light emanating from behind him and he put two-and-two together. *Oh, crap! This is a sacrifice!* Adam wiggled harder and tried to get loose. Just as the thunder quietened down he heard Ah Kin chanting into the storm. Suddenly he heard Ah Kin walking towards him, he was still chanting as he reached down and wiped his brow. Adam flinched in disgust. 'Don't touch me!' he yelled. 'You're going to let everyone in the world die?' He ranted. 'Six-billion people? I can save us! Let me go!' But Ah Kin wasn't paying any attention. 'We had a deal!' Adam yelled.

'A deal?' Ah Kin retorted. 'Well I don't have the stone, so it seems the deal is off.'

'But... but where's my mother?!'

Ah Kin laughed hysterically. 'I'm afraid your mother's been dead all along.'

Adam glared at him in disbelief. 'You monster! I'm gonna kill you!' He screamed. But something had taken over Ah Kin and all Adam could see were the whites of his eyes. He seemed possessed, acting and moving around erratically, all the while chanting in an ancient language the same verse over and over again. Ah Kin placed his hands on Adam's chest and the chanting became louder and louder. Now he was raising his hands towards the heavens and then tapping his chest. He repeated the motion again and again chanting loudly as he did so. The chants became faster and more intense and Ah Kin now began pounding on Adam's chest harder and harder. Adam was completely helpless, writhing around trying to free himself, tensing his chest on each blow. Ah Kin's fists now crashed on his chest so hard that it became hard for Adam to breath. Then, all of a sudden Ah Kin stopped. Adam peeked through squinted eyes wondering what was going on. He watched Ah Kin close his eyes and mutter a final silent prayer before producing a small and elaborately engraved knife from his pocket. The pointed blade glistened in the flickering light behind.

'Ah Kin please!' Adam begged. He did his best to focus, in a weak attempt at stopping time. He didn't care about how bad his head was hurting anymore. *Please God, help me!* He focussed his entire body's energy into forming a time warp. But nothing was happening, the pain in his head drove all other thoughts out and he couldn't focus on anything other than the throbbing in his brain. He closed his eyes and prepared for death as he saw Ah Kin raise the knife over his head. 'Please God.' He whispered to himself. Then suddenly; *Crack!* Adam flinched with his eyes closed but then realised that he didn't feel the blow. He tentatively opened his eyes and couldn't believe who he saw standing before him.

'Am I dead?' He asked Nikkita who stood there wielding a familiar looking log in her hands.

'Not yet handsome.' She joked.

Adam peered down and saw Ah Kin's unconscious body lying a few yards away on the floor. 'Wha-What are you doing here?' Adam stammered in genuine surprise.

'Jee, that's nice, I think the words you're looking for are; thanks for saving my life Nikkita!' She teased as she began untying the ropes around his wrists.

'I mean, how... but when...' Adam's mind was whizzing, she was the last person he expected to rescue him. But here she was, and he was so glad to see her.

'Belkin wanted to bring you the stone, but he was too exhausted, he wouldn't have made it here in time. Good job I stepped up, all that Insanity training really paid off.' She winked whilst focussing intently on loosening the knots in the ropes.

After a while of fiddling and tugging Adam's hands and feet were finally free and he jumped off the stone altar and dusted himself down. 'Please tell me you brought the stone?'

'Guess we know who the real hero is.' Nikkita teased as she waved the balled up rag in his face. 'But don't you think we should tie up...' Nikkita stopped midway through her sentence. She spun around in stunned silence looking for Ah Kin, but he'd mysteriously vanished while she had been focussed on loosening the knots.

Nikkita looked up at Adam in utter shock. 'Where is he?' She whimpered.

Suddenly and without warning a flash of silver darted out from the darkness and Adam fell to his knees clutching at his neck. Everything happened in a flash and Nikkita watched in horror as Adam gripped his neck, blood flowed freely from between his fingers and ran down his arms soaking his clothes as the butt of a knife protruded grotesquely out of his throat. Nikkita stepped back and screamed in shock as she witnessed his blood pool beneath him. Adam's face became pale and his eyes grew wide and distant. He tried to speak but no audible words came out. He tried again but blood oozed from his mouth. He released a hand from his neck and raised it towards Nikkita. She screamed again hysterically in utter shock. *No! This can't be happening!*

Adam somehow managed to get back up to his feet and tried to stand upright. He took a shaky step towards Nikkita and reached out. Suddenly Nikkita understood what he was trying to say. *He needs the stone!* Nikkita reached out, but just as she was about to place it into his palm Ah Kin leapt out of the shadows and shoulder tackled Adam barging him to the edge of the temple until finally shoving him over the side. Nikkita shrieked in horror as she witnessed Adam disappear down into the stormy darkness.

Nikkita's eyes were fixated on the evil man and her blood boiled with rage. Ah Kin stood there laughing hysterically at his victory, but his victory was short lived. With Ah Kin dangerously close to the edge himself, Nikkita ran towards him and leapt onto his back. They both flew off the side and joined Adam into the dark abyss.

As she fell she peered over Ah Kin's shoulder and saw Adam's twitching body sprawled out over the steep stony steps of the pyramid. A flash of lighting burst in the sky above and she saw large pools of his blood spread across the steps. He was alive, but barely. Despite it seeming like a reckless move on her part, her sacrifice would not be in vain. *This was the only way.* With the stone partially exposed in her hand, she carefully took aim as she plummeted over the side of the pyramid on Ah Kin's back. It had to be a perfect shot. *Now!* She tossed the stone at the last possible moment towards Adam's motionless body before they both crashed onto the stony steps. She felt a brief jolt and heard something snap. Everything went black.

THE VOICES

Further down the pyramid Belkin and Sofia were slowly making their way up the steep steps. The climb was tiring and they helped each other as they ascended. Suddenly they heard a scream through the thunderous cracks of the storm. Belkin glanced upwards and suddenly all the blood drained from his face as he watched a figure that looked like Adam fall over the edge and crash onto the steps.

'**NO!**' Belkin screamed with an outstretched hand.

A flash of lighting then suddenly revealed Nikkita jumping on to Ah Kin's back and toppling off the side with him before everything went silent.

'My God...they're all dead.' He gasped.

∞

There was no pain. There was only darkness. Adam was conscious but didn't feel like he was any longer in the realm of the world that he knew. He wasn't sure how much time had passed since he fell off the side of the pyramid and in a strange way, it didn't seem to matter anymore. The memory of being tackled off the edge of the temple kept replaying in his mind over and over.

I'm dead. He surmised. *But I can't be... I was supposed to do more.* His lifelong deeds flashed across his mind. *What have I achieved? What good have I contributed to the world? How have I lived? I'm not ready... I haven't done enough.* Suddenly, he heard something in the darkness; a pair of voices.

Open your eyes. They both said in unison.

Adam heard it as clear as a bell and he now realised that he was consciously keeping his eyes closed. He was afraid. He felt their presence. *If I don't see you, you can still send me back.* He reasoned, keeping his eyes tightly shut.

Open your eyes. The voices ordered in a more stern tone.

But Adam was adamant. *I can't.* He thought. *I've not done enough! I've lived a selfish life. I've never been thankful. I don't help the poor. I only remember God when I need him... please, I haven't done enough.* His mind began to flashback to his youthful misadventures with his friends; smoking weed, drinking alcohol, parties, girls. *None of that is really me... I can do better.* Adam always believed in the hereafter but he assumed he'd live long enough to repent and do good later in life to make up for all the fun he had in his youth. He wasn't ready to be held accountable for his deeds, not when the scales were set so heavily against him. As he floated in his darkness he came to the realisation that old age wasn't promised to anyone. His actions thus far had made him ashamed of himself. He didn't have the heart to face the angels that had come for him.

Open your eyes! The voices boomed.

Please, He begged. *Give me another chance. Let me go back, I will live a better life. I will do better. I haven't seen your faces, I haven't seen anything, it's not too late to send me back. Please!*

Open your eyes. They repeated, softly this time.

Adam couldn't procrastinate any longer. He had to face his fears. He plucked up all his courage and concluded that this was it, no second chances. He had to be brave and accept his fate.

He burst open his eyes prepared to face whatever terrible fate was in store, but he found himself lying face down on a large stone step about four levels below the temple. He was propped up on his left arm, which was hideously disfigured, broken in several places. His ribs felt broken and there was blood pouring from a deep gash in his forehead. But despite all these injuries Adam couldn't help but feel relieved. He smiled as he realised that he was granted his second chance. He looked at his disfigured arm and noticed that the bones in his wrist had completely split apart and the broken bones in his forearm protruded unnaturally. *Guess I'll never play the piano.* He joked to himself wiping the blood from his forehead. He was so happy to be given another chance that none of his injuries concerned him. His ribs ached as he chuckled in relief, and he welcomed the pain. It was confirmation that he was still alive.

Adam looked around and realised that just beneath him a few steps below was the figure of a man. Lightning flashed and Adam immediately recognised him. *Ah Kin.* Adam gazed at him as he lay there lifeless. His legs twisted in an unnatural way. But then something else caught Adam's attention. The Mayan stone lay there glowing in the darkness just a few feet away from him. Adam closed his eyes and made a silent prayer to God, thanking him for the opportunity to make things right. He shifted his body painfully to the right and dragged himself with his good arm towards the stone, every inch of his chest screamed in pain. But he didn't care, he had been given a second chance, and he wasn't going to squander it. He was now just inches away from the stone when another flicker of lightning flashed across the skies illuminating a horrific sight that would be forever burned into his mind. Lying on the stone block above him was Nikkita's motionless body. She was perfectly still and her eyes were wide open staring blankly into the darkness. A thin stream of blood flowed from her head and ran down between her eyes. Adam closed his eyes and squirmed in frustrated grief. *No...I can fix this.* He told himself. He took a deep breath and fixated his gaze on the stone. He used all his strength to shift his body now just inches away. Every muscle and bone screamed in agony as he reached out and finally clutched the pulsating red stone in his palm. The stone blasted a bright red light and its immense power surged through his body. Instantly all his pain vanished.

The power was immense and now strangely familiar. Simply by thinking it, Adam was reversing time. The process wasn't painful and his nose didn't bleed. It almost felt like second nature to him now and the power within the stone seemed to be doing most of the work.

As time rewound, he witnessed Ah Kin and Nikkita rising back up. He didn't realise until now how selfless and brave Nikkita had been to do what she did. As their bodies reversed back to the top, he finally witnessed a ghostly version of his own body elevating back up the pyramid and he cringed as he watched the painful impact he experienced during his fall. His ghostly shadow eventually ascended back up to the top of the pyramid and disappeared into the temple.

Adam got to his feet and discovered that all of his injuries had disappeared. *Of course, as of right now, they haven't happened!* He swiftly climbed back up to the top of the pyramid with cat-like agility. As he reached the top he realised that time was frozen at the exact moment he was being shoulder tackled by Ah Kin. He gently reversed time a little further until the knife in his throat was reversed out and back into Ah Kin's hands. He followed the trajectory of the knife and discovered where Ah Kin was hiding. He decided that this would be a good place to reverse back to. He would ambush Ah Kin when he wasn't expecting it. Adam placed the stone in his pocket and stepped back into his ghostly shadow lying on the stone altar. A bright flash of light engulfed everything.

'Guess we know who the real hero is.' Nikkita said as she waved the balled up rag containing the stone in Adam's face. The déjà vu Adam felt was indescribable. Just seeing Nikkita alive in front of him again filled his heart with bittersweet joy, but he couldn't lose focus right now.

'But don't you think we should tie up... hey where are you going?' Nikkita asked as she watched Adam walk right past her.

Adam didn't reply, he dashed off behind one of the partition walls to where he knew Ah Kin was hiding and snuck up on him unaware. Ah Kin was crouched behind the wall and seemed perplexed as he searched for Adam through a narrow gap with his knife poised for throwing.

'Oi!' Adam yelled from behind him.

Ah Kin spun around like a deer caught in the headlights. His face was a picture of confusion and terror as he realised he'd been discovered. Before he had a chance to do anything Adam front kicked his face as hard as he could knocking him down. Adam didn't know how to kill someone, so he decided to do to Ah Kin, what Ah Kin had done to him. He grabbed him by his shirt and lifted him back up to his feet and marched him towards the edge of the temple.

'No, Adam. Have mercy!' Ah Kin begged.

But Adam was deaf to his plea. Mercy was the last thing on Adam's mind.

Ah Kin was too dazed to fight back. His head was spinning and he barely had any control over his legs. He glanced over Adam's shoulder and saw a confused and scared Nikkita standing close to the southern entrance on the other side of the temple room.

Ah Kin turned his head around and stared down at his impending doom. 'If you'd have shown mercy to me, she'd still be alive.' Ah Kin hissed.

'Who'd be alive?' Adam asked puzzled.

'Her.'

Suddenly the knife appeared in Ah Kin's hand and with all his remaining might he threw it across the temple towards Nikkita. It bolted so fast that she had no time to react and it struck her straight in the chest.

'**NO!**' Adam screamed as he threw Ah Kin over the temple's edge and ran over to her.

Nikkita screamed as she stumbled and fell off the southern temple entrance at almost exactly the same time as Ah Kin fell out of the northern entrance. Adam dashed over to the southern edge and fell to his knees as he saw Nikkita's twisted lifeless body laying on the steps a few levels below.

HOOꞐAAB-KOO

Belkin and Sofia were half way up the pyramid climbing as fast as they could. Since the screams the only other sound they heard came from the angry skies above.

Belkin checked his watch as he helped Sofia up the steps. 'Something's wrong.' He whispered to himself. The celestial alignment between the earth and the Milky Way was due to occur in less than ten-minutes and judging by the chaos brewing in the night sky the alignment was still on course. *What are you doing up there Adam?* The earth's rotation had to be interrupted as soon as possible in order to avoid the alignment and prevent the polarity shift that would ultimately end human civilisation.

Suddenly Belkin noticed Adam staggering down the steps. He looked exhausted and dejected.

'Adam!' Belkin yelled up at him over the storm's thunderous booms and the pouring rain. 'What are you doing? Get back up there! Can't you see what's going on?' He waved towards the menacing dark clouds swirling above. 'You've got to stop all this.' He roared.

'I couldn't do it.' Adam sobbed as he continued to descend the steps towards them.

'You've still got time Adam.' Belkin replied as loudly as he could through the thunder. 'You can still do it!'

'You don't understand.' Adam cried as he approached them. 'I couldn't save her.' Adam broke down and collapsed onto his knees crying uncontrollably.

Belkin suddenly realised that he wasn't talking about saving the world. Something had happened to Nikkita. 'We heard a scream...what happened up there?'

'I couldn't save her Belkin. She's dead!' Adam bawled.

Belkin knelt down and grabbed Adam's shoulders. 'I don't understand. You have the stone, don't you? You can turn back time, go back and save her.'

'You think I haven't tried that?!' Adam screamed back taking his frustration out on him. 'I've turned time back six times. Six times!' He cried. 'Every time she dies in a different way.' Adam sobbed as he looked up towards the skies. 'Why can't I save her? I mean... what's the point of this stupid power if I can't save the people I love?'

Belkin knelt there in stunned silence, unsure how to console him. He felt sorry for him as he watched him cry unashamedly. *Poor kid.*

'I even tried to reverse time so I took the stone with me, hoping she wouldn't follow me up there. I almost died reversing time that far, but she always does.' He sobbed. 'She always comes after me... she always dies.'

In a rare moment of affection Belkin moved in close and hugged Adam. Adam barely had the will power to lift his arms and embrace him back.

'Listen Adam, we're not gods. We don't decide who lives and who dies. All we can do is try, and then hope for the best.'

Adam looked up at Belkin and met his gaze as he wiped his face with his sleeve.

'Now you have to be strong for all the other Adam's and Nikkita's out there who still have a chance. You can still save them. Maybe this isn't your story Adam... maybe it's theirs.'

Adam stared at Belkin as he reflected on his words. *Maybe it's not my story.*

Belkin stood up and helped Adam back to his feet. 'You need to get back to the top Adam, use the stone and stop the world from rotating for just sixty-seconds. Sixty-seconds Adam. That's all I'm asking of you. You've given me six-months,' He gripped Adam's shoulders tightly. 'don't give up now!'

Adam nodded begrudgingly.

Belkin suddenly slapped Adam across the face and Adam instantly snapped out of his daze. 'Now get back up there and finish this! Go!'

Adam took a deep breath and looked into Belkin's eyes. Belkin could see a sliver of determination in his eyes once more. Without a word, Adam darted off back up to the top of the Pyramid. Belkin watched as he dashed up the steps and checked his watch again. He had less than three minutes remaining and the sky looked as though it was being torn apart. *Hoonaab-koo.*

Adam scrambled back to the top of the pyramid once more. Nikkita's body was lying on the stone altar in the middle of the temple room with Belkin's jacket covering her chest. She resembled a fairytale princess in a deep sleep awaiting her true love's kiss before she would re-awaken.

'Now, Adam!' Belkin shouted from a few levels below. 'Do it now!'

Adam dug into his trouser pocket and pulled out the stone, instantly feeling its overwhelming power. He could feel the electricity charging through his mind and body, filling him with strength once more. He walked towards the northern opening of the temple room and stood in the pouring rain. Lightning sparked in the dark sky above followed by a monstrous clap of thunder. Adam gasped at the sight of skies above him. *Armageddon.*

Adam held the stone high above his head. It beamed brightly bathing the surrounding area in its crimson light. He channelled all his energy into his palms held above him. A red orb of energy the size of a basketball began forming around his hands and began growing. But as it grew, its colour transformed into a deep purple. Belkin and Sofia finally reached the top and gasped as they looked at Adam who was now completely consumed by the power of the stone.

'Oh my...' Sofia gasped. She watched as Adam stood there with both his arms stretched out above his head. A large ball of purple energy bursting and crackling from his palms, purple sparks shooting towards the sky as the energy orb continued to grow. Adam's eyes were open wide, but all Sofia saw was a pure white light radiating from his sockets.

Suddenly Adam screamed and the orb of energy reacted immediately and doubled, then tripled in size. The sphere of energy was the size of a large car now and growing exponentially. The ground beneath Adam began to crack under the pressure. Adam's nose was now bleeding profusely. In the chaos, Sofia hadn't even noticed that the rain had now stopped. She looked up at the sky and thunder clapped repeatedly as lightning bolts lit up the sky striking the huge purple orb of energy. Every time the lightning struck, the orb doubled in size. Sofia took a few steps back. Adam was now grinning like a mad man. Whatever energy was within the stone seemed to have taken over and completely consumed him. The orb he held above his head was now larger than a two-story house. It resembled a small planet as it began to rotate on its axis attracting huge bolts of lightning like a giant plasma ball. Adam cackled hysterically. Sofia felt uncomfortable as she watched the spectacle unfold before her. She looked over at Belkin who seemed equally as concerned.

'Shouldn't we do something?' She finally yelled over the thunderous noise.

'We can't...' Belkin yelled back. 'This is the only way!' Belkin checked his watch. The alignment was less than a minute away. 'Come on Adam... Now!'

Suddenly all sound disappeared as the gigantic orb finally burst and swept across the planet at the speed of light. Everything on earth was frozen still and deathly silent.

The purple energy made a complete rotation of the globe at the speed of light before it returned to Adam and began spinning into a vortex drilling into his chest. Adam shuddered uncontrollably and began to levitate as his body absorbed the copious amount of energy being beamed into him. Within moments he had absorbed it all and his body settled back down to the ground.

Adam knelt on one knee as he took a moment. His face was calm, and his breathing stable. There was no more blood and his eyes shone like bright white beacons in the night. There was an inferno brewing inside. Adam calmly stood upright and raised his face to the sky. A howling wind erupted out of him and a single beam of purple light burst out of his entire body and shot up straight into the night sky. The beam of light struck the earth's stratosphere and quickly spread out in all directions coating the entire planet in a protective purple shell of energy. Adam had achieved the impossible and planet earth ground to a halt as it stopped rotating.

With the purple energy still beaming from his body up into the stratosphere, Adam could feel the planet as if they shared a single consciousness as if he and it were one and the same. He felt the alignment with the Milky Way was approaching but he knew that as long as he maintained this position the earth would avoid it. Adam held the position and in his mind's eye witnessed the misalignment. The alignment was out by the slightest degree, but that was all that was required. The Milky Way passed the critical juncture and Adam could feel that it was once again safe for the earth to continue in its orbit.

HOLLOW VICTORY

Open your eyes.

Adam knew that he was unconscious. *Maybe, this time, I really am dead.* It was dark, and he couldn't feel his body.

'Open your eyes!'

He felt a sensation on his face but wasn't sure what it was. Suddenly he heard a faint clapping sound. Clap. There it was again. Suddenly his face began to tingle, and then it started to sting.

'Adam wake up!'

He felt a sharp slap across his face. **CLAP!** His eyes burst wide open. Startled he instinctively shuffled away from the dark figure that had just slapped him.

'It's me Adam, Belkin. Are you okay?'

Adam looked around anxiously and realised that he was still in the temple room on top of the Pyramid. 'Did it work?' He asked.

'You were amazing my boy!' Belkin exclaimed in uncharacteristic glee. 'I've never seen anything like it! It was magnificent!'

'I stopped the planet...' He uttered in disbelief.

'We must have missed the alignment by a hairline. You played it right to the wire. But the power you displayed was spectacular.'

'I-I... saved the world?' Adam chuckled. 'I did it! I saved the world!' But then as his senses began to return to him a chilling realisation dawned on him. Belkin helped him to his feet and he turned around and walked towards the stone altar where Nikkita still lay. Her body was in exactly the same position he had left it. He stood there for a moment looking at her willing her to move.

Belkin finally placed his hand on his shoulder. 'Come on Adam.' He said sympathetically. 'You did everything you could. She made the ultimate sacrifice and saved billions of lives. She's a hero.'

Adam instantly recalled one of the last things he remembered her say. *Guess we know who the real hero is...*

'Oh my God.' Sofia suddenly blurted. 'My dream... it was her. The girl... the girl that was made of light. She was your guardian angel Adam.'

Adam stared at her lying there peacefully. 'She sure was.' He sighed.

'We have to leave Adam.' Belkin ordered.

'But... but what about Nikkita? We can't just leave her like this.'

'While you were passed out Sofia and I staged this crime scene to make it obvious that Ah Kin was responsible for her death; a sacrificial ritual that went wrong.'

'This doesn't feel right.' Adam admitted. 'Leaving her here like this.'

'We have to get her body back to her family.' Sofia explained. 'We have to let the authorities find her. They'll review the scene and everything will point towards Ah Kin.'

Adam glanced over and noticed Ah Kin's body had been moved and was now lying near the far wall with a dagger in his chest.

'As long as we don't touch anything and leave now, it'll be an open and shut case. Missing person units will swiftly identify her and fly her body back to her family in London. They deserve closure too.'

Adam wanted to give her a dignified funeral right here and now, but he couldn't criticise Belkin's logic. His heart ached in his chest and he slumped in defeat as he realised there was no other way. *She deserves better.* Adam sighed heavily as he finally conceded. He looked down at Nikkita and kissed her one final time gently on her lips. 'Goodnight princess.'

Without another word he turned around and began descending the steps of the pyramid. Belkin and Sofia looked at each other silently acknowledging the tragedy of the situation.

'Let's go.' Sofia suggested as she approached the steps. Belkin was about to leave until he saw something red glowing from the corner of his eye.

'You go ahead... I'll be right behind you.'

EVERYTHING CHANGES

The sun was rising and despite being exhausted Adam had barely slept. His body was worn out but his mind was spinning with thoughts of Nikkita. Sofia suggested taking a sleeping pill to calm his mind. He took the pill and within twenty-minutes he was out like a light.

∞

'Adam, yo, dude wake up man, it's time to go!'

Adam rubbed his eyes. He looked up at Raj. 'What time is it?' He groaned.

'11:45 in the AM.' Raj replied. 'We gotta leave now and head back to Cancun if we're going to catch the evening flight back to London.'

Adam recalled the long three-hour drive from Cancun to Chichin Itza and begrudgingly got to his feet. His body was still aching and now his head was heavy with sleep.

Packed, and freshened up, Adam met Belkin, Sofia and Raj outside who were loading up the Range Rover with the last few bits of Raj's equipment. He got into the back of the car with a pillow he stole from the hotel room. Before long the car was loaded and they were ready to set off. Belkin drove with Sofia in the front and Raj joined Adam in the back.

'Hey, man.' Raj turned to Adam and said. 'I heard about Nikkita. I'm really sorry for your loss bro.' Adam didn't know how to respond and simply nodded his head in acknowledgement. 'Sash is gone too.' Raj continued, 'can't believe it.' Raj said as he shook his head in disbelief. Adam didn't know what to say to comfort Raj. He didn't want to talk about anything and hoped that Raj would just let it go for now. Raj extended his fist towards Adam. 'You did awesome last night bro, heard about it from Sofia.' Adam didn't feel like much of a hero but he bumped fists with Raj all the same. 'I was wrong.' Raj admitted. 'Belkin was right to see something special in your skinny arse.' he smiled.

The road back towards the airport seemed different at first, but then Adam began recognising the familiar landmarks and billboards he had noticed on his way here. Leaving felt wrong and he felt like he was leaving behind his soul in Chichin Itza. He was leaving Nikkita. His heart was begging him to stay. All he wanted to do was to run back up that pyramid and hold her one last time. He recalled all the promises he made her. How he told her she'd be fine, how he'd take care of her. He shook his head in self-regret as he recalled the assuring words he had used that day. *I'll get you home in one-piece, I promise.* He hadn't. He'd let her down. She trusted him, and he felt like he had completely failed her.

∞

They'd been on the highway for a while. No one was speaking, the local radio station was playing some old pop songs until suddenly Sofia shrieked. 'Oh my God look out!' she screamed.

SCREEEEECH

The car fishtailed and swerved side to side as Belkin slammed on the breaks and locked up the wheels. But it was too late. **BANG!** The car smashed into the edge of a concrete sidewalk and toppled over and was now skidding on its side. The car finally came to a stop and Adam could smell gasoline. He looked down and noticed that he was strapped in and his seatbelt was keeping him secure. *What the hell, I didn't...* Suddenly Adam saw a large black pickup truck charging right at them. Adam held on tight and braced for impact. BANG! The truck T-boned into their SUV and Adam's neck jerked back violently and he hit his head on the window. Everything went dark and Adam was out cold.

∞

Adam regained consciousness but struggled to focus. The local residents had now surrounded the cars and were trying to get the doors open to help. Adam looked around and noticed that everyone was unconscious. The car was on fire and he coughed on plumes of smoke billowing from the engine bay. The SUV was still on its side and he was suspended uncomfortably by his seatbelt in the back seat. He unbuckled himself and fell down onto the door on Raj's side. Raj wasn't buckled in and he lay there motionless, blood seeping from his ears. Adam looked towards the front of the SUV and both Sofia and Belkin were unconscious. *What the hell?!*

Adam crouched down and grabbed Raj's shoulder. 'Raj... Raj!' He cried. But Raj just laid there, his body completely limp. The front passenger side where Sofia sat seemed to have taken the majority of the impact and she was buried under crumpled metal and plastic that was once the roof and door of the car. Belkin suddenly let out a groan. Adam breathed a sigh of relief. 'Belkin, are you okay?!'

'ARGH!' Belkin groaned. 'My ribs, I think they're broken.'

Adam checked himself for damage. He had a slight concussion and felt dizzy, but other than that seemed to be remarkably unharmed. He looked down at his arms and legs and moved his hands and feet. Everything seemed fine..

'Are you... okay Adam?' Belkin mustered.

'Yeah, I am. Just a little knock on my head.'

Outside, people were tugging on the door handles. The chassis had twisted and the doors had become stuck. Adam watched as the locals threw water on the hood of the SUV to douse the flames. He turned back to Raj to see if there was any sign of life but then suddenly something caught his eye. Outside a few yards away a well built Caucasian man with a shaved head and a scar across his face stood there staring at him. He looked completely out of place amongst the local Mexicans. He wore light blue boot-cut jeans, a white t-shirt and brown leather jacket. But it was the brown leather cowboy boots that really stood out to Adam. *I've seen him somewhere.* The man began walking towards them and he seemed to be staring at Adam.

Suddenly a car came screeching around the man and skidded to a halt next to Adam. The man in the cowboy boots kicked in the rear glass and pulled Adam out of the car with remarkable ease. He checked the pulse on Adam's wrist against his watch for a few seconds and examined his head and scanned his body for any obvious injuries.

'Are you a doctor?' Adam asked. But the man didn't reply. 'My friends!' Adam begged. 'You need to help my friends!'

The man grabbed Adam's arm and led him to the rear passenger door of the car that had just pulled up. 'Get in.' He ordered in a deep gritty voice.

'No!' Adam protested. 'I'm not going anywhere, I-' But suddenly Adam found himself teleported into the back of the car. 'Wait, what?! How did I...?' Adam realised that he was no ordinary man. *He's a Timestopper too!*

Just a few minutes after the car pulled away Adam noticed an ambulance followed closely by a Mexican police car zooming past them with their sirens blaring heading back towards the site of the collision. *God, I hope they're okay.*

They continued to drive another few miles until the car pulled up and the man in the cowboy boots got out and silently gestured for Adam to follow him. Adam did as he was told and noticed an older looking jeep parked beside them. The man then approached Adam holding a black bag.

'Put this on your head.' He commanded. Adam noticed a slight hint of a British accent in his voice. 'If you behave I won't tie your hands up. No peeking. Understood?'

'I-I won't.' He stammered. Adam couldn't stop staring at the man. There was something strangely familiar about him.

'Good lad.' The man said as he placed the bag over Adam's head. Try and get some sleep. It'll be a long drive.

∞

Adam had been sitting in the back of the car in the dark for what felt like an eternity. He tried falling asleep but he felt far too anxious to drift off. His mind whizzed around trying to figure out who his kidnapper was and how he might have been connected with Ah Kin. But none of his theories seemed to fit. *What does he want with me?*

As he sat there in the dark, Adam's mind wandered back to the car accident. He wondered how Belkin, Sofia, and Raj were doing. His heart sank further when he began thinking about his mother, Sash and Nikkita. *So much death.* Adam sighed heavily as he realised that despite saving the world, he'd still lost his.

The car finally pulled up and the man switched the engine off. Adam heard the driver's side door of the car open and slam shut. He then heard his door open. A hand grabbed his arm and pulled him out of the car.

'Watch your head.'

Ushering him around blindfolded, they walked through a series of doors. The last of which used a keypad tone before it buzzed open. Adam was sat down on a wooden chair and the bag was finally pulled off his head. The bright lights were dazzling and Adam winced as he struggled to focus on his surroundings.

He was in a concrete room with no windows that looked like a cross between an interrogation room and a science laboratory. There were now two other men in the room with the man in the cowboy boots. There was a short Chinese man with bulging muscles standing beside the door dressed like a martial arts expert. The other man on the right looked like he was in his late 70's and wore a white doctor's coat. The thick lenses of his spectacles reflected the bright fluorescent tubes. He stood there grinning at Adam as if he'd found a new toy. He approached Adam leaning in and taking a closer look at his face. 'Remarkable.' He said in a thick German accent.

'What's going on?' Adam blurted as he looked around at them all. 'Who are you people? Why am I here?

'Sorry about our style mate.' The man in the cowboy boots replied. 'But we couldn't just let you leave with those people.'

'Those people were my friends!' Adam argued. 'You've practically killed them all!'

'They weren't your friends Adam.' The man replied. 'Belkin had been using you from the start. What you did last night wasn't about saving the world. It was about ending it.'

'What?!' Adam gasped in shock. 'How do you-'

'Ah Kin was deluded too.' The German doctor interjected. 'The Mayan prophecies predicted the alignment, this much is true, but ending the world due to such an alignment? Not scientifically possible.'

'What?!' Adam barked back. 'But the polarity shift... the-the stone...!'

'What you've done,' the German doctor continued. 'is set in motion everything that Belkin wanted. It's the first major sign of the end times. There are six other signs that will now occur in quick succession and you are now pivotal to them all.'

'This can't be? You're lying! Why should I trust you?' Adam asserted sceptically.

'The name's Lukas, Dr Lukas Schneider.' The doctor beamed as he shot out his hand. Adam reluctantly raised his hand and shook it. 'And you don't need to trust me, but maybe you'll trust this man.' He said as he pointed at the man in the cowboy boots. 'Does he look vaguely familiar to you?'

'I've seen you before, I know it.' Adam said as he turned to the man in the cowboy boots.

'You last saw me in that alleyway when you passed out. I carried you home.' The man divulged.

'Wait... that was you?'

'Adam,' the doctor interjected. 'meet your father; Joseph.'

The man in the cowboy boots pulled up a chair and sat in front of him. 'But you should call me Dad.'

THE END OF PART ONE

From The Author

I'd like to thank God for giving me the determination to complete this book. Professionally speaking, writing and publishing this novel was one of the hardest things I've ever done in my life. It's been a five-year labour of love that started off as a simple story that just evolved into something amazing. I'd like to thank my family and friends who provided me inspiration for some of the characters and scenarios, and for supporting me through this ambition of mine. I've loved every minute of writing this story, and I hope you've enjoyed reading it.
If it proves to be a success, I'd love to turn this into a series of action adventure novels, and adapt it for a movie.
So, Spielberg, if you're reading this - call me! ☺

Printed in Poland
by Amazon Fulfillment
Poland Sp. z o.o., Wrocław